The

BOOKMAN'S
TALE

The

BOOKMAN'S TALE

A Novel of Obsession

Charlie Lovett

VIKING

VIKING
Published by the Penguin Group
Penguin Group (USA) Inc., 375 Hudson Street,
New York, New York 10014, USA

USA | Canada | UK | Ireland | Au2stralia | New Zealand | India | South Africa | China

Penguin Books Ltd, Registered Offices: 80 Strand, London WC2R 0RL, England
For more information about the Penguin Group visit penguin.com

LIBRARY OF CONGRESS CATALOGING-IN-PUBLICATION DATA
Lovett, Charles C.
The bookman's tale : a novel of obsession / Charlie Lovett.
pages   cm
ISBN 978-0-670-02647-0 (hardcover) —ISBN 978-1-101-62280-3 (ebook)
1. Booksellers and bookselling—Fiction. 2. Widowers—Fiction. 3. Americans—England—Fiction. 4. Shakespeare, William, 1564–1616—Authorship—Fiction. I. Title.
PS3612.O86B66 2013
813'.6—dc23

Printed in the United States of America
10   9   8   7   6   5   4   3   2   1

Book design by Carla Bolte

ALWAYS LEARNING   PEARSON

For my father, Bob Lovett

Who infected me with an incurable bibliomania.

All that glisters is not gold.

—William Shakespeare, *The Merchant of Venice*

Things are seldom what they seem,
Skim milk masquerades as cream;
Highlows pass as patent leathers;
Jackdaws strut in peacock's feathers.

—Gilbert and Sullivan, *H.M.S. Pinafore*

The

BOOKMAN'S
TALE

Wales could be cold in February. Even without snow or wind the damp winter air permeated Peter's topcoat and settled in his bones as he stood outside one of the dozens of bookshops that crowded the narrow streets of Hay. Despite the warm glow in the window that illuminated a tantalizing display of Victorian novels, Peter was in no hurry to open the door. It had been nine months since he had entered a bookshop; another few minutes wouldn't make a difference. There had been a time when this was all so familiar, so safe; when stepping into a rare bookshop had been a moment of excitement, meeting a fellow book lover a part of a grand adventure.

Peter Byerly was, after all, a bookseller. It was the profession that had brought him to England again and again, and the profession that brought him to Hay-on-Wye, the famous town of books just over the border in Wales, on this dreary afternoon. He had visited Hay many times before, but today was the first time he had ever come alone.

Now, as the cold ache in his extremities crept toward his core, he saw not a grand adventure but only an uncomfortable setting, a stranger, and the potential for shyness and unease to descend into anxiety and panic. Anticipation brought cold sweat to the back of his neck. Why had he come? He could be safe in his sitting room with a cup of tea right now instead of standing on a cold street corner with a sense of dread settling into the pit of his stomach.

Before he could change his mind, he forced himself to grasp the door handle and in another second he was stepping into what should have been welcoming warmth.

"Afternoon," said a crisp voice through a haze of pipe smoke that hovered over a wide desk. Peter mumbled a few syllables, then slipped through an open doorway into the back room, where books lined every wall. He closed his eyes for a moment, imagining the cocoon of books shielding him from all danger, inhaling deeply that familiar scent of cloth and leather and dust and words. His rushing pulse began to slow, and when he opened his eyes he scanned the shelves for something familiar—a title, an author, a well-remembered dust jacket design—anything that might ground him in the world of the known.

Just above eye level, he spotted a binding of beautiful blue leather that reminded him of the calf he had used to bind another book—could it have been nearly ten years ago? He pulled the book from the shelf, reveling in the smooth, luxurious feel of the leather. Taking a closer look at the gold stamping on the spine, Peter smiled. He knew this book. If not an old friend, it was certainly an acquaintance, and the prospect of spending a few minutes between its covers calmed his nerves.

An Inquiry into the Authenticity of Certain Miscellaneous Papers, by Edmond Malone, was a monument of analysis that unmasked one of the great forgers of all time, William Henry Ireland. Ireland had forged documents and letters purporting to be written by William Shakespeare, and even the "original manuscripts" of *Hamlet* and *King Lear.* Peter turned past the marbled endpapers to the title page: it was a copy of the first edition of 1796. He loved the feel of heavy eighteenth-century paper between his fingers, the texture of the indentations made on the page by the letterpress. He flipped a few pages and read:

> It has been said that every individual of this country, whose mind has been at all cultivated, feels a pride in being able to boast of our own great dramatick poet, Shakespeare, as his countryman: and propor-

tionate to our respect and veneration for that extraordinary man ought
to be our care of his fame, and of those valuable writings he left us.

Peter smiled as he recalled reading "those valuable writings" from
an actual copy of the First Folio, that weighty 1623 volume of Shakespeare's works in which many of his plays were printed for the first
time. He was calm now—all sense of dread and panic banished by
the simple act of losing himself in an old book. Remembering how
that First Folio, given the opportunity, always fell open to the third
act of *Hamlet*, he spread the covers of the Malone and let the pages
fall where they would. The book opened to page 289, revealing a
piece of paper about four inches square. The brown foxing on the
pages between which the paper had been pressed told Peter it had
been there for at least a century. Out of habit more than curiosity he
turned the paper over.

The sharp pain that stabbed his chest almost made him drop the
book onto the dusty floor. He thought he had outrun that pain, that
he could escape it with distance and distraction, but even in the corner of a bookshop in Hay-on-Wye it had found him. Knees suddenly
weak, he slumped against a bookcase and watched, as if in a dream,
as the paper fluttered to the floor. The face was still there; he closed
his eyes, willing the face and all that went with it to retreat, willing
his pulse to slow once more and his hands to stop shaking. He took a
deep breath and opened his eyes. She lay there calmly, serenely, looking up at him, waiting. It was his wife. It was Amanda.

But Amanda was dead—buried nine months ago in the red earth
of North Carolina, an ocean away. A heartbeat away. And this painting, so much older than Amanda or her mother or her grandmother,
could not possibly portray her. But it did.

Peter leaned over to retrieve the paper from the floor and examine
it more closely. It was an expert watercolor, almost imperceptibly
signed with the initials "B.B." He looked again at the book from

which it had fallen, hoping for a clue to the watercolor's origin. On the front endpaper was a penciled interlocking "EH," the monogram of some long-forgotten owner. The description printed on a card inside the cover made no mention of a watercolor, only the price: £400. He had seen copies cataloged for half that. Copies that didn't hide a century-old painting of his dead wife.

On the shelf in front of him was a shabby copy of Dickens's unfinished final novel, *The Mystery of Edwin Drood*. The original cloth binding was worn at the corners and spine, the hinges were broken, and a few pages were loose, but nothing was missing. He could easily restore it to be worth two or three times the asking price.

Glancing around, he found himself still alone in the room. His hand trembling, Peter slipped the watercolor into *Edwin Drood*. He could not leave Amanda here, so far from home. He reshelved the Malone and tucked *Drood* under his arm. Twenty minutes later he had purchased a stack of books, including the Dickens, and was walking toward the car park on the outskirts of town, two heavy bags hanging at his sides.

The drive from the Welsh border to Peter's cottage in the Oxfordshire village of Kingham took just over two hours. Peter's cottage was down a narrow lane from the village green and, like the rest of the village, built of golden Cotswold limestone. It was in the middle of a row of terraced cottages, but in five months of residence, Peter had yet to meet either of the neighbors with whom he shared the thick stone walls.

By seven, he had a fire in the grate, a cup of tea in his hand, and the watercolor propped up on the coffee table. Despite Dr. Strayer's advice, he had boxed all his pictures of Amanda and left them in the attic of the house in Ridgefield. So how could she be here, in what suddenly seemed like *her* cottage? She had, after all, picked out the William Morris fabric on the sofa and curtains. She had overseen the renovation of the kitchen and the addition of the conservatory. She had spent weekends in Portobello Road buying the Pilkington vases that stood on every windowsill and the Burne-Jones prints that hung in the upstairs hall. She had gone to country auctions to buy the furniture and had found the carpenter who installed the floor-to-ceiling bookshelves in the sitting room. The shelves had been her gift to Peter, the outward and visible sign of her passion for his passion; but everything else in the cottage was pure Amanda. She had never spent a night here, but that Peter could have lived here for five months and actually come to think of it as his cottage seemed silly now that she stood on the coffee table staring at him.

The painting showed a woman seated in front of a mirror, combing a long tress of dark hair. Her shoulders were bare, and her hair just covered her breasts. The dark hair and the pale skin were Amanda's as were the straight shoulders, and even the insistent way that she gripped the brush, but the most remarkable similarity was in the countenance that stared out from the mirror—teasing and challenging at once. The resemblance was uncanny—the narrow face, the high, pale forehead; and above all the deep green eyes that could laugh and demand to be taken seriously simultaneously. Amanda could do that. Of course the face couldn't be hers. She had been born in 1966; the watercolor was definitely Victorian. Still, Peter sat staring into Amanda's eyes, wondering where she had come from and wishing she had never left.

He lost himself in those eyes, and in the past, for a few minutes, then roused himself, stood up, and began pacing the room. Here was a mystery that demanded a solution. During his years as an antiquarian bookseller, Peter had solved his share of bibliographical puzzles, but he had done so with the same emotional detachment with which he solved crosswords. This was different. The mystery of the watercolor's origins felt deeply personal and Peter could already feel curiosity and grief melding into obsession. He had to know where this painting came from—how a hundred-year-old portrait of his wife, who had been born only twenty-nine years ago, had come to be tucked into an eighteenth-century book on Shakespeare forgeries.

The problem was how to begin. Peter had never worked with paintings before. It took him another hour of staring and pacing to remember what was in the bookcase in the spare room upstairs. He had not set foot in that room since he moved to Kingham. It had been intended as Amanda's sanctum sanctorum, and though she would never spend afternoons sitting there in the armchair reading her books, it still seemed an inviolable space. Now he opened the door slowly and looked into the stale silence. In the distance he heard the church bell toll nine and he waited until the last chime had died in the wet winter air before turning on the light.

In the bookcase by the window were sixty-five nearly identical volumes—Peter's wedding gift to Amanda. Because it had been a Royal Academy exhibition catalog that brought them together, and because Amanda so loved her Victorian paintings, Peter had resolved to give her a copy of the catalog for every year of Victoria's reign—an illustrated journey through seven decades of English art. It had taken him a year to track down all the volumes, but it had taken Amanda almost that long to plan the wedding. Now the books stood patiently on the shelves of the room she would never use.

Peter stood in the doorway for several minutes wrestling with the eerie sense of Amanda's presence. It wasn't just that this was Amanda's room furnished with her books and her favorite chair and the lamp she'd picked out from the antique shop in Stow-on-the-Wold. Peter was used to living with Amanda's taste. This was different. This was a feeling that Amanda might return at any moment—not the evanescent Amanda who sometimes spoke to him, but the real flesh-and-blood Amanda. It was a feeling Peter longed to embrace, but which he knew he must fight. He felt the same nausea and dizziness he had felt when they first met, and he had to lean against the doorway to steady himself.

"It's okay," said Amanda. "You can go in." She stood at the end of the hall and Peter looked up just in time to see her fade away. Her words gave him the courage he needed, though, and he entered the room, crossed to the bookshelf, pulled out the volume labeled "1837," and sat gingerly on the edge of the chair. *These are just books; these are just things; this is just a room; and that was just my imagination,* he told himself. And although he didn't really believe it, he opened the book and began looking at paintings.

Before Peter had left for England, Dr. Strayer had given him a typed list of things he needed to do in order to move on with life. The second item was: "Establish Regular Eating and Sleeping Habits." He had been making progress on this—going to bed by eleven, sometimes falling asleep as early as one, and sleeping until about ten. It wasn't ideal, but it had become regular.

Peter had opened the first Royal Academy volume at nine o'clock P.M. He closed the last one at seven o'clock the next evening. He had not eaten or slept. Now he sat, bleary-eyed and exhausted, amid piles of books on Amanda's floor. He had looked at thousands of paintings, read thousands of captions. He had not seen Amanda's face; he had not seen the initials B.B. or discovered any artist with those initials.

It wasn't until he was standing in the doorway looking back at the books he had left heaped on the floor that he realized that Amanda's presence, which he had felt so strongly when he entered the room, was gone. After twenty-two sleep-deprived hours he honestly felt that this was nothing more than a room. He listened for Amanda's voice telling him not to leave her books on the floor, but he heard nothing. He turned out the light, left the door open, and staggered downstairs.

———

For the first two months, Peter had left the cottage only to buy food at the local shop. He had ventured into nearby Chipping Norton on a couple of errands before Christmas, but had avoided the bookshop, where he might be recognized by the proprietor. The excursion to Hay had been the beginning of his attempt to address the fourth item on Dr. Strayer's list: "Re-establish Your Career," and he had to admit it wasn't a wholly unpleasant experience to discover that the world of books still existed, that he could escape what Dr. Strayer called his "secret lair."

"What do you mean by that?" Peter had asked.

"You've spent most of your life in hiding," said Dr. Strayer. "Your secret lair is the only place you feel truly safe. When you were a child it was your room where you'd hide so you didn't have to interact with your parents. In college it was the rare-books room; once you married Amanda, it was your basement book room. You bury yourself in these places, Peter. You avoid life there."

"I left my lair plenty with Amanda," Peter retorted.

"Yes, *with* Amanda. She was your trusty sidekick, the person who made the world safe for you. Be honest, Peter, the only places you ever really went without her were bookstores and libraries—and there you didn't need Amanda to run interference because you could interpose the books between yourself and any meaningful human contact."

And so he had started the process of emerging from his secret lair in Kingham with an excursion to bookstores. And just as Dr. Strayer had predicted, he had done everything he could to avoid any conversation.

Still, wouldn't Dr. Strayer be pleased that Peter had taken some small step toward restarting his career? He hadn't looked at his own books—the bibliographical reference library he had built over the past several years—since he lost Amanda. Even when he had boxed them up to be shipped to England, they had been only rectangular solids to be fit into empty boxes—boxes now stacked in the stone shed in the garden.

He thought he might have one or two books on Victorian illustrators so he turned on the lights in the tiny back garden, shoved open the door of the shed, and began carrying the boxes into the sitting room. Two hours later, he had opened them all and emptied the contents haphazardly onto the floor-to-ceiling shelves. On the coffee table he left two books: *A Treasury of the Great Children's Illustrators* and Percy Muir's landmark study *Victorian Illustrated Books*. Not sure he could bear another dead end without at least some sleep, Peter left the books where they were, picked up the watercolor, and went upstairs to bed. He slept soundly for the next twelve hours, dreaming of those Royal Academy catalogs and the building where he first encountered them.

Ridgefield, North Carolina, 1983

When it opened in 1957, the Robert Ridgefield Library had been the tallest building in Ridgefield—a nine-story neoclassical behemoth of granite and glass, columns and cornices, with an incongruous cupola perched uncomfortably on top.

The Ridgefields had come to North Carolina from Scotland just after the revolution and had spent the next two centuries going from success to success. A moderately wealthy nineteenth-century merchant family, they had become impressively wealthy in tobacco, then excessively wealthy in textiles, and now obscenely wealthy in banking. Along the way, they had turned a backwater two-year Bible college into the nationally recognized Ridgefield University.

The library had been built atop Ridgefield's highest point—a hill on the edge of campus previously favored by students for late-night trysts. From the upper floors one could view the countryside around Ridgefield for miles—a patchwork of corn and tobacco, clouds of dust rising from the horizon as pickup trucks sped down gravel roads. In the Georgia granite above the library's main entrance were carved the words, "Let those who enter here seek not only knowledge but wisdom."

The moment Peter walked into the library for the first time, passing from the blazing sun of a North Carolina August into the cool dimness of its narrow corridors, its miles of shelving, its million and a half books, he felt at home. He was eighteen and had lived his life on that very farmland that was visible from the top of the library—a world in which he had always felt awkwardly out of place. His family had run a general store in a small town eight miles from Ridgefield, until his father's neglect of the business sent it into bankruptcy. After that his parents seemed more interested in drinking and fighting than in spending time with their son. He had often gazed at the strange white building on the horizon and dreamed of a different life, a life free from the encumbrances of family and the daily interactions at school with people who understood him no better than he understood them. He dreamed of a life protected from everything outside of himself, but protected by what he could not imagine.

He had tried various ways of insulating himself over the years. As a youngster he spent most of his free time in his room with his stamp collection, meticulously mounting stamps and trying not to think of the wider world that those little rectangles of paper represented. During high school, he had taken to sequestering himself in the basement with a pair of headphones and a stack of classical records. But however carefully he mounted the stamps, however loudly he played the music, he could never quite escape. A part of him always knew that the world still existed outside his door and that, ultimately, he could not avoid it.

Peter had won a scholarship to Ridgefield, and freshman orientation had been a harrowing experience, focused on "getting to know" people. Peter did not want to know people. What he wanted was to find that world-within-the-world where he could be himself by himself. Following his tour guide through the foyer of the library into the stacks, he suspected he may have found that place. Lagging behind the tour and slipping into the rows of stacks that disappeared into darkness, Peter discovered exactly what would protect him: books.

It took him only a few weeks to secure a work-study position in the library. It was nirvana. Peter spent four hours a day reshelving books. Technically, he was part of the Circulation department, but he worked alone, wheeling his cart down the narrow aisles between towers of books, easily avoiding contact with anyone who might be browsing.

Even on those occasions when he had to push his cart through the main reading room, with its wide oak tables and banks of card catalog drawers, Peter remained invisible to his fellow students. The cart would glide almost silently across the smooth marble floor and heads would remain bent over books, his passing no more remarkable than a change in the light streaming in from the high clerestory windows as a cloud moved across the sun.

On a dark and rainy October day in his sophomore year—he would later tell her the exact date, October 14—Peter Byerly wheeled his cart into the reading room and first laid eyes on the woman he would marry. She was sitting alone at a table, poring over a biography of William Morris. She sat ramrod straight, with her book propped on the table in front of her, her posture almost daring the work to get the better of her, while all around her students slumped with the weight of impending midterms. She wore, in place of the unofficial uniform of jeans and a T-shirt, an impeccably tailored black suit, with pleated trousers and a crisp white blouse. Not a strand of her shoulder-length black hair was out of place.

She was slim, though not as slim as most college girls aspired to be. She was tall, though not as tall as those girls whose height inspired envy among their peers. Both her figure and her stature were enhanced by the one quality completely lacking in most coeds but which she possessed in abundance—poise.

He did not at first see that she was beautiful—though it would not take him long to notice. What he saw was that she was different, that she seemed, like himself, to inhabit a world on the margins of Ridgefield University. She did not fit in, and this intrigued him, made him want to shout, *Comrade!*

Peter slid quietly into a chair at the edge of the room and pulled a book from his cart. For the next thirty minutes, he pretended to read, while watching her. Except to turn a page, which she did frequently, she did not move. At six o'clock she closed the book, put it on a pile of others, picked up the books and her red leather purse, and headed toward the exit. Peter followed. When she returned several of the books at the circulation desk, he swept them off the counter as soon as they had been processed.

Ten minutes later he was sequestered in the stacks perusing her books. In addition to the William Morris biography there was a book on the Pre-Raphaelite painter Holman Hunt, a volume of Edward Burne-Jones prints, and two volumes of the catalog of the annual exhibit at London's Royal Academy of Arts—1852 and 1853. He glanced through the volumes of artwork and the Holman Hunt biography before reshelving them. The Morris biography he slipped into his bag without checking it out. He wasn't sure what made him do it; for some reason he felt a need to illicitly possess a book she had read. He returned it to its shelf a week later, afraid that if she was as complex and multifaceted as Morris, she was way out of his league.

Over the next month he watched her for at least half an hour every afternoon. Her schedule was precise—she arrived at the library every day at two, spent fifteen minutes in the stacks, and read at the same spot in the reading room until six. She never varied her posture; she always wore smart clothes; she took notes with a fine pen in a black journal.

She read voraciously—biographies of Victorian artists along with poetry of the period and a smattering of history. She worked her way through the Royal Academy catalogs at the rate of one every two or three days. It was three weeks after he first saw her that he noticed, while shelving the volume for 1863, that the front cover of the 1865 volume was completely detached. He couldn't abide the idea that she should find it in such condition, so he carefully removed the book and its detached cover from the shelf and trekked up six flights of stairs to a sturdy wooden door marked CONSERVATION.

The brightly lit room into which Peter stepped looked as he imagined an autopsy room might—but, instead of human cadavers, books lay on the counters in various states of disassembly next to neat lines of knives and piles of various kinds of paper. On a shelf to his left were a dozen or so beautifully restored books, some in leather bindings with gold decoration. The room was not a morgue, thought Peter, so much as an intensive care unit, from which all patients would one day be discharged, if not fully cured, at least substantially improved. A man in a white lab coat leaned over a strange sort of vice that held a disbound book. He was spreading something that looked like cold oatmeal on the exposed spine.

"Can I help you?" he asked, standing up. The man looked at Peter through round gold-rimmed glasses. He looked to be about thirty and had blond, almost white, perfectly straight and groomed hair hanging to his shoulders and an equally pale beard sticking several inches straight out from his face. He smiled through his beard and Peter's first thought was that he looked like a Muppet. Peter couldn't help but smile back.

"I have a book that needs repair," said Peter.

"It has to be referred by library personnel," said the man, his smile fading and his tone of voice indicating that Peter was not the first person to come barging into the Conservation department uninvited.

"I am library personnel," said Peter. "I work in circulation."

"Put it over there," said the man with a sigh, nodding to a high pile of damaged books on a table near the door and turning his attention back to his work.

"When do you think it will be done?" asked Peter.

"We're running about six months right now, assuming nothing major comes down from Special Collections."

"Six months," said Peter. "But I have . . . I mean, we have a client . . . That is, a student who needs this book in a couple of days. It just needs the cover attached." Peter held up the book in one hand and its wayward front cover in the other. The man in the lab coat turned back toward him and considered both the book and Peter for a moment. His face softened and his smile returned.

"I'll tell you what," he said. "I'll put it in the girlfriend pile." He took the book and cover from Peter.

"The girlfriend pile?"

"Usually when a guy comes in here in a rush to get something repaired it's because his girlfriend needs it. What can I say, I'm a sucker for love and chivalry and all that. How about I have it for you Monday afternoon?"

"Monday would be great," said Peter, and he backed slowly out of the room, watching the young man return to his oatmeal paste.

Back in the stacks Peter could not get the Conservation department out of his mind. Suddenly he was seeing damaged books everywhere he looked: a frayed spine here, a torn endpaper there. He had thought of books before only as his shield, but now they seemed to be taking on lives of their own, not so much as works of literature or history or poetry, but as objects, collections of paper and thread and cloth and glue and leather and ink.

When he returned to the Conservation department on Monday afternoon, the book was waiting for him on the counter near the door. Peter inspected the front cover, the spine, and the front endpapers. "I can't even tell it was ever detached," he said.

"What can I say, I do good work," said the man in the lab coat.

"I don't suppose you ever let students work in here," said Peter.

"We sometimes have a student intern," said the man, "but they usually come from Special Collections."

"Special Collections?"

"Yeah, you know, the top floor. The Devereaux Room."

"What's the Devereaux Room?"

"You've never been to Special Collections?"

"No," said Peter.

"You're a book lover, right?"

"Absolutely," said Peter, who had never thought of himself as a book lover before this moment.

"Well, if you love books, you're going to adore the Devereaux Room," said the man. "Listen, I think there's a work-study position available up there right now. I could put in a good word for you with Francis."

"Francis?"

"Francis Leland, the head of Special Collections. I'll tell him we've got a budding bibliophile on our hands and maybe he'll take you on."

"That would be great," said Peter, wondering what exactly one did in Special Collections.

"I'm Hank, by the way," said the man, holding out a hand. "Hank Christiansen."

"Peter Byerly," said Peter, returning Hank's firm handshake. "Thanks for the . . . the recommendation."

"Sure thing," said Hank.

Peter turned to go, but stopped in the doorway. "And thanks for this," he said, holding up the repaired volume of Royal Academy pictures.

"I hope she likes it," said Hank.

Peter returned the book to its place in the stacks. The next day, she checked it out.

On November 15, 1984, a pair of books in the Ridgefield Library transformed Peter's life. He had gone to the library after his ten o'clock class, hoping to finish his shift before his three-thirty interview with Francis Leland in Special Collections. At three he picked up a cart of books to shelve and scanned it for anything that might have been returned by his mystery woman. In a matter of seconds he found the repaired Royal Academy catalog. Smiling, he wheeled his cart toward the elevator.

Not until he pulled the book out and was about to place it in its proper spot did he notice a crisp piece of ivory paper sticking out of it. She had never left a bookmark in a book before. He gently pulled the paper out of the book. At the top, printed in royal blue, was the initial "A." Below that, in a neat script, was a note addressed "To my admirer."

> First of all, thank you for having this book repaired. I so hate having to handle damaged books—I'm always afraid I'll cause further injury. I have noticed you watching me, you know. I even followed you in the stacks one day. I've been hoping you would say "hello," but since it's been a month and you haven't done it yet, I suppose I'll have to be the one to get things started. Meet me tonight at 10:30 in the snack bar at the Student Center.

The letter was signed simply, "Amanda." Peter leaned against the steel bookcase and felt the cold metal through the fabric of his shirt. He had held his breath as he read the letter and now he exhaled heavily as books seemed to swirl around him. After a minute, feeling somewhat steadier, he read the letter again to be sure he hadn't misunderstood. She wanted to meet him, to speak to him. She had noticed him and her name was Amanda. Where had he heard that name before? Suddenly he remembered his appointment. He had only five minutes to get himself to the top floor of the library. He carefully folded the letter and slipped it into his shirt pocket, then set off at a brisk pace for the Amanda Devereaux Rare Books Room.

The Devereaux family was as old in Louisiana as the Ridgefields were in North Carolina, and the family's great maverick was Amanda. Wealthy almost beyond equal by the time she was twenty, due to the early death of both her parents, she began to collect books just after World War I. She started by assembling one of the finest collections of eighteenth-century literature in the world. Then she began on the seventeenth century, and eventually expanded to cover literature in English from all eras.

In 1939 she stunned her family when, at the age of forty and apparently confirmed in her spinsterhood, she became the second wife of sixty-year-old Robert Ridgefield, widower and patriarch of the Ridgefield clan. There were those who suspected she married him because his up-and-coming university would make a perfect repository for her books, but by all outward signs they had a close and loving relationship. Their only child, a daughter, had been born a year after the wedding.

A lifelong smoker, Amanda Devereaux, who kept her maiden name, died of lung cancer at the age of fifty-seven, two weeks before the groundbreaking ceremony for the library. Robert Ridgefield never fully recovered from her death, but he did build a magnificent home for her collection, as he had promised her he would. At the center of the Special Collections department was the Amanda Devereaux Rare Books Room, a monument to the late bibliophile in which her greatest treasures were permanently displayed.

At three-thirty, still slightly light-headed from reading a different Amanda's letter, Peter sat at a massive oak table in the center of the Devereaux Room, waiting to meet Dr. Francis Leland. The carved wooden chair in which he sat was a fine antique, underfoot was a huge oriental rug, and facing him, a large glass case displayed several medieval illuminated manuscripts. Above this case hung an imposing portrait of Amanda Devereaux. Around the room were fourteen mahogany cases, each surmounted by a carved bust. From where he sat, Peter could read the names of Julius Caesar, Augustus, Cleopatra, and Caligula. Each of the fourteen cases was filled with ancient-looking books.

In front of him lay a slim volume bound in worn, dark brown leather with no markings on the cover. Next to it lay a pair of white cotton gloves. After a few minutes of waiting in a silence not punctuated even by the ticking of a clock, Peter decided this must be a test. He pulled on the gloves and carefully opened the book. The pages within were worn at the edges and looked as soft as flannel. Peter turned to the title page and read: *The Tragicall Historie of Hamlet Prince of Denmarke.* At the bottom of the page was the publication date: 1603. Shakespeare had still been alive, Peter thought, and for the second time that day, the simple combination of ink and paper literally took his breath away. He felt thrilled, awed, privileged. How many people ever had the chance to hold a copy of *Hamlet* printed when Shakespeare was still alive? Fingers trembling he turned to the first page of text.

He had read *Hamlet* in high school and again in freshman English, but this text was different. He had turned the page and read almost to the arrival of the ghost when he heard a soft voice behind him.

"Interesting reading?"

"It's not quite the way I remember it," said Peter, gently closing the book and laying it reverently on the table. He turned to see a short man with curly gray hair and horn-rimmed glasses. He wore not the tweed jacket that Peter had expected, but a pair of blue jeans and a red polo shirt.

"It's called a bad quarto," said the man. "It's the first printing of *Hamlet*, but the text is inferior to later editions. Some scholars think it was plagiarized from memory by someone who saw a performance."

"Still, it's the first printing of *Hamlet*," said Peter.

"Yes, quite a find," said the man.

"I didn't mean to touch it, it's just . . ."

"Quite all right," said the man. "There is no point in having these things if we don't ever have the pleasure of looking at them. What do you think of it?"

"It's . . . it's . . ." Peter struggled to find the words to describe the experience of holding that book, turning those pages, reading those words printed while the author still lived and breathed and walked the streets of London. Until recently books had been only something to hide behind, then he had begun to see them as carefully crafted objects, but this was completely different. This was a revelation. This book was filled with history and mystery. Just being near it made Peter flush with emotion. "It's amazing," he said at last. He placed one cotton-gloved hand lightly on the book. He could almost feel its life pouring into his fingertips. "I mean, the person who first owned this book, who first read these pages, might have seen the original production of *Hamlet*. He might have even known Shakespeare personally."

"It's our latest acquisition," said the man. "A newly discovered copy. Miss Devereaux would have been thrilled."

"Did you know her?" asked Peter, nodding toward Amanda Devereaux's portrait.

"Only briefly," said the man. "She was already quite ill when her husband hired me to oversee Special Collections here at Ridgefield. I'm Francis Leland." He held out his hand and Peter shook it.

"Peter Byerly," he said. "It's a pleasure to meet you, sir."

"Two things you should know about life here in Special Collections, Peter. The first is you are welcome to handle anything, as long as you handle it properly. The second is that I am not called sir, I'm called Francis."

"Okay. Thank you . . . uhm . . . Francis," said Peter, feeling awkward at the sudden familiarity. He turned his eyes away from the librarian and back to the book on the table. "So how could something as old as the first edition of *Hamlet* be newly discovered?" he asked.

"People are finding lost books all the time," said Francis. "Scholars didn't even know the bad quarto existed until eighteen twenty-three. We thought there were only two copies until this one turned up in a theological library in Switzerland. No one had taken it off the shelf in a couple of centuries, so no one knew it was there. We bought it privately last month."

"That must be something to discover a book that nobody's ever heard of or that everybody thought was lost."

"It's every bibliophile's dream," said Francis, and Peter knew in a second that it was his own. He could imagine nothing more glorious than finding some lost literary treasure—the manuscript of some unknown Shakespearean play or perhaps an edition of *Hamlet* earlier than the one he had just held—and preserving it for the world. Even the remote possibility that such a thing could happen brought a surge of adrenaline to Peter's veins.

"Now," said Francis, "how soon can you extricate yourself from circulation and begin work here?"

"You mean I got the job?" asked Peter.

Francis pulled a pair of white cotton gloves from his pocket and slipped them on as he spoke. "Peter, you either are or you are not a rare bookman. I can't change that. You felt the power of this." He picked up the *Hamlet* quarto. "Most students just see an old book, but you felt its deeper significance. You don't choose this career; it chooses you. Now, I can help you and I can teach you, but know this—after today you will never look at books the same way again. Nothing I do or don't do will change that."

Peter sat quietly for a moment gazing at case after case filled with books and considering the fact that each of those books might provide him with the sort of emotional jolt he had received from the *Hamlet*. He felt like an addict who has just discovered an endless supply of the perfect drug. Francis slipped the *Hamlet* onto a shelf in a case surmounted by a bust of Cleopatra.

"All the Elizabethan imprints are here in the Cleopatra case," he said. "It was Miss Devereaux's favorite part of the collection. This is her First Folio." He indicated a tall, thick volume lying on its side on the top shelf of the case. "You'll enjoy it, I think."

"Why are there busts on all the cases?" asked Peter.

"Ah, you noticed that, did you," said Francis, smiling. "A tribute by Miss Devereaux to her most admired collector. You see, Miss Devereaux also dreamed of finding an unknown treasure, and she had great respect for those collectors who had saved a piece of culture for future generations. Did you know, Peter, that it was because of a book collector that you were able to read *Beowulf* in your freshman English class? One man saved the only known manuscript of the first great English poem. And he saved a lot more than that. *Gawain and the Green Knight*, the Lindisfarne Gospels, some of the greatest treasures of the book world. His library in London was divided into fourteen bookcases, each with the bust of a Roman emperor or imperial lady above. Miss Devereaux asked me to organize this room the same way."

"Who was this collector?" asked Peter.

"He was one of those who, as you say, might have known Shakespeare personally. His name was Robert Cotton."

Bartholomew Harbottle strode down Borough High Street, burst through the door of the George and Dragon, and shook the dust of the highway off his new doublet. From the back bar he could hear the familiar sounds of carousing—and it had barely gone four o'clock. He stomped across the floorboards, threw open a door, and revealed himself to his friends.

"Barty!" cried Lyly. "We thought you were in Winchester."

"And I thought you were sober," said Bartholomew, taking both a seat at the table and a mug of ale proffered by Peele.

"There's no point in staying so," said Peele. "There's no work."

"But it's the high season," said Bartholomew, "I should think the theaters would be filled every day in such weather."

"He hasn't heard," said Lyly. "The theaters have been closed these two months. First a riot and now the plague."

"I could do without the plague," said Bartholomew. "But I'm sorry to have missed the riot. And what of you, Lyly? Not Master of the Queen's Revels yet?"

"Edmond Tylney absolutely refuses to die. I shall petition the queen again in the spring. Perhaps fifteen ninety-three will be my lucky year."

"Well, tell her that riots are good for business, will you," said Peele with a booming laugh.

"But who's this I see returning from the bar laden like a pack-horse?" said Bartholomew. "Can that be the face of Christopher Marlowe behind all those mugs?"

"None other," said Marlowe, sloshing ale onto Bartholomew as he set the next round on the table.

"I'm surprised to find you here, with the plague in town."

"My visit will be brief, I assure you," said Marlowe.

"If it were me," said Peele, "it would be just long enough for a good drink and a better whore."

"It wouldn't be long at all then," said Bartholomew, "for yours is never long for long." The table erupted in laughter and Bartholomew took a long draught of ale and looked around at the sparkling faces of the educated wits, the very sort of men he had hoped to have as friends when he entered the book business only three years ago. And now here he was, welcomed into the bosom of London's finest—urbane and talented, they made up perhaps the greatest collection of writers who ever drank together.

There was Thomas Nashe sitting quietly in the corner. Bartholomew had sold hundreds of copies of Nashe's pamphlets at his bookshop in Paternoster Row. Then there was George Peele, whose *Arraignment of Paris* had been presented before the queen. Peele's wild antics dated back to his days at Oxford, and he could drink, gamble, and whore as heavily as Bartholomew himself, and that was saying something. Patient John Lyly was as fine a writer as any of them, Bartholomew thought, excepting of course Kit Marlowe. For Marlowe there was no match.

That he, Bartholomew Harbottle, who had been born and raised in a village void of literacy, could be sitting here, at the age of twenty-six, drinking and laughing with the greatest playwright of the age seemed unfathomable. But then Bartholomew always had a talent for improving his lot, first attaching himself to the household of one of the local gentry, then forcing that gentleman to recognize his intellect and send him off to Cambridge, and finally making his way to London where his success in the book business had brought him to such lofty literary circles. He had won money off Marlowe cheating at cards. He had even won whores off Marlowe cheating at cards. He, whose long-forgotten family scraped out a living on a scrap of farmland, had cheerfully romped with bawds paid for by the greatest English writer who ever lived.

"So all the poets are out of work," said Bartholomew. "Even the glove-maker's son?"

"Will Shakespeare?" said Peele. "Not out of work exactly. That is, he's not writing plays."

"What is he writing?" asked Bartholomew, knowing that bashing the upstart Shakespeare, who had come not from Oxford or Cambridge but from a grammar school in someplace called Stratford, was a favorite pastime of the wits.

Peele looked around the table, waiting until every eye was on him before delivering his punch line. "The glove-maker's son is writing sonnets!" A wave of laughter swept the room. "Sonnets, can you imagine. See how many of those you can sell, Barty."

"But you must tell us of Winchester," said Lyly. "I judge by the fineness of your new doublet that your trip was not without its rewards."

"Gentlemen," said Bartholomew, leaning back in his seat. "I have today made more money as a bookseller than in all the past twelve months. I have made enough that not only shall I buy the next round of ale while I tell you the tale, but for anyone who wishes to adjourn upstairs afterward, I shall buy a round of fleshly entertainment as well." He soaked in the cheers of his friends, blew the froth off another mug of ale, and began his story.

He told of how he had met Robert Cotton, a young collector of books and manuscripts, at a meeting of the Elizabethan Society of Antiquaries. Barely a week later he had been drinking with a canon from Winchester when the reverend let slip a local legend that sent Bartholomew packing for Hampshire.

"It took me nearly two months to lay my plan, but one can't rush

these sorts of things. I needed, after all, a brawny imbecile and a senile verger and they both needed an affection for drink. The verger
proved an easy matter. I had only to drink a few nights in the taverns near the cathedral. The imbecile was more of a challenge.
I finally found a farmhand who fit my requirements perfectly. He
wasn't too trusting at first, but after a week or two of my paying for
his ale every night, and a couple of visits to a brothel, he was ready
to follow me anywhere. I chose a Tuesday night when everything in
the precincts was quiet." Bartholomew took two greedy gulps of ale
and continued.

"As you know, my family is from Wickham."

"They're from no such place," said Peele.

"Yes, but that's hardly common knowledge in Winchester. When I
knocked on the door of my old verger, whom I had gotten good and
drunk earlier in the evening, I was a poor pilgrim from Wickham
come to pray for my father's health at the tomb of our town's most
famous bishop."

"William of Wykeham," said Lyly.

"None other. You see, according to the canon I entertained here in
this very inn, a little-known legend in Winchester holds that Wykeham was buried with an ancient book in his arms."

"The sort of book that might appeal to young Robert Cotton?"
asked Nashe.

"Exactly," said Bartholomew, smiling. "The verger didn't seem
concerned that, despite the warmth of the summer night, both my
'brother' and myself were clad in heavy cloaks. He let us in the south
transept and tottered back to his lodgings."

"And under the cloaks?" asked Marlowe.

"Well, I had prayed to Bishop William before, you see. I'd spent
long afternoons in his chantry chapel sizing up his tomb, measuring
every dimension. It took some time to find a good carpenter who
could be trusted, but eventually I found one who made me some-

thing resembling the trestle of a large table. It was in parts so the imbecile and I could assemble it next to the bishop's tomb. Then it took all our combined strengths, along with a couple of iron bars, to prize the bishop's effigy and its marble slab from the top of the tomb and slide it onto the wooden support."

"And what did you find?" said Lyly.

"Dust, the smell of a few centuries of decay, and the good bishop. It was unnerving the way he stared up at me with those empty eye sockets, and I swear I heard moaning echoing through the cathedral when I first looked on him."

"The wind?" said Peele.

"That's what I told myself," said Harbottle.

"And what about the book?" said Marlowe.

"Clasped in his hands right where it had been for nearly two hundred years. It took me a minute to prize it loose, and I'm afraid I broke a few of the episcopal fingers in the process, but when I had it free and blew the dust off, well . . . it was as beautiful an illuminated Psalter as you could ever hope to see. Eleventh century, I'd say, maybe even earlier. Once I had that in my bag, it was just a matter of pushing the top back on the tomb, slipping out of the cathedral, and giving my companion enough to drink that he'd remember nothing in the morning."

"And what did this Robert Cotton think of your find?" asked Peele.

"He had only two things to say," said Bartholomew. "That he didn't want to know where it came from, and would twenty pounds be sufficient."

"Twenty pounds!" cried Peele, sputtering ale all over the table. "For one book?"

"Twenty pounds should keep us all in ale until the plague is long gone," said Marlowe, pounding his empty mug on the table. "What say you buy us another round and we drink a toast to the late bishop of Winchester."

When the next round was served, Bartholomew, blushing with the triumph of his story and with his third mug of ale, turned to the great playwright.

"Now, Marlowe," he said. "You've not yet told me what brings you to London when the plague is abroad."

"I came to bid farewell to our dear friend Robert Greene," said Marlowe.

"Greene? Why, where's he going?"

"As good a question as any," said Lyly. "For he lies this day on his deathbed."

Bartholomew set down his mug and felt the blood drain from his face. Among them all, there had been no better drinker, no better whorer, none more prone to lose half a crown in a card game and laugh at the loss while pissing into the Thames than the poet Robert Greene. Bartholomew had the unusual good fortune never to have lost a close friend, and despite his lifestyle he was capable of affection. That Greene should be no longer there for a friendly night of debauchery hit him harder than he would have expected.

"Plague?" he whispered.

"Hard living," said Marlowe. "He reckons it was a dinner of pickled herring that did him in, but I think we all know it took more than one dinner to push Robert Greene to the edge of this world."

"Where is he?" asked Bartholomew.

"Lodging with a shoemaker in Dowgate," said Marlowe. "A Mr. Isam. The wife looks after him. Seems a bit smitten, I'd say. Greene hasn't a halfpenny to his name to repay her."

"I should like to see him," said Bartholomew.

"You're not the only one," said Peele, laughing. "Emma Ball was here not an hour ago looking for him."

"His mistress?" asked Bartholomew.

"More than that, to judge by the crying bundle in her arms," said Peele.

"I'll show you the way," said Marlowe, draining his mug and pushing back his chair.

Bartholomew had no wish to betray the tenderness of his feelings to his drunken companions and so banged his mug on the table with false enthusiasm. "Lead on," he said to Marlowe. "For though you say he dies in poverty, a bookseller can often find profit on a deathbed."

Bartholomew parted with Marlowe in front of the narrow house in Dowgate where Robert Greene lay dying. Mrs. Isam let him in.

"Quite a lot of company he's 'aving today," she said. "Though none as can pay off his debts."

He was just about to knock on the door at the top of the stairs, when he heard a shrill voice from within.

"Course he's yours, you barnacle. You'd think lying there dying you'd be willing to admit it. Not like he can do you any harm now. Just want the poor bastard to be able to say he 'ad a father once."

Bartholomew pressed his ear to the door but could not quite hear Greene's low reply to this outburst. Soon the woman's voice erupted again. It could only be Emma Ball.

"Fie on you, then, fie. You've only give me two things in me whole life—our son and this useless wad of paper." He heard a thud as she apparently threw something against the wall. "Well, you can keep that, though much good as it'll do you where you're going. Burn up fast there it will. And I'll choose a more decent corpse for my son's father."

Bartholomew heard angry steps coming toward the door and barely had time to throw himself against the wall before the door flung open and a wild-looking woman in filthy clothes, clutching a mewling wad of rags, flew from the room and down the stairs. Waiting until he heard her pass through the outer door, Bartholomew stepped into the room.

"Your mother, I presume," he said to his old friend.

"Barty!" said Greene, bursting into something between a fit of coughing and a laugh. "How good to see you."

Robert Greene's usually florid face was pale and drawn. It was hard to believe that this was the same man who had produced great romances like *Mamillia* and *Pandosto* and written those marvelous pamphlets about life in the underbelly of London. This was the man who had lived with vigor all those rakish adventures he had written about; but now his signature pointed hair was nothing but a wispy tangle, his beard was matted and unkempt, and he wore only a borrowed nightshirt, having sold, he told Bartholomew, his beloved doublet of goose-turd green to offset some of his many debts.

"Still writing I see," said Bartholomew, noticing the pen and paper on the crude table by Greene's bedside.

"My deathbed confessions," said Greene. "You shall enjoy this bit, I believe. It's about the glove-maker's son." Greene reached for the papers beside his bed and read in a weak echo of his formerly robust voice.

"There is an upstart Crow, beautified with our feathers, that with his *Tiger's hart wrapped in a Player's hide,* supposes he is as well able to bombast out a blank verse as the best of you: and is in his own conceit the only Shake-scene in a country." Greene's voice again dissolved into coughing and laughter.

"It will be a shame to see you go," said Bartholomew, "for no one laughs more heartily at your humor than you do yourself."

"True, true," said Greene, falling back against the pillow. "I doubt Mr. Shakespeare will laugh at this."

"And what of your other visitor?" asked Bartholomew.

"Marlowe?"

"The one with the shrill voice and the bundle in her arms."

"Ah, be careful whom you bed, good Barty, for in bedding there is oft breeding."

"Well said, sir," said Bartholomew. "And that bundle that smelled of shite and sour milk—I'm betting that was your breeding?"

"So says his whore of a mother. Fortunatus, she calls him, though she's no cause to. As unfortunate a wretch as was ever brought into this world, and I'll not claim him when I'm on my way out." Greene burst into another coughing fit, this one more prolonged than the others. For the first time, Bartholomew truly felt his friend was about to die. He again felt an unexpected surge of emotion—not for the lost debauchery but, surprisingly, for the lost soul. Surely after the life he had led, Robert Greene could expect no heavenly reward.

"Do me a final favor, Barty," said Greene when his coughing had subsided.

"Anything, old friend," said Bartholomew.

"There's a book on the floor there." He pointed to the other side of the bed and Bartholomew retrieved a thin quarto volume.

"*Pandosto*. One of your romances."

"Indeed," said Greene. "In a moment of foolishness I gave it to that sister of a scoundrel and she returned it to me here on my deathbed. Sell it for me, will you, Barty? It's not worth much, but sell it and give the money to Mrs. Isam. Without her, I should die in the street, and hers is a debt I shan't be able to repay in this world."

"Consider it done," said Bartholomew, tucking the volume under his arm.

"Now, off with you," said Greene. "There are women in South-wark who will miss me tonight, and someone must tend to them." He laughed again and Bartholomew found that he could not answer, so he only bowed low at the foot of the bed and backed out of the room, gently closing the door behind him. In the dim stairwell he looked at the book Greene had given him. It would bring a few shillings, maybe more with the death of its author. As he stepped out into the late-afternoon light, he suddenly thought that he should like to keep this volume himself, as a memento of his soon-to-be departed friend. Digging into his doublet, he pulled out half a crown and tossed it to Mrs. Isam, who sat in front of the house plucking a chicken.

"For the debts of your lodger," he said.

"Bless you, sir," said Mrs. Isam. "It's a start at least."

Bartholomew tucked the book back under his arm and strode off toward St. Paul's, the afternoon sun blurred by the tears in his eyes.

Peter wiped the sleep from his eyes as he waited for the bread to toast and the kettle to boil. He had looked through the indexes of his books on illustrators, but neither helped him identify B.B. Now he stared at Dr. Strayer's list pinned to the message board in the kitchen. His original typed instructions were now almost obscured by the notes Peter had scrawled in the margins over the past several months. Underneath a circular stain of tea and a smudge of marmalade he could still read the list:

1. Grieve for Amanda; Acknowledge Your Feelings
2. Establish Regular Eating and Sleeping Habits
3. Meet New People
4. Re-establish Your Career
5. Use Career to Bring People Closer, Not to Keep Them Away
6. Develop a Passion in Addition to Books
7. Learn Something New
8. Get in Touch with Old Friends
9. Re-establish Relationship with Amanda's Family
10. Don't Run Away, Run Toward

Beside "Develop a Passion" he had written and then crossed out "poetry" and "painting." He had almost forgotten that he had purchased a watercolor set in Chipping Norton two months ago. He had given up after trying one painting. Next to "Get in Touch with Old Friends" was Francis Leland's phone number, though Peter had not dialed it since arriving in Kingham. Beside "Meet New People," he had scrawled the service schedule for the local parish church, but he had no intention of attending. Peter hadn't done a very good job with his assignments.

He would forget about the watercolor portrait, he decided. Today he would work on item number four. He would re-establish his career. After all, he had bought a couple dozen books in Hay-on-Wye for which he had customers back in the United States. He spent the rest of the morning organizing his reference books. He carefully unwrapped his purchases from Hay and put them on a shelf of their own. The *Edwin Drood* in which he had smuggled the watercolor required repair, so he would repair it. Hank had been a good teacher, and though Peter was no expert conservator, he could certainly manage a job such as this. He crawled into the dimness of the cupboard under the stairs and began to pull out the boxes that held his tools and supplies. When he had everything out in the light, he realized that he'd also pulled out his abandoned set of watercolors.

As he was about to put it back, he suddenly remembered something the salesgirl had said when he bought the watercolors. "There's another artist lives round here. Buys paints in here all the time. A regular expert he is. Even sells old watercolors over at the antiques center." Without pausing to move the boxes out of his way, Peter ran upstairs, grabbed the watercolor and his car keys, and bolted outside.

Chipping Norton, or "Chippy" to the locals, was the closest market town to Kingham and the place where Peter did any shopping he couldn't accomplish in the village shop. It was not overrun by tourists, and thus a good deal more pleasant than many more famous Cotswold towns. The market square, on a steep hill, was lined on all sides with old stone buildings. In addition to the standard high street shops there was a small theater, to which Peter had never been, several nice looking restaurants, in which Peter had never eaten, and an antiques center.

The bell on the door that jingled as Peter stepped inside didn't summon any attention, so he set off through a maze of furniture, china, lamps, vases, and more, in search of watercolors. Passing a stall of old books he made a mental note to return some other day and take a closer look. On the second floor he found what he was looking for—about two dozen nicely matted and framed pieces, mostly Victorian, but some eighteenth century. He didn't have an expert eye, but he suspected that only one or two of them were up to Amanda's standards. From the corner of each hung a price tag on the back of which was stamped, M. WELLS, ROSE COTTAGE, CHURCHILL.

Peter had driven through the village of Churchill every time he'd gone to Chippy but had never stopped or paid any attention to the cottages that lined the few streets. Still, it took only five minutes to find Rose Cottage, set back slightly from the Kingham road.

As he stood on the doorstep in that uncertain interval between knocking and hearing movement within, it occurred to Peter that in seeking out M. Wells, he was following Dr. Strayer's third instruction: meet new people. No sooner did he think this than the familiar churning stomach, clammy hands, and dizziness that always accompanied the forced meeting of strangers came over him. With one hand leaning against the stone door frame of Rose Cottage, he did his best to shake it off and concentrate on the square of paper in his jacket pocket. Perhaps if he could make tracing the watercolor his new passion, he thought, he could knock out two items on the list at once.

The door opened to reveal a tall man with swept-back white hair who looked as though he hadn't shaved in a week. He wore a paint-spattered and moth-eaten brown sweater and an irritated expression.

"Selling anything?" he said.

"No," said Peter.

"Come to talk about God then, have you?"

"No, I wanted to talk to you about a watercolor."

The man considered Peter as he might a piece of furniture he was thinking of buying. Finally he turned, and with a slight softening of his expression said, "Right, I've just put the kettle on. Come in and have a cuppa then."

Peter followed the man through a dark and cluttered sitting room and out into a large, sunny conservatory. On an easel stood a watercolor of the view across the fields. A fine Jacobean manor house had been added where a copse of trees now stood.

"Evenlode House," said Peter's host. "You can't see it anymore, the trees have grown up so, but it's still there, parts of it anyway."

"I'd no idea there was such a lovely manor house so close to Kingham," said Peter.

"You from Kingham then?"

"No," said Peter. "That is, I'm from the United States. I live in Kingham. I'm Peter Byerly."

"Martin," said the artist, offering neither his last name nor a hand and disappearing into what Peter assumed must be the kitchen. "You'll not find Evenlode House particularly lovely," came Martin's voice from the next room, "if you find it at all. Family's been out of money for a few generations now. Not sure they even live in the main house anymore. Still, they're not too proud to keep out the curiosity seekers with a nice load of buckshot."

Martin returned with a tray bearing a teapot, two cups, and two digestive biscuits. He put the tray on the table, handed a cup of tea to Peter, and took both biscuits for himself. "So, Mr. Byerly—is it a new watercolor or an old one you're interested in?"

"An old one," said Peter. "But I'm not looking to buy. I thought you might be able to tell me something about this." He pulled out the portrait and laid it on the table. "I'm trying to find out who the artist is. Or who the subject is." Martin frowned, set down the half a biscuit he hadn't yet eaten, and picked up the watercolor. He stared at the painting for nearly a minute, carefully examining both sides.

"Victorian," he said. "Paper looks like eighteen seventies or eighteen eighties. See a lot of it in scrapbooks. Nice work. Good lines. Not easy to do detail like that in a watercolor. Someone who really knew how to handle a brush. A fine artist, I'd say." He paused and squinted at the painting. "B.B. Never heard of him. What day is it?"

"Uhm . . . Friday," said Peter, thrown by the non sequitur.

"Third Friday of the month?"

"I believe so, yes."

"What you want is to go up to London then."

"I beg your pardon?" said Peter.

"Historical Watercolour Society meets third Friday of every month. Six-thirty in the Haldane Room, University College. Might be somebody there who can help you."

"Thank you," said Peter. "I appreciate the advice. And if you happen across any other paintings by B.B., I'd be much obliged if you'd give me a call." He pulled out a business card that read merely "Peter Byerly, Antiquarian Bookseller, Kingham, Oxfordshire" along with his phone number. Martin Wells showed no inclination to take the card from Peter's outstretched hand, so Peter laid it on the table and showed himself out. Twenty minutes later he was stepping from the platform of Kingham station onto the 13:21 for London Paddington.

When he and Amanda had rented a flat in Chippy the previous spring during the cottage renovations, they had ridden this train often—taking weekends in London to visit museums and go to the theater. On their last trip to the city they had taken a long walk along the south bank of the Thames. Peter had taken Amanda into Southwark Cathedral, where they found the grave of Shakespeare's brother Edmund. They had crossed the river at Westminster, and finished the afternoon at Amanda's beloved Tate Gallery. Peter had not visited London since.

How much had changed in less than a year. Before, Peter and Amanda always sat facing each other on the train, so they could tease each other with their feet under the table. As ever, Amanda would sit bolt upright, a book propped on the table in front of her. She liked to ride facing forward, so Peter faced backward, looking across landscape through which the train had already passed. Now he sat alone at the back of the car in a forward-facing seat, staring blankly at what lay ahead.

Although Martin Wells had been a bit gruff and slightly disagreeable, he had been harmless. It was always the anticipation that got Peter in trouble—his pathological dread of the unfamiliar. Dr. Strayer had a thousand explanations for Peter's phobias, but only Amanda had ever been able to put Peter at ease among strangers. With her at his side, he'd been able to not only cross oceans but attend cocktail parties and make small talk. Amanda made it all seem easy. She could feel him tense up from across a room and would appear at his side, lay her hand on his arm, and siphon all his tension away.

Peter arrived at Paddington at three o'clock and realized two things: he had over three hours to kill before the meeting of the Historical Watercolour Society, and that the meeting would probably be very much like a cocktail party. Without giving the matter much thought, he let his feet lead him to the tube station, a habit he had developed when he and Amanda would part ways for the afternoon before meeting at Fortnum's for tea. Amanda would go off to the Victoria and Albert Museum or the National Gallery or the Tate. Peter always went to Bloomsbury.

He emerged from the Piccadilly Line at Russell Square, and ten minutes later he was climbing the steps of the British Museum. A million things to see in London, and Peter always came back not just to the same museum but to the same set of galleries—the British Library displays to the right of the main entrance. He knew every case by heart. When the manuscript book of *Alice in Wonderland* moved from the Children's Books case to the English Literature case, Peter noticed.

Today, *Alice* was opened to the scene where she grows so tall she can barely fit into the corridor. Opposite Lewis Carroll's meticulous printing was his own full-page illustration of Alice folded up into a space too small for her body. The drawing made Peter shiver, not just because of his own bouts of claustrophobia, but because, as he looked at it, Amanda whispered "See the Pre-Raphaelite hair? Carroll was a friend of Rossetti's." Amanda was like this, she would rest for a while, leaving Peter in peace, and then, without warning, she would be at his elbow with a comment.

Peter paused only briefly to admire Alice. He always did this— looked quickly at some well-loved artifact like Handel's manuscript score of *Messiah* or the Gutenberg Bible—as an appetizer to his main course, his real reason for coming to the museum. That entree was the collection preserved for posterity by Robert Cotton. Although only a few of Cotton's treasures were on permanent display, they kept Peter coming back again and again. He had been intrigued by Cotton from the moment Francis Leland first mentioned the great collector. He had learned Old English so he could read a facsimile of the *Beowulf* manuscript Cotton had rescued. Now he stood before the original, paying silent tribute to his idol. Though the pages were scorched around the edges from a 1731 fire, he could read the careful brown lettering with ease. This was not a translation or even a facsimile, but *the* Beowulf, the manuscript that forever altered English literature.

Somehow communing with Cotton always made Peter feel better. Cotton's accomplishments made Peter believe that anything was possible, not just in book collecting but in life. Amanda had understood that. She would wait for him on the street in front of Fortnum's and when he would come striding confidently down the pavement, she would say, "Been visiting Robert, I see."

Peter thought he could use a little of that Cotton-induced swagger as he sat in a sandwich shop on Great Russell Street at ten past six, knowing he would be late for the meeting, but in no hurry to finish his ham-and-cheese toastie. It was nearly six-thirty when he finally ventured out into the night and began the short walk to University College.

The meeting of the Historical Watercolour Society was well under way when Peter slipped into the Haldane Room. The room was unpleasantly overheated and as dim as the side streets of London through which he had just walked. At the front a voice droned away while a series of slides was projected on the bare wall. In several rows of chairs, which may once have furnished an elegant dining room but were now what Amanda would have called "not fit for the yard sale," sat perhaps thirty people. Some took notes, some watched motionless, some squirmed, at least two appeared to be asleep. Along the walls were a few overstuffed sofas and armchairs, but these attracted only two people.

On a sofa across the room from where Peter sat tentatively in an armchair lounged a woman who struck Peter as the precise opposite of Amanda. Whereas Amanda would have sat up straight in the front row, a notebook perched on her knees, her right hand racing across the page recording nearly every word the speaker uttered, this woman relaxed back in the corner of the sofa, her legs propped on an ottoman. A mélange of books and papers was scattered next to her, along with a wool scarf and a rumpled sweater. Like the sofa on which she reclined, her body curved invitingly. Her pale brown hair was streaked with blond and unkempt enough that Peter guessed she had not combed it since standing on a tube platform where arriving trains swept the wind down the tunnel and across the waiting masses. What he could see of her face in the dimness seemed pleasant: it was rounder and softer than Amanda's, but no less attractive. She stared at the wall at a spot someplace above Peter's head, and the light from the slide projector occasionally glinted off her elaborate earrings. Amanda had only ever worn the simple diamond studs her father had given her on her sixteenth birthday. The woman did not seem to notice Peter, and although she looked at neither the speaker nor the slides, he sensed she was paying closer attention to the presentation than anyone else in the room. In this one detail only she was like Amanda.

Somehow the idea of meeting just one person, especially a person so utterly different from Amanda, was less intimidating than the thought of playing the role of American guest to an entire roomful of eccentric British watercolor enthusiasts, so when the lecture ended and the speaker began to take questions, Peter followed the woman, who had gathered up her belongings as soon as the slide projector had been shut off, into the spacious lobby outside the Haldane Room. She had pulled on her sweater and was winding the scarf around her neck when he caught up to her. Her bag, overflowing with papers, sat on the floor by a folding table laden with tea, coffee, and biscuits.

"Excuse me," said Peter.

"You too?" said the woman, not looking at him but still adjusting her scarf. "I always get claustrophobic in there, especially when it's a slide lecture, and with the Watercolour Society it's always a slide lecture. What did you think of Richard?"

"I beg your pardon?"

"Professor Richard Campbell—our speaker this evening."

"To be honest, I didn't really listen. I don't know much about watercolors."

"He knows his stuff, but he has all the personality of a jacket potato," she said. Peter pictured an upright baked potato in a bowler hat lecturing to a group of sleeping students. It looked like a Magritte painting; Amanda hated Magritte. She said that painting died with the Armory Show.

"I'm Peter Byerly," he said, holding out his hand.

The woman shook it firmly. "Byerly," she said slowly, rolling the word around in her mouth as if she were tasting a fine wine. "There was an Amanda Byerly who wrote an article for our journal once. American woman. Bloody good scholar." Amanda had a way of doing this, of cropping up unexpectedly and surprising him with some previously unknown accomplishment. He remembered suddenly a night in London three years ago when she had said she was "off to a meeting of art enthusiasts." Peter had stayed in the hotel room and watched a bad American movie. Perhaps Amanda had gone off to the Haldane Room. He had never asked her.

"My wife," Peter mumbled, and then, almost reflexively as he noticed the bare fingers of the woman's left hand, he added, "my late wife."

"Well, Peter Byerly, mysterious American widower who comes to a meeting of the Historical Watercolour Society despite not knowing or apparently caring much about watercolors, how do you feel about getting something to eat?"

Peter was taken aback by the casual, almost flippant, nature of the invitation, but he was intrigued by something else. When he had said, "my late wife," she hadn't said, *I'm sorry.* People always said "I'm sorry," and Peter had found that sympathy was wearing a little thin these days. It had a way of intruding on conversations and setting tight boundaries for relationships. Even though his only relationships right now were with the postman and the gardener, he was still tired of being handled like some delicate glass sculpture.

"You see," said the woman, "in a minute, they're all going to come pouring out that door and they'll spend about ten minutes making sure they eat every biscuit and drink every drop of tea and then they'll toddle off to the Spaghetti House, where they'll spend more time arguing over who should put in an extra fifty pence because he had a bread stick from the second basket than they will actually eating dinner. So I like to slip out early, but that means I nearly always

eat alone. You're a man of mystery and you don't look much like a se-
rial killer, so I ask again—how about some dinner? There's an Indian
place not far from here."

Peter was torn. If this Richard person "knew his stuff," as she said,
perhaps Peter should wait and waylay him while the others drank
their tea and ate their biscuits. On the other hand, if this woman read
the society's journal carefully enough to remember Amanda, maybe
she could help him, or at least point him in the right direction.

"Do they have curry houses in America?" She seemed oblivious to
his hesitation. "They do a great vindaloo. Americans like spicy food,
right? If not you can get it mild."

Why not, thought Peter. Why the hell not. Here he was talking, or
at least listening, to this perfectly nice woman and for whatever reason his palms weren't sweating and his stomach was calm. In fact, he
was hungry. He'd had precious little to eat the past two days. Besides,
eating spicy food while trying to talk to one person seemed a much
more pleasant prospect than being lost in a crowd of thirty arguing
over bread sticks.

"That sounds nice," said Peter.

"Brilliant," she said. "I'm Liz, by the way. Liz Sutcliffe. And no, I'm
no relation."

"No relation to whom?" asked Peter.

"Stu Sutcliffe," said Liz, adding when Peter only stared at her
blankly, "the fifth Beatle."

"I thought there were only four," said Peter, opening the door and
letting Liz pass out into the cold.

"An American who knows nothing about watercolors or the Bea-
tles," said Liz with a laugh. "What *will* we talk about?"

It occurred to Peter as he followed her down the empty street, coat
pulled tightly against the wind, that he had not reacted in any unusual way when he felt the soft flesh of her hand. He could not recall
touching a woman in the months since he left North Carolina, but

shaking hands with Liz Sutcliffe had not been momentous. It was a nice hand, he thought now, comforting. But at the time he had only thought, *How do you do.*

In the restaurant, Peter decided he liked Liz. He was not attracted to her, but he felt comfortable with her. He wondered if he might be learning to make a friend. Dr. Strayer would be thrilled. What he liked most was that she got straight to the point as soon as they sat down. Peter was therefore not required to make small talk.

"So," she said. "You don't give a toss about watercolors; you didn't listen to the speaker. Why did you come tonight?"

Peter reached into his coat and withdrew the watercolor, which he had placed in an acid-free envelope. Carefully drawing it out he laid it on the table in front of her.

"Pretty lady," said Liz, without touching the picture or even leaning over it. "Exquisite work. She looks familiar."

"Indeed," said Peter.

Liz picked up the watercolor and examined it more closely. "Jesus, I met her, didn't I? I met your wife. It was two . . . no, three years ago. She came to a meeting and sat in the front row and took notes the whole time and asked about six questions afterward—cracking good ones, too. She was nothing like you, was she?"

"Not a bit," agreed Peter.

"This is her, isn't it? This is your wife."

"Yes," said Peter, "except that it's a hundred-year-old watercolor."

"She aged well," said Liz, deadpan, as she laid the painting on the table. Peter felt as if she'd slapped him in the face, and then, unable to stop himself, he began to laugh. He laughed long and hard enough that he attracted the attention of several nearby diners. He hadn't laughed so freely since . . . well, since the last time Amanda had said something funny.

When he finally caught his breath, Liz, looking slightly abashed, said, "Sorry. I can be a bit insensitive sometimes."

"It was funny," said Peter. "Thank you for that."

"So you came to the meeting because you want an expert to tell you how your late wife ended up in a hundred-year-old painting?"

"Something like that."

"Why does it matter?"

Peter pondered the question for a moment. It was one he had been careful not to ask himself so far—it was easier to simply be swept along by the mystery—but he knew Liz had gotten right to the heart of the matter. "I think it's because I've been trying to say good-bye for so long," he said, picking his words carefully, "that I need this not to be her. I need to find out who it is so it won't be her anymore. And then maybe she really will be gone."

Liz picked up the watercolor again and looked at it in silence. Peter took a long pull on his beer. He had never had Indian beer before. It was cold and tasted of home.

"Is that a signature?" asked Liz.

"Yes," said Peter. "It's B.B."

"I beg your pardon?"

"B.B. Not much to go on, I know."

"Jesus fuck," said Liz, suddenly flustered. Her head disappeared below the table and when she popped back up, she was holding her large canvas tote bag, one arm shoved into its depths. She withdrew a pair of reading glasses and fumbled them on. Peter watched as the color drained from her face.

"What is it?" he said, strangely afraid of what she might answer.

"You're really Peter Byerly?" she asked, leaning back in her chair and crossing her arms across her chest. "And your wife is really dead?" Her voice had the slightest edge of accusation.

"Yes," said Peter coldly. "I can show you my passport if you like; I left the death certificate at home, silly me."

"And you really know fuck all about watercolors, Victorian painters, and B.B.?"

"I wouldn't say I know 'fuck all,' as you so delicately put it," said Peter. "Amanda was passionate about Victorian art, and some of her knowledge rubbed off. But I've certainly no idea who B.B. was."

"Well, it's a damn good thing you didn't pull this out of your pocket at the meeting."

"Why?"

"Mr. Byerly, can I trust you?"

"You can call me Peter." He crossed his arms on the table and leaned toward her. "And yes, you can trust me."

Ridgefield, 1984

Peter stood inside the door to the snack bar at the Ridgefield Student Center, lurking in the shadow of the Coke machine. In a booth against the far wall, he saw the familiar figure of the girl he now knew to be Amanda. Her back was to him, and as always she sat straight up, but now instead of propping a book on the table in front of her, she merely stared at her neatly folded hands.

Peter's palms were sweating. He watched her as the clock on the wall ticked past 10:35. He followed the second hand around another slow, agonizing minute. His stomach somersaulted and his body seemed to lurch to one side. He leaned against the wall and chanced another peek at Amanda. Two girls walked in, laughing, and Peter quickly turned his attention to the Coke machine.

"You gonna buy anything?" asked one of the girls.

"Uhm . . . n-no," stammered Peter. He turned and took a step toward Amanda, then pivoted and ducked out the door into the cool night air. He loitered in the courtyard until his pulse slowed slightly. When he reentered the snack bar, the clock read 10:40. Amanda had not moved. *It's like pulling off a Band-Aid*, he thought. *I just have to do it.* Without further thought, he took a dozen rapid steps and was standing next to Amanda's booth.

She turned to look at him and for the first time he saw her eyes— deep and green and flecked with gold, filled with both confidence and fear. For a moment he could do nothing but return her gaze. She finally broke the silence by holding out a hand toward him and saying, "I'm Amanda."

Peter knew he was meant to shake her hand, but his palms were sweating again, and besides, he felt like he might fall over any minute and he needed his hands to steady himself. Glancing down, he planted his feet firmly apart, drew a deep breath, wiped his hand on his jeans, and held it out toward her. His vision was starting to blur when he felt her cool, delicate fingers slip around his and squeeze gently.

"Don't worry," she said softly, "I'm nervous, too." Peter tried to answer her, but found he could not speak. It was as if every atom of his being was focused on that place where her flesh made contact with his. All else disappeared, including his roiling stomach, his spinning head, and his unsteady feet. "Why don't you sit down?" she said. She slipped her hand out of his and Peter returned to reality.

He managed to mumble, "Okay," and slid into the booth opposite her. He sat for an eternal minute staring at her hands on the table. "I'm a little nervous," he managed to say at last, mentally cursing himself for stating what she already knew.

"It's funny," said Amanda. "I didn't expect to be."

"I'm Peter, by the way. Peter Byerly."

"Hello, Peter," she said. He looked up to find her smiling and suddenly felt as if a great burden had been lifted from him. Amanda's smile simply dissolved his anxiety.

"You're not a freshman," said Amanda. "I would have remembered you from orientation."

"Sophomore," said Peter. "I'm sorry I'm late."

"I was a little worried," said Amanda. "You didn't watch me today. You know, in the library."

"I had an interview. I have a new job."

Amanda remained perfectly still, smiling at him. He looked into her eyes again and he felt himself relax further. He leaned back in the booth and finally looked down with a shiver from the intimacy of her stare. Amanda bit her lip ever so slightly and looked at his hands, folded like hers on the table.

"Tell me about your new job, Peter Byerly," she said. And so Peter told her everything about his afternoon in the rare-books room. He told her how Francis had pulled volume after volume from the shelf, showing him just a few gems of the collection. He did his best to explain how it felt to hold Shakespeare's First Folio, or the original monthly installments of *David Copperfield*. He confessed his dream of finding and preserving a great literary artifact, of having scholars and students know something wonderful that they wouldn't have known without him. Above all, he tried to convey to her his unexpected emotional reaction to the bad quarto of *Hamlet*.

"It was like when I saw you for the first time," he said. "Not just the discovery of something beautiful and precious, but the opening up of a whole new world."

"Is that what it was like when you first saw me?" asked Amanda, beaming.

"Well," said Peter, "yeah. I can't explain it. I just knew right away there was something special about you. To be honest, I've never really been interested in a girl before."

"I'm glad you're breaking that habit," said Amanda.

"Me too," said Peter.

"Now," said Amanda, when their plates had long been cleared and their glasses stood empty, "tell me about something that has nothing to do with books. Tell me about your brothers and sisters."

"Haven't got any," said Peter.

"Okay, about your best friends, then."

"Haven't got any of those either."

"So are you lonely, or just a loner?"

Peter had never considered this before, but without thinking answered, "A little of both, I guess."

Amanda reached across the table and took his hand in hers. Her soft skin enveloping his felt just as electric as it had before. "Why are you so alone, Peter?" she said.

For the first time since he sat down, Peter felt uncomfortable. She had found the question he didn't want to answer, didn't even want to ask himself, and he could see in her face that she must sense his discomfort.

"You don't have to tell me," she said, giving his hand a squeeze, but not letting go.

"I'm not sure," said Peter. "If anybody other than you asked, I'd just say that I spent my childhood hiding from my drunken parents, but that's not really the whole answer. The truth is, it's my fault as much as theirs. I was always scared to meet people. Scared or maybe lazy."

"Lazy?"

"Yeah, like I couldn't be bothered to put in the effort to get to know someone, when I could be sitting in my basement listening to records or collecting stamps. That was easy."

"You're making an effort with me," said Amanda.

"Maybe I was waiting for you," said Peter. "Saving that social energy for this moment."

"Are you trying to be romantic on a first date?" said Amanda, smiling.

"I, I didn't mean," said Peter, stammering. "That is . . . I just meant that . . ."

"It's okay, Peter," she said. "I don't mind."

"Oh," said Peter, and they sat in silence for a minute, both looking at their hands still clasped together on the Formica table.

"You know," said Peter, "I've discovered two things in the Ridgefield Library that fascinate me—rare books and you."

"I'm glad I fascinate you, Peter Byerly," she said. "I don't even mind being second on your list."

Peter loved the way she gently teased him. He didn't feel the need, for now, to tell her that he would give up his dream, give up rare books, even give up the safety of the library if it meant he could be with her. "I have a feeling this is an important day," he said.

"The most important," said Amanda, and leaning forward she kissed him lightly on the lips. For a moment, Peter thought he might faint from sheer joy.

By the middle of spring semester, Peter was spending much of his time with the two Amandas. In Special Collections he studied and worked under the steely gaze of the portrait of Amanda Devereaux. As for the living Amanda, she was anything but steely. Warm and welcoming, Peter would have said of the smile that greeted him every night at the snack bar.

Francis Leland was not only head of the Special Collections department, he was also a member of the faculty, and he arranged for Peter to create his own major through the Humanities department: Bibliography and the Book Arts. In addition to an English course in Shakespeare, Peter was taking a directed study with Francis that they had titled vaguely "Introduction to Rare Books," as well as a class with Hank Christiansen on book repair and restoration. "We'd better call this one-oh-one," Hank had said, "because it will take me at least two years to give you even a proper introduction to the subject." Peter could not have been happier.

He read all his Shakespeare assignments from Amanda Devereaux's copy of the First Folio, and when the class read *Hamlet,* he also read the complete text of the bad quarto. When he mentioned this in class, the professor had no idea what Peter was talking about.

"They don't know what's here," said Francis, when Peter told him about his professor's ignorance. "Faculty members are caught up in the here and now; they just don't have time to explore Special Collections."

"But if you teach *Hamlet*," said Peter, "in a building two hundred yards from a copy of the first printing, how can you not want to read that, to hold it in your hands?"

"We're a special breed, Peter," said Francis.

Peter was often embarrassed by his own ignorance. One day he pulled a 1607 first edition of Thomas Dekker's *The Whore of Babylon* out of the Cleopatra case. He tried to open the volume but had been unable to.

"It's not a book," said Francis, coming to his aid. "It's a slipcase." From what ought to have been the fore edge of the book, Francis withdrew a folding cloth case. Peter saw that what he had taken to be a book was merely a leather-covered box with one edge open to slide in the case that Francis now unfolded on the table. The case was elaborate in its design, but once unfolded it revealed a somewhat worn copy of Dekker's play.

"It's not just to protect a fragile book," said Francis. "It has the added benefit of making the book look a lot bigger than it really is." Peter saw how this was accomplished by the clever design of the interior folding case. One side was built up nearly an inch thick, while the other side held the slim Dekker volume.

"By the time you finish with Hank," said Francis, "you'll be able to make one of these."

"Why do you like me?" Peter asked Amanda one night as they walked from the snack bar back toward Amanda's dorm. The smell of spring hung richly in the air and though few students were about, Ridgefield seemed more alive than ever, more filled with potential. It was the new life all around that gave him the courage to ask the question.

"I had a boyfriend in high school," said Amanda. Peter loved the way she responded to a question with a long story that seemed unrelated to the topic until the answer would suddenly emerge at the end of her narrative. "He was a football player, but he was not a star. He got decent grades, but he was not a scholar. He drank a beer once in a while, but he was not a drunk. He was a nice average guy and I liked him in a nice average way. I saw what most girls considered extraordinary in high school and it didn't interest me. Big jocks, fast cars, booze and pot, and worse. Inept sex on your parents' bed with some boy you hardly know. I was perfectly happy with my ordinary guy."

"So what happened to him?" said Peter. They had stopped under a sprawling maple tree away from the artificial lights that spilled onto the paths across campus. Only the moonlight filtering through the leaves illuminated Amanda's face; her hair looked almost silver, and Peter longed to pull her into his arms and bury his face in those tresses.

"We graduated," said Amanda, twirling a stray wisp of hair on her finger. "He went his way and I went mine. He called me once over the summer about going to a concert, but I told him I was busy. I think he was relieved. It was just easier. I mean, I liked that he was ordinary, but so was the relationship."

"You still haven't answered my question," said Peter, reaching up and pulling her hand away from her hair, clasping it in his, and pulling her close enough that he got light-headed from her scent. "Why do you like me? Is it because I'm ordinary?"

"On the contrary," said Amanda, leaning her head against his shoulder. "I like you because you're extraordinary—but a kind of extraordinary I never knew existed."

Southwark, London, 1609

Bartholomew Harbottle pulled his cloak tight despite the sticky summer heat. The smell of incense hung in the air as it often did during a plague year, but Bartholomew had come to think of himself as immune to the plague. After all, he had survived the outbreak in 1592, when there had been death all around him. Extraordinary that all those friends who had celebrated his triumphant return from Winchester that summer were dead, but none from the plague. Greene had died the day after Bartholomew's visit. He left a note to his abandoned wife asking that she pay ten pounds to Mr. Isam, but the debt was never settled. Peele had died a few years later, of the pox, and Nashe had succumbed to a batch of bad fish near the end of Elizabeth's reign. Over the years Bartholomew had lost track of Lyly, who never did become Master of the Revels, but he heard that his old friend had died poor and neglected, from no cause in particular. Perhaps he had died of shame or impatience.

Marlowe's death had been most shocking of all. Less than a year after Greene had died, Bartholomew had swaggered into the George and Dragon to be greeted by a bar full of downcast faces and the news that Christopher Marlowe had been stabbed to death in a fight at Deptford. He had been only twenty-nine. Bartholomew had taken to his bed for a week and had later walked all the way to Deptford to stand at Marlowe's unmarked grave.

Batholomew had made new friends, but life in the taverns of Southwark was never quite the same without Greene and Marlowe. He still stopped by the George and Dragon on occasion and was still

known among the theatrical set. He and Richard Burbage, the great
actor and owner of the Globe, had bought drinks for each other, and
on several occasions Bartholomew had sat listening to Will Shakespeare tell the story of his next play. The glove-maker's son had out-
stripped them all, and Bartholomew had known it the day he sat in
the summer sun at the Globe watching the King's Men perform the
tragedy of *Hamlet*. Compared to the glove-maker's son, most of Bartholomew's old friends had been insignificant. But to Shakespeare,
Bartholomew guessed, he was nothing more than a second-rate
hanger-on. The great playwright would allow Bartholomew to buy a
round of drinks and to sit in the firelight with a few of the King's Men
listening to him weave a tale, but Bartholomew knew he would
never be in Shakespeare's inner circle.

It hardly seemed twenty years since he had begun his career as a
bookseller in 1589, but life had a way of slipping by quickly. In all
those years he had never had another find the likes of the stolen Psalter he sold to Robert Cotton. Cotton was still collecting and had
moved into a fine house in Westminster, but Bartholomew had yet to
sell Cotton another book. Still those heady days of youth, when all
London seemed to be at his feet, were as fresh in his memory as his
visit last week to a new girl named Penelope in a room above the
George and Dragon.

Today's trip to the tavern was a rare bit of business south of the
river, for today Bartholomew would meet Will Shakespeare himself,
and show him the book that was tucked into his cloak—a book Bartholomew had kept for nearly seventeen years. He had thought he
would never part with it, but when he chanced to see Shakespeare
and a small knot of actors outside the closed Globe Theatre a few
days earlier, the playwright was complaining of lack of source material for a new play. Bartholomew told him he had just the thing.

As he slid onto a bench in the back bar of the George and Dragon,
Bartholomew was keenly aware that this was the first time he had

ever been alone with the great playwright. Here was a man he and his friends had once ridiculed, and Bartholomew's heart raced as if he had been granted a royal audience.

"So," said Bartholomew, "any word on when the theaters might re-open?"

"The season is lost," said Shakespeare. "We shall have to hope for better luck in sixteen ten. Still a fresh season, whenever it happens, must mean a fresh play or two. I can't expect them to keep coming back for *Hamlet* and *Romeo and Juliet* forever."

Bartholomew, who thought it very likely that they would keep coming back to those two great tragedies forever, only nodded his agreement.

"Now, what have you got for me?" said Shakespeare.

Bartholomew pulled the slim quarto volume out from under his cloak. It was a tad worn around the edges, for he had pulled it off his shelf many times when sleep would not come to him late on a winter's night. He laid the book on the table. "It's by Robert Greene," he said.

"Greene," said Shakespeare with a laugh. "He was a friend of yours, was he not?"

"He was," said Bartholomew.

"A friend who once called me an upstart crow, as I remember it."

"And what better revenge," said Bartholomew, leaning forward, "than to use his story for your next play. A story no one reads any-more becomes a play everyone in London flocks to see. The upstart crow has the last word."

"What's it about?" Shakespeare asked.

Bartholomew picked up the book, opened to the first page, and read. "'Among all the passions wherewith human minds are per-plexed, there is none that so galleth with restless despight, as the in-fectious sore of jealousy.'"

"I've written a play about jealousy," said Shakespeare. "Burbage proposes a revival for next season."

"This one is different," said Bartholomew, who wasn't sure it was that different. After all, just like Desdemona, the main character's wife in Greene's *Pandosto* dies in the end. Still Bartholomew pressed his case. "Besides, you can change it. You could make it a comedy. The wife is restored and all are happy."

"You are a bit of a rogue, are you not, Harbottle?"

"I enjoy my drink and my visits to the upper floors of this fine establishment, though not as often as in my youth, but I am a businessman."

"The greatest rogue of all," said Shakespeare, laughing. "I have heard of your adventures in Winchester Cathedral."

"A story which no doubt grows in the retelling."

"And now you wish to sell me this book so I can have my revenge on poor forgotten Robert Greene. Perhaps I should put you in the play. A thief, a rogue, but a likeable man. A comic rogue, if you will. Not quite a clown—darker than a clown—and a schemer. A salesman."

"You do me honor, sir, though I doubt that I am all that."

"The stage makes us all what we are not," said Shakespeare. The two men took deep drafts of ale as this proclamation hung in the air. Finally Bartholomew pushed the book across the table.

"Your revenge will be all the sweeter knowing this," he said. "Greene himself gave me this copy of *Pandosto* the night before he died."

Shakespeare picked up the volume and let it fall open on the table. "And you expect me to buy it?" he said.

"You misunderstand," said Bartholomew. "I do not wish to sell you this book. I wish to lend it to you for as long as you require."

"But you are a bookseller."

"Most days I am. Today I am merely a member of the audience who will delight in a new play by William Shakespeare."

"That and a sycophant." Shakespeare laughed.

"Granted," said Bartholomew.

"Very well," said Shakespeare, closing the book and pulling it toward him. "I shall read what your friend Mr. Greene had to say. But I warn you, if I decide to make this story into a play, I may have to mark up your book a bit."

"By all means," said Bartholomew, "mark it up as much as you require."

"*Pandosto* is not a name for a play," said Shakespeare.

"I always read it in the winter," said Bartholomew. "Why not *A Midwinter's Tale*? To go with *A Midsummer Night's Dream*."

Shakespeare tucked the book under his arm and drained his mug of ale. Standing, he winked at Bartholomew and said, "I'd stick to bookselling if I were you."

Bartholomew sat back and smiled after Shakespeare had left the room. For the bookseller was indeed a scheming rogue, and proud to know so, and he was laying deeper plans than just the writing of another play by the upstart crow.

The street outside the Globe roiled with humanity. No plague, perfect weather, and a new play by Shakespeare had drawn enough Londoners across the bridge to fill the playhouse to its capacity of three thousand. Bartholomew Harbottle feared that if his companion did not arrive soon, there would be no space for them in the galleries, and he could not imagine that Robert Cotton would be willing to stand with the groundlings for three hours.

It had taken Bartholomew weeks to persuade Cotton to make this outing to the Globe, and only the collector's affection for the Winchester Psalter and Bartholomew's intimation that another grand acquisition might be on the horizon had convinced him to make the journey from his home in Westminster. The clattering of hooves and rattling of coaches occasionally rose above the din of the crowd as some noble or other was disgorged near the theater's entrance, but

Bartholomew's eyes were trained toward the river. From Westminster, surely Cotton would make the trip by boat. It was nearly two o'clock when Bartholomew finally glimpsed the familiar doublet of blue and gold glinting in the sunshine as Cotton strolled toward the theater in no hurry, it seemed, to arrive betimes. Bartholomew fumbled in his purse for the four pennies that admitted himself and his guest to the galleries, and the two had just squeezed into the end of a row when a trumpet sounded, the roar of the crowd lowered to a murmur that would underscore the entire performance, and two men, exquisitely attired in richly embroidered garments, stepped onto the stage.

"What does he call it?" asked Cotton.

"It's called *A Winter's Tale*," said Bartholomew, and Cotton settled back on the bench and watched the play unfold without further comment.

Bartholomew did not mention his own part in the genesis of the play, though he did mark how closely it followed the story of *Pandosto*. He had not spoken to Shakespeare since that day almost three years ago when he had suggested Greene's romance as a source. He had heard that a new play, presented at court last November, was titled *A Winter's Tale*, and he had some hope, the title being so similar to what he had suggested, that Shakespeare had taken the bait. Not until April had he known for sure. On a cold and dank day, a messenger brought a package to his shop in Paternoster Row. Inside, Bartholomew found the copy of *Pandosto* he had loaned Shakespeare and a short letter.

Harbottle,

Pardon the messenger, but I have business in Stratford. I think you will find something of yourself in *A Winter's Tale*. I beg forgiveness for defacing your *Pandosto*, but return it herewith with my thanks.

W. Shakespeare

Bartholomew opened the book and turned rapidly through several pages. The margins were filled with the scrawled notes of the playwright. That very afternoon he set off to Westminster to pay a visit to Robert Cotton.

Bartholomew almost forgot Cotton as he watched *A Winter's Tale*. The story of King Leontes, who falsely accuses his wife, Hermione, of adultery, imprisons her, and banishes her presumably bastard child Perdita, kept most of the audience attentive, though there was an occasional scuffle or outburst from the yard. When, in the waning stages of the third act, news came first of the death of Leontes's young son Mamillius and then of Queen Hermione herself, Bartholomew saw tears glisten on many faces, and even heard cries of woe from one or two of the groundlings. He began to wonder if Shakespeare had taken his advice about changing the ending, for the story had all the marks of a tragedy. Nor had Bartholomew seen any character fashioned in his own image. Still, these matters were trifles. Shakespeare had written the play, and Bartholomew now had everything he needed to secure his fortune.

Lost in his thoughts, Bartholomew did not at first notice a new character appear onstage early in the fourth act, singing. When Autolycus, the traveling merchant, called himself a "snapper-up of unconsidered trifles" and bragged how he made his living by cheating the foolish, Bartholomew sincerely hoped that Cotton would not recognize his companion the bookseller on the stage. "A thief, a rogue, but a likeable man. A comic rogue, if you will," Shakespeare had said. Bartholomew forgot for a moment all his well-laid plans, and imagined only an audience, years hence, watching this play and seeing a thinly disguised Bartholomew Harbottle tread the boards, laughing, singing, and thieving.

As the last two acts unfolded, Bartholomew watched in awe as he, so it seemed, took over the play in the character of Autolycus. This rogue did not sell books, but he did sell ballads. Bartholomew at first took some slight offense when Autolycus, deciding not to help out young Perdita and her beloved, said, "If I thought it were a piece of honesty to acquaint the king withal, I would not do't. I hold it the more knavery to conceal it, and therein I am constant to my profession." Was knavery really Bartholomew's profession? Surely the proudest moments of his career did not drip with honesty, but Bartholomew did not believe he had ever done anyone real harm, nor, he was glad to see as the play raced toward its conclusion, did Autolycus. As Perdita was restored to her father and Hermione brought back to life to give the play the happy ending Bartholomew had suggested, the schemings of Autolycus ultimately contributed to the happiness of the characters.

As the crowd surged into the street after the performance, Bartholomew pulled Cotton toward the George and Dragon. Most of the playgoers were heading back toward the bridge, but enough spilled into the taverns of Southwark that Bartholomew was glad he had made arrangements in advance with the barman for a private nook to await him. A mug of ale for himself and a cup of wine for Cotton stood on the table as the two men took their seats.

"Did you hear that crowd's roar of approval?" said Bartholomew.

"Hardly a surprise," said Cotton. "Shakespeare is popular. But you still haven't told me what this afternoon is all about. I enjoy a good play as much as the next man, but you led me to believe there was an acquisition in the offing."

"And so there is, but patience, good friend. Now tell me, will you grant that Will Shakespeare is the greatest playwright of our time?"

"I would not argue the point," said Cotton.

"I would say he is the greatest playwright of any age," said Bartholomew, "and that he is likely to remain so." He could imagine the laughter of his old friend Robert Greene if he had heard such a claim, but Greene had not lived to see the meteoric rise of the upstart crow.

"I have some medieval manuscripts of the Greek dramatists that might belie that assertion," said Cotton. "But I will grant you he is an important writer. Though I do not think today's effort was his best."

"There's a reason for that," said Bartholomew, sensing his opening. "The word among the players is that Shakespeare is ill. He plans to retire to Stratford at the end of the season and is not likely to survive the winter." Bartholomew had heard no such rumor, though it occurred to him that it might be useful to start one.

"I am sorry to hear that," said Cotton. "He used my library once, years ago. I believe he was working on *Henry V.* One of his best, I thought. Stirring. He was a quiet man—not taken to drunken carousing and immoral behavior like so many of these theater folk."

Bartholomew reflected that it was just as well that Cotton was unfamiliar with the less savory of Will Shakespeare's escapades. He took a draught of ale and wiped his mouth on his sleeve with a broad gesture. "There will be quite a scramble for his manuscripts when he dies," he said. "Some will want to publish them, I imagine, but as many will want to destroy them."

"Destroy them?" said Cotton. "Why would anyone want to do such a thing?"

Bartholomew knew that Cotton would view the destruction of any literary relic as heresy. "Jealousy, of course," he said. "We certainly saw the power of that emotion in today's performance. But perhaps you don't know what the other playwrights think of Shakespeare—a grammar school boy outshining the finest lights that Oxford and Cambridge can offer. And why should the King's Men object? If the plays are published they can be performed by anyone. As it stands, the players know their roles. Why should they not destroy the manuscripts and ensure themselves a monopoly?"

"But his plays have been published. I've seen them," said Cotton.

"Some have," said Bartholomew. "A dozen perhaps. But there are at least thirty more that have not." He knew that no fewer than eighteen of Shakespeare's plays had been published, and the rest numbered no more than twenty or so, but Bartholomew trusted in the power of exaggeration. "And there are others," he went on, warming to his deception, "not yet performed. I have seen the pages of a tragedy that will eclipse even *Hamlet* and *King Lear*. And it can be yours."

"I beg your pardon?" said Cotton, not realizing that Bartholomew had finally arrived at the crux of the matter.

"I have an opportunity, a brief one, to acquire all of Shakespeare's manuscripts. He has debts in Stratford he would like to see settled before his death, and he wishes to provide for his family."

"And you are offering to obtain these manuscripts on my behalf?" said Cotton, leaning forward for the first time in the conversation.

"Precisely," said Bartholomew.

"But you know I don't collect contemporary literature."

"Think of the future. You could be the man who saved the works of England's greatest playwright. Think how those manuscripts would look on your shelves next to your beloved Greeks. They belong in your library, not in someone's kitchen fire." Bartholomew had years of experience in salesmanship, and he knew when a customer had passed the point of no return. Cotton teetered on the edge. "If not for the glory of your own collection," he said, "do it for England. So that the world will know none can outshine our poets."

This twin appeal to patriotism and poetry seemed to tip the balance, for the salesman caught that familiar twinkle in the eye of his victim. Cotton bit his lip for a moment and then asked, "How much?"

"One hundred pounds," said Bartholomew calmly. "Half on deposit, the rest on delivery."

"One hundred pounds!" said Cotton. "This is highway robbery. You are as much a rogue as the salesman in that play."

Cotton's shock did not concern Bartholomew. He knew that once the customer began to complain about the price, the sale had been made. "What can I say, the man has debts. I assure you my share of the price is a pittance. I only do this out of friendship with Shake-speare and a love for English literature."

"You know I do not carry fifty pounds with me through the streets of Southwark."

"Of course not."

"And I shall need some indication that you can actually provide the merchandise."

"A sample," said Bartholomew.

"Tuesday then," said Cotton, rising from his seat. "Bring your sample to my house. If it suits, I shall be prepared to make the first payment, but only if the balance of the materials is delivered within the week." He did not wait for Bartholomew to bid him good-bye, but pushed his way through the crowded bar toward the door.

On the table where Cotton had left it stood his cup of wine, untouched. Bartholomew thought perhaps he should try his hand at acting on the stage of the Globe. Without script, costumes, or props he had pulled off the performance of a lifetime. And his audience had been as sober as a bishop.

"**M**r. Byerly," said Liz, taking off her glasses, laying the watercolor on the table next to her glass of wine, and leaning toward Peter conspiratorially. "Peter. My world is a small world. It may not seem very important to anyone who does not inhabit it, but I assure you for those of us who do, it is all important. You apparently do not inhabit this world. Your late wife perhaps did, or at least she understood it. Mine is the world of Victorian art. It's a world of collectors and professors and dealers and amateur enthusiasts and a few people like me—editors at small publishing houses hoping to find that one manuscript that will leave a lasting mark. There are not many secrets left in the world of Victorian art. So can you imagine what it would mean for a person like me to be involved in the publication of a secret that will rock this little world, a scandal people will be talking about for years to come."

Peter thought he could imagine exactly what it would be like. It would be like finding an undiscovered edition of *Hamlet* that predated the bad quarto. It might not mean much in the larger world, but in the world of rare books it would leave a mark forever. "Yes," he said. "I can imagine that."

"Well," said Liz, "B.B. is supposed to be *my* bombshell."

"So you know who painted this?" said Peter, suppressing a quaver that tried to slip into his voice.

"Not exactly," said Liz. "You see, we have a member who lives down in Cornwall, an older gentleman who's quite the amateur scholar. My company has published two of his monographs—well researched, well written, and dull. Two years ago he rang me and told me he had a lead on a Victorian painter who signed himself 'B.B.' He wouldn't tell me much about it, only that if his hunches were right, this book would not be boring. It would be sexy. That's the word he used. Since then he's been teasing me with clues once in a while—always on the phone, never anything written down—and from what he's told me I can tell two things. B.B. was involved in some sort of scandal that will make a little monograph about an obscure painter into a book that people might actually read."

"And that's why you're glad I didn't show the painting around at the meeting?" said Peter.

"If Richard Campbell had seen your watercolor, he might have started sniffing around trying to find out about B.B."

"What's the second thing?" said Peter.

"My Cornish scholar would kill to have your bloody painting as an illustration in his book. Apparently he's had trouble getting permission to reproduce B.B.'s works."

"Who was this B.B.?" asked Peter

"I can't tell you."

"You don't trust me?"

"It's not that. It's that I don't know any more than I've already told you—just enough to know it's a good story."

"So you propose that I hand over this painting to you and then wait patiently until the book comes out to find out how my late wife managed to be in two centuries at once?"

"I wouldn't have to keep it. I would just get it photographed and return it to you in a couple of days."

"And how long do I have to wait to read this scandalous story?"

"Actually I'm expecting the finished manuscript in the mail any day. We'll put a rush on it, so it should be out in about six months."

"Miss Sutcliffe," said Peter, leaning on his crossed arms and preparing to make a speech of his own. "I am a man of passions, some might even say obsessions. From what you say about your infatuation with Victorian art, I think you can understand that. I've had two passions in my life. No, that's not a strong enough way of putting it. For a decade, two passions *were* my life; there was nothing else. Those passions were rare books and Amanda Byerly. Since my wife died, my life has been empty. My capacity for passion died with her, or so I believed. Now, just when I begin to feel the faintest glow of my passion for rare books returning, I discover this." He tapped his finger on the watercolor. "Inside a rare book, I find a portrait of my wife that cannot be my wife. My two passions united in a single square of paper. And this paper—well, somehow I feel it has the potential to release me from one of those passions and launch me back into the other. It's already accomplished incredible things. It's made me excited and curious again; it even made me sit here and talk to you, a perfect stranger. So you see, this is not idle curiosity, Miss Sutcliffe. This is not a casual chat. This is a matter of life and death for me; or if not life and death then at least life and no life. Because living the way I've been living for the past nine months is no life."

"How did you know it was Miss Sutcliffe?" said Liz, smiling.

"No ring. I just assumed."

"You assumed right. But you're not right about everything. It doesn't sound to me like your capacity for passion is dead. I admire passion, Peter, and you have it. So I propose a compromise."

"A compromise?"

"Exactly. You let me borrow this painting and photograph it for my Cornish gentleman's book. I'll return it to you next week and as soon as the page proofs of the book are ready, I'll send you a set. You'll see it before the reviewers."

"That sounds fair," said Peter, trying to keep the disappointment from his voice. He was not feeling particularly patient.

"That's not the whole deal," said Liz.

"Oh?"

"You also have to finish having dinner with me, start calling me Liz, tell me honestly what you think of the vindaloo, and take me for a walk on the Embankment before you catch your train home." She smiled and whisked the watercolor off the table as a waiter set down two dishes of fragrant curry.

And so Peter had done exactly that. He had forgotten all about the watercolor and rare books and Amanda and spent a pleasant evening with Liz Sutcliffe. After dinner they had walked down to the river and along the Embankment toward Westminster. The wind had died down and the moon came out from behind the clouds just as Big Ben struck ten o'clock.

"It must be nice living in London," said Peter. "To be able to walk along the river, watching the boats and looking at that amazing view of Parliament."

"I suppose," said Liz. "The truth is I hardly ever come here. I live in Hampstead and work in Bloomsbury and it's pretty rare that I go anywhere else."

"That's too bad," said Peter, who immediately felt like a hypocrite for criticizing someone else's cocooned existence.

"Well, that's the thing about London," said Liz. "Everything you need is right in your neighborhood. The sights we just take for granted." She stopped at the top of the stairs to Westminster Bridge and looked up at the famous clock face glowing overhead. "But you're right—it is pretty wonderful."

It was just past midnight by the time Peter turned his latchkey and stepped from a cold drizzle into his sitting room, lit only by the flashing message light on his answering machine. He nearly fell over the box of book repair supplies that he had left in the middle of the floor, as he stumbled toward the light switch. Quietly cursing the electrician who had seen fit to put the switch across the room from the front door, he flicked on the lights and began to fumble with the thermostat. The cottage's heating system was temperamental at best. Right now it felt more like twenty degrees Fahrenheit than the twenty degrees Celsius claimed by the thermostat. Amanda would never have put up with this. Too tired to wait and see if his fiddling would return heat to the house, he filled a hot-water bottle in the kitchen and trudged upstairs to a cold, empty bed. Downstairs, the answering machine flashed in the darkness.

Peter didn't receive messages often, and when he did they were usually from Francis Leland or Hank Christiansen or Amanda's best friend Cynthia. Peter could imagine the three of them meeting for coffee and drawing straws to see whose turn it would be this week. Whoever it was always had a legitimate-sounding question, but Peter knew their real reason for calling was to check that he was alive and capable of returning a phone call. He never did. On rare occasions, a client would call, asking advice on a purchase or for help in finding a particular volume. Those calls he sometimes returned.

Not until Peter finished breakfast the next morning did he think to check the answering machine. He hoped the message might be from a customer giving him some excuse to return to Hay. He had awoken early and as he lay in bed listening to the rain, he couldn't get the copy of Malone's *Inquiry,* the book in which he had found the watercolor, out of his mind. Why had he not looked through every page for margin notes? Why hadn't he just bought the thing? He could certainly afford one overpriced book. And it would have kept him from being a thief.

The message was left by an unfamiliar voice—English, male, crisp, and upper class. "Mr. Byerly," said the voice. "I hope I've reached Peter Byerly. My name is John Alderson. I've heard from a friend that you know a little something about rare books. Do a bit of dealing I gather. And to think you're right here in Kingham. I've been thinking of selling a few choice items from my library and wondered if you might like to handle the job for me. I'm home most mornings. Feel free to drop by for a cup of tea and you can see if you're interested. It's John Alderson, We're on the road toward Cornwall. Evenlode..." The machine clicked off. Like the heating system, it seemed to have a mind of its own and did not like being overworked.

Could he have meant Evenlode House, the dilapidated manor house that Martin Wells had told him about? John Alderson had not sounded like the sort of man to keep visitors away with buckshot. The rain had stopped and Peter had been in England long enough that by midmorning on a cold day he rather fancied a cup of tea. Cornwall was only two miles away, so Evenlode House must be closer. He decided to walk it.

The road to Cornwall was barely wide enough for a single vehicle and lined with tall hedgerows that shut out not only the wind but the world. Peter felt a delicious solitude as he walked the mile to a rusted iron gate on which a sign in large red lettering proclaimed EVENLODE HOUSE—KEEP OUT! The gate hung loosely from two crumbling stone pillars and Peter easily stepped inside, hoping the sign did not apply to invited guests. He followed a deeply rutted mud track uphill across a field and then down through another hedgerow where it turned suddenly to the left, revealing what was left of Evenlode House. It appeared to have once been a grand Jacobean manor, but was surely not habitable in its current state.

One wing had collapsed into a pile of rubble through which a pair of dogs nosed—looking for rats, Peter imagined. Most of the windows were broken, and grass and small trees grew on the roof, except where the slate tiles had caved in. Several of the chimneys that rose above the roofline had fallen into heaps of stone on the ground below, leaving ragged stumps from which no smoke rose. It did not impress Peter as the sort of estate where he was likely to encounter great bibliographic rarities.

Still, Peter had been to more than one house in North Carolina where the exterior belied the value of the books within. As he came around the side of the house, Peter realized that it must, indeed, be uninhabited, for parked in what had once been the kitchen garden were two large camping trailers—*caravans*, he had heard the locals call them. Here, he thought, was the actual home of John Alderson. Knocking did not seem like a good plan. He was already worried that the dogs might have outflanked him.

"Mr. Alderson!" he called out, half hoping no one would answer. Then, without warning, the air erupted in a roar. Without thinking, Peter fell to the ground, feeling the cold seep instantly through his khakis. His ears rang with pain as he rolled over to see a grizzled old man standing astride the pile of rubble that had been the west wing. The two salivating hounds crouched in front of him, and he held a smoking shotgun in the crook of his arm.

"That was a warning," spat the man.

"Mr. Alderson, you rang me," sputtered Peter. "I'm Peter Byerly."

"Shotgun or dogs, you can take your choice, Yank, if you say that name one more time. Keep out means keep out." The man cracked the shotgun in half and pulled a pair of cartridges out of his coat pocket. Peter decided that further negotiation was useless and got to his feet.

"I'm sorry to intrude, sir," he said. "I must have made a mistake." Peter turned and began to walk back up the muddy track toward the gate. He heard a metallic crack as the man snapped the shotgun back together.

"You can move faster than that, Yank!" the man yelled, his voice echoing through the valley. "Dogs'll show you how."

Peter did not wait to see how the dogs might impart these instructions. His feet slipping in the mud, he ran up the hill as fast as he could. Behind him he heard the sound of laughter and barking, but he did not turn to see if the dogs had taken chase. Just as he crested the hill, another shot rent the peaceful air. Peter slid down the hill toward the gate and stumbled panting onto the road.

As he made his way back toward Kingham, cold, wet, and muddy, but with his breathing gradually returning to normal, it occurred to him that he had not been nervous that morning when he'd gone to meet the mysterious Mr. Alderson. The one time, he thought, when being afraid of a stranger would have proved worthwhile.

Two hours later, having bathed and put on a fresh set of clothes, Peter listened again to the answering machine message. The voice was certainly not that of the inhospitable man at Evenlode House. This voice sounded inviting, the sort of voice Peter hated to ignore. He thought he might ask the proprietress of the village shop where Mr. Alderson lived, but he had nodded mutely to this woman nearly every day for the past five months as he bought his bread and milk and newspaper and he could not imagine anything more awkward than suddenly breaking that well-established silence. The only two people in the neighborhood with whom Peter could claim to be on speaking terms were the gardener, who puttered around in Peter's tiny backyard once a week in exchange for a twenty-pound note, and the postman. He could not recall either man's name. Then it occurred to him that perhaps Martin Wells might be able to help. Martin was listed in the local phone directory, and Peter was pleased to hear the exasperated sigh with which the painter accepted an invitation for tea. "To repay you for your hospitality and your advice about the Watercolour Society," Peter said.

"Best go on and get it over with," said Martin. "I'll be round in half an hour."

"John Alderson," said Martin, reaching for his third biscuit. "You'll not be wanting Evenlode House to speak with him. Mr. Alderson lives in Evenlode Manor, farther up the road. Surprised you made it off the premises of Evenlode House if you used his name."

"I almost didn't," said Peter.

"Aldersons and Gardners have hated each other for centuries," said Martin. "Not sure when it started, but they haven't spoken a civil word to each other since before Victoria."

"And they're neighbors?" asked Peter.

"Live on opposite sides of the river," said Martin. "Nothing to stop them killing each other but a few feet of water. You'll be safe with Alderson, though. Evenlode Manor's nice enough, I've heard."

"So how did it happen that Evenlode Manor is a fine house with a library and Evenlode House is a pile of rubble?"

"Depends who you ask. Gardner would say it was the Aldersons drove them to poverty, though he'd not say why. Alderson would say his family went to work in the past century while the Gardners drank, grumbled, and shot pheasants. Not that the Aldersons are living like kings. I hear they've had to sell off all sorts of things to keep that house in good nick. You can tour it on Tuesdays in the summer."

Martin seemed in a hurry to leave once the chocolate digestives had been exhausted, but his facade had mellowed somewhat during the half hour of his visit. He did not say thank you as he stepped back out into the winter sun, but he did say something much more generous to his host. "First American I ever met who could make a proper pot of tea."

Ridgefield, 1985

Part of Peter's job in Special Collections was playing host to visiting scholars. It was one of his favorite tasks for two reasons: it often gave him the chance to examine books and manuscripts he might not otherwise have come across as he pulled them for researchers, and it showed him that there was some purpose to Special Collections other than mere preservation. Though he was frustrated by how seldom members of the Ridgefield community used the materials in Special Collections, the regular visits by scholars from as far away as Europe and Japan comforted Peter with the thought that the collection was a living, breathing thing—taking in new information as acquisitions were made, and sending out knowledge in the form of new scholarship.

It was during his preparation for one such visit that Peter handled the first edition of *Greene's Groatsworth of Wit*, a 1592 deathbed confessional by the minor author Robert Greene, which included the first printed reference to William Shakespeare as a member of the London theatrical community. Dr. Yoshi Kashimoto of the University of Tokyo had requested this pamphlet along with a number of other Elizabethan items.

Peter lifted the delicate pamphlet out of its folding case and began to read Greene's text. His understanding of the Elizabethan idiom was still far from fluent, but he had no trouble finding the reference, near the end of the text, to Shakespeare as an "upstart crow."

"Everything ready for Dr. Kashimoto?" said Francis, who stepped into the room as Peter was returning the Greene pamphlet to its case.

"Absolutely," said Peter. "I saw he was interested in minor Elizabethan dramatists, so I also pulled a few items we have that aren't in the standard bibliographies."

"I'm sure he'll appreciate that," said Francis. "You're taking Connelly's Shakespeare survey this semester, so you might want to attend Kashimoto's public lecture. I think you'll find him thought provoking."

"Funny," said Peter, "Connelly didn't mention anything about a Shakespeare lecture on campus."

" I'm not surprised. Kashimoto is an Oxfordian."

"So he's from England?" said Peter.

"No," said Francis. "An Oxfordian is someone who believes that Edward de Vere, the Earl of Oxford, wrote the works commonly attributed to William Shakespeare of Stratford."

"I beg your pardon?" said Peter.

"There's a significant and legitimate question about the authorship of Shakespeare's plays," Francis explained.

"They never taught us that in high school English," said Peter.

"Well," said Francis, "the Oxfordians have had trouble making inroads in the academic establishment."

"How can they say that Shakespeare wasn't Shakespeare?" said Peter, bewildered by such nonsense.

"Two reasons, essentially," said Francis. "To begin with, the Stratford businessman known as William Shakspere, who never spelled his name with an *e* after the *k*, has a reasonably well-documented life, and yet there exists no evidence from his lifetime that he was even a writer, much less the great William Shakespeare—whose name always had an *e* after the *k*."

"But it was a long time ago," said Peter. "People didn't know then that they should save letters or manuscripts."

"True," said Francis. "That is just what the Stratfordians argue. They're the ones who believe the plays were written by William Shakespeare of Stratford."

"Well, they were, weren't they?" said Peter.

"The other problem," said Francis, "is that there is no evidence that Shakespeare ever received any education, though he probably attended the Stratford Grammar School. He certainly never attended Oxford, Cambridge, or any other university in Europe."

"So," said Peter, puzzled that he seemed to be, for the first time since they had met, in an argument with Francis. "He was a genius, he didn't need to be taught how to write."

"Again, well argued," said Francis. "But it's not the quality of his writing but the content that presents a problem. The writer of Shakespeare's plays had a significant knowledge of law and art, of music, medicine, military tactics, philosophy, and a dozen other specialized fields, and especially of life in the Italian court. He used sources in several languages, including Latin and Greek. One can be born with genius, but where did Mr. Shakspere of Stratford acquire all this information?"

"So you really think Shakespeare didn't write his own plays?" said Peter, not sure how to refute this argument.

"Alas, no. I myself remain a Stratfordian. But I do admit there is room for doubt. I might even say it would be unreasonable not to doubt."

"Do you think we'll ever know?" asked Peter.

"Perhaps," said Francis, "when some enterprising book hound discovers solid evidence in favor of Mr. Shakespeare, or Edward de Vere, or Christopher Marlowe, or Francis Bacon. They've all been suggested as possible authors."

Peter felt the usually solid floor of the Devereaux Room shifting beneath him. He stared down at the stack of books and pamphlets awaiting the arrival of Dr. Kashimoto. He had expected to have his preconceived notions about the world challenged when he came to college, but to have his mentor introduce a doubt like this, on such a basic tenet of Western culture, was like being told that truth wasn't true or reality wasn't real. But then he felt Francis lay a hand on his shoulder and he heard a calming voice turn a bizarre nightmare into a glorious fantasy.

"Wouldn't it be something, Peter, to discover a page of manuscript written by the Stratford Shakespeare? Or a letter to Anne Hathaway where he complains about what trouble the third act of *Hamlet* is giving him?"

"The Holy Grail," said Peter reverently. He was surprised to hear the words coming from his mouth. The comparison had been instinctual.

"Exactly," said Francis. "The Holy Grail."

Peter took the car this time. If he had to make a second getaway, he had no interest in doing it on foot again. A few hundred yards past the unwelcoming entrance to Evenlode House the road humped over a small stone bridge. Below, the River Evenlode flowed—a dozen feet wide and muddy and swollen from the recent rains. Another quarter mile down the road on the right he came to a pair of stone pillars surmounted by ornamental urns. An engraved stone on a pillar read EVENLODE MANOR. The iron gate was open, and a neat gravel drive led through a row of trees to the crest of a small hill. Peter turned his car into the drive and shortly crunched to a stop in front of Evenlode Manor. It was no Blenheim Palace, but it was a far cry from its decrepit neighbor. Looking up at the three-story Georgian facade, with stairs sweeping up to the huge wooden doors, Peter felt as if he had entered a Jane Austen novel. The grass was immaculately trimmed and a croquet lawn to the left of the house was backed by ornamental shrubs that led into further gardens. Peter felt confident that this time he had come to the right place.

The door was answered by a housekeeper who led him into a drawing room and told him in a deep Irish brogue that he should make himself comfortable while she informed Mr. Alderson of his arrival. The furnishings were a little French for Amanda's tastes, Peter thought, but the view she would have loved. Tall windows looked out across the wide green Evenlode valley. He wondered why, during the summer they had spent in Chipping Norton, Amanda had never come here on a Tuesday, and then he thought perhaps she had, some day when he was deep in a book and she had announced only, "I'll be out for a while."

"Mr. Byerly," said a crisp, friendly voice behind him. Peter turned to see an exceptionally tall man with a neatly combed wave of white hair.

"I'm John Alderson," said the man, extending a hand.

"A pleasure to meet you, Mr. Alderson," said Peter, taking Alderson's firm handshake.

"Please, call me John. We don't stand on formalities here at Evenlode Manor, despite what Miss O'Hara might have told you."

"She was most kind," said Peter.

"I won't waste your time, Mr. Byerly. The fact is I'd like to sell some books. I happened to mention that fact to the vicar on Sunday and he said there was an American chap in Kingham who was in the book business. I presume that's you."

"It is," said Peter, pulling a card out of his pocket and presenting it to John. It was the only one he could find that morning, a bit crumpled and with one corner torn off, but it would do the job.

"Well," said John, "I have a modest library filled with old books that I have no use for, and I have three bedrooms in which I've piled all my books on gardening and art and the law—books I actually read. The present arrangement seems a rather inefficient use of both funds and space. So I thought perhaps you could take a look through the library and see if there are some things there worth selling. Clear out a case or two, perhaps."

"I'd be delighted," said Peter, who suddenly felt a familiar, but nearly forgotten, excitement pulsing through his veins—that anticipation of a treasure hunt. Rarely had he bought books in an environment that seemed as conducive to treasure finding as Evenlode Manor.

John showed Peter into the library where eight bookcases of deep cherry lined two walls of the room, while two others flanked the fireplace. On a large table in the center of the room lay a stack of oversized volumes. The cases by the fireplace ran from floor to ceiling; the others extended to the ceiling from solid built-in cabinets.

Most of the bindings looked nineteenth-century, though some were clearly older. Peter knew immediately that he would have no trouble moving a case or two of these books fairly quickly. Even if they turned out to be mediocre in content, he could sell them to another dealer for the bindings. It seemed likely he would find a few rarities. Only one shelf was not filled. From the lack of dust, Peter guessed that some books had been removed recently. Then he remembered the strict face of Miss O'Hara, and decided she must dust the library at least twice a week.

"Well," said John, "if you're perfectly happy having a look around, I'll get back to my work. Perhaps we could meet for tea in a couple of hours."

Peter knew it would take a lot longer than two hours to examine the library in enough detail to recommend a course of action, but he could at least do some browsing and get an idea of what he was up against. He felt the rusty wheels of his bookseller's mind slowly begin to turn, and thoughts of the mysterious watercolor faded away.

His first find came almost immediately. Because they were already laying out on the table, he started with the oversized books. At the bottom of the pile Peter saw two matching volumes. The deep brown calf binding was clearly at least a hundred years older than the other volumes, and on the spine, stamped in gold, were the words *A Dictionary of the English Language*. Any other bookman might have been disappointed that the set, though in excellent condition, was not a first edition; Peter was thrilled to read on the title page of Samuel Johnson's magnum opus, "Fourth Edition." The fourth edition, Francis Leland had explained years ago, included Johnson's final corrections and additions. "I'd love to have one for the Devereaux collection," Francis had said.

Peter decided in that moment that he would not sell the volumes to Ridgefield; he would buy them from Alderson at a fair price and donate them to the Devereaux Room in memory of Amanda—his Amanda. Though he had thousands of books to look at, he could not resist lingering over the Johnson for a few minutes. In the "Advertisement" he read words of comfort to a twentieth-century widower who fears his own weaknesses: "Perfection is unattainable, but nearer and nearer approaches may be made; and finding my dictionary about to be reprinted, I have endeavoured, by a revisal, to make it less reprehensible." A noble undertaking, thought Peter. He wondered if he would have made quicker progress if Dr. Strayer had simply told him, *Peter, I believe that by revisal you could make yourself less reprehensible.*

With cases full of books beckoning him, Peter set the Johnson aside and turned to his work. After an hour he had found a few fine eighteenth-century titles and sorted through several shelves of worthless volumes of nineteenth-century sermons. He had just sat down on the floor to begin work on the lower shelves when he heard a knock on the open door. He looked up to see a mousy woman, shoulders hunched, strands of hair flying in all directions, standing in the doorway. She wore a plain gray dress that had all the tailoring of a potato sack and her feet were encased in a pair of muddy Wellington boots. He thought at first she must be one of the gardeners, but then she brushed the strands of hair away from her face and he saw the same high forehead and sharp chin as his host. She was too old to be his daughter; Peter could only assume this was John Alderson's sister.

"Been walking," she said, almost inaudibly, as if these two mumbled words would explain not only the mud on her boots but everything about her, from her choice of wardrobe to her defensive stance, arms clasped across her insubstantial breasts.

"Is the sun still out?" asked Peter, who knew that in England, whenever a social situation left one at a loss for words, one could always bring up the weather. He used this rejoinder to pull himself up from the floor, but neither her stance nor her tone of voice invited him to move any closer.

She stared at him for a long moment, then looked around the room, her eyes resting on the one shelf that had been empty before Peter set to work. Then, when Peter had nearly forgotten his query, she growled, "No."

"Pity," said Peter, forcing a smile. In a conversation with a stranger, he was used to being the one who was socially inept. He found it unnerving that he should be better at making small talk than someone else.

After another long pause, and still without moving, she said, "Brother show you the box?" Her eyes did not stray from her own feet as she muttered this enigmatic question.

"No," said Peter, unable to elaborate as he had no idea what she was talking about.

The woman gave a small grunt of disgust, then shuffled across the room to the desk by the window. Not the gait, Peter thought, of someone who takes walks in the countryside. She opened a drawer, removed a small brass key, and shuffled back across the room where she inserted the key into the door of a cabinet. With a click she unlocked the door and then stooped and withdrew a hinged wooden box, its edges covered in brass straps faded to a dull grayish brown. A label pasted to the top of the box had nearly peeled away and the woman quickly ripped it off and crumpled it in her hand—but not before Peter could read the nineteenth-century script: NEVER TO BE SOLD.

She set the box in the middle of the library table and opened the lid. "Save you the trouble of looking through all that muck," she said, nodding toward the shelves where Peter stood. "Give you a week to make an offer, then I'll get brother to call someone else." And with this cryptic threat she turned and left the room.

Peter opened the dusty lid of the box and soon felt that even being shot at this morning had been worthwhile if it brought him to this. The box was a gold mine. Despite his limited experience with documents, Peter suspected its contents might be worth more than all the bound items in the library combined. Just a quick perusal of the papers in the box revealed a commission signed by Charles I, a letter from Walter Raleigh, and a deed signed by Francis Bacon. There were church documents signed by archbishops of Canterbury and a stanza of manuscript poetry signed by Robert Greene. Of course they would all need careful study and authentication, but there was enough here to keep Peter busy for months.

He took the documents from the box one by one, carefully stacking them on the library table, and just as he was about to return them, he saw there was something else in the bottom of the box. At first, Peter thought it was a book, but then he realized it was a custom-made folding case, much more elaborate than any he had seen on the shelves of the Devereaux collection. The work appeared nineteenth century—mid-Victorian, Peter guessed. It took him several minutes to open, and he was careful to memorize each step of unfolding so that he would be able to reassemble the case. Inside was a slim quarto volume in a simple leather binding.

Peter gingerly lifted the front cover. When he read the title page, he stopped breathing. He knew he had found something that made the rest of the contents of the box pale in comparison. If the text was complete, it could be the sort of treasure he had always dreamed of finding. When he began to turn the pages, and his eyes suddenly comprehended the scribbled markings that filled the margins, the breath spurted from his lungs as suddenly as if he had been punched in the gut. Without his realizing it, that expelled breath voiced two words.

"Holy Grail."

Thick clouds hung over London, and for them Bartholomew was grateful. The heavy oaken door of Robert Cotton's house had presented no more problem than the stone lid of William of Wykeham's sarcophagus that Bartholomew had prized open all those years ago. This bit of prizing he managed all on his own. Not until he was safely inside, with the door closed behind him, did he light his lantern.

Bartholomew had been to Cotton's house several times—first a few months ago, when he began to talk to the collector about Shakespeare, and most recently three days ago, when he delivered the *Pandosto*. Now he made his way quickly up the stairs and into the library. In the dim light of his lantern the busts of emperors glared down upon him, their uplit faces menacing as he began to scan the shelves in search of his quarry. It had been a stroke of great luck that Cotton had let slip he was going to Cambridge for a few days, but Bartholomew did not fool himself that the collection was unguarded. Surely some burly local to whom Cotton had paid a few shillings would be checking the outer door at any time; he needed to work quickly.

In the Nero case he recognized the Winchester Psalter he had sold Cotton twenty years ago. He wondered if he ought to take it, too, and replace it in Wykeham's tomb—as penance for his other misdeeds. But the Psalter was a large book, and surely Cotton would immediately notice its absence. Besides, Bartholomew reasoned, taking the Psalter from the tomb had not been a crime—he had saved a beautiful book for future generations. Better it be preserved in Cotton's library than decay to dust in a stone box in Winchester.

Bartholomew tried not to think of what he was doing as stealing. After all, he had not exactly sold the *Pandosto* to Cotton; rather, he had presented it as proof of his access to Shakespeare's papers. That he had thus relieved Cotton of the fifty-pound down payment on papers that might not even exist Bartholomew thought of as an act of knavery rather than thievery. He hoped he might live up to the standard set for him by Shakespeare in the person of Autolycus—if a thief, a harmless thief; when a knave, a clever and amusing knave, likeable if not wholly moral.

On the second shelf of the Augustus case, Bartholomew spotted *Pandosto*. He pulled it out, wrapped it carefully in a cloth, and had just turned to leave when he heard voices at the door below. In another second heavy boots were pounding up the stairs. There was a single window at the far end of the library, looking out toward the Thames a hundred feet away. Bartholomew did not have time to think, and as the door to the library flew open, he leapt from the window to the cobblestones below.

He heard the crack of the bone an instant before the pain seared through his leg, and in that instant came a peace Bartholomew had never felt. There was no longer any question of whether his plan would succeed, whether he would escape and retire and live out his days comfortably in the country. Some people recovered from broken legs, some avoided the infection that so often poisoned the body, but Bartholomew knew with a fiery certainty that he would not. In that instant he knew that he had failed, that he would die, probably within a few days, but the peace that came with that finality surrounded him like a cocoon as he lay on the stones, his leg crumpled beneath him. Then the pain arrived.

His boatman waited for him a few dozen yards away, and Bartholomew knew he must hurry to elude capture. It would take per-

haps a minute for his pursuers to realize where he had gone and to
run out the front of the house and along the lane that led to the river.
Without a thought for his agony, and without a sound, he pulled
himself up on the side of the house, and hopped toward the water.
Each movement sent the pain to greater heights than he thought
possible, but Bartholomew focused his entire being on silence, bit-
ing the inside of his mouth until he could feel warm blood flow-
ing freely. Reaching the boat, he collapsed over the gunwale and
murmured to the boatman to fly downstream. As the craft moved
toward the center of the river and was enveloped by darkness, Bartholomew heard the clatter of boots on the stones and then knew
no more.

He awoke in his lodgings, the pain from his leg radiating through
his body. His landlady held a damp cloth to his head and the boatman stood nearby. Bartholomew knew he must accomplish one
more task before he drifted back into darkness. He whispered his instructions to the boatman and gave him the cloth-wrapped book
and the bag of gold he pulled from within his doublet, along with a
note he had prepared for just such an eventuality.

When the boatman had gone, Bartholomew fell back against the
pillows and surrendered himself to the ministrations of his landlady,
who tended him with the gentle attention of one who had fond
memories of, on occasion, sharing his bed.

Over what he only guessed were the next several days he drifted
in and out of the world. He was agonizingly awake when the bone-
setter came to see to the break. As his leg became more and more
swollen and inflamed, the apothecary paid several visits—each time
bathing Bartholomew's leg in vinegar to fight the infection, each
time shaking his head at the landlady as he left.

It was morning when Bartholomew awoke, feeling clearheaded
for the first time since the accident. The pain had subsided somewhat, but he felt the blackness beckoning him. It occurred to him

that this might be a good time to repent of his sins, but before the thought had formed itself into any action, the rising darkness washed over him and he slipped into its embrace.

Bartholomew's grave in St. Paul's churchyard was not marked with a stone. Though his landlady had been fond of him, she had kept the few shillings he had given her for such a purpose to settle part of his debt to her. She did, however, weep as he was lowered into the cold earth.

Matthew Harbottle had never known the origin of his surname. Before his mother had died, two years ago, she had always changed the subject whenever he asked about either his father or his name. His mother had only ever called herself Lil. She had died in childbirth in a room above the George and Dragon; the child had died, too. By then Matthew was sixteen and had been working for years as a stable boy at the tavern. His mother, he knew, conducted other business there, but he had always lived with this knowledge and it seemed neither shameful nor immoral to him. Shortly after her death, he had begun his new career among the players. A man from the Globe Theatre had come to the inn asking for Matthew, and though Matthew never learned why the man had come looking for a specific stable boy, he gladly accepted the job he was offered.

Matthew was small, but years of work had made him strong and he was perfectly suited for his new career. Crouched in the atticlike space above the heavens of the Globe, Matthew rolled cannonballs when thunder was required and lowered actors who were playing fairies or gods to the stage. For other productions he would work below the stage, making the sound of approaching horses and pushing props up through trapdoors. When the company traveled, Matthew looked after props and costumes, stabled the horses, and did whatever else was needed.

Matthew never saw a play, and he had never learned to read, so he could not comprehend the scripts he sometimes delivered to actors, but he did hear snatches of plays as he listened for his cues. To him plays were bits of dialogue that drifted into darkness and the undulating sound of the crowd—now a murmur, now a roar, now the unmistakable sound of three thousand people gasping in unison.

Occasionally the players would invite Matthew to come along to the tavern for a drink. Then he felt like a king, stood to a mug of ale by the men who brought words to life in an inn where once he had been a stable boy and the son of the whore upstairs. He was wise enough to know, from the winks of the players and their nods toward the upper floors, that many of them had enjoyed his late mother, but whenever he asked one of the players about his father and his name, the response was always the same—a hearty laugh and an offer of another mug of ale. Thus it came as quite a surprise when early one morning, as he slept in a room filled with costumes and props, a stranger shook him awake and whispered, "Your father has sent these for you."

Matthew pressed the messenger, as best he could in his groggy state, for news of his father, but the man would only point to the folded paper he had delivered along with a cloth-wrapped package and a heavy cloth bag. "The letter explains everything," he said. The messenger left before Matthew could ask him to read this mysterious letter from a father he had never known. To him, it was unintelligible scratches.

He understood well enough, however, the meaning of the cloth bag. He counted the money three times. Fifty pounds, all in gold. More money than he had ever seen, or ever expected to see. He hid the money and the book with all the writing in the margins in his mattress. He could imagine no possible use for the latter, but it seemed wise to keep it hidden, at least for the time being.

Later that day he asked one of the players to read him what was written on the piece of paper. He sat quietly on the edge of his bed as he listened to the almost incomprehensible words.

My Dear Son,

This shall be both the first time you hear from me and the last, for if I am compelled to send this letter, then know that death is near and will have overtaken me by the time this reaches you. Had things gone differently, I might perhaps have sent for you, but that is for neither of us to know. I send with this letter two treasures. The money I trust you will use to secure your future. That you will live comfortably in this world is comfort to me as I prepare for another. The other I advise you to keep as long as you can, and if you are ever forced to part with it, do not do so here in London. I wish you well.

Your affectionate father,

Bartholomew Harbottle

P.S. Though we have not met, I have heard you at work. As recently as last week I attended a play at the Globe and knew you to be in the heavens. Would that I were bound there now.

Thus did Matthew Harbottle become a silent, illiterate partner in the Red Bull Theatre in Clerkenwell with an investment of fifty pounds. The job he had done at the Globe he did at the Red Bull for Prince Charles's Men for many years. As before, he accompanied the players on their provincial tours, and it was on one such tour, late in his life, that he found himself in Exeter and in greater debt at the end of a card game with a local nobleman than he would have liked. Recalling his father's words about selling the strange book away from London, he offered the volume as settlement of the debt. The man accepted this offer, and even agreed to write Matthew's name in the front of the book, beneath what he said was a list of others who had owned it. He thought his father would have liked this, for one name on the list, the man told him, was "Bartholomew Harbottle." Matthew asked the man to write *Matthew Harbottle, Red Bull Theatre*, and then handed over the book without further thought. Early the next morning the company departed for Bath.

Ridgefield, 1985

Peter marked his progress through Ridgefield University not in courses or semesters but by his encounters with certain books—and he held a special place for the Kelmscott *Chaucer*.

At the snack bar one night during final exams, Amanda had asked him if Special Collections had any works printed by William Morris.

"Sure," said Peter. "I couldn't tell you all of them off the top of my head, but we've got a good collection of Kelmscott Press." Kelmscott was the private press owned and operated by Morris, the Victorian author, artist, and designer. "I know we've got the *Chaucer*."

"The Kelmscott *Chaucer*?" said Amanda in awe. "With the Burne-Jones illustrations? An original, I mean, not the facsimile."

"Yeah," said Peter, taking a bite of his hamburger. "Why do you ask?"

Amanda had just finished writing a paper on Edward Burne-Jones for her art history class. She had used the facsimile edition of the *Chaucer* to look at the artist's medieval-style illustrations. When Peter asked her if she would like to see the real thing, she ran her foot up his calf and whispered, "Yes, please."

The week of exams the library was open all night, but Special Collections still closed at five. Peter unlocked the door and disabled the alarm system before ushering Amanda into the narrow corridor that opened into the Devereaux Room, now lit only by the green glow of the EXIT sign. He turned on a reading lamp on the massive library table and pulled out a chair for Amanda. Then he disappeared for a moment into the dimness and returned with the oversized volume, bound in white leather with delicate blind stamping. From a box on the table he pulled two pairs of white cotton gloves, then he sat by Amanda and opened the book.

It was hard to believe it had been printed less than a hundred years ago. The thick paper; the exquisite foliage design wrapping around the text; the illustrations, so reminiscent of illuminated manuscripts; even the ancient typeface all spoke of a fifteenth-century volume, and of course that was exactly what Morris had intended. The pages were heavy between Peter's fingers as he gently turned them. Even through the cotton tips of his gloves he could feel the texture of the hand-set type and the wood-block illustrations. He adored the feel of a hand-printed book. The love and care positively radiated off the pages. He turned to a page spread that included two of Burne-Jones's illustrations and leaned back, letting Amanda soak in the beauty of the artistry and craftsmanship. She gave a short, soft sigh as she ran a cotton-gloved fingertip slowly across the page.

"It's so beautiful," she whispered reverently, and Peter looked from the page to Amanda's face.

"So are you," he mouthed silently, for though he had always found her face lovely, she had taken on a special glow as she pored over the book. She was enchanted, Peter thought, and he was thrilled that he had helped her feel that way. He wondered how it had never occurred to him to bring Amanda to the Devereaux Room before. Suddenly his mind was crowded with images of books from the collection that would delight her—works of the Victorians and of the medieval artists who had inspired them. In no volume, however, could the intersection of his passion for fine books and her passion for Victorian art more perfectly intersect than in this most famous example of nineteenth-century printing.

Almost hypnotized by the interplay of text, illustration, and design, Peter did not hear Amanda shift in her chair, and so the only warning he had was the slightly rough texture of her cheap cotton glove slipping across the bare flesh above his collar. Peter's physical contact with Amanda had previously been limited to holding hands as they walked each night from the Student Center to the residential quad, an occasional embrace, and short, chaste good-night kisses at the door of Amanda's dormitory. Like everything else about Amanda, the kisses were regimented, and Peter liked that. That quick kiss was the highlight of his day, every day, but if he had stopped to consider what else it might lead to, and how it might lead there, his dread of the unfamiliar would have invaded the peace Amanda had created in his life. But she moved so quickly in the quiet isolation of the Devereaux Room that Peter did not have time to fear the unknown. He did wonder afterward if she had planned that moment, knowing that in that room Peter would feel more comfortable than anywhere in the world.

Her cotton-gloved hand pulled his head toward her and she pressed her lips to his—not the quick, dry kiss he was used to, but an endless, open kiss with damp lips and the unmistakable feel of her tongue darting into his mouth. Her other hand reached down and pulled Peter's arm around the small of her back and he tightened his arm around her, pulling her body into his. Peter's eyes were closed and he had lost all sense of where they were; only Amanda's warmth in his arms and against his lips existed. They kissed for what seemed like both an eternity and an instant. He nibbled her neck and she drew her fingers through his hair and he caressed her back and they kissed and everything disappeared except Amanda and her lips and hair and body. And then she pulled away and did the last thing he expected. She began to laugh. Peter sensed immediately that she was not laughing at him but laughing with sheer joy. Even in the dim light her eyes sparkled, and the smile he had seen briefly every night after the kiss in front of her dorm played across her face with such enthusiasm, it seemed like it would never fade.

Finally she fell back in her chair. "Look at us," she said. "Mr. Timid and Miss Methodical, nuts about each other and making out in the rare-books room." Only later did Peter realize this might have been a profession of love; at the time it seemed like only her delighting in the absurdity of it all. And then Amanda said the most surprising thing of all. Leaning conspiratorially into Peter, she nodded to the portrait of Amanda Devereaux watching over them and whispered, "What would Grandmother think?"

"Amanda Devereaux was your grandmother?" said Peter, removing his gloved hand from the small of Amanda's back and turning to look at the portrait. "I can't believe I didn't see that. You have her eyes. Did you know her? What was she like?"

" 'What was she like?' " Amanda repeated. "Peter, I've just told you my big secret—the one piece of information that has chased away every guy I ever liked and attracted a bunch of creeps I couldn't stand. Don't you get it? I'm a superrich heiress. You're now supposed to form all sorts of preconceived notions about me."

Peter leaned forward and kissed her wetly on the neck, pulling her toward him. "I'm afraid all my notions about you have already been conceived."

"Peter," said Amanda, laughing and pushing him away. "This is a big deal for me. It's why I enrolled in Ridgefield under my middle name. I'm not Amanda Middleton; I'm Amanda Ridgefield. You're the first person I've told, and I sort of expected a reaction."

"Look," said Peter, settling back in his chair. "It's no big deal. I mean it's nice that you don't have to worry about money and everything, but I certainly don't want you to judge me by my family, why should I judge you by yours?"

"It is a big deal," said Amanda. "You think so, too, I can tell. You're smiling." Peter could not deny it. "See, you can't stop grinning, and you can't even look me in the eye."

"I'm not looking you in the eye because I'm looking at the hickey on your neck, and I'm grinning because I'm remembering how you got it."

"You honestly don't care that I'm like Ridgefield royalty and that I've got scads of money and that lots of people are going to treat me and anyone I'm dating in certain ways because of it?"

"I don't," said Peter, who was getting over the initial shock of discovering that his two Amandas were connected. "Let's kiss some more."

"And you don't care that when you meet my parents they're going to put you through every test you can imagine to make sure you're good enough for precious Amanda of the Ridgefields?"

"I'd expect nothing less no matter who your parents were." Peter leaned toward her, but she gently pushed him away.

"And you don't care that when everybody finally figures out who I am, and they will soon enough, they'll all think you're after me for my money?"

"Amanda," said Peter softly, taking her hands in his and feeling the warmth of her nervousness through the thin glove, "I don't care about any of that stuff. I love you." He had said it without premeditation and it seemed like the most natural and truthful thing in the world, but his declaration unintentionally brought the conversation to a much more serious level. Peter felt the tension in her hand, and grasped for a way to change the subject before she felt pressured into a response. He glanced up at the portrait of Amanda Devereaux, gazing down on her granddaughter. "Now seriously," said Peter, standing up and pointing to the portrait. "I want to know all about Amanda Devereaux."

He heard the tiny sigh of relief escape from Amanda's lips as she relaxed into her chair. "Well," she said, "she died before I was born, and Mom doesn't talk about her much, but from the few stories I've heard, I gather Gran was pretty amazing."

Peter did not go home that summer. He rented Francis Leland's basement apartment, where he would live for the remainder of his undergraduate career, and spent his mornings at the library assisting Hank Christiansen with restoration work and continuing to commune with the Devereaux collection. In the afternoons he mowed Francis's yard or washed his car to help offset the rent. The two of them would sit on the broad front porch sipping iced tea and talking about books or anything else that took Francis's fancy.

Peter saw Amanda every day. They took long walks in Ridgefield Gardens, the grounds of the former family estate now owned by the university. They went to the movies on hot afternoons and swam in the pool at Amanda's house when her parents were out of town. "You'll have to meet them eventually," Amanda said, "but let's enjoy the summer." Other than this one mention that Peter must one day meet her parents, they did not speak of the future; they merely lived in the present. It was a perfect summer.

One weekend they drove to Wrightsville Beach in Amanda's car, staying in separate rooms in a cheap motel three blocks from the beach. Peter had insisted on paying, and the Seaside Inn, whose glory days were long past and not particularly glorious, was the best he could afford. Amanda did not complain. They lay in the sun and ate hot dogs and ice cream and over-fried seafood, and they walked on the beach, standing ankle deep in the surf, kissing expertly. Peter had never kissed a girl before Amanda, but their frequent late-night visits to the Devereaux Room that spring had given them plenty of practice.

"Have you ever been to the beach before?" asked Amanda as they walked hand in hand through the edge of the surf.

"Fifth-grade field trip," said Peter. "Boy, was that a miserable three days."

"Oh? Do tell."

"I had this crush on Rebecca Ferguson, but of course I didn't have the nerve to do anything about it."

"You never told me you had a girlfriend."

"Believe me, I didn't," said Peter. "She only had eyes for Glenn Bailey, but I was doing that fifth-grade thing where you think if you do a grandiose enough job of brooding, the girl will notice you and take pity."

"I would have taken pity," said Amanda, slipping an arm around his waist.

"Trust me, you wouldn't have. I was the world's mopiest fifth grader. Following them while they walked on the beach holding hands, staring at her from the next table at dinner, sitting in the dark crying while they sat next to each other at the bonfire. If we'd all been thirty years older, they would have taken out a restraining order. As it was, nobody noticed."

"Crying in the dark. You poor thing," said Amanda. She stopped walking and wrapped both her arms around Peter, pulling him into a long, warm kiss. "So do you like the beach better this time?" she asked.

"Just a little bit," said Peter.

Amanda gave him another quick kiss and then was off and running through the surf and Peter was chasing her and they were both laughing and he had a feeling that overcame him about once a day with Amanda—that he had never been happier in his life.

That night Peter lay awake in his room. He was still adjusting to the newness of a companion and of passionate, if chaste, physical contact. He was pleased with their tacit agreement not to sleep with each other for the time being, but his body ached for Amanda as he lay in bed replaying the sight of her in her pale blue bikini. He embraced the ache. It reminded him that Amanda was real. For the first time in his life, he knew exactly what he was aching for.

Peter took to reading love poetry, not just from the elegant cases of the Devereaux Room but from simpler shelves in the other rooms into which Special Collections spilled—rooms filled with manuscript materials and books from floor to ceiling. Occasionally Peter

came across a book that he thought deserved the more honored position of a spot in the Devereaux Room. He would make his case to
Francis and almost always be overruled, but Francis nonetheless en-
couraged Peter in this endeavor. "The best way to learn about books,"
he said, "is to spend time with them, talk about them, defend them."

Late in the summer, but not so late that the thought of the end of
that idyll had yet crept into his dreams, Peter discovered a book that
certainly belonged in the Devereaux Room. It was a slim pamphlet
of sonnets by Elizabeth Barrett Browning. If Peter had not sought out
these poems, later known as *The Sonnets from the Portuguese*, in their
purported first edition of 1850 only a few days earlier, he might not
have realized the significance of the year 1847 on the title page. Here
was a private edition of some of the most famous poems of the last
two centuries, printed a full three years before they made their public appearance. It was a candidate for promotion to the Devereaux
Room that Francis would not be able to refuse.

"It's a Wise book," said Francis, when Peter showed him the pamphlet.

"I beg your pardon?" said Peter.

"Thomas Wise was one of the most distinguished bookmen of the
late nineteenth and early twentieth centuries. He was a bookseller
and bibliographer and he had a spectacular collection of nineteenth-
century pamphlets by George Eliot, Charles Dickens, John Ruskin,
and just about every other prominent Victorian writer."

"Sounds impressive," said Peter.

"It was," said Francis, "until nineteen thirty-four, when two young
booksellers named John Carter and Graham Pollard proved that
these supposedly rare pamphlets were forgeries and that Wise was
the forger. This book"—Francis tapped his forefinger on the *Sonnets*
laying on the table—"was one of them."

"How did they prove it?" asked Peter.

"Two ways. First they looked at what they called negative evidence. What was lacking in terms of provenance, contemporary mentions, contemporary inscriptions, anything that, had it been there, might indicate that the pamphlets really did date from the period that was claimed for them. Then they turned to positive evidence, and they really pioneered the use of scientific analysis in this field. They had the content of the paper analyzed, they compared the typeface to foundry catalogs to see when it had been cast. It was a remarkable job."

"It sounds like Wise fooled a lot of people," said Peter.

"He did. He was smart enough to let the pamphlets out on the market one or two at a time, so it wouldn't be obvious they were all from the same source. Unfortunately, he seemed especially fond of preying on American collectors."

"Like Amanda Devereaux."

"Exactly. She was collecting at the height of Wise's deception. The result is that we have one of the best collections of Wise forgeries outside the British Library."

Peter picked up the now maligned copy of the *Sonnets*. "So I guess this belongs in the back rooms," he said.

"I don't think so," said Francis. "When I first shelved the collection, it had only been about twenty years since Wise had been exposed. People still thought of his pamphlets first and foremost as fakes for which they had paid too much. But now Wise is considered among the great forgers of all time, and ironically his pamphlets are as rare as he claimed them to be. I'd say you're quite right. It's time we devoted a little shelf space in the Devereaux Room to Mr. Wise."

Peter had seen a copy of Robert Greene's *Pandosto,* on which *A Winter's Tale* was based, before, but not the first edition. He had read the 1607 edition at Ridgefield when researching a paper for his sophomore Shakespeare class. The copy that lay before him now on the broad library table of Evenlode Manor was dated 1588. As soon as he saw the date he recalled a sentence in a footnote of his Shakespeare anthology. "The original 1588 edition of *Pandosto* is known only in a single, incomplete copy in the British Library."

Discovering the first complete copy of the first edition of a book upon which Shakespeare based one of his plays would have been enough for Peter to feel he had fulfilled his dream of changing the course of literary history. If this copy proved genuine, and not a clever forgery, he could probably sell it with one phone call to the Folger Shakespeare Library in Washington for at least six figures. But the printing history of the unique book in front of Peter was perhaps the least interesting, and certainly the least valuable, thing about it. As he slowly turned the pages and examined the book, Peter heard the voice of Dr. Yoshi Kashimoto, the great Japanese champion of Edward de Vere: "If anyone could show me a single contemporary document linking the plays published under the name Shakespeare with William Shakspere of Stratford, I would recant my position and bow at the feet of the Stratfordians." It was a sentiment that had been repeated in various forms for over a century and a half by those who claimed a variety of authors for Shakespeare's plays. "Show us a single document," the cries had rung out, "and we will proclaim the greatest literary mystery of all time solved." In his trembling hands, Peter held that document.

The only previously known surviving handwriting of William Shakespeare consisted of six signatures and, possibly, a three-page manuscript passage of the play *Sir Thomas More*, written in collaboration with several other playwrights. Peter had examined the originals of all the examples of Shakespeare's hand in person. The brown ink in the *Thomas More* fragment seemed to dance across the page in its profusion of loops and oddly angled lines, and the text sloped up as it approached the right side of the page.

Filling the margins of every page of the *Pandosto* he now held was that same brown ink, those same loops and lines, that same sloping text. And both the handwriting and the content of the marginalia gave every indication, under Peter's admittedly cursory examination, that it had come from the pen of William Shakespeare. Most astounding of all was what was written on the front endpaper. Third on a list of names that Peter assumed to be owners of the book, written in the same hand as the marginalia, were the words, "W. Shakspere, Stratford." Peter pictured Dr. Kashimoto standing before a crowd of international Shakespeare scholars and recanting his position. *Mr. Peter Byerly has provided all the proof we need that William Shakspere of Stratford was the true author of the plays.* Peter only wished that Amanda were waiting for him back at the cottage so he could share with her this astounding discovery.

The thought of Amanda, of how she was not waiting for him and would not share in his exaltation, brought Peter back to reality. True, the book in front of him might be among the most important artifacts in English literature, but the world would want proof of its authenticity. There were too many stories of successful forgers for such a significant artifact to be immediately taken at face value. And with this thought came the echo of another voice—the mousy woman in the drab gray dress. "Give you a week," she had said. If Peter couldn't prove the authenticity of the *Pandosto* in seven days, Alderson would call in another bookseller and that person would make the greatest literary discovery of the past century.

Peter couldn't imagine getting much sleep in the next week. He would need to do textual analysis of the marginalia, trace the provenance of the book, and find a lab that could test the paper and ink. He probably couldn't prove its authenticity absolutely in so short a time, but he might be able to accomplish enough that he could make the discovery public and be sure that he was the intermediary between the Aldersons and the rest of the world.

Among the most important of his tasks would be to find out where this book had come from—how had such an important artifact escaped notice for over four hundred years? Peter looked back at the list of names on the front endpaper. They were all written in different hands. If these were, in fact, the owners of the book, then tracing the provenance might not be too hard. As he read over the list his breathing faltered at the fourth entry, and stopped altogether at the last. The fourth entry read, "R. Cotton, Augustus B IV." Peter understood the abbreviations perfectly. At some point this book had sat on the second shelf of the Augustus case in the library of the great Robert Cotton. The final entry on the list was in pencil, not ink, and was considerably more cryptic, but, to Peter, equally intriguing: "B.B. / E.H." The handwriting was unmistakably that of the artist who had signed Peter's stolen watercolor with the same initials, B.B.

Peter closed the book for a moment to allow himself to breathe. He could not hold still and he got up and paced the room, stopping to mindlessly adjust books on a shelf every few seconds. Now that he had some distance, even if it was only a few feet, on the *Pandosto*, the excitement and curiosity he felt were tempered with a slow surge of fear. For whatever reason, he had been entrusted with a priceless artifact. What if he lost it, or spilled tea on it? What if he was wrong and made a fool of himself? What if he was right and people expected him to make speeches and appear on television? Every vision of the future seemed fraught with peril.

In an attempt to calm himself, Peter began putting the documents back into their box. It was not until he got to a commission signed by Lord Nelson that he happened to glance at the upper-right corner of one of these documents. Barely visible, in the lightest pencil, were two of the same initials he had read in the *Pandosto*, "E.H." Here they were written in interlocking cursive—the sort of monogram one sometimes found in Victorian books. Peter began to sift through the other documents, and found that every one had the same lightly penciled monogram in the same corner. He hadn't seen it on any of the other books he had examined that morning—those that did have ownership markings said simply "Alderson." Who was E.H.? How had his collection of autographed material come to the Aldersons' library? And what relationship did he have to the elusive B.B.? Peter looked up from the E.H. monogram and saw the empty shelf in the case in front of him. He felt the first pieces of the puzzle click together, like the tumblers of a successfully picked lock.

He had seen this monogram before, in the book from which he had stolen the watercolor—a book about forging Shakespeare materials. And if you had such a book in your library, signed by the same hand that inscribed your priceless Shakespeare artifact, it might not look good. He remembered the mousy girl's surreptitious glance toward the empty shelf. She had known about the box and possibly about the *Pandosto*. Had she removed Malone's book on Shakespeare forgery from the library? Was she setting him up? Did she know the *Pandosto* was a fake, but want her brother to be able to sell it without suspicion to some patsy of an American? Or did she know it was real, and simply want to avoid distracting Peter with unnecessary concerns? And what did John Alderson know about all this? Two things seemed certain to Peter—the mousy woman should not be trusted, and her deadline could not be ignored. She obviously knew something about the book world—maybe enough to go to Hay to sell the forgery book and perhaps whatever else had been on that shelf. He had an odd feeling that she was more in charge of this library than her brother, and that Alderson would listen to her if she said the American was cheating them and needed to be replaced.

Peter glanced at his watch. It was past four, and Alderson would be returning soon. Peter needed the brother to trust him, and in his experience there was nothing like a nice fat check to earn people's trust. He folded the *Pandosto* back into its elaborate case and quickly put the rest of the documents back in their box and returned it to the cabinet. He locked the cabinet door and replaced the key in the desk drawer. From the case to the right of the fireplace he pulled three volumes at random and stacked them on top of the *Pandosto*. Then he returned to some pretense of examining books until he heard footsteps approaching through the drawing room.

"Getting on well, I hope," said John Alderson, striding into the room.

"Yes, quite well," said Peter. "There are some very nice things here."

"Well, I'm glad to hear it."

"In fact," said Peter, "there's one item I'm quite eager to purchase. A friend of mine has been looking for it for years. It's your Johnson's *Dictionary*."

"But it's not even a first edition," said Alderson. "I shouldn't think it would be worth much." Peter thought it interesting that John Alderson, who had pretended to know very little about books, knew the edition of his *Dictionary*.

"I can give you two thousand pounds for it," said Peter. It was a strong retail price, but Peter could easily afford it. He would be delighted to present the book to Ridgefield, and John Alderson, whom Peter suspected knew exactly what the book was worth, would now believe that the local American bookseller had more money than sense—a belief that could be very helpful if the sister started agitating for his removal.

"Two thousand?" said Alderson, clearly taken aback.

"There will be a lot more that I'll want to buy," said Peter, "but I have an especially eager customer for that particular book."

"Well, then, two thousand it is," said Alderson, with a chuckle.

"I'm afraid I might not be able to get back for several days," said Peter, as he pulled out his checkbook and began writing out a draft. "I hope that won't be a problem." He tore the check out and held it out to Alderson. Peter could see a flash of greed in his eyes that he had seen before in those who thought they had just been paid more than their old books were worth.

"No," said Alderson, "that's not a problem at all." He took the check from Peter and tucked it into his shirt pocket.

"And I wonder," said Peter, "if I might be able to take a few items with me." He picked up the *Pandosto* and the three books on top of it. "My reference materials are back at my cottage, and I'd like to do a little further research on these." It was a delicate moment. Alderson hesitated more than Peter would have liked, enough that each man, perhaps, sensed that the other was not entirely what he seemed.

Alderson's eyes darted to the locked cabinet that held the box of documents and then he smiled at Peter. "Of course," he said, with what Peter felt certain was false jollity. "Take whatever you need. Now, can you stay for tea?"

"I'm afraid not," said Peter. "I'm expecting a call from America at five, so I need to be getting home. Shall I ring you in a few days?"

"Lovely," said Alderson. "I'll show you out." Peter was halfway down the front steps, descending into the early evening gloom, when he heard Alderson's voice behind him. For the first time since Peter met him, his voice quavered almost imperceptibly. "I don't suppose you met my sister, Julia."

"No," said Peter steadily. "I haven't had the pleasure."

"Well, then," said Alderson, brightening. "We shall have to introduce you the next time."

Loath as he was to return to the scene of his crime, Peter felt he had to examine whatever books Julia Alderson had removed from her family library. A quick call to the shop in Hay-on-Wye confirmed that though the next day was Sunday, the shopkeeper would be in most of the afternoon. Peter also confirmed that his refrigerator was nearly empty, so he pulled on his coat and stepped into the darkness for a walk up to the village shop. He found walking to the shop once or twice a day to buy food as needed a comforting routine.

Peter selected a frozen dinner of chicken tikka masala, and then did his usual trick of pretending to read the cooking instructions while he stood in the short queue at the cash register so he wouldn't accidentally make eye contact with anyone. He had cooked enough of these dinners that he could have recited the instructions from memory, but they had successfully protected him from making conversation with his fellow shoppers for months. Thus it took him a moment to realize he was being addressed by the Irish brogue behind him, which said, "It's Mr. Byerly, isn't it?"

"I beg your pardon?" said Peter, for whom this phrase was an instinctive reaction to any form of public address. It bought him time, if nothing else.

"You're Mr. Byerly," said the woman, who now stepped beside Peter.

"Yes," said Peter, glancing up just long enough to recognize the housekeeper from Evenlode Manor before turning to study the display of crisps.

"You're not the first person to come poking around the manor, you know," said Miss O'Hara.

Peter's avoidance of conversation with the housekeeper had been more out of habit than a particular feeling of nervousness. Being shot at earlier in the day had made public conversation less intimidating. Now it suddenly occurred to him that Miss O'Hara might be an excellent source of inside information on the Alderson family. He turned and looked her in the eye.

"And who's come before me?" he asked.

"Old man come up from Cornwall and wanted to look at paintings. Miss Julia was none too happy about that, I can tell you."

Peter tried to conceal his amazement. The old man must have been Liz Sutcliffe's secret scholar, and therefore the paintings must be by the mysterious B.B. The connections between the Amanda painting, Evenlode Manor, and the *Pandosto* seemed to be multiplying.

"So Julia's not married," he said.

"Never has been," said Miss O'Hara. "Disappointed in love, she is. Always falling for the wrong person, Mr. John says."

"When the old man was visiting from Cornwall," said Peter, "did Miss Julia show him anything in the library?"

Miss O'Hara did not seem to think this question unduly prying for an idle conversation in a shop queue. "Couldn't have done without me knowing. I was dusting books that week. Take every one off the shelf and dust it twice a year. I was in the library the whole day."

"So you'd know if any books went missing."

"Miss Julia took a shelfful up to her room a few weeks back. Probably trying to impress some man. She doesn't let me in her room, but I suppose she's still got them in there. Mr. John never lays a finger on the downstairs books."

"Next," said the shopkeeper from behind the counter. Peter tried not to grin as he stepped forward. He was beginning to feel like a genuine detective. He didn't know if any crime had been committed, but the mousy Miss Julia was certainly shaping up as a prime suspect. He was more certain than ever that he had to return to Hay. He only hoped that the book in the familiar blue binding was still there.

Ridgefield, 1985

Peter wanted Amanda's birthday to be perfect.

"It's a weird day to have a birthday," she had told him. "I mean, everyone is always celebrating on Halloween, but it doesn't have anything to do with me." She had already planned the evening; that left him to find a present, and he wanted to give her something that would reflect her passions and his and thus be unique to their relationship. Jewelry did not fit the bill. Amanda happily wore the same pair of diamond stud earrings every day, and that seemed to be the extent of her interest in adornment. Scarves, handbags, chocolate, and flowers—all of which Francis Leland suggested—seemed equally inappropriate.

In a box in the dusty back room of a local antique shop, Peter discovered an early edition of George MacDonald's 1870 fantasy novel, *At the Back of the North Wind*. The book was illustrated by the Pre-Raphaelite follower Arthur Hughes. Amanda, he knew, considered Hughes on a par with her idol Edward Burne-Jones. This would be the first book Peter would give Amanda. The front cover and about half the spine were missing. Several signatures were loose, one such gathering of pages literally hanging by a thread from the middle of the book. Many pages were torn at the margins. To any serious collector it was worthless. Peter bought it for a dollar.

When he showed the book to Hank Christiansen, Hank agreed it was a perfect candidate for rebinding.

"It'll be a great project," said Hank. "And if you screw it up, it's no big deal since the book belongs to you."

"I'd rather not screw it up," said Peter.

"Don't worry," said Hank. "By the time you're through with this book, it will be elegant. When is Amanda's birthday?"

"Halloween," said Peter.

"That gives you a month," said Hank. "We'd better get to work."

Peter had become something between a student and an assistant in Hank's workshop, often working alone with Hank after the rest of the staff had left. They seldom spoke about anything other than book repair, frequently working side by side for hours in companionable quiet. It was usually Hank who broke the silence, with a gentle instruction for Peter or sometimes a witty remark he seemed to have spent an hour thinking up. On these occasions his eyes twinkled behind his glasses as he waited for Peter to laugh. Peter always did. He found Hank wise and funny and, because of the long periods of silence, easy to be around. If pressed, he might have even called Hank a friend.

Though he had assisted Hank in several binding jobs the previous spring, Peter had never done a full binding by himself. As he lay the *North Wind* on the counter to plan an attack, he hoped a month would be enough time.

The first task was to remove what was left of the original cover. Peter clamped the text block of the book in the job backer, the same upright vice he had first seen Hank leaning over a year earlier. Using a lifting knife, Peter sliced away the remnants of the spine and rear cover. He placed a few dollops of gloppy paste on the spine and allowed the moisture to loosen the glue on the backs of the pages. Within thirty minutes the glue was soft, and Peter peeled it away with his lifting knife. Taking the now disbound book from the job backer, Peter began the process of pulling the text—separating the signatures from one another and from the thread that had bound them together. By the end of the afternoon the book lay scattered on the counter in unsewn signatures.

Peter spent the next week mending the tears in *North Wind*'s pages. There were more than he had at first realized, but few of them affected the text and none extended into the illustrations. Peter was happy about this because the *kozo*, the thin but fibrous Japanese paper that he pasted across the tears to repair the paper, dried an opaque white. An expert could use tiny enough pieces of *kozo*, even individual fibers, that a torn illustration could be repaired without the repair being visible, but Peter was no expert. Though some would have found the process of fixing one margin tear after another with a tiny brush, a special paste, and a slender piece of *kozo* tedious, Peter achieved an almost Zen-like state during these hours of careful repetitive work. He worked for seven hours one day, missing his English seminar and having no idea of the time until Hank turned the lights out and announced it was closing time.

Before he began resewing the sections of the *North Wind*, Peter picked out material for the new endpapers. Because he planned to do an elegant full leather binding, Peter chose a hand-marbled paper with swirls of blue, gold, and white. Then he arranged the sections of the book in order and began sewing them onto three strips of linen tape, stretched tautly into a sewing frame. The linen strips would form the inside of the book's spine. After a long day of work, Peter had a tightly sewn text block. The pages turned easily but did not pull loose when he tugged gently on them. Peter began to feel that the resurrection of the *North Wind* had truly begun.

"Come on," said Amanda, "at least give me a hint." They were sitting on a bench behind the library enjoying the cool air of an autumn evening during a study break.

"No hints," said Peter, turning his back to her in mock indignation.

"I'll bet I can make you talk," said Amanda, tickling him around his sides, but though Peter laughed and squirmed, he didn't tell her a thing.

"It's no fair," said Amanda in a pouty voice, as she slipped her arms around him from behind and rested her head on his shoulders. "I don't want to have secrets from each other."

"We don't," said Peter, suddenly much more serious. "Not real secrets. But this is your birthday present. You've got to let me have a little fun."

"Oh, all right," said Amanda, kissing his cheek and then disentangling her arms and standing up. "But you have to let me get a little work done."

"Hey," called Peter at her back, as she skipped back toward the library, "this study break was your idea!"

"This is nice work," said Hank the next day, fanning through the pages of the *North Wind* and nodding in approval. "You can tell when work like this is done with real love."

Peter blushed deeply, never considering that Hank may have been referring to Peter's love for books rather than his love for Amanda. "Thanks," he managed to mumble.

"Have you thought about what sort of leather you want to use?" asked Hank.

"I thought maybe the blue calf if we have enough left," said Peter. "I mean, I wasn't sure how much that would cost but . . ." Peter let his words hang in the air. He had been trying to decide how to approach Hank about the costs of the materials he was using in this job. The leather would be the most expensive single item, but everything from the *kozo* to the banding tapes cost money. Most of Peter's hours of work in the library were classified as work-study time. He had started to do a little book dealing and had made some modest profits in these fledgling efforts, but almost all of that he had spent buying up more books from various charity and antique shops. His parents grudgingly sent him twenty or thirty dollars a month as an allowance, though the only thing it allowed him to do was pay for coffee with Amanda some evenings. He wasn't sure how he was going to pay for the materials for the *North Wind* rebind, but he at least needed to know how much he was going to owe.

"Well," said Hank, "I figure a piece of blue calf big enough for this job should run about four hours."

"I beg your pardon?" said Peter.

"You give me an extra four hours' work this semester and I'll give you a piece of calf."

"What about the rest of the supplies? Boards, endpapers, gold leaf?" Peter saw a familiar twinkle in Hank's eye—a twinkle he had first seen when Hank mentioned the girlfriend pile.

"I figure by the time you screw up cutting your binder's board a couple of times, you'll owe me about three hours, plus the four for the leather. Of course you've already put in about thirty or forty hours of extra time since August, so it seems to me I owe you."

"Thanks," said Peter, smiling. He could think of nothing more to say, so he turned to his work.

He did not, in the end, screw up cutting the binder's boards, the dense cardboard that would form the covers of the book. Once these had been attached to the linen tapes onto which the text block was sewn, Peter left the book in a book press for the rest of the week. "A book needs to get used to its new cover," Hank had told him.

It was October 20 and Peter had reached the most delicate and nerve-racking stage of the rebinding—covering the book with the expensive blue leather he had picked out. While the book was under the press, he had carefully cut the leather to the proper size and shaved the edges thin with a bookbinder's paring knife. Pasting the leather onto the covers was the work of a single afternoon, and Peter had to work quickly and carefully. The paste wet the leather, making it easier to stretch across the boards and wrap around the edges, but also easy to mark or tear. Peter could feel Hank watching from across the room as he pulled and stretched and wrapped and smoothed the leather onto the book. He knew Hank must have been dying to say, *Would you like a hand with that?* especially as Peter reached critical points when he did wish for an extra hand to hold one corner while he folded another, but Hank resisted the temptation to offer assistance, and Peter, stubborn in his wish to be the sole craftsman of the *North Wind*, resisted the temptation to ask. By the end of the afternoon, the leather-covered book was back in the press, drying out.

With trepidation, Peter removed the book from the press the next day. Despite his nearly sleepless night spent fretting about puckers in the leather or creases marring the cover, the binding was smooth and clean. He finished the process of attaching the marbled endpapers and put the book in the finishing press, a vice that gently held the felt-wrapped volume in place so that Peter could tool the spine. With heated brass tools, he stamped the title and author on the spine in gilt lettering, with a decorative fleur-de-lis separating AT THE BACK OF THE NORTH WIND from GEORGE MACDONALD.

It was still nearly a week before Amanda's birthday when Peter put the finishing touch on the book, stamping a gold A.R. on the front cover. Intensely proud of his work, he presented it to Hank the next day.

"This is an excellent job, Peter," said Hank, opening the covers and admiring how smoothly they moved on the new hinges, how the pages turned effortlessly. "A lot of first timers end up with a book that's too tightly bound, but this is a real pleasure to handle." Peter felt a surge of satisfaction as Hank handed the book back to him.

For the next few days Peter left the *North Wind* on a shelf in the conservation lab, but pulled it down to feel the cool, supple leather every time he came in to work. On the thirty-first, just before he left the lab, Peter took out a calligraphy pen and a pot of deep black ink. He had been practicing his lettering for several months. On the half title of the *North Wind* he wrote, in his best simulation of a nineteenth-century script, "To Amanda, with love, from the binder, Peter, October 31, 1985."

Peter opened the delicate binding of the *Pandosto* and began an examination that would take most of the night. He started with the provenance. The line of ownership, from the author himself to the mysterious B.B., could be one of the strongest pieces of evidence in favor of authenticity. Peter knew enough of the history of English book collecting to recognize several of the names on the list, but he would need to research the connections between the owners and try to identify names such as Em Ball, Bartholomew Harbottle, and William H. Smith. The list read:

R. Greene to Em Ball

Bart. Harbottle

Wm. Shakspere, Stratford

R. Cotton, Augustus B IV

Matthew Harbottle, Red Bull Theatre

John Bagford

John Warburton

R. Harley, Oxford

B. Mayhew for William H. Smith

B.B. / E.H.

Ten entries. Ten clues that might tell the story of how a priceless volume survived undetected for over four centuries.

From his frequent nocturnal visits to the Devereaux Room with Amanda, Peter knew that Francis never came in after hours, but he always worked in his office from two until five on Saturdays. Special Collections was not officially opened during these hours, and Francis said it was often the only uninterrupted time in his work week. After Peter finished his dinner and confirmed, in his copy of De Ricci's *English Collectors of Books and Manuscripts*, his memory about the identities of Bagford, Warburton, and Harley, he phoned Francis Leland's private number.

He did this without thinking that he had not spoken to Francis since leaving Ridgefield. As the phone rang four thousand miles away, Peter also did not think about the eighth item on Dr. Strayer's list, "Get in Touch with Old Friends," even though Francis's phone number was written on the list next to this entry. When Peter had gone to the kitchen to look up the number, he hadn't even noticed the list, only the scrawled digits in the margin.

Since arriving in Kingham, Peter had not called or written any friends in the United States—not Hank or Amanda's parents or her best friend, Cynthia, though all had begged him to keep in touch when they had last seen him at the funeral, and all had left repeated messages on his machine. In his effort to escape every reminder of Amanda, Peter had severed all contact with his life in America, and he had given little thought to how those left behind might interpret his long silence. Thus Peter, who was focused wholly on identifying the names on the *Pandosto*'s endpaper, did not comprehend the mixture of excitement and relief in Francis Leland's voice.

"Peter, thank God. We've been so worried about you. Are you well?"

It seemed to Peter a completely irrelevant question, as if Francis had asked what shoes he was wearing. "I'm trying to track down some people," said Peter.

"Is it the Ridgefields?" asked Francis. "They're in New York, but they left numbers with me in case you called. I know they'll be so relieved to hear from you. You can't imagine what we've all been thinking, Peter."

Frustration crept into Peter's voice. He and Francis had always understood each other before. Why were they now talking at such cross-purposes? "No," said Peter, "you don't understand. I need to track down some people." Single-minded as he was, he could think of no other way to phrase his request, but without waiting for Francis to respond, he plowed on. "The first three I suspect are Elizabethan or Jacobean. One of them had some connection to Robert Greene. Her name was Em Ball. Then there are two named Harbottle—Bartholomew and Matthew. Matthew had something to do with the Red Bull Theatre. And then there are two much later names, eighteenth or nineteenth century—Benjamin Mayhew and William H. Smith. I know the last one's pretty common, but he was probably a book collector."

"Peter, are you all right?"

Had he stopped to consider Francis's question, Peter would have recognized the tone of parental condescension that used to creep into Dr. Strayer's voice when Peter was being obstinate. He chose, instead, to ignore Francis. "Oh, and I have some good news. I found a copy of the fourth edition of Johnson's *Dictionary*. I know you would have bought it, but I've decided to give it to the Devereaux collection in memory of Amanda." Peter paused for a moment and thought of the portrait of Amanda Devereaux. "My Amanda," he added.

"That's wonderful. Listen, Peter, are you seeing anyone over there. I mean a doctor?"

"Why would I see a doctor?" said Peter, completely missing Francis's point. "I'm in perfectly good health. I mean other than getting shot at."

"Getting shot at?" said Francis. "Really, Peter, I think you ought to—"

"So do you think you can help me with those names?" Peter interrupted.

There was silence on the line and then Francis spoke again, this time in a quieter, calmer voice. The old Francis, Peter thought. "Well, Em Ball was Robert Greene's mistress," he said. "A prostitute and sister of a gangster. Rumor was that she showed up when he was on his deathbed and tried to make him admit to fathering her illegitimate son, which he refused to do. Bartholomew Harbottle I'm surprised you don't know. His name is in one of your favorite books. He was a bookseller, died around 1610 or 1620. His ownership signature is in our bad quarto of *Hamlet*. The other two I'll have to look up for you, but I do know the Red Bull Theatre was in Clerkenwell. Burned down in the great fire, I believe."

"Listen," said Peter, "can you leave a message on the machine if you track down Matthew Harbottle or William H. Smith? I may be out."

"Peter, what's this all about?" asked Francis.

"I think I may have found the Holy Grail," said Peter and hung up.

So Robert Greene had given this copy of *Pandosto* to his mistress. It was easy to imagine that she would have sold it to Harbottle and he would have sold it to Shakespeare as the source material for *A Winter's Tale*. There had never been any proven connection between Shakespeare and Robert Cotton, but most scholars agreed that it made sense that the playwright might have consulted Cotton's library. Perhaps the *Pandosto* had been a gift? And Cotton was a notorious lender of his books. Perhaps the Red Bull Theatre had mounted a production of *A Winter's Tale* and this Matthew Harbottle borrowed the book and never returned it. This bit of conjecture seemed less likely to Peter. After all, seventeenth-century theatrical troupes didn't hire dramaturges, and this scenario wouldn't explain the coincidence of the name Harbottle.

Peter spent the night making a careful transcription of the *Pand-*

osto's marginalia, stopping only for a nap before breakfast. The rear endpaper was crowded with a hodgepodge of scribbles surrounding a preliminary version of the song performed by Autolycus in Act IV of *A Winter's Tale*. It took Peter hours to sort out the mess, and even then he wasn't sure of the meaning of many of the markings and abbreviations. Peter detected a short phrase, almost obscured by other writing across it, just above the words to the song. With the help of a strong light and a magnifying glass, he finally managed to decipher it. "B. Harbottle = Autolycus."

If Bartholomew Harbottle had been the model for the merchant and knave Autolycus, a number of possibilities for how the *Pandosto* moved from Robert Cotton's hands back into the Harbottle family now presented themselves. Bartholomew Harbottle might have borrowed it with no intention of returning it or simply stolen it. *A Winter's Tale* was written late in Shakespeare's career, when he was an established playwright. If Harbottle suspected the volume might be valuable someday, he might have passed it on to a relative.

As Peter fell asleep on the sofa in the sitting room, he felt he had a reasonable handle on the journey of *Pandosto* from Robert Greene to his mistress, to an unscrupulous bookseller, to William Shakespeare, to Robert Cotton, and finally to the unknown Matthew Harbottle. But if Matthew had been alive when Bartholomew died—not later than 1620, Francis had said—it was unlikely he lived much past the great fire of 1666, and the book would almost certainly have been out of London by then. Yet the next name on the list was John Bagford, a collector and dealer who was at his peak of activity around 1710. So where had *Pandosto* hidden for forty-five years? And if the book had belonged to Robert Harley, Earl of Oxford, why hadn't it ended up in the British Museum with the rest of his collection?

Wakefield, Yorkshire, Northern England, 1720

John Warburton took a long drink of whiskey and set down his glass. While it was true that whiskey had lost him his job, if tonight's meeting went well, he should have enough money to keep him in drink and under roof a while longer.

On the large table in the center of his library he had created two piles of manuscripts from his ever-growing collection. On the left were those he anticipated would bring him five hundred guineas by night's end. They were medieval works, including some fine examples of Anglo-Saxon and Early English writing—just the sort of thing to tempt his dinner guest. On the right were manuscripts he did not wish to sell—his collection of Elizabethan and Jacobean plays. Several of these he had bought from his old friend, now departed, the bookseller and great collector of printing samples John Bagford. He remembered well the day that Bagford had arrived on his doorstep with a cache of Elizabethan materials he had found languishing in a manor house near Exeter.

Warburton spent the afternoon compiling a list of the plays represented in his collection. This he would keep in his desk, while the plays he would hide elsewhere, to protect them from the prying eyes of his guest. The list ran to fifty-five titles, including works by Robert Greene, Thomas Dekker, Christopher Marlowe, and William Shakespeare. All but a few of the plays were unpublished, and most of Warburton's copies were unique.

After completing the catalog, he picked up the pile of manuscripts and carried them into the kitchen where he would store them in the highest cupboard—an unlikely place for even the most persistent bibliophile to go hunting for treasures. He did not realize that one item from his theatrical collection—a printed volume with marginalia by William Shakespeare—remained on the table next to the medieval manuscripts.

Humfrey Wanley, keeper of the library for Robert Harley and his son, Edward, arrived at the home of John Warburton at eight o'clock.

"Mr. Warburton," said Wanley, extending his hand. "A pleasure to meet such a distinguished collector."

As the two men entered the library after dinner, Wanley did his best to hide his enthusiasm, for although many of the manuscripts laid out on the library table were quite ordinary, several were exquisite.

"This, I think, must be the finest example of ninth-century English in any collection," said Warburton, opening a codex of extracts from the Gospels.

"Fine, to be sure," said Wanley, "though certainly not the finest."

"Still, that alone should be worth a hundred guineas," said Warburton.

"Let's not talk of price just yet, my dear man. How about some more of that excellent port?" Wanley saw to it that the wine continued to flow as the hour passed midnight. He took only a sip for every glassful downed by his companion, so that by the time the two men had begun to pack the manuscripts into an empty chest, Warburton was weaving on his feet. The host finally collapsed into a chair, letting Wanley finish the job.

Wanley saw that now was the moment, and though there were a few items on the table he had not yet examined, he swept everything into the chest and shut the top firmly.

"I can give you cash," said Wanley.

"Five hundred guineas," said Warburton, slurring his speech.

"Not quite that," said Wanley crisply. "You'll need to sign the bill of sale here." He laid a piece of paper on the desk and placed a pen in Warburton's hand.

"How much then?" said Warburton, squinting at the paper. "Three hundred?"

"A hundred guineas," said Wanley. "It's a fair price, as you well know." It wasn't an unfair price, thought Wanley, though it was certainly a bargain.

"A hundred?" said Warburton. "But I can't—"

"It's that or nothing," said Wanley. "Shall I leave them here?"

"No, no!" cried Warburton, for he was not too drunk to realize that his arm lay across a pile of bills that a hundred guineas would more than settle. He picked up the pen and dipped it into the inkwell, scrawling his name on the bill of sale. The next morning he awoke with his head on his desk and a hundred guineas clasped in his hand.

A year went by before Warburton had occasion to seek out his sequestered theatrical manuscripts. Pushing open the kitchen door he saw the ingredients of one of Betsy Baker's pies laid out on the table. Betsy, his cook, made superb pies. Reaching into the high cabinet where he had hidden his manuscripts from the prying eyes of Humfrey Wanley, Warburton was surprised to find barely a handful of papers in place of the armload he expected. He was just beginning to canvass the other cabinets for the missing manuscripts when Betsy came in from the garden.

"Morning, Mr. Warburton. Not enough for breakfast then?"

"No, no," said Warburton, "breakfast was lovely."

"Ooh, thank you, Mr. Warburton," said Betsy, relieving him of a page of *The Queen of Corsica* from the manuscripts he held. "I do get so tired of reaching into that high cabinet to get to them papers."

"I beg your pardon?" said Warburton. "Do you mean to say . . . ," he started to ask, but he found he could not finish his sentence.

"Them papers as you put up there for me. Have to strain me back every time I need one. It's the secret to a perfect pie, you know," she said, pressing the page into the pie pan. "You've got to line the pan."

Humfrey Wanley pulled the last few Warburton books out of the chest and noticed one he did not remember buying—a tatty and marked-up copy of an old romance. Since there were markings on the endpapers, he did not place the library's bookplate in the volume but instead added the name of his employer to a list of previous owners—"R. Harley, Oxford."

Before Wanley could more closely examine the old romance and enter it into the library's catalog, Lord Harley entered the room with a visitor, a collector from Cambridgeshire.

"Mr. Wanley," said Harley. "My friend here would like to borrow a few items from the library to assist in his research on Elizabethan costumes."

"Of course, my lord," said Wanley. "The library is completely at his disposal."

"Excellent, Mr. Wanley," said Harley, and he swept out of the room, leaving the librarian and the visitor alone.

"I think you'll find what you want just over here," said Wanley, indicating a shelf above the table where he had been unpacking the manuscripts.

"Thank you, my good man," said the visitor. "I shan't take a minute."

It did, in fact, take little more than a minute for the visitor to find the books he sought. He showed them to Wanley, who carefully recorded the titles in a log of borrowed books. As he did so, the visitor picked up the slim volume lying on the table. It was a romance called *Pandosto*. He fancied he would take it up to his room to read before retiring that evening.

As it happened, Robert Harley entertained his visitor well into the evening and the port that followed dinner was of such quality and quantity that the guest felt neither the inclination nor the ability to read before turning in. The next morning he departed for home with *Pandosto* in his bag.

Six years later, in 1726, Humfrey Wanley was dead. The library he had spent much of his later life building for Robert and Edward Harley was one of the great collections of books and manuscripts of its time. The manuscripts were eventually sold to the nation in 1753 and were one of the foundation collections of the British Museum and later of the British Library.

But the slim volume that a visiting collector had borrowed one summer day in 1720 never returned to the Harleian collection. The man who had borrowed it died two weeks after returning home, leaving the book on his desk next to the three volumes on Elizabethan costumes that bore the bookplate of the Earl of Oxford and Mortimer. His grieving widow returned the costume books, but the other volume she shoved onto a shelf in the house's library and there it remained, nearly invisible between two thick folios, for more than a hundred and fifty years.

Ridgefield, 1985

The annual Ridgefield University Halloween Masquerade was first held in 1958 to celebrate the completion of seven new buildings made possible by the Ridgefield family, in whose honor the school had been renamed. Older members of the faculty murmured that the ball symbolized the fact that the formerly conservative Baptist school had sold out, but they didn't murmur this very loudly. They liked having spacious faculty lounges, private studies in the new library, and significant increases both in the intelligence of their students and in their own salaries.

Though it was a campuswide event, held in the cavernous and highly decorated gymnasium, Peter had never attended the masquerade. Now Amanda wanted to go for her birthday, and Peter could not very well say no. He had loved the solitude of their relationship thus far, but he also knew that Amanda had a social life outside her dates with him in the snack bar or the Devereaux Room. She told him about parties she went to and plays she saw. When she invited Peter to escort her to any such event, he always claimed he had to study, that his work in the library gave him limited time to keep up with academics. She indulged him in this fantasy up to a point, but she would not be dissuaded from entering the Halloween ball on his arm.

"Besides," she said, "the great thing about a masquerade is you can hide behind your costume. You won't be Peter Byerly, you'll be Romeo."

"You do know that Romeo dies in the end," said Peter.

"Yes," whispered Amanda, "but he also gets to sleep with Juliet." Peter did not dare ask if this were a promise. Though he continued to tell himself that he was happy not to be sleeping with Amanda for now, he was finding it harder and harder to convince himself this was true. On the evening of the ball, Peter did his best to think only of the gift that awaited Amanda in the Devereaux Room.

She had borrowed their costumes from the Theater department, and Peter had to admit, as he looked at himself in the long mirror on the back of her dorm-room door, that he looked nothing like Peter Byerly. Gold slippers, green tights, and an elaborately gilded doublet hid the real Peter quite nicely. He had never been in her dorm room before, but Amanda had said he could dress there, since her room-mate had gone to dinner, while she dressed in the bathroom down the hall. There was no question, Peter said, of his dressing at his apartment and then walking eight blocks through Ridgefield as Romeo.

There was a knock on the door and Peter flicked the lock and let Amanda back in. She looked magnificent: a rich tapestry of blue and silver cascaded from her shoulders to the floor, and matching ribbons were woven skillfully into her hair. Best of all, they were dressed for the ball scene at the Capulets' house—a masquerade itself—so they wore decorative masks. This made Peter feel he really might be able to step into the crowd at the gymnasium without breaking into a cold sweat.

"You look handsome," said Amanda, smiling as she adjusted his doublet. "Are you excited?"

"Nervous," said Peter.

Amanda took his hand and leaned forward to kiss him lightly on the lips. "Nothing to worry about," she said. "We can still kiss with the masks on."

"That's not what I was worried about," said Peter. "All of your friends have been waiting to meet me for months now. Even in the mask, I feel like I'll be on display."

"First of all, I don't have that many friends, and second of all, you don't even have to talk to anyone. Just dance with me and look handsome."

"Afterward," said Peter, "you can unwrap your present."

"I have a present for you, too," said Amanda, taking his hand in hers.

"But it's *your* birthday," said Peter.

"Well, really, it's for both of us," she said, pulling him toward the door.

Peter had imagined Amanda having scores of friends who would mob him on their entry to the masquerade. He had steeled himself for this eventuality by focusing on his identity as Romeo, running over lines from the play in his head. Not until they had entered the gym and stood alone for ten minutes, glasses of punch in hand and unable to converse because of the loud dance music, did it occur to Peter that Amanda had been telling the truth earlier when she said she didn't have many friends. He realized that he had only ever heard her mention three—her roommate, Jill; Cynthia, a childhood neighbor who had also come to Ridgefield; and Alison, a fellow art history major. Three friends more than Peter had, but not exactly the mob of glamorous socialites he had dreaded.

As the music changed to a slow ballad, Amanda set down her punch and intertwined her fingers in his.

"Dance with me," she said. Peter allowed her to lead him into the middle of the gym, amid hundreds of swaying bodies draped over one another. She pulled his hand to her waist and placed hers on his shoulder and they began to dance. After a few steps, Peter realized she was leading—he knew nothing about dancing—but the result far exceeded in elegance the hunched and shuffling couples around them. Peter relaxed his body just enough to say to her, without speaking, *Yes, lead me, I will follow you anywhere.* He could see the sparkle in her eyes through the mask. *She speaks, yet she says nothing,* thought Peter. Unlike Romeo, he understood his love's silent speech perfectly, as she swept him in a wide arc across the dance floor.

Later, standing in the rush of cool air by the door, Amanda introduced Peter to her friends, one at a time.

"So this is your Romeo," Cynthia said. She was dressed as Marie Antoinette, complete with a bloody slit across her neck. "You're a lucky man to capture our Juliet."

"She doth teach the torches to burn bright," said Peter, finding that the combination of the mask, the costume, and the words that were not his own made meeting Cynthia much easier.

"She won't tell us much about you," said Cynthia. "But then Amanda always was good at keeping secrets. All I've been able to get from her is a name."

"What's in a name?" said Amanda, squeezing Peter's hand.

"Call me but love and I'll be newly baptized," said Peter.

"You two are a pair," said Cynthia, laughing and embracing Amanda. Before she disappeared back into the crowd, she shook Peter's hand and said, "Someday, you'll have to let me see who you really are." Peter wondered if anyone other than Amanda would ever know who he really was. For now he was happy to be known only as the masked Romeo. The young Montague had helped him survive his first real college party. He wondered how soon he would be called on to repeat the performance without the costume and the mask.

He and Amanda both lowered their masks as they walked hand in hand across the campus in the cool October air. In the distance the bells of Ridgefield Chapel tolled midnight.

"Sounds like your birthday present is going to be late," said Peter.

"I don't mind waiting," said Amanda. "You know you were wonderful tonight."

"I just followed your lead," said Peter.

"You have no idea how heavily I lean on you, do you? I mean, when I went to that ball last year I was miserable. I stood in a corner for two hours and turned down every guy who asked me to dance. I just felt out of place. Tonight just felt natural—the dancing and the kisses in the shadows and even the silly conversations with my friends. I just let you hold me up for everything."

"I thought you were holding me up," said Peter.

"I guess that's why it's called mutual attraction," said Amanda.

In the Devereaux Room, Peter handed Amanda her birthday present, wrapped as meticulously as it had been restored.

"So this is what all the secrecy was about," said Amanda, weighing the package in her hand.

"Open it," said Peter solemnly.

Amanda carefully undid the wrapping—Peter was not surprised that she was not a ripper of wrapping paper.

"A book," she said with a smile. "I guess I should have known it would be a book."

"Open it," said Peter again.

Amanda opened the volume, carefully reading the title and then turning the pages, stopping at each of the stunning illustrations.

"It's beautiful, Peter," she said. "And this binding is amazing. How could you . . . I mean, I know I shouldn't ask this, but how could you afford something so . . . so elegant?"

"It was only a dollar."

"Oh, Peter, don't be silly," said Amanda. "Who would sell a book like this for a dollar?"

"Well, it didn't exactly look like that when I bought it. It was kind of falling apart and I repaired it and bound it for you."

"You . . ." Amanda closed the book and saw, for the first time, her initials on the front cover. She seemed to lose all ability to complete her thought as she ran her hands gently across the supple leather. In Peter's company Amanda was rarely at a loss for words, and he felt a great surge of pride in his accomplishment. He felt himself blushing and glanced down at his doublet in a vain attempt to hide his embarrassment. He need not have bothered, he realized, when he looked back up and saw Amanda's eyes clouded with tears.

"I didn't mean to make you cry," he said. In an instant her arms were around him and her body was shaking with sobs. Peter thought for a moment that he had inadvertently hit upon some unknown sorrow in her life. Her uncle had been killed in a tragic bookbinding accident, that sort of thing. But Amanda finally managed to speak through her tears.

"It's the most perfect present in the world," she said, loosening her grip on him so he could see her smiling as she wiped her tears away with her sleeve. "I just can't imagine how much you must . . . must love me to do something like this."

"A lot," said Peter simply, who now fought to keep his own tears away at the thought that something he did could have such a profound effect on the woman he loved.

"Oh, Peter," she said, locking her watery eyes on his. "I love you, too."

"I know," said Peter, smiling, because although he knew, it was the first time she had ever said it. "I know you do."

"Okay, enough crying," said Amanda, taking a deep breath. "It was a perfect gift, let's just leave it at that before things get any mushier. Besides, it's time for you to unwrap your gift."

"I don't see any packages," said Peter.

"I don't think you quite understand, Romeo," said Amanda, taking Peter's hand and guiding it to the laces that bound the front of her dress. "It's time for you to unwrap your gift."

There was no need to leave for Hay until midmorning, in pursuit of whatever books Julia Alderson had sold, so over breakfast Peter stared once more at the list of owners of the *Pandosto*. True, it would be nice to know if the book had been a gift from Shakespeare to Cotton or how it had gotten from Matthew Harbottle to John Bagford, but the much more pressing questions were, Who were B.B. and E.H.? and How did the book come to Evenlode Manor? If the book was a forgery, it was most likely to have been forged in the nineteenth century when Shakespeare's reputation was exploding. Peter had to understand the connections between the cryptic initials, Evenlode Manor, and the strange behavior of Julia Alderson if he hoped to prove the book's authenticity. Unfortunately, his only reliable source of information on the Aldersons was the housekeeper, whom he could hope to encounter only by chance. Martin Wells might know something about the family, but Peter didn't think the painter would welcome an unannounced visit on a Sunday morning.

It was not until he had finished his second cup of tea and his third slice of toast that Peter realized that Sunday morning meant a ready-made opportunity for mixing with the locals. Dr. Strayer had mentioned church as a good way to meet the villagers, but the only thing that had interested Peter less over the past few months than meeting strangers had been spending time with God. He often thought it would be easier if he could simply lose his faith, but Peter remained a believer and what he believed was that God was a bastard.

The eight o'clock service had already begun as Peter slipped into the back row of St. Andrew's, well away from the small congregation who huddled in the first few pews. He had walked past the lych-gate a hundred times on solitary evening strolls to the edge of the village but had never ventured into the churchyard, much less the church itself. The interior was dim and dank and held the cold with thermos-like efficiency.

Peter's family had attended a nearby Baptist church only on the occasional Christmas Eve and Easter, but Amanda had introduced Peter to the Episcopal Church during his junior year. At first he went only to please her, but eventually he came to appreciate the beauty of the liturgy and the music. Over the years his unquestioning child-hood acceptance of God grew into a deep and mature faith, nurtured with Amanda at his side. When he lost Amanda, Peter did not lose his belief in God—after all, if he didn't believe, then how could he blame God for what had happened?

The Anglican service was similar enough to the Episcopal liturgy that Peter knew exactly when to kneel or stand and when he was ex-pected to join in a prayer or response. But he merely sat silently, his coat pulled tight against the cold and the Almighty. He did not take communion.

The congregation and the organ wheezed their way through the final hymn, then quickly the center of activity moved to the back of the nave, where a tray of coffee seemed to appear out of nowhere and cups were handed around. Peter timidly joined the huddled circle and reached for a cup. No one seemed to notice him at first and he was just beginning to think he had been foolish to believe he was going to strike up a conversation with a group of total strangers in a church, of all places, when a man's voice beside him said cheerfully, "You're the American chap who did up the cottage in West Street." Before Peter could respond, or even discover who had addressed him, a woman said, "Oh yes, I've seen you round the shop."

Suddenly Peter was the center of attention, a mini-celebrity and welcome diversion in what was generally a predictable ritual. The man who had first spoken to him introduced himself as Alan, the verger. He was a tall and broad white-haired fellow, wearing enough tweed to account for several denuded sheep. He took Peter by the elbow and guided him around the circle, introducing him to the geriatric population of Kingham.

"So what does an American get up to here in Kingham?" asked a short man whose hand shook as he sipped his coffee.

"I'm a bookseller, actually," said Peter. "Antiquarian," he added, as if this would explain exactly why he had settled in the village. This revelation caused a surge of approval around the circle that could hardly have been more enthusiastic if Peter had said he was a philanthropist or a Nobel Prize winner.

"And have you found any good books round the village?" asked Alan, giving Peter just the opportunity he needed.

"I did look at some nice things up at Evenlode Manor yesterday," he said. "Though I must admit, I went to Evenlode House first by mistake." This brought a roar of laughter from the circle.

"That *was* a mistake," said one man.

"Evenlode House and Evenlode Manor in one day. You've seen our 'ancient grudge' then," said another, quoting *Romeo and Juliet*.

"How do you mean?" said Peter.

"There's been bad blood between the Aldersons and the Gardners for centuries," said a woman whom Peter had not previously noticed. She was so stooped and short that she seemed lost below the elbows of the other parishioners, but she spoke in a strong, clear voice.

"Isn't there some fellow writing a book about it?" asked the man who had cited Shakespeare.

"That there is," said the short woman. "Cornish gentleman was here a few months ago. Had a long chat with my older sister. She's the one who really knows the story." That this woman, introduced as Martha, could possibly have an *older* sister seemed almost absurd to

Peter, but the mention, once again, of the enigmatic Cornish gentleman made him certain that the feud between the inhabitants of the elegant Evenlode Manor and those of the dilapidated Evenlode House was somehow related to the identity of B.B.

"It sounds fascinating," said Peter. "Positively Shakespearean."

"It's sad what's happened," said the vicar. "Neighbors shouldn't act like that."

"You'll not see any of them darken the door of this church," said Alan. "And they certainly won't be inviting you to tea, vicar. So they won't be learning your lessons on neighborly behavior." This brought another outburst of laughter from the circle, and somehow was also the signal that the weekly socializing was over. Coffee cups clattered back onto the tray that was whisked away and the parishioners headed for the door, wrapping scarves around their heads against the morning wind sweeping across the fields from Churchill.

The vicar followed his modest flock to bestow his official good-byes, and Peter found himself alone, or so he thought. "Come back for a slice of cake and Louisa will tell you all about it," said a voice. Peter looked down to see Martha standing beside him, pulling on her gloves. He glanced at his watch. It was 9:30. He would have liked to get on the road, but the chance to delve a little deeper into the history of the Aldersons and their neighbors was too great a temptation.

"Cake would be lovely," he said, as he offered his arm to Martha and led her out the door.

Martha and her sister lived in a three-room cottage a hundred yards down the lane from the church. Within a minute of their arrival, Martha had piled fresh wood on the fire in the grate, served Peter a thick slab of ginger cake, and disappeared into the bedroom to retrieve her sister. Louisa was even shorter and more hunched over than Martha. She reminded Peter of Alice of Wonderland when her chin is pressed against her shoes. From his chair by the fire, Peter looked down on her as he said hello, giving him the feeling of addressing an extremely wrinkled eight-year-old. After Martha settled her sister in a chair she disappeared again, returning a moment later with a tray of tea. She poured a cup for each of them, then turned to Louisa, who had not yet spoken a word.

"Mr. Byerly wants to know all about the Aldersons and the Gardners," she said. A smile of delight crept across Louisa's face, as if her sole purpose at this late stage of life was to share the gossip of centuries past with whomever might listen.

"That's a story, that is," she said, and she paused to sip her tea before plunging into her tale.

"Grandfather worked for the Gardners at Evenlode House starting in the eighteen seventies, when he was just a boy. He used to tell me stories about the family when I was a little girl and we would go walking on the grounds. They was a kind and peaceful family, my old granddad always said." These were not the adjectives that came to Peter's mind as he recalled his encounter with the current Mr. Gardner.

"On only one subject did my granddad ever hear a Gardner raise his voice, and that was the Aldersons. There was real hatred there, I tell you."

"Why?" asked Peter.

"I don't know how far back it went. Story is they were both royalists in the Civil War, supposed to have hidden two hundred troops between them, but I've no idea where. The houses weren't so large then. But somewhere along the way they stopped agreeing. I do know they both wanted to build a mill on the Evenlode at least two hundred years ago. You see, the Gardners owned all the land south of the river, and the Aldersons owned the land to the north, but nobody could decide who owned the river. But even before that I'm not sure they got along. By the time my granddad was working there, Mr. Phillip Gardner was the head of the house. Oh, the tales Granddad used to spin about Mr. Phillip. Fancied himself a painter, he did."

Peter nearly choked on his tea at this revelation. Could Phillip

Gardner have been B.B.? Was that the reason the Cornish man had been asking questions around Kingham? "What sort of painter?" Peter asked.

"Not a very good one, I suppose," said Louisa. "Granddad said Mr. Phillip tried and tried to get into the Royal Academy or the Watercolour Society, but he never could. Said he always blamed it on Mr. Alderson. Of course by then the Gardners blamed anything that went wrong on the Aldersons. Granddad says they blamed the Aldersons for the flood that came roaring through the valley and killed all those sheep in the eighteen sixties. Not sure how the Aldersons could control the weather."

"But this Phillip Gardner was a painter?" asked Peter, eager to get back to that subject.

"Well," said Louisa, "he painted. Whether that makes him I painter, I couldn't say. Truth is he found a more reliable way to support the estate. Married a rich widow from down Witney. Not that that worked out so well either."

"Tell him about the mistress," said Martha.

"Now we never knew about that for sure," said Louisa, "but there were certainly mutterings among the servants that Mr. Phillip took a mistress after he was married. But this I can tell you. Four years after he marries the widow, she disappears and he dies under mysterious circumstances."

"It was ruled an accident," said Martha.

"It weren't no accident," said Louisa. "At least Granddad didn't think so. Either way, once Mr. Phillip was dead and buried at the family chapel, no one seemed to take much interest in the house. That's when the place just started falling down."

"I hear the mistress is buried with him," whispered Martha.

"Don't believe a word of it," said Louisa.

"But how would you know? Even Granddad never set foot in that chapel."

"I wonder if it's even there anymore," said Louisa. "When I was a girl, Granddad would point it out to me, and even then it was covered with vines and crumbling."

"Where was it?" asked Peter, wondering if uncovering the scandal of Phillip Gardner's marriage might give him some further clue about B.B.

"Down the hill past the house," said Martha. "Though I doubt Thomas would be offering to take you for a tour."

"Thomas? Is he the one who lives in Evenlode House now?"

"Lives in a caravan in the garden, from what I hear," said Martha.

"Yes, that's him," said Louisa. "Mr. Phillip's great-great-nephew."

"So," said Peter, "this Phillip Gardner was a frustrated painter, he married a rich widow, and four years later he died mysteriously?"

"That's right," said Louisa. "No one ever accused the wife of murder, but they buried him awfully quick, from what Granddad said."

"Was Phillip the one who collected all those papers and things?" asked Martha.

"Oh, yes, I nearly forgot about that."

"What sort of papers?" asked Peter, trying to contain his excitement as another piece of evidence seemed about to fit into place.

"Once he had the widow's money, Mr. Phillip thought he'd show off a bit, you see. Now he knew that Mr. Alderson fancied himself a collector—furniture, artwork, and he had a special weakness for . . . what would you call them? Letters and autographs of kings and that sort of thing."

"Historical documents," prompted Peter, picturing the cache at Evenlode Manor.

"I suppose that's what they were," said Louisa. "Anyway, Mr. Phillip took to collecting them sorts of things himself. Used to show them off to Granddad. It only went on for a couple of years."

"He just did it to annoy Mr. Alderson," said Martha.

"He certainly did that," said Louisa with a laugh.

"So what happened to the collection?" asked Peter, almost certain he knew the answer.

"I've no idea," said Louisa.

"Do you think they might have sold it to the Aldersons?" asked Peter.

"A Gardner would sooner burn them in the grate, no matter what they were worth," said Louisa.

"And you told all this to the man from Cornwall?" asked Peter, now almost certain he had stumbled into the scandal that Liz Sutcliffe was so eager to spring on the Victorian art world.

"Oh, yes," said Louisa. "Older gentleman, but still young from my point of view." Louisa and Martha laughed and Peter joined in as best he could, for his mind was pulling at the strands of Louisa's story and trying to unravel them into a narrative that fit all the evidence.

"You don't happen to remember the gentleman's name, do you?" asked Peter.

"Oh yes," said Louisa. "His name was Graham. Had a big white beard."

"And his surname?" asked Peter.

"His surname," said Louisa, suddenly scowling. "Oh, I've no idea."

"Nor have I," said Martha.

London, 1856

Phillip Gardner stepped out of the Oxford train into the glass-and-steel cavern of the recently completed Paddington station. He was twenty-four years old and it was the first time he had visited London alone. Under his arm he carried a portfolio of paintings, which he hoped would launch his career. He strode down the platform to the station entrance and hailed a hansom cab.

"Royal Academy of Arts," he told the driver, and with a crack of the whip, the cab clattered away, bearing Phillip toward his future.

Benjamin Mayhew arrived at Paddington ten minutes before his train was due to depart. He was bound for a book auction at Oxford's Holywell Music Room—the dispersal of the library of a recently departed don. Benjamin knew from a contact in Oxford that there would be a substantial number of important books under the hammer, but when one of his fellow booksellers had come in to Benjamin's shop yesterday, asking if the sale was worth the trip to Oxford, Benjamin had claimed the library was nothing more than a collection of dull religious tracts—no point in having more competition than necessary.

With a few minutes to spare before his departure, Benjamin strolled over to W H Smith, one of a chain of bookstalls that had become ubiquitous in England's railway termini. Benjamin perused the racks of newspapers and books, and his eye happened to fall on a small pamphlet written by William Henry Smith himself. It was not this coincidence but the title—*Was Lord Bacon the Author of Shake-*

speare's Plays?—that caught his eye. Benjamin Mayhew had never come across the notion that someone other than William Shakespeare had written the plays attributed to that name. Curious to see what the kingdom's most successful newsagent had to say on the topic, Benjamin bought a copy of the pamphlet, along with the *Times*, and was soon ensconced comfortably in a first-class carriage bound for Oxford.

In *Was Lord Bacon the Author of Shakespeare's Plays?* Benjamin read Smith's argument for Francis Bacon as the author of the Shakespeare canon. Smith called Shakespeare "a man of limited education, careless of fame, intent upon money-getting, and actively engaged in the management of a theater," but said that this was not enough for us to suppose "from the simple circumstance of his name being associated with these plays, that he was the author of them." Of Bacon, however, Smith wrote, "His history is just such as we should have drawn of Shakespeare, if we had been required to depict him from the internal evidence of his works." Smith conjectured why Bacon would have wanted to disassociate his name from the theater and how his training as a lawyer could explain the obviously extensive legal knowledge of the author of Shakespeare's plays.

By the time the train steamed into Oxford, Benjamin had read the pamphlet over three times. A wealthy merchant with an interest in literary controversy might make an excellent client for an antiquarian bookseller, he thought. That afternoon he bought heavily at the sale in the Holywell Music Room. He paid more than he wanted for a first edition of Malone's *An Inquiry into the Authenticity of Certain Miscellaneous Papers*, in which Malone exposed the great Shakespeare forger William Henry Ireland. It seemed a good book, he thought, to offer to Smith at a low price—and in Benjamin Mayhew's experience there was no better way to hook a regular customer than by tantalizing him with an underpriced copy of a book closely related to his passion.

Hay-on-Wye, Wales, Sunday, February 19, 1995

Peter's mind was aswirl as he headed out of Kingham toward Hay-on-Wye, the *Pandosto* nestled in an acid-free envelope inside his leather satchel on the backseat. Phillip Gardner had been a frustrated painter who blamed his failure on his neighbor Reginald Alderson. Gardner married a rich widow and took up document collecting to annoy Alderson. Four years later he was dead, with rumors of a mistress and murder circulating around the neighborhood. Somewhere in this mysterious narrative Peter felt sure was the key to both the stolen watercolor and the authenticity of the *Pandosto*. Might Reginald Alderson have murdered Phillip Gardner in order to get his hands on the collection of documents? Or was Alderson in cahoots with the mistress? And what secrets lay in that family chapel?

Of one thing Peter was nearly certain. Somehow Phillip Gardner's collection of rare documents had ended up in the hands of his enemy. After Peter left Martha and Louise's cottage, as he was walking down the lane, he suddenly remembered the interlacing initials E.H. penciled on the corner of each of the documents at Evenlode Manor. He had thought it had been the monogram of a previous owner; now he realized that E.H. stood for Evenlode House. And the *Pandosto* resting securely in his satchel bore the same initials.

Peter loitered in front of the window of Church Street Books in Hay-on-Wye, feigning interest in the same display he had stared at just four days earlier and hoping for someone to enter the shop and distract the shopkeeper. He had no interest in being subjected to an unnecessary conversation beginning with, *Aren't you the fellow who stole that watercolor?*

Five minutes later a customer went into the shop and attracted the book dealer's attention. Edmond Malone's book was still where Peter had reshelved it four days ago. Next to it were two volumes by William Henry Ireland detailing his forging of Shakespeare manuscripts and a copy of Ireland's play *Vortigen*, which he had tried to pass off as Shakespeare's. All four books had the interlacing *E.H.* on the front endpaper.

The next two books on the shelf were by another famous Shakespeare forger, John Payne Collier. Again, both books were marked with the monogram of Evenlode House. Peter was detecting an unsettling pattern. In all likelihood, Julia Alderson had removed this collection of books by and about Shakespeare forgers from the library of Evenlode Manor to avoid casting suspicion on the authenticity of the *Pandosto*. These books had all the hallmarks of the library of a forger in training, a forger whose greatest achievement was in the satchel next to Peter's feet.

The next book on the shelf only increased Peter's suspicions: *Notes and Emendations of the Text of Shakespeare's Plays*—the book that Collier based on his boldest forgery, which bore a strong resemblance to the *Pandosto*. In 1852, Collier had announced a remarkable discovery. He had obtained a copy of the Second Folio of Shakespeare's plays, printed in 1632. In the margins of this volume were thousands of notes and textual annotations. Collier claimed these annotations came from "purer manuscripts" of Shakespeare's plays. The folio promised fodder for generations of Shakespeare scholars. Collier, however, refused to submit the volume to scrutiny, hiding it away in the library of the Duke of Devonshire. When the old duke died, his son allowed the British Museum to make a careful examination of the volume. The marginalia were clearly forged, and all evidence pointed to Collier as the perpetrator.

Peter now held a copy of Collier's notorious book, lushly rebound in green morocco. In a corner of the inside back cover was a small stamp in the shape of a butterfly—the binder's mark. On the front endpaper was the familiar E.H. monogram and something that cast the greatest doubt yet on the marginalia in the *Pandosto*. At the top of the page, in an uneven script, was the inscription, JOHN PAYNE COLLIER TO PHILLIP GARDNER, 1877. Collier, the notorious forger of Shakespearean marginalia, had known Phillip Gardner, Peter's most likely candidate for the painter B.B. and onetime owner of the *Pandosto*. Was the *Pandosto* another forgery by Collier, hidden among Gardner's documents as he had hidden the Second Folio in the Duke of Devonshire's library? Did Collier never "discover" the *Pandosto* because he had, long before 1877, been unmasked as a forger?

Peter still hoped the *Pandosto* might be authentic, but he had already begun to adjust his expectations. Discovering an unrecorded Shakespeare forgery by Collier, especially one of this audacity, would make a small ripple in the pond of Shakespeare studies, rather than the tsunami that the marginalia would cause if genuine, but it would be a discovery nonetheless, worthy of an article in a scholarly journal. The book might still attract spirited bidding, especially if it was, in fact, a complete first edition. Even without the priceless Shakespearean marginalia it would be a unique copy of an important book.

The collection of books on Shakespeare forgeries formerly of Evenlode House, and presumably most recently of Evenlode Manor, numbered ten. The final three titles were the books that had unmasked Collier and revealed his forgeries. Peter carried all ten books in a neat stack to the front room and set them on the counter.

"Ah, come back then, have you?" said the shopkeeper.

Peter kept his head down as he pulled out his checkbook. "Yes, I have a new customer who's interested in literary forgery and I remembered seeing these. I'll take the lot."

"Yes, quite a nice little collection that is. Funny couple brought it in about two months ago. Not exactly literary types. But I don't imagine they're stolen. Titles are a bit obscure for a book thief."

"I don't suppose you remember the names of the people who brought them in," said Peter, wondering if John Alderson was in on the deception with his sister. "I thought I might try to find out something about the provenance." It wasn't exactly kosher for one dealer to ask another about his sources, but if the reason was scholarly rather than commercial, rules could be bent.

"Let me see," said the man, pulling a large register out from under the counter and flipping the pages. "She was a quiet lady, not much personality, if you know what I mean."

"Mousy?" said Peter.

"Exactly that," said the man. "That's exactly what I'd call her. But I made the check out to him. Ah, here it is," he said, running his finger along an entry in the register. "Fellow by the name of Thomas Gardner."

Everything about his loss of virginity had felt safe to Peter—not just the familiar surroundings of the Devereaux Room and the familiar arms of Amanda, but even the residual role-playing that served as a protection against too much revelation of his most intimate self. As for other sorts of protection, Amanda had taken care of that, as she took care of so much. As they made love on the soft carpet amid their discarded costumes, she had guided him as she had guided him on the dance floor. Afterward he had curled up against her and rested his hand on her bare belly, feeling her skin gradually cool under his touch. They lay in a silence broken only by their breathing in unison, and Peter felt a sense of belonging deeper than any he had ever felt.

Finally Amanda placed her hand on top of his and spoke softly, her voice muffled by the carpet in spite of the cavernous space above them. "That was my first time," she said.

"Mine, too," said Peter.

She took his hand gently in hers and moved it lower across her smooth flesh. "Let's see if the second time is just as good," she said.

On Saturday morning, two days after Halloween, Peter was walking across campus to the library, his head down, his shoulders hunched, and his books clasped tightly against his chest—a posture with which he had successfully shielded himself from the outside world since middle school—when he heard a cheerful voice at his side.

"Good morning, Romeo. Do you recognize me with my head attached?"

Peter had no choice but to look up and see Amanda's friend Cynthia, who had fallen into step next to him, smiling broadly.

"Morning, Cynthia," he muttered. "I've really got to get to the library." He picked up his pace, but Cynthia matched his stride and kept smiling at him. It was unnerving.

"Me, too," she said brightly. Peter knew this must be a lie. He was practically the only student at Ridgefield who went to the library on Saturday mornings. "It'll give us a chance to talk. It's so hard to have a real conversation at that masquerade." Peter was thinking that this was exactly what he had liked about the ball. "You know Amanda talks about you all the time, but it's always 'Peter and I did this' or 'Peter and I did that.' She's very cagey when it comes to telling me what you're actually like."

"I guess I'm kind of a private person," said Peter, gripping his books a little tighter. Although he wanted to escape this conversation as soon as possible, he couldn't deny the thrill that rushed through him when Cynthia said that Amanda talked about him all the time. Then he suddenly felt a jolt in his stomach when it occurred to him that Amanda might have said to her friend, *Peter and I made love.* He stared intently at the patterns of the bricks in the path as they walked.

"Well that's okay," said Cynthia. "To be private. I mean, I'm not that way. Everybody always knows how I'm feeling, whether they want to or not, but then I guess Amanda has always been a little on the private side."

"I guess Amanda and I are alike that way," said Peter.

Cynthia put a hand on Peter's arm and gripped lightly, pulling him to a stop. He felt it would be rude to keep staring at the ground, so he looked up at her, but still avoided making eye contact. His hands began to sweat and he was afraid he might drop his books. "Listen, Peter," said Cynthia. "I understand you're a private guy, and I'm sure you have your reasons. But I'd like to be your friend, I really would, and there's a real simple reason for that. I've known Amanda since we were six. She's the best friend I've ever had. And I've never seen her as happy as she's been since she started seeing you. Now maybe you haven't dated a lot, so you don't have much to compare Amanda to."

"I haven't dated at all," mumbled Peter.

"Well, let me tell you, what Amanda feels for you—that's not just what a girl feels for some guy she's dating. She's head over heels, Peter. And here's the thing. Either you're head over heels, too, in which case I'd really like to be friends with the man who's going to spend the rest of his life with my best friend; or you're not, in which case I need to know right now so I can tell Amanda that I had to kick your ass for breaking her heart."

Cynthia didn't stop smiling, but Peter sensed that this final threat was not a joke. He also realized that, at some point during this speech, his hands had stopped sweating and he found himself looking directly into Cynthia's eyes.

"It feels a little weird to be telling you this," said Peter. "I mean, I hardly know you. But yes, I'm head over heels. She may not know it yet, but I am the guy who's going to spend the rest of his life with your best friend." Peter felt his cheeks grow hot with the pride of this declaration, but he did not drop his gaze from Cynthia.

"Good," she said, linking her arm with his and pulling him down the path toward the library. "Then I won't have to kick your ass."

"And even though I'm not very good at it, I would like to be your friend."

"Peter," said Cynthia, "I think you're going to make an excellent friend." They walked the rest of the way to the library in companionable silence, and Cynthia deposited him on the doorstep with a kiss on the cheek before heading back across campus toward the dormitories. Peter laughed as he pushed his way through the heavy doors and wondered how long she had been lying in wait for him.

Peter was surprised to see the light on in Francis Leland's office as he tossed his books onto a table in the Devereaux Room. He had expected to have Special Collections to himself until Francis came in for his afternoon of work. Peter slid into his usual chair and noticed a copy of that day's *New York Times* open on the table and folded back to an article with the headline, "Gallery Said to Possess First American Imprint." He picked up the paper and began to read.

The article described how a Salt Lake City rare-documents dealer named Mark Hofmann had discovered a copy of the earliest document printed in America, a broadside titled "Oath of a Freeman." Supposed to have been printed in Cambridge, Massachusetts, in 1638 or 1639, the "Oath" had been recorded but no copy was known to have survived.

"It's the Holy Grail of Americana," said Francis, as Peter lay the paper back on the table.

"Is it really worth a million and a half dollars?" asked Peter. This was the asking price of the New York book dealers who were handling the "Oath" for Hofmann.

"Who's to say what it would sell for at auction," said Francis. "It's the only one. I'd say a million and a half is a bullish price, but not ridiculous. The question is, who can afford it?" According to the article, the Library of Congress and the American Antiquarian Society had performed extensive forensic tests and concluded that the "Oath" was authentic.

The article also described how Hofmann, who had exhibited a penchant for digging up historical documents, especially those related to the Mormon Church, had recently been injured in one of three pipe bomb explosions in Salt Lake City. The local police seemed to be considering Hofmann a suspect in the bombings but did not draw any connections between the violence and the amazing discovery of the "Oath."

"What would you do if you found something like that?" Peter asked Francis.

"I'd do the same thing these folks have done," said Francis, tapping the newspaper with a pencil. "I'd suspect it and send it to the experts."

"Do you think these experts used the same techniques as Carter and Pollard?" asked Peter.

"Forensic science is a little more advanced now than it was fifty years ago, but yes, I'd imagine basically they looked at three things. First is provenance, the history of ownership. With something that old and valuable you have to ask where it came from and how it remained undiscovered for so long. Next you have to look at the content. Is there anything in the text that's inconsistent with the time period—spelling, word use, anachronisms, and so forth? That's not so much of an issue with this piece because the text of the "Oath" is recorded in historical sources. Anyone can look it up. Last is materials. Is the ink as old as it purports to be? Is the paper from the right time period? Do the printing process and the typeface fit the timeline as well?"

"So you think it's authentic?" said Peter.

"I'd like to see the forensic reports myself," said Francis, "before I decide for sure it's not a forgery. But it looks like it could be the real thing."

"The first document ever printed in America," said Peter. "That would be something."

"Yes," said Francis, "it certainly would."

London, 1875

He saw her for the first time seated before a canvas by John Everett Millais at the Royal Academy exhibit of 1875. He had come to the exhibit on his way to meet with his favorite bookseller, Benjamin Mayhew, with whom he would arrange the purchase of a rare document. Phillip Gardner had once hoped that his own work might hang on the walls of a London gallery, but he had come to accept, after repeated rejections by both the Royal Academy and the Historical Watercolour Society, that he had no great talent as an artist. His technical abilities were unmatched—and had he not had the foresight to marry as he did, he might have scratched out a reasonable living as a copyist—but he lacked the artist's vision to create original work. Rejected by the art world, he painted his mediocre watercolors in private, hung them on the walls of his country home, and paid an annual visit to the Royal Academy to remind himself of his own shortcomings. Every year he walked through the rooms, occasionally stopping at a canvas that had attracted a crowd to see if he could detect what made it so special. He never could.

In her gloved hands she clutched a small booklet that appeared to be heavily marked with underlinings and marginalia. She was a tall woman, stately, Phillip would have said, with dark hair and an intensity to her stare that he found both riveting and unnerving. The lines of her face were sharp and angular, yet her dress clearly contained the curves of a woman. Phillip was not in the habit of staring at women in public. Though his marriage was a sham that provided him with an income and his wife with a country home, he was able to obtain whatever sexual relief he required with a few shillings and a walk to a certain street near Covent Garden. So he could not have said why, exactly, this woman fascinated him—perhaps because she was as still as the figure in the painting, or because she seemed so confidently self-possessed. Or because she was so obviously alone.

Her eyes were fixed on the canvas, and did not seem to flinch when another exhibit goer juxtaposed himself between her and the image of a man, who looked something like a toreador, carrying a woman up a rocky path. The woman's hands were linked behind the man's neck, and her face, visible over his shoulder, did not seem to indicate, as far as Phillip could tell, whether she was being kidnapped, rescued, or merely carried up the hill from a picnic because she had hurt her ankle. Phillip must have spent longer than he had intended trying to puzzle out the possibilities, for when he heard a voice at his side, he realized that the woman he had been watching had risen from her seat and was addressing him.

"Ruskin doesn't like it," she said, still looking at the painting but holding up her booklet. "He says it's a defect of industry that one lover should have a body without a face and the other a face without a body." Phillip was taken aback that an unaccompanied woman should so brazenly address an unaccompanied man in public, but this breach of protocol was tempered in his mind by other factors. First, she was, much to his surprise, an American. Second, she was clearly intelligent—and intelligent conversation with a woman was something he sorely missed since the twin tragedies of his sister's death and his own wedding. Third, and perhaps most overpowering, was her intoxicating aroma—he didn't know how to describe it, but her scent enveloped him as he turned to look at her, and he knew at that moment that he had to have her.

"Are they lovers?" he asked. "I wasn't sure."

"Well of course they are," she said with a laugh. "It's called 'The Crown of Love.'" She took a step closer to the painting and squinted at the canvas, then turned back to him and fixed him with her eyes for the first time. "But I see what you mean. They could just as easily be enemies. It's a fine line."

Phillip Gardner was too delighted to have his own ignorance misconstrued as a keen critical eye to realize that he had an uncanny ability to confuse love and danger.

Peter spent the night at an anonymous hotel near Heathrow airport—he had driven from Hay toward London but had no wish to navigate the metropolitan traffic. He would park his car at the airport and take the tube into town. He slept little, and not just because he was trying to wrap his mind around the fact that the supposedly mortal enemies Julia Alderson and Thomas Gardner were apparently in cahoots. Had the man at church who had cited *Romeo and Juliet* in describing the "ancient grudge" between the two families been more accurate than he knew? Peter felt he was beginning to detect a plot.

Somehow Julia and Thomas meet and fall in love. They are kept apart not just by their families' feud but by Thomas Gardner's poverty. Julia uncovers a rare book in which a famous Victorian forger has scrawled marginalia in the hand of William Shakespeare. She hears that an American bookseller is living nearby. She and her beloved plot to dupe this American into selling the *Pandosto* at an enormous price to an unsuspecting client, so they can afford to rebuild Evenlode House and live happily ever after, despite the scorn of their surviving kin. But what if the American bookseller detected the forgery? How far would they go to protect their plan? Peter needed to find out everything he could about the *Pandosto*, but he also needed to go back to Evenlode Manor as soon as possible and pretend nothing was wrong.

That morning Peter would go to the one place where he might be able to get some answers—the British Museum. When he and

Amanda had first come to England on their honeymoon, Francis Leland had arranged for Peter to meet Nigel Cook, a librarian at the British Museum. "You've got to have a contact there if you're going to deal in English literature," Francis had said. "They have things there you won't find anywhere else." It had seemed odd to spend an afternoon of their honeymoon in the musty rooms and cluttered offices of the book department—not exactly as romantic as the boat ride to Kew Gardens or the dinner at the Savoy—but Peter had indulged Amanda's passions as she made her first visit to the Tate and the Victoria and Albert Museum. She was happy to do the same for Peter, letting him grip her hand with nervousness and excitement as Nigel Cook led them through a maze of rooms into his office.

Nigel had given Peter one of the great bibliographical thrills of his life—on a par with his first encounter with the bad quarto of *Hamlet*. He had allowed Peter to handle a manuscript from the library of Robert Cotton—an eleventh-century stunningly illuminated Psalter that, according to a Latin inscription, was connected to Winchester Cathedral and Bishop William of Wykeham. Nigel had also given Peter and Amanda a brief tour of the facilities—the cataloging rooms, the areas for visiting researchers, a laboratory for testing ink and paper, and a conservation lab much like the one at Ridgefield.

"If there's ever anything I can do for you," said Nigel as he bade them good-bye back in the public galleries, "don't hesitate to call." He had presented a business card and Peter had stashed it in his wallet. Seven years later it was still there.

Peter phoned Nigel from the hotel room at 9:05. He hesitated to press the final digit of the number, the familiar fear of contact rising within him, but he wiped his damp palm on the duvet, and completed the call. Nigel remembered him immediately and unquestioningly agreed to provide what Peter asked for. Of course Peter had not told Nigel the whole truth. It would have been unfair to make the librarian keep such a secret.

"I have an early edition of *Pandosto*," Peter said, "possibly unrecorded." Nigel had agreed to provide Peter with the museum's unique but incomplete copy of the first edition and a Hinman collator. The lab, Nigel said, would be happy to do a paper and ink analysis. They should be able to get results in a few days.

"And, Peter," said Nigel, "it's nice to hear from you. I spoke to Francis a couple of months ago and he seemed worried about you. Are you all right?"

Peter was surprised at the careful consideration he gave this question. He had certainly made great strides in the past few days—striking up conversations with total strangers on purpose, delving back into the book world, allowing a new passion to pull him out of his secret lair. But to say he was all right—that was taking things a bit far. After a long pause, he answered the question the best way he knew how. "I don't know," he said.

Peter's hesitation before dialing the next number was considerably longer. Though he had always hated making phone calls to anyone other than Amanda, he at least knew that Nigel would be receptive to his inquiries. He had no such reassurance about Liz Sutcliffe, in fact, quite the contrary—he needed to ask her for something she had already refused him. After ten minutes of sitting on the bed staring at her card, he gave up planning what to say and dialed the number, picturing the way she had smiled at him over the vindaloo. He was both startled and comforted to hear Amanda's voice.

"She likes you," said Amanda. "She'll be happy to hear from you." Peter thought he sensed encouragement to do more than just make this phone call, but before he could respond to Amanda, Liz answered the phone.

"Peter Byerly, what a surprise," she said. Peter found himself without a voice and the line was silent for a moment. "You're not having second thoughts about our arrangement, I hope," Liz prompted.

Peter felt overwhelmed by the sudden feeling that the phone was inadequate for what he needed. If he was to have any chance of convincing Liz to help him, he had to talk to her face-to-face. "I'm coming to London today," he managed to say at last, "and I wondered if you might like to have lunch. I mean, you know, have lunch with me."

"Lunch would be brilliant," said Liz. "My office is in Bloomsbury, but I could meet you anywhere you like."

"I'll be working at the British Museum," said Peter.

"How would it be if I meet you on the steps of the museum at one o'clock?"

"Fine," said Peter. "That would be fine. I'll see you at one, then."

"Super," said Liz cheerfully, and hung up.

Peter stopped by W H Smith for the morning paper, then settled himself into a seat on the Piccadilly Line train into London. Only after he had read the entire front page of the *Times* did Peter realize that Liz Sutcliffe might think he had asked her on a date.

The morning fog had burned off and the winter sun shone on Russell Square when Peter emerged from the tube. He gulped in the crisp air as he walked briskly the few blocks to the British Museum. It was ten-thirty when he presented his reader's pass to the attendant at the door leading to the book department.

"It's excellent to see you, Peter," said Nigel, as he showed Peter into a modest-sized reading room with a library table in the center and books lining the walls. "It's been far too long."

"Seven years," said Peter. He was afraid for a moment that Nigel might ask him what had transpired in those years, but he needn't have worried. Nigel, Peter should have remembered, was quintessentially British, and thus only one topic of conversation would suffice with a relative stranger.

"Remarkably fine weather today," he said, "though I don't expect it will last."

"Still, we can enjoy it for now," said Peter, knowing that deep in the bowels of the British Museum, neither man was likely to do anything of the sort.

"I've called up the first edition of *Pandosto* and a few other Robert Greene items for you," said Nigel. "You'll find the collator just down the corridor in the room to your right. I'm having an assistant make some printouts of the 1592 and 1595 editions of *Pandosto*—those we only have on microfilm, but you can still do a collation if you need to. I hate to leave you unoccupied, but I really must get back to work. I'll have the materials sent in as soon as they arrive."

Thus Peter found himself alone in a book-lined room far below the tourists and the schoolchildren who now surged through the galleries on their way to the Rosetta Stone and the Elgin Marbles. He set his satchel, containing the *Pandosto*, on the table and began to scan the shelves. The books were primarily standard reference works— the thick, heavy volumes of the *Oxford English Dictionary*, shelves of bibliographies, and long rows of the short, squat volumes of the *Dictionary of National Biography*, known to scholars as the *DNB*.

Peter thought he might as well do a little research on the *Pandosto's* provenance while he was waiting; the *DNB* might well give him further clues on several of the owners. He took the book out of his bag, wishing as he did so that he had returned it to its folding case before he had left home. The acid-free envelope in which he had placed it seemed insufficient to protect such a treasure. Opening *Pandosto* on the table, he positioned his satchel so that anyone entering the room would not see the book. Once again he read through the list of owners, trying to construct a story that would connect them to one another.

R. Greene to Em Ball

Bart. Harbottle

Wm. Shakspere, Stratford

R. Cotton, Augustus B IV

Matthew Harbottle, Red Bull Theatre

John Bagford

John Warburton

R. Harley, Oxford

B. Mayhew for William H. Smith

B.B. / E.H.

The author had given the book to his mistress who had subsequently sold it to the bookseller Harbottle. Harbottle had then sold or given the book to Shakespeare, who had been inspired by the bookseller to create the character of Autolycus. Shakespeare had given the book to Robert Cotton, perhaps in thanks for allowing him access to his library. Harbottle had then gotten the book back from Cotton, by means legitimate or illegitimate, and passed it on to a relative, probably his son. The younger Harbottle had disposed of the book sometime in the seventeenth century, probably outside of London, thus avoiding the great fire of 1666, and it had eventually been purchased by John Bagford, who then sold it to John Warburton.

Peter pulled down the *DNB* volumes for Bagford and Warburton. Bagford, he confirmed, was a sometime bookseller, who had also compiled a famous collection of printing samples. Warburton's biography noted that he had, "after much drinking and attempting to muddle Wanley, sold in July 1720 to the Earl of Oxford many valuable manuscripts on Wanley's own terms." Humfrey Wanley was librarian to Robert Harley, first Earl of Oxford. The collection formed by Harley and his son was donated to the British Museum and became part of the British Library. So how had *Pandosto* escaped?

Peter took a microcassette recorder from his bag and began to dictate notes. He had gotten into the habit of using the recorder at Ridgefield. Rare-book rooms forbade the use of pens, and Peter had a habit of breaking sharp pencil points almost immediately. A recorder provided him with an easy way to take notes without posing a risk to delicate materials.

Peter could find no listing in the *DNB* for a "B. Mayhew," and he was on the verge of pulling down the volume containing the Smiths when a young man entered the room with an armload of books.

"Mr. Byerly?" he asked.

"Yes," Peter answered.

"I believe these are for you," said the man, setting the books on the table.

Peter left the volumes of the *DNB* scattered on the table and rushed to examine the pile of books. Most were in simple protective folders, nothing like the complex and elegant cases created at the behest of Amanda Devereaux, but sufficient to protect four-hundred-year-old books and pamphlets from the stresses of being pulled off shelves. Despite several tantalizing rarities, Peter searched the pile for the one book that held his interest—the only recorded copy of the 1588 first edition of *Pandosto*.

As Peter saw it, the question of the authenticity of the Evenlode Manor *Pandosto* was twofold: was the printed book genuine and were the marginalia genuine? His task that morning was to begin answering the first question. The British Library copy of *Pandosto*, which he now removed carefully from its folding case, was not complete—it lacked the second signature. If Peter could prove that the Evenlode Manor copy was a complete and genuine first edition, it would be a significant find even if the marginalia proved to have been forged.

Peter carried the two copies of *Pandosto* from the reading room down a narrow corridor to a room not much larger than a closet and almost completely filled by the six-foot-tall, five-foot-wide gray metal bulk of the museum's Hinman collator. The collator, an optical comparison device, had been invented by Shakespeare scholar Charlton Hinman in the late 1940s to assist with his research in comparing copies of texts to one another. A researcher placed two copies of a book on the machine's two platforms, then looked through a binocular viewer and adjusted the image so that, through a series of mirrors, the two copies overlapped exactly. In this way one could tell at a glance if the texts were identical or if there were some variation, as differences would seem to dance before one's eyes. Hinman had used his collator to compare copies of Shakespeare's First Folio, meticulously cataloging the various changes and corrections that had been made during the course of the press run.

Peter carefully opened the two copies of *Pandosto* to their title pages and clamped each gently onto one of the collator's platforms. He flicked the power switch, and the machine hummed as lights illuminated the texts and fans whirred. Peter leaned over the binocular viewer and adjusted the knobs until the two pages that floated before him gradually merged into one crisp image. It was a perfect match. Over the next hour, Peter repeated this process with every page, excepting of course those that were missing from the British Library copy. Everything matched precisely.

Until he reached the final page, he did not realize that his back ached from leaning over the viewer. Leaving the books in the collator, he stepped back into the reading room, where his eyes took a moment to adjust to the light. He stretched to relieve the tension in his back and had walked several laps around the library table when he noticed, next to his bag, a pile of photocopies—the printouts of the later editions of *Pandosto* that Nigel's assistant had made from the microfilm copies.

Peter now knew that all the pages of the British Library first edition matched the Evenlode Manor copy, but what about the missing signature? If the Evenlode Manor *Pandosto* were a forgery, the text must have been copied from extant copies—and the only recorded copy of the first edition was incomplete. If the text of the missing signature matched a later edition, the Evenlode Manor copy would be suspect indeed.

He returned to the collator and removed the British Library *Pandosto*, replacing it with the photocopy of the 1592 edition. This time he compared only the pages that had been missing from the library's first edition. On each page the jiggling text that indicated differences on almost every line swam before his eyes. The same was true of the 1595 edition. Finally removing the Evenlode Manor *Pandosto* from the collator, Peter exhaled a long sigh of relief. He had found exactly what he had hoped for. There now seemed only two possibilities. Either the text of the Evenlode Manor *Pandosto* was a genuine first edition, or it had been brilliantly forged from a complete copy of the first edition. Of these two possibilities, the former was not only more appealing but more likely.

Peter switched off the machine and removed the Evenlode Manor *Pandosto* and the photocopies. The latter he placed in his bag, in case he needed to refer to them later. He sat at the table in the reading room and opened *Pandosto* to the final page—the rear endpaper crowded with notes. There was a large smudge of brown ink in the lower-right corner. Taking a pair of scissors from his satchel, Peter carefully snipped a tiny piece from this corner and placed it in an envelope. The sample should be sufficient to test the age of the ink and paper. He slipped the book into its protective envelope and back into his bag.

Peter knocked on the open door of Nigel's office to attract the attention of the librarian and gave him the envelope containing the sample.

"I'm hoping it's sixteenth century," said Peter, "but there's a chance it's a nineteenth-century forgery."

"We'll check the ink and paper for you," said Nigel. "Don't know if we'll be able to prove anything conclusively, but I'll let you know what we find out."

Peter jotted his number down on a scrap of paper and handed it to Nigel. "If there's any way to get results by the end of the week, I am under a bit of a time crunch," he said.

"I'll do my best," said Nigel, smiling. Peter would have liked a more definitive promise, but he didn't want to seem like a pushy American, so he let the matter drop. "And how's the collating coming?" asked Nigel.

"Quite well," said Peter.

"I'm just off for lunch," said Nigel, "but if you need anything, my assistant James should be back in a few minutes."

At the mention of lunch, Peter felt a jolt of panic. The clock on Nigel's wall read 1:10. "I must be going," said Peter, backing out of the office. "I've an appointment myself. Call me as soon as you hear anything." Peter dashed back down the hall and grabbed his bag. Without stopping to reshelve the volumes of the *DNB* scattered across the table, he made for the door and took the stairs toward the galleries above two at a time. By the time he reached the front doors of the museum, it was 1:15.

Peter burst through the doors, breathless from his dash up the stairs and through the galleries. The sharp winter air struck his cheek with the force of a slap, as a gust of wind rushed up the wide stone stairs to meet him. A mass of schoolchildren loitered on the steps. Peter scanned the crowd for Liz, wondering if she had given up and left. He was suddenly struck by the vivid memory of another day, years ago, when he had met Amanda on these steps. He had been late then, too.

"I suppose Robert Cotton is to blame," Amanda had said, smiling and giving Peter a quick peck on the cheek. That day had been even colder, and he felt the kiss on his face long after Amanda had led him down the steps.

"Looking for someone?" said a voice, jerking him back to the present. "I guess if your watch is set to American time, you're four hours and forty-five minutes early," said Liz, winking at Peter as he turned to her.

"Sorry," he said. "Got caught up in some research."

"Well," said Liz, slipping her arm through his in exactly the way Amanda used to do, "that's at least an excuse I can understand."

Liz looked different from when he had seen her three days ago, and it took Peter a minute to realize that her hair, which had been a dirty brown streaked with blond on Friday night, was now a rich, even honey color. She must have had it cut, too. It wasn't much shorter, but it was considerably less frizzy, the ends were even at her shoulder, and even when the wind swirled around and strands of hair whipped her face, it stayed altogether more kempt than it had on Friday. Peter's arm was tensed almost to the point of pain where Liz's was draped through it. Every muscle in his body seemed to be crying out to him—*she thinks this is a date; don't lead her on.* Yet in spite of this, Peter found himself saying, "I like your hair."

"Thanks," said Liz. "I got home on Friday night and I thought, Jesus, this guy had to sit across from me all night looking at this crap hair, so I decided what the hell, I'd do something about it."

Peter felt like he was in a wrestling match between his body, which now tried to pull slightly away from Liz, and his mouth, which was just on the verge of saying something else nice. True, he had had a pleasant enough time with her on Friday night, but if he had been driven by curiosity about the watercolor then, his motives today were far more powerful, and he needed her to understand that this lunch was not a social engagement. "A lot's happened since Friday," he said, finally managing to disengage his arm from hers as they got caught in a crowd of tourists crossing Great Russell Street.

"You'll have to tell me all about it," said Liz, grabbing Peter's bare hand in the softness of her suede glove and pulling him past Museum Street. "I know a fab little Italian place just around the corner." Peter resigned himself to the hand-holding, reasoning that it was necessary to avoid separation in the crowds that surged along the pavement. In another moment they had turned a corner into the comparative calm of Coptic Street—its bookshops and art galleries of little interest to the bulk of the tourists that teemed along Great Russell Street. Yet Peter did not drop Liz's hand; it would be impolite, he thought.

He followed her around another corner and through the door of a tiny Italian bistro, but neither of them spoke again until they were seated at a table by the front window.

"I have something for you," she said, reaching into her voluminous bag and pulling out a stiff buff envelope. "Your watercolor. Thanks for the loan."

Peter took the envelope from her. In all the excitement of *Pandosto*, it seemed somehow less weighty than it had when he had handed it to her three days earlier. "You're welcome," said Peter, slipping the envelope into his satchel.

"You don't want to look at it?" Liz asked.

"I trust you," said Peter.

"It's not that," said Liz. "It's just . . . it seemed to me you sort of, I don't know, needed to look at it every so often."

Though the watercolor, and what Liz knew about it, was his reason for wanting to see her today, Peter's obsession with the image had faded considerably since his discovery of the *Pandosto*. The painting was a worthless artifact of interest only to him because of its coincidental resemblance to Amanda; the book was quite possibly one of the great discoveries in the history of English literature.

The waiter set two glasses of red wine on the table and Liz raised hers to Peter. He responded to the toast, clinking his glass against hers slightly too hard, the wine almost sloshing onto the crisp, white tablecloth. He took a gulp and set the glass on the table.

"Easy does it there, cowboy," said Liz. "So what is it that's happened since Friday?" Her voice seemed tinged with insecurity, and Peter felt suddenly ashamed that he should be thinking only of trying to get information from her, not of how she might legitimately feel about going out for two meals with the same man in three days. He felt a surge of tenderness for her, such as he had not felt for anyone since he lost Amanda. It was a feeling as frightening as it was unexpected.

"I have a problem," he said. "Maybe two problems."

"I'm listening," said Liz, crossing her arms over her chest and leaning back in her chair.

Peter wasn't sure how to start. He desperately wanted the name and address of the mysterious scholar from Cornwall who seemed to be the only person in the world who knew anything about the identity of B.B., and now he had some leverage in trying to pry this information out of Liz. On the other hand, he couldn't help thinking, as he looked at her defensive posture across the table, that the air was rife with unspoken feelings, and if he didn't address those first, she would never tell him anything.

"I'm having a hard time dealing with this," said Peter finally, making a limp gesture with his hand meant to encompass the two of them but looking more like a request for the waiter to clear the table.

"This?" said Liz.

"You and me, I mean."

"What about us?" Liz seemed to draw her arms more tightly across her chest.

"Well, I think it's possible, I mean, I think maybe I might . . . I might like you."

"Wow, you sure know how to sweep a girl off her feet," said Liz.

"You see, this is my problem. I'm absolutely no good at this," said Peter. "I've only ever been out with one woman in my entire life and I'm not . . . I don't think I'm over her, and I don't want you to get the wrong idea."

"What idea would that be?" said Liz coldly.

"That I like you. I mean that I like you . . . you know, that way."

"Well, you're honest. When you said you're no good at this, you knew what you were talking about."

"Look," said Peter, feeling the sweat bead on his forehead and his appetite drain away. "I don't really know how to explain this, but there's a big part of me that doesn't want you to think this is a date. But then there's this other part, this part I didn't even realize was there until I saw you on the steps, that does want you to think it's a date. Does that make any sense?"

"First of all," said Liz, "you can relax, because this is not a date; it's just two friends meeting for lunch. And secondly, that's all we are, Peter, two friends. I know you come with a lot of baggage, and apparently being friends is not one of your great talents, but trust me here—it's not that hard. Besides, to be friends all you have to do is sort of think that you might like me." She finally smiled and uncrossed her arms, reaching for her wineglass and holding it up toward Peter again.

"Now, gently this time," she said. "To friendship."

Peter tapped his glass lightly against hers and took a long drink of wine. As he set down his glass, Liz picked up his napkin and wiped the sweat off his forehead. Peter shivered from the intimacy of the gesture, but before he could think of what to say, Liz settled back in her chair and went on.

"You still want to know about B.B., don't you?"

"But it's not for selfish reasons anymore."

"Not for selfish reasons?"

"Well, it's for reasons that are less selfish than the original reasons."

"That's reassuring."

"Listen," said Peter, struggling to explain. "I found something else signed by B.B., not a painting but more of a . . . a document. It was in a house that I'm pretty sure your mysterious Cornish scholar visited, only I don't think he saw this item."

Liz leaned forward, a glint in her eye. "What sort of document?"

"I can't tell you."

"I thought you trusted me," said Liz.

"I do," said Peter. "It's just that I need to find out more about this . . . this document before I tell anyone. This may sound crazy, but there's a chance it could be dangerous to know about." Peter thought of the cold eyes of Julia Alderson and the cold steel of Thomas Gardner's shotgun. If the *Pandosto* was a forgery, he could imagine those two doing a lot to keep that fact a secret.

"It sounds less crazy than you think," said Liz. "I had a call this morning from my Cornish scholar. I can't call him because he doesn't have a phone, but every now and then he goes into town and rings me from the phone box. He said he sent the final manuscript to me by overnight post, but I've never heard him sound so . . . well, so jittery. He told me he was afraid."

"Of what?" asked Peter, the image of Thomas Gardner, prowling the wilds of Cornwall with a shotgun slung over his shoulder, springing to mind.

"He wouldn't say. He just said he kept hearing strange noises and he was worried. I told him he was being paranoid. He lives on the edge of Bodmin Moor, for Christ's sake, of course he hears strange noises. I mean as big a deal as the manuscript about B.B. is to him and me, most of the world will never even notice it. And as jealous as they'll be, no one in the Historical Watercolour Society has the imagination or the balls for academic espionage. Still, I'm worried that he should be so scared."

"You mean Graham?" said Peter.

"How did you know his name?" said Liz.

"Like I said, a lot has happened since Friday," said Peter, smiling over the rim of his wineglass.

"There's more than one Graham in Cornwall," said Liz, returning Peter's smile.

Graham's manuscript may not be a big deal to the world at large, thought Peter, *but a book filled with Shakespearean marginalia would be front-page news. And if the book Liz was about to publish somehow threatened that news, it might be worth . . . well, making strange noises over.* "Look," he said. "I'll make a deal with you. If you'll tell me how to find this Graham, I'll go and check on him. I'll ask him what I have to ask him, but I'll also do my best to be sure he's not in any danger. And I promise you, as soon as I think it's safe, I'll tell you about what I found. You'll be the first to know, and I guarantee it's a really good story."

"You'll go to Cornwall today?"

"My car's at Heathrow—it'll be evening by the time I get down there, but yes, I'll leave as soon as we finish lunch."

"And if you think he's in danger, you'll get him to come up to London?"

"Of course," said Peter.

"It won't be easy. He's a stubborn son of a bitch."

"Just tell me his surname and how to get there and leave the rest to me," said Peter, confident that one look at the *Pandosto* together with hearing the account of Thomas Gardner's temper would convince anyone to move someplace safer than rural Cornwall.

"After lunch," said Liz, as the waiter set two bowls of pasta in front of them. "I'll tell you after lunch."

"Really?" said Peter, who had expected more resistance.

"Let's get back to your other problem, shall we, Peter?" she said.

"My other problem?"

"You know, the fact that you . . . how did you put it, that you might like me."

"Oh, that," said Peter, twirling pasta on his fork as his appetite evaporated once more.

"You obviously haven't gotten over Amanda." Peter nodded his head. "And since this is a lunch between friends, you can talk to me about her. So tell me something about the late Mrs. Byerly."

Peter saw Amanda standing across the restaurant smiling at him. She wore a full-length black dress with a tight-fitting sequined bodice. Peter had forgotten that dress. He supposed the Italian opera music playing in the background must have resurrected it. "Tell her about the opera," Amanda mouthed to him, before fading away.

"I'd never been to the theater before I met Amanda," Peter began, still looking over Liz's shoulder at the spot where Amanda had appeared. "My junior year she took me to a student production of *The Mikado*—she loved her Victorians. And it was fun. About halfway through the second act, I actually noticed I was having a good time, which is unusual for me in a roomful of people. So we started going to the theater. First it was just student shows at Ridgefield, then once in a while a trip into Raleigh to see a professional touring production. I remember our first Shakespeare. I was already infatuated with the plays, but I'd never seen one on the stage. It was *A Midsummer Night's Dream*. I'd never laughed so hard in my life. It just put me in even greater awe of Shakespeare that he could write jokes that would make me laugh four hundred years later.

"Anyway, we were planning a summer visit to London about three years after we were married, and Amanda read that the English National Opera was performing *The Marriage of Figaro*. Now Amanda had always loved Mozart and *Figaro*, but she'd never been to the opera. When she found out that they were doing her favorite opera in London, she called up and got tickets, and then she went to her mom's and borrowed her grandmother's old records of *Figaro* with the libretto, which she must have listened to every night for a month. She wanted to learn all the Italian, she said, so she could enjoy the performance the way the composer intended.

"So we get to London, and Amanda can't wait to go to the opera. She's bought this beautiful full-length gown and she's rented me a white-tie outfit. We're way overdressed, but Amanda doesn't care.

We're sitting in a box and she's so excited and the lights go down and the overture plays and Amanda is gripping my hand with anticipation. Then the curtain opens and there they are—Figaro and Suzanna—and Figaro is measuring the room for his marriage bed and he sings. 'Five, ten, twenty, thirty . . .'

"Well, Amanda's hand just goes slack. I glance over and there's this look of horror on her face. She's been learning Italian for the past month and they're singing the opera in English. Now I'm trying hard not to laugh because I love her so much, but there's also something genuinely hilarious about this moment. And then I start to watch the opera—which I have to say I was more or less dragged to. And I can understand what's going on because it's in English. And I start to get into it and pretty soon I'm laughing at the jokes and having a really good time.

"When it's over, before I even know it I'm on my feet clapping, and I feel Amanda sort of reluctantly standing up giving a perfunctory ovation, but I just can't help myself. I shout 'Bravo' with everybody else and I'm feeling great in my white tie—like I was born to be a gentleman in an opera box. When the curtain calls are over, I look and Amanda is sitting down again and she's crying. So I sit down and take her hand, and I tell her I'm so sorry they ruined her favorite opera and maybe we can go to Milan sometime and see a proper production. And she looks at me and she says—and I'll never forget this—she says, 'It's not that at all. I'm just so happy that you had a good time.' She had spent hundreds of hours getting ready for this night and from her point of view Mozart had been butchered, but what she felt when it was all over was happiness that her reluctant husband had actually enjoyed himself. That's love." Peter swept away a tear with the back of his hand as he looked at Amanda's glistening cheeks across the room. As she faded away again, he realized he had never told anyone that story—not even Dr. Strayer.

"God dammit," said Liz, yanking Peter back to the present. "You made me cry. That wasn't supposed to happen." She wiped her eyes with her napkin. "It must be hard without her," she said.

"Yes," said Peter. "It is." It felt good to admit—not to pretend that everything was okay. He reached across the table and grasped Liz's hand. "Thanks for listening," he said.

Peter's pasta remained uneaten in his bowl when he signaled for the bill. Liz wrote out elaborate directions and drew a map to help him navigate his way to the home of Graham Sykes on the fringes of Bodmin Moor.

As they walked toward Russell Square, Peter suddenly remembered that in his haste to leave the British Museum, he had forgotten to look up William H. Smith.

"Do you know anything about W. H. Smith?" he asked Liz.

"Well, they don't carry the sort of books we publish, I know that much," said Liz.

It took Peter a moment to realize that she was talking about the chain of newsagents. Funny that he should have posed the question that way instead of saying William H. Smith.

"Actually I was talking about a person," said Peter. "William H. Smith. I think he may have been a Victorian."

"The monarch of the sea," said Liz.

"I beg your pardon?"

"I think his father started the family business—selling newspapers in train stations. But it was the son who made W H Smith a household name. He was a member of Parliament and became First Lord of the Admiralty, I think under Disraeli. I guess he was generally seen as a wealthy landlubber who didn't deserve the appointment, so Gilbert and Sullivan made him into Sir Joseph Porter in *H.M.S. Pinafore*. You know, 'I am the monarch of the sea, the ruler of the Queen's Navee,'" Liz sang. "We had a talk about him at the Victorian Theatre Society a few months ago."

"How many societies do you belong to?" said Peter.

"Several," said Liz, laughing.

"I wonder if it's the same William H. Smith. The one I'm looking for was probably interested in Shakespeare."

"I'll ask Lawrence for you," said Liz. "Lawrence Smith—he's the one who gave the talk. I think he's a great-nephew or something." They were now standing outside the Russell Square tube station, and Liz went over the directions to Graham Sykes's house once more.

"He's a night owl," she told Peter, "so go see him when you arrive no matter how late it is."

"I will," said Peter. Without realizing it had happened or knowing who had initiated it, he found himself in a hug with Liz.

"And call me," she whispered in his ear. Then she turned and disappeared around the corner, leaving Peter to descend into the windy depths of the tube alone.

London, 1875

In a sumptuously appointed office above his retail premises just around the corner from St. Paul's, Benjamin Mayhew sat at a wide desk composing correspondence. He had expected a visit from Phillip Gardner, his most profitable client, but one o'clock had come and gone and there had been no sign of the collector. Perhaps, thought Benjamin, his train had been delayed.

Benjamin had worked in the book business for over twenty years now, and had built a wealthy clientele who made him a very good living. He well remembered his first encounter with his favorite client, William Henry Smith—the businessman who now served as secretary to the treasury under Benjamin Disraeli. Smith had indeed been intrigued by the book on Ireland's Shakespeare forgeries and had, over the years, been a steady customer. Though he was by no means a collector, Smith was an intelligent and ambitious man with a level of intellectual curiosity that made good books an essential part of his life. He had become more than a client to Benjamin; he had become a friend and a man for whom the bookseller bore the utmost respect. Benjamin had provided several volumes of source material for Smith's 1857 book, *Bacon and Shakespeare,* an expansion of the ideas set forth in the pamphlet that Benjamin had read all those years ago on the train to Oxford. Benjamin had a copy of this book, presented to him by the author, on an honored shelf in his office. The two men had enjoyed a good laugh together when, at Smith's club, the author had read aloud the second chapter of the book, titled "A Brief History of Shakespeare."

William Shakespeare's is indeed a negative history.

Of his life, all that we positively know is the period of his death.

We do not know when he was born, nor when, nor where, he was educated.

We do not know when, or where, he was married, nor when he came to London.

We do not know when, where, or in what order, his plays were written or performed; nor when he left London.

He died April 23rd, 1616.

"Is that the whole chapter?" Benjamin had asked, laughing.

"Well," said Smith, "It's all we know for sure, so it's all I need say."

Phillip Gardner had first approached Benjamin several months earlier because of his neighbor. "I should like to begin collecting historical documents," he had told Benjamin on the floor of his shop.

"What sort of documents?" asked Benjamin.

"Any that might be of interest to Mr. Reginald Alderson," said Gardner.

Thus Phillip Gardner became the best sort of client—one motivated not by intellectual curiosity or literary passion but by hatred. Reginald Alderson was a passionate collector of historical documents, Phillip Gardner was bound by birth to hate Reginald Alderson, therefore Phillip would use his wife's money to pay any price to outbid Alderson at auction and go to any lengths to outfox him in other means of acquisition. All this he told Benjamin at their first meeting. Since then, Benjamin had been Phillip Gardner's primary supplier of material. Gardner paid his bills promptly and had no objections to providing Benjamin with a substantial premium on items bought from under the nose of his rival.

That afternoon Benjamin would make just such a purchase in the salesrooms of Sotheby's—a manuscript stanza of poetry by the Elizabethan writer Robert Greene. Benjamin knew, from his informant at Sotheby's, that Alderson had registered as a bidder for the sale, and the only item on the block that could possibly interest him was the Greene poem. Benjamin had expected to dine in the city with Phillip Gardner and then make their usual jaunt to the sales-room where they would publicly humiliate Reginald Alderson as they had done so many times before. Benjamin sometimes wondered why Alderson kept showing up rather than bidding through an agent, for the results were always the same. As the bidding went up, Phillip Gardner nodded to Benjamin; Benjamin nodded to the auctioneer; eventually the lot was hammered down to Phillip; and Reginald Alderson stormed from the room, to the suppressed snickers of those regulars who knew what was happening.

Usually Gardner took Benjamin to his club following an auction, but when the time came for Benjamin to leave for Sotheby's and his client had still not arrived, he resigned himself to the fact that today he would celebrate his victory in solitude. No matter—the Greene fragment would fetch a high price, especially with Reginald Alderson driving up the bidding, and a high price meant a high commission. Benjamin was perfectly happy to be friends with Phillip Gardner, but what he liked most about the man was his wife's money.

"**I** think it's time," said Amanda to Peter as they lay entwined on the carpet of the Devereaux Room, their pulses and breathing returning to normal after their lovemaking. It had been five weeks since Halloween. Five wonderful Saturday nights of passion—for Amanda was as organized about her sex life as she was about everything else. Not that Peter minded. There were no awkward attempts on his part to initiate, no fumbling fondling in the back of a car wondering how far it might go. There was only the keen edge of anticipation as they made their way through the dark halls of the library to the Devereux Room just after eleven o'clock every Saturday. After their first time, there had been no more costumes, and the past five weeks had been a gradual unfolding of each to the other, leading to this perfect moment—Amanda's damp body pressed against Peter's own, her arm draped across his stomach, her still erect nipple grazing his chest as she whispered to him, "I think it's time."

"You might have to give me a few more minutes," said Peter. Usually Amanda drifted off to sleep after sex, and Peter would wake her an hour or two later with a kiss, a caress, and a whisper of desire.

"That's not what I meant," said Amanda, giving him a teasing swat on his flank. She propped herself up on one elbow and fixed him with a serious look. "I mean I think it's time for you to meet my family."

"I was kind of hoping I could just meet them when our kids graduate from high school," said Peter, a nervousness rising in his gut that he had never felt in the safe confines of the Devereaux Room.

"They're not that bad," said Amanda. "In fact, they're actually pretty nice."

"But they're the Ridgefields," said Peter. "You know I have a hard enough time meeting people who aren't royalty with a daughter I'm in love with."

"Say that again," said Amanda, kissing him lightly on the chest.

"What, the part about their being royalty?"

"No, the other part."

"About how I'm totally head over heels in love with their precious daughter Amanda?"

"Yeah," said Amanda, kissing her way down his abdomen. "That part." As her lips flitted across his skin, Peter forgot about the Ridgefields, forgot about being nervous, and thought only of Amanda— her lips and her tongue and her mouth and her flesh and how much he loved her.

As they walked across campus toward Amanda's dorm in the hours after the last Saturday night party had ended but before the first obsessive premed student had arisen to study for an approaching biochemistry final, Peter squeezed Amanda's hand and said what he knew she wanted to hear, and what, at that moment of peace and darkness when the night air had taken on a tinge of winter cold, he almost believed himself.

"I would love to meet your family."

On Monday night, as they sat in their usual booth at the snack bar, Amanda officially invited Peter to her parents' house for dinner the following Saturday.

"Saturday night?" asked Peter. It would be hard enough to meet her family, he thought, but to meet them on a Saturday night, when all he could think of was Amanda wrapped around him on the floor of the Devereaux Room, just might be unbearable.

"We'll just have to visit the library on Friday," said Amanda, running her foot up his leg. "I wouldn't want you to be . . . tense."

"Trust me, there is nothing you can do that will keep me from being tense," said Peter, adding hastily, "not that you shouldn't try."

"It's just Mom and Dad," said Amanda. "They'll like you, and you'll like them. They don't bite, except my dad a little."

"What'll we talk about?" said Peter. "I mean, I'm from a family who couldn't even keep a general store open in a town where there was no competition, and they're the Ridgefields—only the most successful businesspeople in the South. We have nothing in common."

"Well, first of all, you all love me. And there's something else you and my mom can talk about. You probably know as much about her mother as anyone."

"Her mother?" said Peter.

"Yeah, you know, Amanda Devereaux."

"Amanda Devereaux was your mother's mother?" said Peter. "But then why are you named Ridgefield?"

"The Ridgefields couldn't die out," said Amanda. "My mom was the last of the line. Her dad was Robert Ridgefield, and before he died he made her promise to name her children Ridgefield. My dad was a Middleton, but he changed his name—I think it gave him clout." Peter wondered what it would be like to be named Peter Ridgefield, if Amanda's parents insisted on her carrying on the family name.

"How old was your mom when her mother died?" asked Peter. In his nervousness about meeting the Ridgefields he had completely forgotten he would be meeting someone who had known Amanda Devereaux, and known her well.

"Eighteen," said Amanda. "She was halfway through her first semester at Wellesley when they called her to come home. She transferred to Ridgefield so she could look after her father. He died three years later. I think he stayed alive to see Gran's book collection in-stalled in the new library and then just gave up."

"So she must remember her mother well."

"I think so," said Amanda. "She doesn't talk about her much. Mom has always been one of those 'live in the present' sort of people. I guess losing two parents so quickly when you're so young will do that to you."

"So I shouldn't ask her about the other Amanda?" asked Peter.

"No, you should. She's really proud of what Gran accomplished. She always reads the *Friends of the Ridgefield Library* magazine from cover to cover, and once in a while she even buys a book to add to the collection—you know, something that Francis finds that she thinks Gran would have been especially happy about. Just let her see how much you love Gran's books, and I'll bet you can get her to tell some stories."

"And should I let her see how much I love you?" asked Peter.

"As if you could hide it," said Amanda, slipping her fingers around his hand.

The next day Peter entered the Devereaux Room to find Francis Le-land and Hank Christiansen poring over a single piece of paper.

"What's so fascinating?" said Peter.

"It's a handwritten poem by Emily Dickinson," said Francis.

"Previously unpublished," said Hank.

"We've had that for a while," said Peter, looking over Hank's shoul-der at the familiar paper. "I used it when I was writing a paper for my nineteenth-century poetry class."

"Do you know where it came from?" said Francis.

"No," said Peter.

"We bought it a couple of years ago with a little help from Sarah Ridgefield," said Francis. "It came from Mark Hofmann."

"The guy who found 'Oath of a Freeman'?" asked Peter.

"One and the same," said Hank. "Only now with these bombings in Salt Lake City there are whispers in the business that not everything he sold may be what it claims to be."

"You think the poem could be a forgery?" said Peter.

"It seems unlikely," said Francis.

"The paper checks out," said Hank. "The ink is nineteenth century as far as I can tell, and the handwriting certainly matches Dickinson's."

"If this is a forgery," said Francis, "then Hofmann is one of the most brilliant forgers of all time."

Cornwall, Southwestern England, Monday, February 20, 1995

By the time Peter had been driving an hour it was nearly dark—the early winter sunset aided by the increasing cloud cover. He did not usually drive on motorways; he felt he missed too much and he was rarely in a hurry, but tonight was an exception. The drive to Cornwall would take about four and a half hours, and then he would have to follow Liz's intricate directions to Graham Sykes's house in the total darkness of sunken Cornish lanes.

As he flew along at seventy miles an hour, Peter glanced to his left and saw Amanda seated quietly in the passenger seat, the map perched on her lap. She had loved to navigate when they traveled the British countryside. Peter recalled the first time he had gotten up the nerve to rent a car. The pound was cheap and they had come to England on a book-buying trip.

They kept to two-lane roads, stopping in every town and hunting through the local bookshops. They had gone to provincial book fairs in town halls every Sunday afternoon. They had spent entire days in book towns like Oxford and Cambridge and Bath, but Peter had especially enjoyed those days spent in smaller towns where the single bookseller would welcome the young American couple, often even closing up shop for an hour or two to take them out to lunch. Always comfortable when Amanda was by his side, Peter even enjoyed conversations with these relative strangers.

Peter had made his first visit to Hay-on-Wye during that trip. Amanda had navigated via what she called "the scenic route," and they had crossed the River Wye on an ancient toll bridge, where an old man came out of a booth to accept their coins and raise the barrier so they could pass. The entire journey had been suffused with a sense of adventure that Amanda especially had relished.

"I love not knowing what tomorrow will bring," she had said. One day began in Bath and ended on the beach at Southhampton at sunset. In Salisbury and Winchester they found themselves at Evensong in the local cathedrals after the bookshops had closed. Another day they finished the bookshops of York more quickly than anticipated and took a long drive across the moors, ending with dinner at a fish-and-chips shop overlooking the bay at Whitby.

Peter smiled at the memory and turned to ask Amanda what she had liked best about that trip, which now seemed like a journey of such innocence. But Amanda was gone and the road map lay on the passenger seat alone.

The roads became narrower and narrower as Peter skirted the edge of Bodmin Moor, until he found himself jouncing down a steep, rutted lane, overhung by gnarled trees. He hoped he had followed Liz's directions properly, because he had little hope of getting the underpowered Vauxhall back up the lane in darkness. He wondered if he'd even be able to do it in daylight. At the bottom of the hill, the lane ended in front of a gate giving on to a small pasture in which Peter's headlights illuminated a few sheep. Across this pasture he saw the lights of a small stone cottage—the home of Graham Sykes, he hoped. Peter swallowed a lump of panic. He couldn't imagine that anyone who lived in such an isolated place was likely to welcome nighttime visitors—especially when Graham was concerned he might be in danger.

Peter pulled his satchel from the car, climbed a stile, and set off toward the cottage. The overcast sky obscured any moonlight, and in the near pitch darkness he picked his way slowly across the field, feeling the dampness from the grass wetting his trouser legs.

By the time he reached the door of the cottage his shoes were covered in mud. When his first timid knock went unanswered, he banged more loudly.

"Be off!" said a voice from within. "Ya can't be up to any good this time of night."

"Mr. Sykes," said Peter, trying to match the volume of the voice from within, "my name is Peter Byerly. I'm a friend of Liz Sutcliffe's. She sent me here because she's worried about you."

"A likely story," retorted the voice.

"It's true, sir. I've driven down from London. I could use a hot cup of tea," said Peter, hoping that the British inability to refuse tea to visitors might soften the old man.

"They got no tea in London?" said the voice. "Be off."

"There's something else," said Peter, for whom the most pressing something else was that it had now begun to rain and he didn't relish the idea of spending the night in his car, soaked to the skin. "I have a book with me. Something that used to belong to B.B. I was hoping you might help me figure out whether or not it's a forgery."

There was silence within for a long minute, as the rain continued to pelt Peter. Finally the voice returned, its belligerent tone replaced with something approaching curiosity. "What do ya know about B.B.?" it asked.

"Not much, to be honest," said Peter. After another long pause, he added, "I found a watercolor that he painted, but I think Liz told you about that. This other item could be something a lot more valuable. Unless this rain starts soaking into my bag, that is."

After another pause, there was a sound of locks being undone and at last the heavy wooden door swung open. In the doorway, framed by yellow lamplight, stood a man who looked well able to protect himself. Over six feet tall and broad shouldered, Graham Sykes had thick arms that strained at the seams of his flannel work shirt. His upper body leaned forward slightly, like a bird of prey. In one hand he clasped an iron poker. His deep-set eyes glared intently out at

Peter from a sea of white hair that covered his head and his face and stretched across his brow in a single unbroken line. His wide body completely blocked the door as he appraised Peter, now dripping wet on the doorstep, and clutching his satchel under his topcoat, hoping to keep the contents dry.

Finally Graham growled, "Well, don't be standing there in the rain, then. I'll put the kettle on." He stepped aside and Peter came through the door, which opened directly into a small sitting room. A fire was dying in the grate, but the room was warm and bright. His reluctant host shut the door and disappeared through another doorway, leaving Peter dripping on the stone floor. He took off his coat and hung it with several others on the wall by the door, ascertained that his satchel had remained dry, and then stepped toward the fire, warming his hands over the glowing embers.

Graham Sykes returned from the kitchen with two mugs of tea—no frilly china cups for him. Though he usually drank his black, Peter took the mug of heavily milked and sugared tea without complaint and drank deeply as Sykes did the same.

"Sit," said Sykes, pointing to a sagging armchair under the window. Peter sat and found himself sinking into the depths of the chair. Sitting on the sofa, Sykes towered over him. "Now what have you to tell me?" said Sykes.

Peter started slowly, fixing his stare at his mug rather than daring to look at the intimidating figure of his host. He told of how he had discovered the watercolor of a woman who resembled his late wife, though he knew Liz had already explained this. He told of how he had been chased off the Evenlode House estate and how he had been led by Julia Alderson to discover a cache of documents at Evenlode Manor. Finally he reached for his satchel and withdrew the *Pandosto*, laying it on the coffee table.

Sykes donned a pair of reading glasses pulled from his shirt pocket and opened the book. His face remained impassive for several minutes as he pored over the volume, slowly turning pages and frequently returning to the list of owners on the front endpaper.

Peter felt panic rising within him as he saw his precious *Pandosto* in the hands of this rough and, it seemed, potentially violent man. He tried to calm himself with the thought that Sykes was a scholar, but he could feel the cold sweat on the back of his neck.

"The same library where I found this book," said Peter, as evenly as he could manage, "had several books on Shakespeare forgery."

"So you have your doubts," said Sykes, re-pocketing his glasses, but keeping the book in his brawny hand.

"Yes," said Peter. "I've tracked down most of the names on the list of owners, but all I know about B.B. was that he painted watercolors and you wrote a book about him."

"And you want to know whether B.B. was a forger."

"I'd love to hear that he wasn't," said Peter, still hoping that he could prove the authenticity of the *Pandosto*. "If that is a forgery, it's a brilliant one."

"It would be strange for a forger to sign his work, wouldn't it?" asked Sykes.

"Strange, but not unheard of," said Peter. "Especially if he used a pseudonym." Peter had thought of this, though. He had imagined himself in a future where he had discovered that B.B. was a forger, had forged all the documents at Evenlode Manor. If that were the case, why did he sign this book when he hadn't signed anything else but his own watercolors? The signature on the endpaper of *Pandosto* might allow him to hold out hope that the marginalia were genuine.

"And tell me this," said Sykes. "Who gets the credit?"

"I beg your pardon," said Peter, feeling the sweat trickle down his back.

"Who gets the credit? Who gets to break the story? If this thing is for real," said Sykes, tapping a finger against the *Pandosto*, "who gets to stand in front of the world on telly and say, 'I am the man who solved the greatest literary mystery of all time'? You or me?"

Though Peter had mentioned nothing about Shakespeare or the debate between Oxfordians and Stratfordians, it was clear that Sykes fully comprehended the importance of the book. And Peter had to admit, he had imagined the exact scenario Sykes described. Peter Byerly lauded by every Stratfordian in the world as their great savior. Peter Byerly—the bookseller who made the greatest contribution to English literature since Robert Cotton. A horrible thought flashed through his mind as he looked at the hawklike form of Graham Sykes, holding *Pandosto* in his talons. People had killed for less.

"It was my discovery," said Peter simply. His words hung ominously in the air for several seconds before Sykes responded.

"Without me, you'll never know what you really have here."

"I could just wait for your book to come out," said Peter.

"It won't come out now," said Sykes. "I'll phone Liz in the morning and tell her I have to do a complete rewrite in light of new evidence."

"Look," said Peter, "you're not the only person I need to help me with this. I've got forensic experts looking at ink and paper—it's a team effort. But I'm the leader of the team."

"We'll see," said Sykes, holding out the *Pandosto* toward Peter, who snatched it out of the old man's hands with a feeling of relief. Sykes might be difficult, even a dead end, but at least Peter still had the book.

"Maybe a good night's sleep will mean more level heads at breakfast," said Sykes.

"I'm not sure I can get my car back up your lane in the dark and the rain," said Peter, for whom the prospect of spending the night in the home of a man he didn't trust was only marginally more appealing than that of spending it in his car in a Cornish ditch.

"You'll have to doss in the barn," said Sykes gruffly. "I'll get you a blanket."

Ten minutes later, Peter lay under a thin blanket in a pile of hay, his body curled around his satchel. The roof above him dripped as the rain continued outside, and the blanket did nothing to keep out the cold that seeped into his bones. He supposed the old man sent him to the barn to try to break his spirit. It was infuriating to think that all the evidence he needed to unravel the mystery of B.B. probably sat snugly in a desk drawer not thirty yards from where he lay—yet he was powerless to discover those secrets.

Toward dawn, Peter slept fitfully for an hour or so, but he was awake when he heard the door of Sykes's cottage slam shut. He lay still and silent for a few minutes, clutching his bag against the possibility that Sykes was now striding to the barn, his poker, or something worse, in hand. When he heard no more sounds, he suddenly remembered Sykes's promise to call Liz Sutcliffe. Liz had said that Sykes didn't have a phone, that he had to go into the nearest village to make a call. And if Sykes was walking into the village, any secrets kept in his house were now completely unguarded.

Ridgefield, 1985

"It's a panic attack," said Francis Leland.

"It's social anxiety disorder," said Hank Christiansen.

"Don't you think it's normal that I should be nervous about meeting my girlfriend's parents?" said Peter. The three men sat in Francis's office drinking coffee and flipping through book catalogs as they talked.

"Yeah, but, Peter," said Hank, "you don't just get nervous about meeting girls and their parents like normal people. You get nervous about meeting anyone. I've seen you cross the quad to avoid passing a stranger on the sidewalk."

"How do you know I do that?" said Peter, who thought he did a good job of hiding his anxiety. He felt almost violated that Hank should so accurately know what he was feeling.

"Because I do exactly the same thing," said Hank, laying a hand on Peter's shoulder.

"Impossible," said Peter. "I've seen the way you greet strangers in the conservation lab; hell, I remember the way you treated me when we first met. No way were you nervous."

"Yeah," said Hank, "in the conservation lab. Ever see me talk to a stranger anywhere else? Ever see me out in a restaurant or a bar?" Peter had never actually seen Hank anywhere outside the library.

"So you have . . ." Peter could not think of how to end his sentence. He simply couldn't wrap his mind around the possibility that other people reacted to the world in the same fearful way that he did. He had always assumed it was a unique, if unpleasant, facet of his personality.

"I have a social anxiety disorder," said Hank. "And I also have a good doctor and some excellent drugs, so if I actually want to go to a restaurant, or the theater, or on a date, I can do it."

"You should see Dr. Strayer, Peter," said Francis.

"It sounds like yours isn't as bad as mine," said Hank. "I mean, you said when you're out with Amanda you usually feel okay."

"She's his natural drug," said Francis, smiling, and he and Hank broke into laughter.

Two days later, Peter emerged from his first appointment with Dr. Strayer with a prescription for antianxiety medication and a completely new worldview. Irrational anxiety was not unique to Peter Byerly. This discovery both excited and frightened him. What he had thought of as his personality was now suddenly a treatable disorder. His concern that his identity would somehow be lost when he took the drugs was not strong enough, however, to keep him from swallowing the first of the tiny white pills an hour before Amanda picked him up to go to her parents' house that Saturday.

The medication did not keep him from being nervous as Amanda drove up the long, winding drive to the white-columned portico of the Ridgefields' quintessentially southern mansion, but it did keep him from feeling sick. On the wide steps leading to the front door stood Sarah Ridgefield and her husband, the former Charles Middleton. Sarah bore a striking resemblance to her mother, Amanda Devereaux. Her face combined feminine beauty with masculine strength, and although her husband was tall and broad enough to have played football in college—Peter later discovered he had been a linebacker for Ridgefield—it was Sarah who was clearly in charge. When Amanda and Peter got out of the car, Mr. Ridgefield stepped forward to hug his daughter, but it was Amanda's mother who thrust her hand in Peter's direction and said crisply, "Peter Byerly, we meet at last." Her grip was firm, and Peter returned the pressure and met the gaze of her green eyes. He was stunned to find that he felt perfectly at ease as they shook hands. No drug could do that, he thought. There was something in Sarah Ridgefield's eyes that Peter had seen before only in the eyes of her daughter.

"You look so like your mother," said Peter. "I'm a big fan."

"I gather you're also a fan of my daughter," said Sarah, dropping Peter's hand and brushing a bit of lint from his shoulder.

"More than a fan," said Peter.

"Mother, are you frightening Peter already?" said Amanda, turning to embrace Sarah.

"On the contrary," said Sarah. "As Peter here is a devotee of Amanda Ridgefield and Amanda Devereaux, I was hoping he might find something to admire in the middle generation."

"I'm sure I shall," said Peter, as Sarah Ridgefield winked at him over her daughter's shoulder. And Peter had a sudden flash, as Sarah took him into her confidence, that here was the mother he had never had. He felt a swelling of love toward Sarah that he had never felt toward his own mother. Was it possible, he thought as they walked up the steps and into the house, that this was meant to be his family all along? And was this warmth inside, this feeling both protected and protective, how it felt to have a real mother?

Dinner was lovely. Peter had half expected liveried servants and silver platters, but they ate fried chicken off plastic plates on the back deck, overlooking a sloping garden that led to a small pond backed by a copse of trees that still retained a tinge of fall color on their branches.

"Won't be able to eat out here much longer," said Charlie, "and we do love the fresh air."

Peter spent the evening plying Sarah for stories about her mother—though it didn't take much encouragement to get Sarah to hold forth on the topic of Amanda Devereaux. At one point in the evening Amanda took her mother's hand and said, "Why didn't you ever tell me any of this?"

"I don't know," said Sarah. "I guess because you never asked." She told Peter about the time when she was a girl and her mother took her to Sotheby's in New York to bid on a Shakespeare First Folio. "I was so nervous," she said. "I thought if I moved a muscle the auctioneer would think I was making a bid, so I sat on my hands and stayed perfectly still. The folio was the last item in the sale, so I must have sat like that for two hours. Mother thought she was giving me this great treat, and I ended up with sore muscles for the next week because I had been so tense."

"And did she buy the book?" asked Amanda.

"She did," said Peter. "I was reading *Lear* from it just the other day."

"Were you?" said Sarah with delight. "How marvelous."

The next week, Peter and Amanda lay on the floor of the Devereaux Room after their usual Saturday night lovemaking. For the first time ever it had seemed just that to Peter—usual. Not that he hadn't enjoyed himself, but the act hadn't connected him to Amanda as it had before. She had seemed passive and eager to get things over with. Now she lay on her back, her fingers lightly entwined in his, staring at the ceiling.

"Is something wrong?" asked Peter at last.

"I'm sorry," said Amanda.

"Don't be sorry, just tell me what's the matter."

"It's stupid."

Peter lifted himself up on one elbow so he could look Amanda in the face. "I'm sure it's not stupid," he said.

"I think I'm jealous," said Amanda.

"Jealous?"

"I spent my whole life trying to find a way to be close to my mother," said Amanda. "I mean, she was this glamorous society lady always going off to charity balls in Atlanta and New York, and I was trying so hard to just be normal. She didn't understand me and I didn't understand her." Amanda fell silent for a moment and Peter looked at her quizzically. "And then," she said, pulling her arm away from him, "you waltz in and the two of you are best buddies in five minutes."

"I thought you wanted us to get along," said Peter.

"I did," said Amanda. "But I guess I didn't want it to be so easy when for me it's been so hard."

"Hard?" Peter said harshly, sitting up and pulling away from Amanda. "Having a relationship with your mom is hard? You do know that I've spoken about three sentences to my mother in the past year, right? Not that she was sober enough to understand any of them." He felt an unexpected surge of anger toward this spoiled little rich girl complaining that she had a hard time getting along with Mommy— and Mommy was the lovely Sarah Ridgefield, not some sad drunk.

"I know, Peter," said Amanda, as she lay a hand on his back. He turned back to look at her, and as quickly as the anger had come it melted away and he pulled her into his arms.

"I'm sorry," he said. "And I'm sorry things have been hard with your mother."

"Peter, you don't have to be sorry because of my insecurity. I'll get over it. And I do love you—God, I love you so much." A tear crept down her cheek as she grasped his hand again, this time gripping it with all her strength. "But sometimes you're just going to have to let me hurt."

Peter enfolded her in his arms and she cried against his shoulder for what seemed like hours, and then they made love again and it was beautiful. It was also different, since Peter now saw that Amanda, like him, was not perfect. He had not realized the extent to which he had idealized her, and while making love to an ideal woman was fantastic, making love to a real woman was even better.

Over the next few months, Peter made every effort to bring Sarah Ridgefield and her daughter together. He gave Amanda extended tours of the treasures of the Devereaux collection, taught her about rare books, and included her in the many conversations he had with Sarah about Amanda Devereaux. Peter also became friends with Amanda's father. Though they shared few interests—Charlie was a banker and a golfer—the two developed a backslapping relationship primarily based on drinking imported beer and discussing sports scores. Peter had never followed sports before but found that he liked basketball.

Peter spent most of his Christmas vacation at the Ridgefield house—he had invented a fiction about his parents going to visit his mother's sick sister to explain why he didn't return home for the holidays. He slept in a guest bedroom far from Amanda's room, but not so far that she didn't creep into his bed on several occasions.

On Christmas morning Sarah served eggs Benedict and they sat down to breakfast next to the ten-foot tree that Peter had helped decorate.

"I'll bet you miss being with your family on Christmas," said Sarah to Peter, and he was at a loss for words. How could he say that no, he didn't miss them, that Christmas at his house—with rarely a tree, few presents, no love—was the most depressing day of the year? How could he explain that, as far as he was concerned, he *was* with his family? And so, finally, he said the only thing he could think of to say.

"Yeah, I sure do miss them. I'll call them later and see how their Christmas was."

"Have some more bacon," said Charlie, and, burning with guilt, Peter heaped another serving on his plate.

On New Year's morning Amanda snuggled in bed with Peter and asked when she was going to meet his family. He tried to imagine Amanda Ridgefield sitting down for dinner in the tiny kitchen of his dilapidated clapboard childhood home. Of course he knew she could carry that off with aplomb—the problem was his parents would be there, too.

In early February, Peter walked into the Devereaux Room to find Francis Leland and Hank Christensen huddled over a newspaper.

"Have you heard?" said Hank. "They arrested Mark Hofmann."

"The guy who found the 'Oath of a Freeman'?" said Peter.

"Forged it, is more likely," said Francis.

"He's been arrested for murder and fraud," said Hank.

"Looks like a lot of the documents he sold were fakes," said Francis. "The guy was a brilliant forger. But apparently some of his customers were suspicious about a big deal that he claimed to be putting together, so he delivered pipe bombs to them."

Peter was stunned. Hofmann's discovery of the "Oath" had been proof to him that Holy Grails were still out there waiting to be found. Its revelation as a fake would threaten Peter's dream of one day finding his own grail.

"I'll bet you never thought the book world was so dangerous," said Hank with a sardonic smile.

"Well," said Francis, "forgery is telling lies. And no matter how good a liar you are, if you tell enough of them, you can dig yourself a hole so deep that the only way out seems to be murder."

That night Peter and Amanda had dinner at the Ridgefields'. Struck by what Francis had said, and after fidgeting with his napkin under the table for the entire meal, Peter lay his hand on Sarah's arm and said, "I have a confession to make; I haven't been completely honest about my parents." And it all poured out—the drunkenness and the neglect and the lies that Peter had invented so he could be with Charlie and Sarah and Amanda for Christmas.

"Because, honestly," said Peter, as he felt tears in his eyes, "you are my family." And the Ridgefields did exactly what parents are supposed to do. Sarah hugged him and told him everything would be okay and that he could talk to her about anything anytime, and

Charlie slapped him on the back and said, "Let's go watch the Duke game."

In the months following Mark Hofmann's arrest for murder in Salt Lake City, details of his activities as a forger began to trickle out. Any document sold by Hofmann became suspect, including items that had altered the early history of the Mormon Church. Despite the bald-faced deception and the grisly murders, Peter couldn't help but admire Hofmann's artistry. He had fooled everyone, even the most experienced document experts in the country.

In the case of the "Oath," he had established a provenance by planting a page with a hymn printed on it at the Argosy Bookstore in New York City. He wrote the title "Oath of a Freeman" on the hymn, then returned to buy it. That gave him a receipt from a reputable bookseller.

He then set to work to forge the "Oath" on a piece of seventeenth-century paper he had stolen from a rare book. He wrote out the text, copying a typeface of the period, then had his lettering made into a zinc plate that he used to print the "Oath." He used a seventeenth-century recipe to mix his ink, and added to it carbon that he had captured in a glass chimney while burning a piece of paper from the same period. This gave him an ink that would pass all tests, including carbon dating.

It was a brilliant job, Peter had to admit, and it fooled a lot of people. The "Oath" was finally revealed as a fake by a new technique measuring the migration of ions in ink over time, but Hofmann had come very close to pulling off the greatest forgery ever. Peter wondered if there was someone out there in rare-book history who had achieved what Hofmann almost did—if there were forgeries sitting on the shelves of the Devereaux Room that were so perfect they would never be detected.

Peter and Amanda lay entwined on the floor of the Devereux Room on the quietest Saturday night of the year. Graduation had been the previous Sunday and summer school didn't start for another week.

"I have a graduation present for you," said Amanda.

"I'm only a junior," said Peter. "I didn't graduate."

"Well, it's a present and it comes right after graduation, so what else am I going to call it?"

"What is it?" Peter asked.

"It's in the pocket of my jeans," said Amanda.

"But your jeans are all the way across the room."

"Whose fault is that?" said Amanda.

"Okay, okay," said Peter. He crawled across the room to where he had pulled off Amanda's pants just as they had stumbled in the door. Final exams and graduation festivities had kept them away from the Devereaux Room for two weeks, and they had been more than a little impatient. "There's nothing here but your car keys," said Peter.

"Those are your car keys."

"I don't have a car, how can they be my car keys?"

"You do have a car," said Amanda. "It's your nongraduation present."

"You bought me a car?" Peter had spent the first three years of his college life walking the streets of Ridgefield. On those rare occasions when he did go home, he had the choice of asking someone for a ride or calling his parents and hoping one of them would actually show up sober.

"Well, it's not like I got you a Porsche or anything. It's a six-year-old Volvo station wagon, but I thought it would be good for hauling books around. You said you wanted to spend the summer going around to bookstores—well, now you can."

Peter crossed the room, Amanda's pants in one hand, the car keys in the other. Her nakedness nearly distracted him from the question he had been burning to ask since he first found out she was a Ridge-field. He had told himself over and over that the answer didn't matter, that his love for Amanda had nothing to do with her bank account, but still, he was curious. More than curious.

"So do you have, like, a gazillion dollars?"

"Not exactly," said Amanda, welcoming him back into her arms. "I have a trust fund that I'll get when I turn twenty-one and I have an allowance. It's a good allowance for a college student, especially since I don't eat out all that much or buy a bunch of junk—but I still had to save up most of this year to get you the car."

"You are the sweetest," he said, kissing her shoulder. "I didn't get you anything."

"Maybe you can take me for a drive sometime," said Amanda, running her hand down his chest. Her hand traveled slowly lower and lower, and Peter knew what she was up to, but he wasn't quite ready to let the subject drop and return to lovemaking.

"This trust fund," he said, "does it mean you'll be . . . I don't know, rich?"

"Why, are you going to leave me if I only have five million?"

"No, it's just, I know you come from a rich family and all . . . ," said Peter, his words trailing off.

"Peter, seriously," said Amanda, sitting up and crossing her arms over her breasts. "You're the only guy I never thought was after me for my money, and now you want to know how rich I am?"

"It's not that at all. I don't even care about the money—I mean, not exactly."

" 'Not exactly?' "

"It's just that this career plan of mine—becoming an antiquarian bookseller—it's not exactly a get-rich-quick scheme. And I want to be able to support you, but you're used to certain things and, well, I don't want you to feel like you're living in squalor."

"Will you be there?" said Amanda, softening.

"Always," whispered Peter.

"Then it will never be squalor. You're the only thing I'm used to that I couldn't give up." And she leaned over and kissed him for a long minute, her breasts grazing his chest. "Besides, I'll be working, too—until we're ready for kids, at least."

Peter shivered. It was the closest they had ever come to seriously discussing marriage and family. Peter assumed Amanda wanted to get married, but he was still saving money for a ring so he hadn't officially asked her. As for children, he knew she loved them and he relished the thought that he might be able to succeed where his own parents had failed. Amanda's tongue on his nipple brought him back to the present.

"Now," she whispered, her tongue sliding down his chest, "let's talk about the things I can't live without."

The first few times Phillip Gardner met the young woman who referred to herself only as Isabel, the two merely walked in Hyde Park and Kensington Gardens. She had told him of how she came to Europe for a grand tour, chaperoned by her former governess, Miss Prickett. Isabel had been so captivated by London and its vibrant world of art and theater that she had abandoned the planned tour and insisted that she and Miss Prickett take a flat in Chelsea. Miss Prickett had argued that Paris, Florence, Rome, Vienna, and Berlin had their fair share of art as well, but Isabel had been adamant—London was the city for her. She had already met the Rossettis, who lived a few blocks away in Cheyne Walk, and had, through their acquaintance, begun to circulate among the painters, poets, and actors of the day.

"Do you know," said Isabel as they strolled the banks of the Serpentine, "the other day I walked up to the home of Mr. Leighton, knocked on the door, and was admitted to his studio merely on the strength of being a visiting American interested in art?"

"Remarkable," said Phillip, who had found that one-word responses to Isabel's rambling narratives were enough to prod her into further anecdotes and helped divert the conversation from the twin topics of his own history and his growing desire for her. The first he had no wish to reveal to her, including, as it did, the fact of his marriage; the second he hoped might be reciprocated in time. Phillip had also visited Leighton's studio in Kensington, to lobby the great painter and associate of the Royal Academy for admission into that august body. Leighton had been kind, but unimpressed by Phillip's portfolio.

"And last week I saw Ellen Terry as Portia in *The Merchant of Venice*. I sent her a note backstage during the interval and she invited me around to her dressing room after the performance. We spoke for twenty minutes about Shakespeare and Shylock and Henry Irving. Twenty minutes while the luminaries of London waited for her. Can you imagine? And she didn't even know who I am."

"And who are you?" asked Phillip, always quick to detect any hint of Isabel's true identity. She was curiously silent about any part of her life prior to her arrival on English shores. Whenever Phillip asked her about her family, she changed the subject to poetry or sculpture or pointed out some sight that was far more mundane than she made it seem. *She must be from a wealthy family,* thought Phillip, *or else she could not have undertaken a grand tour of Europe; and she must have had some education, or else she could not discourse on art and literature as she did.*

"I'm a young lady who's quite worn out with walking, thank you, sir," said Isabel. "Shall we turn toward Chelsea?" Phillip flagged down a cab just outside the park and they were soon rattling toward Isabel's lodgings in Wellington Square. In the open air of Hyde Park, he had not been as overcome by her scent as he was here in the cab. As the driver turned onto King's Road, she was thrown up against him for a moment, and he thought he might swoon from the combination of her aroma and the pressing of her soft body against his.

In the quiet of Wellington Square, Phillip told the cabby to wait while he showed Isabel to her door. He did not care for the way the driver winked at him when he said this.

"Miss Pricket does not approve of my walking in the park alone," said Isabel, as they stood on the steps of the elegant white row house with its wrought iron railings.

"But you were not alone," said Phillip.

"She would approve of that even less, I daresay." Isabel nodded obliquely to a window above where the drapes were pulled back ever so slightly. "No doubt she is watching us even now," she said. "Who knows what she writes in her letters to Mother."

"Our relationship may be somewhat unconventional, but surely it is completely innocent," said Phillip, wishing it were anything but.

Isabel leaned forward as if to look into the gated garden at the center of the square. With her head parallel to Phillip's, but her eyes fixed in the distance, she whispered. "Miss Prickett is taking a day off next Thursday to visit her second cousin in Brixton. I shall not be feeling well, so I shall remain at home. Perhaps you would care to call on me."

Before Phillip could respond, Isabel had whirled around and was at the top of the stairs, opening the heavy door and disappearing into the house. The intent of her words could not have been clearer, and the reaction they called forth was so instant and powerful that he staggered back to the cab and demanded immediate transport to Covent Garden where he might seek relief.

Cornwall, Western England, Tuesday, February 21, 1995

Peter walked across the sodden ground toward Graham Sykes's cottage where he was surprised to find the front door unlocked, especially after Sykes's reluctance to let him in the night before. The fire had died, and the sitting room was nearly as cold as the barn had been. Peter stood listening for a moment but heard nothing.

"Mr. Sykes," he called gently, and then he repeated the name more loudly, but no answer came. Either Sykes was sound asleep or he had left. To the left of the fireplace was the doorway through which Sykes had disappeared to make tea the night before. In place of a door hung a piece of pale blue cloth spattered with paint. Pushing the fabric aside, he found himself in what could only have been Sykes's study.

One wall was lined with rough pine bookcases; on the others hung Victorian watercolors and prints—mostly landscapes, but also the occasional portrait or religious scene. Opposite the doorway was a wide farm table, apparently used as a desk, with a computer printer on one side of it. Everywhere there were papers. Stacks of papers on the floor, papers on the desk, papers cascading down bookshelves, papers on the windowsill. For a moment, Peter thought that Sykes must be a far less organized scholar than he had imagined. It wasn't until the fact registered that every painting and print on the wall was askew on its hook that Peter began to suspect something was wrong.

His stomach began to churn and he felt the sweat forming on his forehead in spite of the chill in the room. Books had been pulled from their shelves and lay facedown on the floor, spines broken. A filing cabinet next to the table had all its drawers pulled open and manila file folders and their contents were strewn across the room. A lamp lay on its side on the table, its bulb shattered. Graham Sykes's study had been ransacked, and judging by the tea that still dripped from the edge of the table, it had happened recently. There was little hope now of finding any evidence of Sykes's scholarship on B.B. Even if whoever had done this had left such papers behind, it would take hours to sort through the mess in the study. Peter drew a sleeve across his sweaty brow and then saw something that made his hopes sink further. In the center of the table, next to the printer, was a neat square of clean wood framed by an accumulation of dust. Someone had stolen Graham Sykes's computer.

Peter felt certain that whoever had done this had come to Sykes for the same information he sought. There would be no papers here about B.B., about whether he was a forger, because Thomas Gardner or Julia Alderson or someone whose identity Peter had yet to discover had taken those papers away. And what reason was there to cover up the trail of B.B. if the *Pandosto* were genuine?

Across the room from the bookcases was another crudely curtained doorway—Peter assumed it led to the kitchen. Though he had completely lost his appetite, he thought a glass of water might calm his nerves, especially if he used it to wash down one of his anxiety pills. He pulled the curtain aside and stepped into a tiny kitchen, with room just for a stove and a sink. A single window sunk through a thick stone wall let in barely enough of the gloomy morning light for Peter to see, sprawled across the floor, the body of Graham Sykes.

At first he did not comprehend the scene. All he could think was how uncomfortable Sykes must be sleeping on a stone floor, with one arm bent behind his back. As Peter's eyes adjusted to the light, however, the grim truth struck him. Sykes's skin was ashen, his eyes were open and unmoving, and a dark pool of blood spread across the floor. A neat red line was carved across the front of Sykes's neck.

And in the sink, to which Peter now turned to be sick, lay a bone-handled carving knife, covered in blood.

Peter heaved violently but produced only a sour taste of bile. He pulled his wallet from his pocket and yanked out a small envelope in which he always kept several pills. He feared the present situation was beyond medicating but shoved two of the tablets in his mouth anyway, not bothering with water but chewing them to a bitter powder. When he stepped back into the study, his foot slid on the floor and he looked to see that he was now tracking blood through the house.

He staggered across the study and through the sitting room, not bothering to close the cottage door behind him as he lurched into the cold, wet air of morning. He stopped for a moment, drawing deep breaths in an effort to stop his head from spinning. As soon as he felt slightly steadier, he began running across the field, skidding on the wet grass. He pulled his keys from his pocket, fumbling to get them into the car's lock. He had started the engine and was backing up, trying to point the nose of the Vauxhall toward the menacing slope of the lane that he had traveled down the evening before, when he realized he had left his satchel in Sykes's study.

Peter sat for several minutes in the idling car, willing his medication to take effect, turning off the engine only when he felt slightly less irrational, though no less ill. No matter what the consequences, he knew he had to retrieve the *Pandosto*. The killer was certainly gone by now, and the police were unlikely to arrive for many hours. Who knew, it could be days before someone else discovered Sykes's body. Peter's fingerprints were already all over the house, his footprints already in the garden and the field, his tire tracks already in the lane. Another trip back to the house would not give the forensic investigators anything they didn't already have. Peter pulled himself out of the car and trudged slowly back toward the house. The satchel was just where he had left it, on the floor of the study. Just as he was picking it up, he noticed something on the floor that he had not seen before—the business card he had given to John Alderson, with the same torn corner, but now speckled with the blood of Graham Sykes. Here, surely, was proof that Julia Alderson had been involved in the murder.

Peter's first effort to navigate the steep, muddy lane ended with the Vauxhall sliding back to where he had started, but the second time he gunned the engine and managed to make it to the top, wheels spinning and mud spewing until he finally gained traction. He was halfway to Exeter, when it suddenly occurred to him that the killer had not found what he was looking for. Thomas and Julia may have succeeded in silencing Graham Sykes, and they may have stolen his computer, but there was still an extant copy of his manuscript. Sykes had posted it to Liz Sutcliffe, and Peter realized that she was now in danger of meeting the same fate as Sykes. At the next service area he screeched to a halt next to a phone box and leapt out of his car to call Liz.

The answering machine at Bloomsbury Art Publishers informed Peter that the office was open from nine until four on weekdays. Peter's watch read 10:15. He tried the number again and got the same message. Liz Sutcliffe's home phone had no answering machine—it just rang and rang. Could Thomas and Julia have made it to London already? Peter had assumed that the sound he heard that morning had been the murderers making their escape, but what if Sykes had been killed late the night before, and Thomas and Julia had headed straight to London in search of the B.B. manuscript? If all were well in London, wouldn't someone answer the phone at Liz's office? Should he call the police? If he did so, he would have to explain that Liz was in danger without revealing himself as the prime suspect in the Sykes murder. As the panic rose within him, Peter slammed down the phone and ran back to his car. Two minutes later, he was racing down the motorway at eighty miles an hour.

He had gone over the events of last night and this morning again and again and had come every time to the same conclusion—he was to blame for the death of Graham Sykes. The murder could only have been an attempt to cover up something that Sykes knew about B.B., something that would cast enough doubt on the authenticity of the *Pandosto* that Julia Alderson and Thomas Gardner would not be able to sell it for millions through the gullible American bookseller whom they had so far duped into believing that he had found the Holy Grail of English literature.

They had given Peter only a week to evaluate the *Pandosto*, knowing that was insufficient time to detect its flaws—for it was undoubtedly a forgery. Why else would they have murdered Sykes? They assumed Peter would test the ink and paper, but they knew that B.B. was a master forger and that his work would pass the basic tests. But there were two things that Julia and Thomas hadn't counted on. They hadn't expected Peter to discover the books proving the connection between B.B. and the forger John Payne Collier, and they hadn't expected him to find out about Graham Sykes's upcoming book on B.B., which no doubt exposed him as a forger. They must have known about Sykes and his work, because the old man had come nosing around Evenlode Manor. Peter supposed that Julia Alderson and her lover had panicked when that happened, knowing they had to sell the *Pandosto* before Sykes published his book. The presence in Kingham of an American bookseller provided them the perfect opportunity. Julia suggested to her brother that he sell off some of the old family library, giving her the chance to put the *Pandosto* in Peter's hands. No doubt she and Thomas had been watching him ever since, and when Peter went to Cornwall and found Graham Sykes, there was only one way to be sure the old man didn't give away the game—murder Sykes and steal his manuscript.

Suddenly the presence of his business card in Sykes's study made sickening sense. It hadn't been dropped there by accident. Not only had Peter left forensic evidence all over the crime scene, he was being actively framed for the murder of Graham Sykes.

If Peter hadn't come to Cornwall, Graham Sykes would probably still be alive and snoring loudly in his bed—and Peter was supposed to have protected Sykes, not endanger him. When he thought of the neck of Liz Sutcliffe falling open under the pressure of a kitchen knife, his panic transformed into anger. He was surprised to discover how possessive he felt toward Liz and how furious it made him to think of anyone harming her. But he liked the anger; it pushed away the nausea and dizziness and left him with determination in the face of his fear.

As he sped toward London, he glanced frequently at the passenger seat, hoping Amanda might show up and tell him what to do, but she seemed farther away than ever. If she were here, he thought, she would calm him, she would convince him that everything would be okay, that the police would discover the real killer. In her absence, all Peter could see was a Hitchcock movie running in his mind—the innocent man is convicted, the metal door slams, the gallows are prepared. True that the man was always saved at the last minute, but that was the movies. There might be no gallows anymore, but that didn't mean innocent people didn't spend their lives in prison.

He was surprised to find, when he glanced to his left for the tenth time, that Liz Sutcliffe was sitting in the passenger seat, twirling spaghetti on a fork.

"Speeding may not be the best idea for a man who's wanted for murder," she said teasingly.

"I thought of that," said Peter. "But I thought it was more important to get to you."

"You don't think I can take care of myself?"

"I just don't think you'll be expecting a visit from a murderer."

"I wasn't expecting to meet you and I handled that well enough."

"Why didn't you answer your phone?" asked Peter, but when no response came, he turned and found the seat empty again. He passed a sign saying he was one hundred miles from London and nudged the speedometer up to eighty-five.

Ridgefield, 1986

Peter spent much of the summer after his junior year in the Volvo station wagon that Amanda had given him. The upholstery on the backseat was badly scratched and the parking brake sometimes stubbornly refused to disengage, but as far as Peter was concerned, only two things about the car mattered: it made him independent, and it had been a gift from Amanda. He didn't turn the key, close the door, or shift the gears without thinking of her.

He took several excursions that summer, starting with day trips to Raleigh and Charlotte, then a weekend in Atlanta, and culminating with a three-week visit to New England.

"Three weeks?" said Amanda, as they lay in the sun side by side next to the Ridgefields' pool.

"Hey, you gave me the car," said Peter. "And you decided to get a job." Amanda was working three days a week at an art gallery in Raleigh.

"I know, but I'll miss you."

"I'll miss you, too."

"You'll just miss the bed," said Amanda. Peter had confessed to her that he planned to sleep in the back of the Volvo to save money. Charlie Ridgefield had offered to invest in Peter's business, but Peter wouldn't hear of it.

"The bed and who's in it," said Peter, grinning.

"Yeah, I notice you haven't spent much time at your apartment this summer." Amanda's parents seemed happy to have Peter around and either didn't know or didn't mind that Amanda joined him in the guest room every night.

"Do you want me to go back to my place?" said Peter.

"No," said Amanda, smiling. "I want you right here."

"And I'll be right here."

"Yeah, in three weeks," said Amanda, pretending to pout.

"Well, we can have some fun saying good-bye tonight," said Peter.

"You have fun," said Amanda, tossing her towel over Peter's head. "I'm going for a swim."

Peter pulled the towel away in time to see Amanda's bikini-clad body slice into the water. He wished he were an artist, that he could paint her. He couldn't imagine being able to capture her beauty.

That night they did have fun, but Amanda refused to say good-bye.

Heading north, Peter found bookshops in every small town. He drove through Pennsylvania and New York and spent five days in Connecticut and Rhode Island before heading out to Cape Cod. He ventured into Boston, and on his way back south he parked his car in Hoboken and took a train into New York. His bunk in the back of the Volvo gradually shrunk as the boxes of books multiplied.

His usual trepidation about meeting strangers did not seem to extend to fellow book enthusiasts, and one of the most glorious parts of the trip was the long conversations he had with booksellers. Peter felt as if he'd finally joined a fraternity—not the beery, raucous clubs at Ridgefield, which had had no more interest in him than he in them, but a real brotherhood of men and women with a shared passion.

Peter had saved up his money from extra hours worked at the library, and even though he wouldn't take Charlie Ridgefield's money, he had allowed both Francis and Hank to invest small amounts in his fledgling company. When Amanda had tried to do the same, Peter would not allow it. "You bought the car," he said. "That's investment enough." He did allow her to make one other financial contribution to his summer. Every night he called her collect.

He would share each day's discoveries with her—underpriced gems found on a dusty shelf, charming villages with greens where he had eaten lunch, booksellers who welcomed him into their midst. Amanda would gush about her work in the art gallery and the artists and collectors she had met. But mostly they talked about nothing, talked just to hear each other's voices, to be together.

"Mother says she misses you," said Amanda one night, as Peter stood in a phone both at a back-roads gas station in Massachusetts. "Isn't that sweet?"

"Tell her I miss her, too," said Peter. In fact, he realized, he didn't miss just Amanda; he missed the family he had become a part of. "And tell Charlie I drove by Fenway Park the other day."

"And do you have any messages for me?" said Amanda.

"Yes," said Peter, "but I'm not sure AT&T would approve."

He was in a phone booth in Princeton the night Amanda did not pick up on the first ring and he heard someone else's voice accepting the charges after nearly a minute of ringing.

"Peter, is that you?"

"Who's this?"

"It's Cynthia," said the voice. "Sorry I took so long to answer. I came over to wait for your call, but I had trouble with the damn key. Jesus, I'm sorry, Peter. It was getting dark and I couldn't see the lock and it was just . . . just the goddamn key." Peter could hear both tears and hysteria in Cynthia's voice.

"Cynthia, are you all right? You sound like you're kind of flipping out."

"It's Amanda. Peter, you've got to get down here right away. It's Amanda."

Peter felt a jolt in his stomach—that old familiar knot he hadn't felt in weeks but that could hit him like a thunderclap, without the warning of gathering clouds. "What about Amanda?" She hadn't felt well the past few days. She thought she might have had a bout of food poisoning—she'd said something about bad clams at a cookout. But it had been passing, she said. Last night it had been nothing but cramps; her period was on the way and it had just knocked her out this time.

"Is she there?" said Peter, trying to keep his voice even. One hysterical person on the phone seemed quite enough.

"She's in the hospital." Peter's stomach tightened another notch, and sweat broke out on his brow and palms.

"Give me the number," he said tersely. "I want to call her. I need to talk with her right now. What's the number?"

"You can't talk to her," said Cynthia. "She's in surgery." Peter now felt the onslaught of a full-blown panic attack, Later, after he hung up, it occured to him that perhaps this was what genuine, justifiable panic felt like. The only way it differed from his usually irrational attacks was that Amanda was in trouble.

"What the hell is she doing in surgery?" said Peter, giving up all pretense of calmness.

"They think her appendix ruptured," said Cynthia. It sounded like she was crying now. "She felt so bad this morning and you know her parents are in France so she called me and I took her to the doctor and he said . . . he said . . ."

"Take a breath, Cynthia," said Peter, who was having a hard time doing so himself. "What did the doctor say?"

"He said he thought she had some sort of infection," said Cynthia. "And they did these tests and an ultrasound and they say they think her appendix might have burst and so this afternoon they sent her to the hospital outside Raleigh and now she's in surgery and they won't tell me what's going on because I'm not family." Cynthia's crying was steady now.

"Bullshit you're not family," said Peter, surprised at his own anger. "What did they say before she went in?"

Peter could hear Cynthia drawing a deep breath. "They said she could be okay, but it depends how far the infection has spread. They said . . . they said there's always a chance in cases like this that . . . that—"

"I'm on my way," said Peter, before Cynthia could finish her sentence. He had no desire to hear her say aloud what he knew they were both thinking. Even though he had been up since seven and it was now nearly ten o'clock, he swallowed one of his anxiety pills, got in the Volvo, and headed south.

Phillip Gardner lay in the arms of his lover, the waning light of the winter sun playing across her pale, perfect skin. Miss Prickett had taken a liking to her second cousin, and Isabel had convinced her governess to make the journey to Brixton every Thursday. It had been the most glorious three months of Phillip's life. On the one occasion after Phillip's wedding when Mrs. Gardner had condescended to share Phillip's bed, her performance had been perfunctory and dispassionate. Isabel was anything but. She threw herself into lovemaking with a passionate abandon that thrilled and sometimes even frightened Phillip. On more than one occasion he had feared her cries might cause the neighbors to send for the police; other times, when she collapsed on the bed, spent from her exertions, he feared for her health. How such a delicate creature could be capable of such energetic coupling was a mystery that both intrigued and delighted Phillip. Now she rolled atop him, slipping him into her with a dexterous hand and moving languidly above him. He reached for her breasts and dug his fingers into their softness as she increased her pace. He thrust uncontrollably, gripping her tighter and tighter, unsure if she was crying out from pain or pleasure or both, until finally, with a cry of his own, he reached his climax.

Nearly an hour later he awoke to see Isabel sitting at her dressing table, running a brush through her waist-length hair. He loved seeing her hair unclasped and free, loved the way it cascaded over her still uncovered breasts, teasing her nipples to hardness with her every stroke of the brush. Though he was too spent to consider luring her back to bed, he was never too tired to watch. There on the stool before her mirror, turned partially away from him so that he could see not only hair and hand and brush and breasts but also the whiteness of her bare shoulder, the curve of her hip, the narrowing of her lower back, and even a hint of the cleft of her bottom, she was transformed from a woman into a work of art, as perfect as anything he had seen at the Royal Academy. He wished only that he could paint her in a way that would begin to do justice to her beauty and to the perfect happiness he felt in that moment.

"When must you go?" she said, catching his eye in the mirror.

"When must *you* go?" said Phillip teasingly.

"I live here," she said.

"You mean you are visiting here," said Phillip, sitting up in bed and taking a more serious tone. "Surely your parents expect you to return from your grand tour someday."

"I'd rather not think about it," said Isabel.

"Nor would I," said Phillip. "But I cannot bear the thought that every time with you could be my last."

"This won't be the last," she said, her reflection smiling at him. At least he had extracted that promise—that he would lie in ecstasy with his beloved Isabel again. He rose and pulled on his clothes, all the while watching her hair sweep across her breasts as she brushed.

"I'd best catch the five seventeen from Paddington," he said, answering her original question. He leaned forward and pressed his lips gently onto a bit of exposed shoulder, sliding his hand up her side to cup a breast and run his thumb lightly across a nipple.

"You don't mind showing yourself out?" she said.

"Not at all," said Phillip, and he left her in front of the mirror, a smile on her lips and the dying light of day shimmering off her hair.

Peter had never driven in London before, and this didn't seem like the morning to try. He saw a sign for the Reading train station, and decided the most efficient way into town would be to take a train to Paddington.

He left the Vauxhall in the multistory car park and took his satchel with him, not wanting to let the *Pandosto* out of his sight for a moment. As he stood in the queue for a ticket, he could hear the morning news playing over a television that hung near the ticket office. He felt a sudden chill when he heard the headlines.

"In Cornwall this morning, police discovered the body of an elderly man brutally murdered in his remote cottage. Investigators are currently on the scene." Peter had left Sykes's house only three hours ago. If the murder was already being reported on the news, he must have made a narrow escape indeed. But how could Sykes have been discovered so quickly? His house was miles from the nearest village. As Peter took his ticket and turned toward the platforms, he felt another jolt of dread slam into his body. The police knew about Sykes because Julia Alderson and Thomas Gardner had reported the murder they themselves had committed. No doubt an anonymous call had come in in a strong Cornish accent: *we saw a strange American man round Mr. Sykes's place last night, driving a beige Vauxhall. Then this morning, we're out for a walk, and we hear screaming.* There was no other explanation.

He slumped into a seat on a London-bound train and half expected, in another Hitchcockian moment, to see his own face on the newspaper of the man sitting opposite him. How much had Alderson and Gardner told the police? Peter picked up the stray newspaper on the seat next to him and hid behind it for the half-hour journey to Paddington. His fellow passengers, if they noticed him, must have thought he was fascinated by rugby scores.

At Paddington he did his best to immerse himself in the crowds that poured from the mainline station into the Underground. He was now utterly convinced that every law enforcement official in the British Isles was holding a copy of his picture and had received orders to "detain at all costs." When he emerged from the tube into the relative calm of Russell Square, he came face-to-face with a uniformed officer just outside the station. After the policeman passed him with indifference, Peter allowed himself to think that, perhaps, he was safe for a bit longer.

Bloomsbury Art Publishers was in a narrow building on Bury Place, just around the corner from the British Museum. Two stories up, on a small window, were painted the initials B.A.P., the only indication from the street of the presence of Liz Sutcliffe's office. Peter pushed open the door and entered a cramped corridor that led to a tightly wound staircase. Beside the stairs was an elevator, but Peter supposed that walking would probably be quicker and mounted the steps. Taped to the door of Bloomsbury Art Publishers was a note on the company's letterhead: TUESDAY—B.A.P. CLOSED FOR STAFF TO ATTEND SEMINAR OF INDEPENDENT PUBLISHERS' GUILD. PLEASE CALL AGAIN.

So there was a reason Liz had not answered her phone. Peter leaned against the door in relief, but was surprised when it swung open and he stumbled into the dim offices. As soon as his eyes adjusted to the light, his relief evaporated. Papers were strewn everywhere, chairs were overturned, and desk drawers lay haphazardly on the floor. The office had been ransacked. Peter ventured farther and found a door with Liz's name on it. Inside, her office was chaos. It was eerily reminiscent of the scene he had left in Graham Sykes's studio a few hours earlier.

Peter knew they had been looking for her copy of Sykes's manuscript. What he didn't know was whether they had found it. If so, then any hope of finding out the truth about B.B. through Sykes was probably gone; if not, then Liz was still in danger. He flicked on the light and surveyed the damage for any clues, but the office was in such disarray he could spend hours searching through its scattered papers, and he didn't have hours. On the floor by the window he found a large desk calendar. On February 21, Liz had written, "Work at home, Bob & S. to IPG seminar." Work at home. But Liz had not answered her phone at home. Peter felt the nausea and dizziness returning. He riffled through the papers on the floor, looking for anything that had Liz's home address. He had just picked up an envelope addressed to her at a flat in Hampstead when he heard police sirens outside. He dashed back into the reception area and saw a small red light high in a corner, steadily flashing. A silent alarm, he thought. That meant two things: Thomas and Julia couldn't be more than ten minutes ahead of him, and the police would be here any second.

He ran into the hall and was just about to head down the stairs when he heard voices below. In desperation he hit the button for the elevator and was stunned when it slid open immediately. He fell into the elevator, pushed the button for the basement, and held his breath. The doors closed and the lift slowly descended. Peter could hear footsteps clattering up the stairs as he and the police passed one another, separated only by the doors of the elevator. When he was disgorged in the basement, he stood at the bottom of the steps and listened for a moment. Hearing nothing, he slipped quickly up the steps and out the door, past two police cars. As soon as he reached the end of the block and was out of sight around the corner, he broke into a run down New Oxford Street toward Tottenham Court Road. There he could catch the Northern Line for Hampstead.

Ridgefield, 1986

Peter had been at Amanda's bedside for nearly two days, holding her hand and sleeping for only a few minutes at a time, when Sarah and Charlie Ridgefield finally arrived from France. The doctors had kept Amanda unconscious, "So she can use all her energy to get better," they had said. But this was all they would say about her condition to either Peter or Cynthia. Even Peter's claim to be Amanda's fiancé hadn't helped. Medical information could be released only to family members. Peter was lucky, they told him, that they were letting him stay in Amanda's room beyond normal visiting hours. Since arriving at the hospital, sleep and food had been incidental, and, in this intensity of focus, even his anxiety had abandoned him. He refused to imagine anything for Amanda other than a full recovery from whatever it was the doctors weren't telling him.

"We removed a burst appendix from the patient," said Dr. Harris.

"Her name is Amanda," said Peter. "The patient has a name—Amanda." Harris had been stern and often downright rude over the past two days; Peter refused to meet his now cheerful demeanor with anything approaching forgiveness. He sat on a sofa in the waiting area, his hand clasped tightly by Sarah Ridgefield; Charlie stood by his wife. Only the promise of finally hearing Amanda's prognosis had lured Peter from her side. Harris had said it was best to discuss these things away from the patient, even though she was still, as he put it, "sleeping."

"Of course," said Harris, looking at his chart. "Amanda. We took out a burst appendix and there was already an extensive infection."

"How can that happen?" said Peter. "How can her appendix just burst?"

"She did have some symptoms," said Harris, "according to the young woman who brought her in."

"Cynthia," prompted Peter.

"Yes, Cynthia. According to her, the patient . . . I mean, Amanda had been ill for two days and was experiencing what she thought was menstrual pain."

"And how is she now?" said Charlie.

"She's battling a major infection," said Dr. Harris, adding quickly, "and she's battling it well. We've been keeping her on massive doses of antibiotics and we have every reason to believe that we can wake her up in another day or two. If everything goes well, we'll still need her here for another week or so, but her white cell count is already much lower. She's strong."

"What is it you're not telling us?" asked Peter, gripping Sarah's hand a little more tightly. Harris had been fidgeting with the chart and had not made eye contact with either of Amanda's parents.

"It was a massive infection, Mr. . . . ."

"Byerly," said Sarah gently. "His name is Peter Byerly."

"Well, Mr. Byerly," said Dr. Harris. "As I said, it was a massive infection. It's not unheard of in cases like this for PID to develop."

"PID?" said Charlie.

"Pelvic inflammatory disease," said Dr. Harris. "Basically it means that the infection spreads to the pelvic region where it can affect the fallopian tubes and the ovaries."

"And did it affect the fallopian tubes and the ovaries?" asked Charlie.

"We think so," said Dr. Harris. "It's hard to be one hundred percent sure at this stage, but I'm afraid it's very likely . . . extremely likely that the patient . . . that Amanda will be sterile."

Peter saw tears slipping down Sarah's cheeks, and he pulled her to his shoulder, where she wept quietly.

An hour later, Peter left the hospital for the first time in nearly three days. He had insisted that he be the one to give Amanda her prognosis, and that he would do it when he felt she was ready. The Ridgefields had agreed.

On the floor of his apartment, under the mail slot, a pile of mail had accumulated in his absence. Peter sat on the floor and sifted through the coupons and sale advertisements, looking for what he knew must be there. He was surprised to find a postcard reproduction of Amanda Devereaux's portrait on the back of which was written, "Welcome home, Sweetheart. I missed you. All my love, Amanda. P.S. Grandmother missed you too!" Peter's mind flashed to an image of himself and Amanda, lying naked beneath Amanda Devereaux's portrait and fumbling with a condom, laughing as they rushed to get the thing in place. That precautions would no longer be necessary suddenly seemed an immeasurable loss to Peter, and, for the first time since arriving at Amanda's bedside, he was overwhelmed by tears.

He slumped back against the door, sobbing as he continued to look through the mail until he found what he needed. Clutching the envelope to his chest, he cried copiously for another ten minutes. Amanda had told Peter about needing a good cry now and then, what a cleansing feeling it could bring, but he had never experienced it himself. He still felt a deep sense of loss, but no longer the hopelessness that had been building in him since Dr. Harris gave his prognosis.

He tore open the envelope and read: "You have been preapproved for a $5,000 line of credit." *That ought to be enough*, he thought.

It felt strange to borrow money from the Ridgefields, but Peter told himself that Ridgefield Bank and Trust was, after all, a publicly traded company. It wasn't as if he were asking for a personal loan from Sarah Ridgefield. Besides, he felt confident that within a few weeks he could turn the contents of the boxes in the back of the Volvo into more than enough cash to repay the loan. He left the bank, made one stop on the way to the hospital, and was back at Amanda's bedside less than three hours after he had left her.

The next day he awoke when Amanda's hand began to twitch gently in his own. She opened her eyes, slowly focused on him, smiled, and whispered, in a tone of great contentment, "Peter."

Kingham, 1876

Phillip and Isabel had an agreement: if she needed to contact him outside the parameters of their regular Thursday meetings, she would send a message through Phillip's bookseller, Benjamin Mayhew. Phillip knew Mayhew would be discreet about passing along messages, and a letter or telegram from the bookseller would arouse no suspicion at Evenlode House, where Mrs. Gardner was usually first to sort through the morning post.

Phillip was lucky, therefore, that the letter from Isabel arrived in the afternoon post, when his wife was napping, and that he happened to recognize, in the pile of letters that sat on the silver tray in the morning room, the gentle looping handwriting he had glimpsed once on the writing table in Isabel's sitting room. He snatched up the letter and rushed to his studio where Mrs. Gardner, more scornful of his artistic efforts than even the Royal Academy, rarely ventured.

Darling Phillip,
I must speak with you at once. Please meet me at the tearooms, Fortnum & Mason, Piccadilly tomorrow afternoon at three o'clock.
Your Isabel

Phillip wadded up the letter and hurled it into the grate, where the fire quickly consumed it. How could she have taken such a risk, when they had made a perfectly good plan? Had she become, suddenly, a fool? Or was she hoping Mrs. Gardner would catch him out, hoping to force his hand? He had told her in the clearest possible terms that there was no hope for a long-term relationship. Though he did not love Mrs. Gardner, he would never consider ending his marriage. He owed it to his family to keep her money invested in Evenlode House.

He grabbed his topcoat and asked the housekeeper, as he met her on the stairs, to inform Mrs. Gardner that he had been called into London by his solicitor and would be spending the night at his club. When he arrived in London two hours later, he went straight to Covent Garden where he spent a night of debauchery with two women he suspected were mother and daughter. He was determined that when he met Isabel, he would have not a drop of sexual energy left. This, he thought, would remove the one weapon she had against him, and he could properly rebuke her for her actions without being tempted into her bed.

She was sitting prim and upright at a table near the back of the room, blissfully unaware, so it seemed, of the disaster she could have caused had her letter arrived a few hours earlier. He was further irritated by her demand that they meet in public. When their relationship had been innocent, he had been more than happy to be seen with her in Hyde Park or Kensington Gardens. But once he had something to hide, he became sensitive to the need to constantly hide it. Yet now she insisted on meeting him not just in public but in a tearoom frequented by the social acquaintances of Mrs. Gardner.

Isabel had her back to the entrance, so he was able to walk up behind her and slam his newspaper onto the table in an attempt to startle her. That she did not even flinch or turn to look at him he took as a bad sign.

"Good afternoon, Phillip," she said.

"Do you have any idea how much trouble you could have caused me?" he spat at her in a whisper as he took his seat. "You're a fool to send a letter to the house like that."

"I don't care," she said flatly, gazing toward the window.

"No, clearly you don't," said Phillip. "Nor, I suppose, do you care whose money it is that bought you that diamond brooch you wear all over London."

"We have a problem greater than money or diamonds," she said, still not rising to his venom. It annoyed him that she could remain so placid while he railed at her. He had taken great satisfaction in the imagined fight they would have—his anger prodding her to return fire, the battle waging long and hard, her ultimate capitulation and begging for forgiveness, his leaving her to contemplate her sins before finally returning to her arms a couple of weeks hence. But she seemed unwilling to play her part.

"Nothing is more important than money," he said. "You seem to forget that the future of the Gardner family rests on my shoulders."

"The future of the Gardner family rests someplace else altogether," she said, finally turning to meet his eyes.

"You've no idea what you're talking about," said Phillip.

"On the contrary, Mr. Gardner," she said. "I know exactly what I'm talking about. It's been two months." She had not called him Mr. Gardner since shortly after they met, and it unnerved him.

"Two months since what?"

"Since I began to carry your child."

For a moment, Phillip couldn't breathe. He was unable to focus on Isabel, on either her face or her figure, even the tea things that arrived at that very moment seemed a blur. All his bluster had been ripped away and he was left with ... with what? With a child out of wedlock? With the ruination of his marriage, his estate, his family?

"Are you certain?" he whispered.

"Quite certain," said Isabel. "A woman knows these things, as I now discover."

"Does Miss Prickett know?"

"Not yet," said Isabel coldly. "But she soon must. I will take my confinement here in London."

"And what will you tell your parents?"

"That I have enrolled in an art school."

"That seems a bit unconventional."

"Don't you think, Mr. Gardner, that we have previously established my unconventionality?"

"You seem to have thought of everything," said Phillip.

"Not everything, Mr. Gardner. I've no idea what the relationship will be between the child and its father."

So blindsided had Phillip been by her revelation that it took him a moment to absorb the fact that *father* referred to him. It was a word he had long ago dissociated from himself. Mrs. Gardner had made plain shortly after their marriage that she would not bear him an heir. His brother's children would inherit Evenlode House along with Mrs. Gardner's wealth, and Phillip would have restored the family fortune at the sacrifice only of his own happiness. After all he had given up, nothing could be allowed to interfere with that plan.

"And how do I know that I am the father?" said Phillip.

Had the tearoom been more crowded, perhaps she would not have done it; yet she seemed to react instinctively. She slapped him hard across the face, and even though her hand was gloved, he felt a sting of pain in his cheek. He had raised his own hand to return the blow when he heard a shrill voice from beside him.

"Why, Mr. Gardner, is that you? It is you. I thought it was. I told Mr. Thompson that is Mr. Gardner, you mark my words, I know it is." The voice belonged to an oversized acquaintance of Mrs. Gardner's, whose name Phillip had forgotten, if indeed he had ever known it. "I do hope we shall see you and Mrs. Gardner at the Royal Ascot this season. I do so love the Royal Ascot, don't you, Mr. Gardner? I was just saying to Mr. Thompson how much I enjoy the Royal Ascot. And who is this lovely young lady?"

The apparent Mrs. Thompson finally stopped for breath and to assess Isabel and await an explanation for her presence at tea with a married man. Almost without thinking, Phillip said, "A young woman from America. My brother has asked me to interview her as a possible governess for his children."

"An American governess, how unusual," said Mrs. Thompson.

"Yes, well now, if you will excuse me, Mrs. Thompson, I really must get on with the interview."

"Of course, Mr. Gardner, of course. I quite understand. Give my regards to Mrs. Gardner, will you, and tell her we shall see her at the Royal Ascot." Mrs. Thompson headed back across the tearoom, not pausing in her monologue but only increasing her volume. "It was Mr. Gardner. I told you it was Mr. Gardner. He says we shall see them at the Royal Ascot."

"So, Mr. Gardner," said Isabel, when Mrs. Thompson had finally disappeared. "Am I to remain your brother's governess, or are we to make other arrangements?"

Since his first visit to London, Peter had loved riding the tube. Amanda always preferred taxis—she said you could see the architecture of the city that way, but Peter claimed the tube was cheaper and, often, quicker. What he liked most, though, was the anonymity. He didn't have to tell anyone where he was going or make small talk with a driver. And he loved the map. Aboveground, London was utterly confusing, but belowground, in the hands of the exquisite tube map, Peter understood the city.

As he rattled toward Hampstead on the Northern Line, the adrenaline that had been driving Peter seemed to have worn off, and he slumped in his seat, settling into a dull dread. The train was just pulling out of the third stop when Liz Sutcliffe appeared beside him once again, still twirling her pasta. She spoke not from Peter's imagination but from his memory. At some point during their Italian lunch, Peter had asked Liz what sooner or later he asked every Londoner that he met: "What's your tube stop?" He had found this a great conversation starter, and though he often caught Amanda giggling when he asked it, she would later tell him what a good job he had done of initiating conversation. "Tube rescues American from social anxiety," she would say.

"Belsize Park," Liz Sutcliffe said, before popping a forkful of pasta into her mouth and disappearing. Her address was Hampstead, but the closest tube station was one stop closer to central London. If Thomas Gardner and Julia Alderson were only a few minutes ahead of him and going all the way to Hampstead, he might still have a chance to reach Liz first.

Peter leapt off the train at Belsize Park and found Liz's street on the tube station's local area map. He sprinted out of the station and up the hill, realizing that although Thomas and Julia might have farther to go from the Hampstead station, they would be going downhill. He turned into a quiet residential street that led to Liz's flat and peeked back around the corner and up the hill to see if he could spot Thomas and Julia. He didn't even notice the parka-clad figure that strode past him, then suddenly reversed and stopped beside him.

"Peter, is that you?" Her cheeks rosy from the cold, and the mist of her warm breath dissolving in the midday sun, Liz Sutcliffe stood next to Peter, a perplexed smile on her face. "What are you doing here?" she asked.

Peter leaned forward, his hands on his knees, trying to catch his breath. Liz waited patiently, as she might for a dog or a small child. Finally he was able to gasp, "Murder."

"I beg your pardon?" said Liz, still smiling maternally, as if Peter were playing some sort of game that proved him an exceptionally clever six-year-old.

"Sykes," said Peter. "Graham Sykes has been murdered."

Liz yanked Peter up by his arm so she could look him in the eye. "What the bloody hell are you talking about?"

"I went to see him," said Peter, still panting, "and this morning he was murdered."

"Fuck," exhaled Liz. "How do you know?"

"I saw him," said Peter. "It was awful. It was so awful." He felt the nausea and chills returning as he remembered the scene; this time he felt not panic but revulsion and grief. A tear ran down his cold cheek. "They cut his throat," he whispered.

"Jesus fuck," said Liz, the color draining from her face. "Bollocks!"

"I'm so sorry," said Peter. "I was supposed to keep him out of danger. I was supposed to warn him but he was . . . we were arguing and . . ." He recalled the argument with Sykes the night before. If Peter hadn't been so stubborn, he might have remembered to warn Sykes about the threat from Thomas Gardner. Now all he could see was the face of the dead man, and all that blood. "It was horrible," he said.

"How could this happen?" said Liz.

Her question hung in the crisp air for a moment as Peter tried to banish the image of Sykes's body. "I'll explain everything," he said at last, taking a deep breath and feeling he was pulling himself back from an abyss. "But we've got to get you out of here first."

"What do you mean?" said Liz. "What does this have to do with me?"

"They ransacked your office, Liz," said Peter. "And they may already be at your flat." Before he could stop her, Liz fled down the road. Peter caught up to her just as she stopped across the street from her home. A glass panel in the street door had been smashed, and a window on the second floor flung open. Below the window several piles of books and papers lay on the pavement. Liz stood wide-eyed before the scene. Afraid that Thomas and Julia might still be in the flat, Peter slipped an arm around Liz and guided her farther down the block.

"We have to leave London," he said when they were around the corner. "Now."

"My car's in the next street," said Liz quietly, and she slipped her hand into Peter's and pulled him down the block. When she had edged her Citroën into the line of traffic moving up Haverstock Hill toward Hampstead, she asked Peter where they were going.

"Kingham," said Peter, who had already given the matter some thought. Even though that meant going back to the murderers, he thought he might be able to keep up the pretense of doing business with John Alderson long enough to solve the mystery of the *Pandosto* and perhaps find some evidence that would both exonerate himself and implicate Julia Alderson and Thomas Gardner in Sykes's murder.

Not until they were well under way did Liz ask, "What were they after?"

"They were after Sykes's manuscript," said Peter. "They didn't find it at his cottage because he had already posted it to you. I assume they didn't find it at your office, or they wouldn't have come to your flat, unless . . ."

"Unless what?" said Liz.

"Well, they didn't just try to get the manuscript from Sykes, they killed him—I think because he knew what was in it. It's not so bad if they found the manuscript at your flat. I'm just glad they didn't find you."

"They didn't find the manuscript either," said Liz.

"How do you know?" said Peter.

"Because I spent my morning on Hampstead Heath reading it," said Liz, reaching into her bag and pulling out a bound sheaf of papers. "It's right here."

Peter had replayed in his mind a hundred times in the past two days the conversation that he and Amanda had had just a few weeks ago on the night she had given him the Volvo. After a second round of lovemaking, they lay side by side, their hands loosely nestled together, gazing at the high ceiling.

"Did you like being an only child?" Amanda had asked.

"I don't know," said Peter. "I guess if I'd had a little brother, I would have had someone to talk to. I might be more . . . socialized. But then I would have worried about him growing up in that house. I'm good at worrying."

"I'd have liked a little sister," said Amanda.

"Not an older one?" said Peter.

"No. I guess since I was first and I always thought another might come along, I never dreamed of an older one. But I used to wish I had a baby sister. To take care of, you know. I want my kids to have siblings."

"How many?" said Peter, after a long pause.

"Do you mean how many kids would I like?"

"Yeah."

"Three or four," said Amanda. "If the first three are all boys, I might try once more for a girl."

"So you'd like girls?" Peter asked, suddenly seeing himself and Amanda walking through a park with two dark-haired toddlers wearing frilly pink dresses. He found the vision equally frightening and enthralling.

"I'd like at least one of each," said Amanda. "But I'm realistic. What about you?"

"I'd like any kids that had you as a mother," said Peter, and Amanda lay her head on his chest and fell almost instantly asleep.

After that, Amanda would sometimes make a seemingly offhand comment—though Peter knew there was no such thing with her—about wanting her daughter to take ballet lessons or hoping that her son would apply to schools other than Ridgefield. Peter began to picture himself as a stay-at-home dad, writing antiquarian book catalogs in his home office while the children napped.

Now he sat at the bedside of the woman who would never bear children and gently woke her.

"How are you feeling?" said Peter.

"Better," said Amanda. "Stronger. I think I can sit up." Peter pressed a button and the bed raised Amanda to a sitting position.

"Not as bolt upright as you like," said Peter.

"Still," said Amanda, "I feel more human."

"We need to talk," said Peter.

"That doesn't sound good," said Amanda. "Besides, I thought the girl was supposed to say that."

"A couple of things have happened while you were sick."

"Peter, you're scaring me. Did somebody die?"

"Nobody died," said Peter. "It's just that you had a pretty bad infection."

"But they said it was clearing up."

"It is. It is clearing up. You're going to be fine. It's just that . . ."

"I'm not going to be fine, am I?"

"The infection got into your ovaries," said Peter, taking her hand. "We're going to have to rethink the whole children issue."

"Oh," said Amanda softly, looking away from Peter for the first time in the conversation. She stared out the window at the pale blue summer sky for a long minute before Peter pulled her back toward him. He made no attempt to wipe away the tears trickling down her cheek. "It's just that I . . ."

"I know," said Peter. "We both did." They sat quietly for a long time, Amanda's hand resting limply in his. Peter felt he should give the news a chance to settle before he went on. Finally, when he could bear the silence no longer, he said, "There's something else, too. Some good news."

"I could use some good news," said Amanda, forcing a smile as she drew her sleeve across her eyes. Peter gripped her hand more firmly and slipped out of his chair. "Did you lose something?" asked Amanda, as he knelt on the floor by her bed.

"Yes," said Peter. "About two years ago. I lost my heart."

"Peter, what are you doing?"

"Amanda Ridgefield," said Peter—and to his own surprise he felt not panic but supreme peace as he said it, "will you marry me?"

Amanda began to cry again, but Peter thought he saw a smile behind her tears. He got back up and pulled a ring from his pocket. "What do you think?" he said. Before she could stop him, he slipped it onto her finger.

"Peter, it's . . . it's beautiful." She was sobbing now, and Peter waited patiently for her to compose herself. After a few moments, she slipped her hand from his and reached for a tissue.

"I don't want you to marry me because you feel sorry for me," said Amanda.

"I don't feel sorry for you," said Peter. "Look, we can adopt, we can do all sorts of things. I'm prepared to do a lot of things to make you . . . to make us happy. The one thing I'm not prepared to do is leave this room without being engaged to you."

"And this isn't a sympathy proposal?"

"Amanda, you know me. You know us. You know how much I

love you. Why do you think I've been buying and selling all these books? To make money for this." He pointed to her ring, which already looked like a natural part of her hand.

"Really?" said Amanda.

"Really," said Peter.

"Okay then, Peter Byerly. Yes."

Though Peter often mourned the scar on Amanda's heart left by her inability to bear children, he never regretted choosing that moment to propose to her. He had been planning to buy the ring after he had sold his Volvo full of books and to propose on Halloween in the Devereaux Room, but he felt a need to balance Amanda's grief, and her family's grief, with joy. Charlie and Sarah were nearly as happy as Amanda when they saw the ring on their daughter's finger and heard the news.

"I'm gonna call you 'son' now," said Charlie, clapping Peter on the back in a gesture that failed to hide the depth of his emotion. "I hope you won't mind that."

"No," said Peter, "I won't mind at all."

Peter drove Amanda home five days later. He spent the rest of the summer in a guest room in the Ridgefield house, helping nurse his fiancée back to health. Amanda seemed to be her old self, sitting in the study reading, laughing and teasing Peter in the kitchen and around the pool, even making love when her parents had gone to New York for the weekend. But from that time on there was between Amanda and Peter a small unspoken barrier, which had not been there before, around the topic of children. He rarely noticed it, but once in a while, when they saw a baby in a restaurant or flipped past a channel playing a Disney movie, Peter felt it—this slight awkwardness, as if they were friends who had accidentally seen each other naked. Peter would learn that marriages acquire such scars, but it was this blemish on their absolute intimacy, even more than Amanda's barrenness, that grieved him. That he never had the courage to talk to Amanda about it was something he would regret for the rest of his life.

By the time his son was born, Phillip Gardner had finally persuaded Isabel to be reasonable, though it had not been easy. The first several times he had visited her following the meeting at Fortnum's, she had insisted that she did not want money from him but affection and a father for her child. He had explained that these were the only two things he could not provide. It was Miss Prickett, in the end, who helped Isabel to see the hopelessness of her situation, and for that Phillip had been grateful.

When the child was old enough to travel, it was decided that Isabel would return to America. The child would be presented as a foundling whom Isabel had discovered outside her art school and from whom no power of Miss Prickett could part her. Isabel conceded that her parents would willingly adopt the child and raise it as part of her family. In the meantime, Phillip would be available for whatever Isabel might need, within reason. He would arrange for a doctor, should that prove necessary, and he agreed to pay a small stipend not to Isabel, who would not accept it, but to Miss Prickett, who would use it to buy clothes and such for the baby.

Isabel could continue to contact him through Benjamin Mayhew, but Phillip had directed Mayhew not to forward messages to Kingham. Phillip could find an excuse to come up to London and check in with his bookseller at least once a week—for anything that required more expedient attention, Miss Prickett would have to do.

Since their conversation in Fortnum's, Phillip and Isabel had continued to meet on a regular basis, though those meetings were entirely chaste. As Isabel reached the last months of her confinement, Phillip's visits to her lodgings were generally limited to a short conversation with Miss Prickett confirming Isabel's health. As for the needs of the flesh, Phillip had felt curiously uninterested in such activities since his discovery of Isabel's condition. He avoided Covent Garden.

The child, known to his father only as Phillip, was born on a cold morning in late November. Miss Prickett dispatched a letter to Benjamin Mayhew at once, but Phillip had accompanied Mrs. Gardner on a trip to Yorkshire to visit her niece and did not arrive in London until just before Christmas. The first time he laid eyes on his only son, the boy was three weeks old. Isabel had expressed, in Phillip's prolonged absence, an intense desire not to see her son's father, so Miss Prickett carried the sleeping child into the sitting room, where she offered the bundle to Phillip.

"I think it's best that you hold him, Miss Prickett," Phillip had said. He was appalled at the thought that such a young child should be offered by its de facto nurse to what amounted to a total stranger.

"I suppose you're right about that, Mr. Gardner." She sat with the child in her arms for a few minutes, then returned to the nursery. In her absence, Phillip showed himself out.

Walking the cold and dim streets of London, up to Hyde Park where he had once strolled so innocently with Isabel under the summer sun, then on the long walk to Trafalgar Square and up Fleet Street to Benjamin Mayhew's office, Phillip decided that he must not see his son again. He had barely glimpsed the boy's face, but seeing the child, coming face-to-face with the reality of what had happened, had left him torn. This evidence of his sins engendered in Phillip the most horrific feeling of shame and disgust he had ever experienced. At the same time, he was overcome by the sense of connection he felt with that peaceful infant. This was his son, his rightful heir, whom he must never know. Phillip could not bear the thought of returning to the emotional blackness that lay in that narrow space between love and shame. In a few months Isabel and the boy would be gone forever. Until then, he would avoid London.

The wind blowing down from Churchill howled around the eaves of Evenlode House on a March afternoon, as the sun hung low in the pale blue Cotswold sky. Phillip did not envy the workmen who were laying stone high up on the top floor of the new west wing. Mrs. Gardner was once again in Yorkshire visiting her niece, who was not well. Phillip had stayed behind to supervise the work, though today it needed little supervising, and he had remained in his study all day, answering correspondence and reading. He had just put another log on the fire and had settled into his favorite chair when the house-keeper—she was new and Phillip *would* keep forgetting her name—appeared in the doorway, silent as a ghost.

"Yes, what is it?" said Phillip, not pleased at the disturbance.

"A young woman and her companion to see you," she said. "Not knowing the young lady or your wishes, I asked she stay at the door. She's got a . . . well, I was not sure you'd be wanting her in the parlor, sir."

From an upper window of Evenlode Manor, Reginald Alderson squinted into the eyepiece of a long brass telescope, trained on his neighbor's front door a mile and a half away. It had proved useful to pay the stationmaster a few pounds to inform him whenever Mrs. Gardner left the village, but he did wish that she might have left sooner. Nonetheless, Reginald was a patient man. He had been pa-tient all the days he had followed Phillip Gardner through the streets of London, and had been rewarded by seeing him speaking with a young American in the Royal Academy. He had been patient in fol-lowing the girl and discovering her lodgings. He had been patient in waiting for the girl's companion to take a day off—a day when he had placed himself next to Miss Prickett on the train to Brixton and had the first of several useful conversations.

"It's quite a coincidence," he had said, "that I travel to Brixton by this route every Thursday as well."

He had been patient in waiting for Mrs. Gardner to take an extended journey without her husband, but once she had departed, the final phase of his plan had swung into action. Phillip Gardner had written Reginald a taunting letter two years ago, not long after he had married Mrs. Gardner, offering to purchase Reginald's collection of historical documents. Thankfully, Reginald had saved this obscenity, and he had little trouble copying the script in writing the letter that now summoned Isabel, Miss Prickett, and the child to Evenlode House. When Gardner had turned them out, knowing as he must that Mrs. Gardner was due to return that evening, Reginald would conveniently meet them just outside the gate and offer his dear friend Miss Prickett and her young charges lodgings for the night. Once the trio were ensconced in Evenlode Manor, the rest would be easy.

Early in the fall of his senior year at Ridgefield, Peter was reading an assignment for his medieval history class in the Devereaux Room when Francis Leland dropped a dusty cardboard box on the table in front of him.

"How would you feel about getting some extra hours this year?" asked Francis.

"Are there any more hours in the day?" asked Peter. He was already spending most of his waking time either in class or in the library. Francis had him working fifteen hours a week in Special Collections, and he worked with Hank in Conservation when he could. His time had become more limited as he worked to fulfill his academic requirements. The dean had grown tired of Peter's inventing classes—this semester he was taking a full load of courses in English, history, and economics.

"Well, there are six more boxes where this came from, and I think it's time we got this stuff cataloged," said Francis. "Given your . . . personal circumstances and your cataloging talents, you're the perfect man for the job."

"What is it?" Peter asked, his curiosity piqued.

"The personal letters and papers of Ms. Amanda Devereaux," said Francis.

"Are you serious?" said Peter, lunging for the box. "Why didn't you tell me about these before?"

"To be honest," said Francis, "they're not a high priority. Researchers are more interested in Ms. Devereaux's collection than in the lady herself. But now that you're marrying into the family, I thought you might like to learn about manuscript cataloging and Amanda Devereaux at the same time."

"You bet I would," said Peter, pulling open the box while his history text lay on the table, forgotten.

Over the next several months, Peter worked with the Devereaux papers, carefully sorting through correspondence with book collectors and dealers. Every day he told Amanda something new about her grandmother, and Amanda quietly indulged his passion, despite the fact that she could not keep straight the maze of collectors and dealers with whom her grandmother had interacted. On Saturdays, when he and Amanda spent the afternoon at the Ridgefields' house, Peter would sit by the pool or in the sunroom regaling Sarah Ridgefield with tales of her mother's collecting. Sarah showed a genuine interest in what Peter discovered.

"By the time I was old enough to understand what book collecting was, she had slowed down a bit," said Sarah. "I remember that one trip to the auction house in New York, but other than that she didn't share that part of her world with me."

"But didn't you ever look through the papers?" asked Peter.

"It wouldn't have done any good without you to explain who Rosenbach was or Huntington or any of the others. You're an excellent tour guide, Peter," said Sarah, kissing him gently on the cheek.

"I was reading her correspondence with Henry Folger this morning," said Peter.

"You mean the founder of the Folger Shakespeare Library?" asked Sarah.

"Exactly. Folger was *the* Shakespeare collector. They seemed to be pretty good friends. I guess Folger could be a nasty rival when it came to book collecting, but his letters to your mother are really kind."

Amanda Devereaux, Peter discovered, never bid on a Shakespeare First Folio while Folger was alive—a courtesy to her friend who collected dozens of First Folios, by far the largest assemblage in the world. A letter to Amanda from Emily Jordan Folger, written two weeks after her husband's death, read, in part, "He valued your friendship, and will no doubt rejoice in your finally acquiring a First Folio." It was more than fifteen years later that Amanda bought the First Folio from which Peter had so often read.

"So many of the big collectors were kind to her," said Peter, "and treated her like an equal—even though book collecting in those days was pretty much a boys' club. Of course she couldn't join the Grolier Club. She was pretty angry about that."

"What's the Grolier Club?" asked Amanda, who had just come into the room with a look on her face that told Peter she was determined not to let Sarah monopolize her fiancé's conversation.

"It's a club for book collectors in New York," said Peter. "The oldest book-collecting club in America, and it was all boys until the nineteen seventies."

"That must have pissed her off," said Amanda, slipping onto the couch next to Peter.

"Amanda!" said Sarah. "Your language." Peter had noticed that Amanda's speech had become more colorful around her mother lately. When he'd asked her about it, she had shrugged and said she was only trying to see if her mother would notice, but Peter thought there was more to it than that. Since Amanda's parents hadn't been shocked by her choice of a socially unsuitable husband, she was determined to shock them some other way. Peter saw it as part of a plan Amanda seemed to have implemented since her illness to put herself into Peter's world, rather than that of her parents, at every opportunity. He supposed that was what engagements were for—to allow the bride time to move from the world of her parents to the world of her groom—and, of course, Peter was not surprised that his friendship with Sarah Ridgefield, which threatened to make those two worlds one, still annoyed Amanda at times.

"Sorry, Mother," she said, taking Peter's hand and giving him a gentle squeeze. "Do go on, Peter."

"Well, she was so pissed off about the Grolier Club," said Peter, squeezing Amanda's hand back to let her know where his ultimate loyalties lay, "that she became a founding member of the Hroswitha Club."

"The what?" said Sarah.

"The Hroswitha Club," said Peter. "It was a club for lady book collectors founded in nineteen forty-four."

"Ladies?" said Amanda, with a hint of politically correct scorn in her voice.

"That's what women called themselves in nineteen forty-four, dear," said Sarah.

"They met at your mother's apartment in New York one time," Peter continued. "Apparently the Hroswitha Club was suitably impressed."

"The ladies in my family have always known what to do in a roomful of rare books," said Amanda, surreptitiously pinching Peter.

"Whatever can you mean by that, dear?" asked Sarah, but Peter was spared the embarrassment of Amanda's answer by Charlie's call to dinner.

Liz insisted on hearing Peter's account of his trip to Cornwall before she would share with him the contents of Graham Sykes's manuscript, so as they inched through the London traffic, Peter told her of his visit with the old scholar. He skirted around the issue of the *Pandosto*, saying only that Sykes had taken an interest in the document Peter showed him, but even as he danced around the truth, Peter began to see that he had no choice but to trust Liz Sutcliffe. Like it or not, she was now a part of all this. She needed to know the whole story.

"I just don't understand," said Liz. "Graham's manuscript is about a hundred-and-thirty-year-old scandal. Outside the world of Victorian art nuts, who's going to give a toss? There's just nothing in there that's worth . . . worth killing for."

Peter took a breath, then the plunge. "What about the most valuable relic in the history of English literature—would that be worth killing for?"

"How valuable?"

"Millions."

"And where is this relic?" said Liz.

"In the backseat of your car," said Peter.

"Well, now I feel safe," said Liz. "Do you want to tell me what's going on here?"

And so Peter told her everything, from his finding of the painting to his visit to Evenlode Manor and the discovery of the *Pandosto*, to his suspicions that Thomas Gardner and Julia Alderson were trying to cover up the fact that the book was a forgery just long enough to get a few million pounds from some gullible American institution like Ridgefield University. They had reached the M40 by the time he finished his story, but the traffic was nearly at a standstill.

"So if B.B. is a forger," said Liz, "then the *Pandosto* is very likely a fake."

"Exactly," said Peter. "So what can you tell me about B.B.? Was he Phillip Gardner?"

"I don't know," said Liz.

"But I thought Sykes had written a whole exposé of this guy," said Peter.

"To be honest," said Liz, "I was a little disappointed with the manuscript. He seemed to be missing some key information."

"Like the actual identity of his subject?" asked Peter.

"He said he didn't want to tell me that until just before we went to press," said Liz. "He just calls him 'Mr. X.' But here's what I do know. B.B. was an amateur artist who was kept out of the Royal Academy and the Watercolour Society by someone named Reginald Alderson."

"John Alderson's ancestor," said Peter. "So it does come back to Kingham. B.B. must be Gardner."

"According to Sykes, B.B. married a wealthy widow who was keeping him in clover and financing the rebuilding of his house. Then he took up with an American woman in London and made the mistake of getting her pregnant. Rather a big mistake for a kept man to make in eighteen seventy-six."

"Just like the old sisters told me," said Peter, "but they didn't know about the pregnancy."

"Alderson found out about the affair and started blackmailing B.B., but Sykes is a little fuzzy on exactly what Alderson was extorting. Alderson was pretty well off, and blackmail seems a big risk for a wealthy man to take just to become more wealthy. Apparently most of B.B.'s surviving output is hanging on the walls of Evenlode Manor, but Sykes says they're fairly unimaginative paintings—watercolors mostly—and since Alderson kept B.B. out of the Royal Academy, why would he have extorted paintings he could have bought for next to nothing?"

"I know exactly what he extorted," said Peter. "I've held it in my hand."

"The *Pandosto*?" asked Liz.

"Maybe," said Peter. "But that wasn't the only thing in Evenlode Manor that came from Evenlode House. Every document in that box that Julia Alderson showed me was marked 'E.H.' Alderson and Gardner were rival collectors; Alderson must have blackmailed Gardner out of all his best material."

"Would a collector really stoop to blackmail just to get some old documents?" asked Liz.

"You haven't spent much time around bibliophiles, have you?" asked Peter. He recalled the lengths to which Thomas Wise and Mark Hofmann had been driven by their passions. Perhaps B.B. wasn't a forger, but simply a victim of blackmail. Perhaps the *Pandosto* was genuine.

"One thing Sykes is firm on," said Liz, "is the dates. He says the child was born in late eighteen seventy-six; the blackmail began the following spring and continued for about two years. Then whatever trail of evidence Sykes was following apparently went dry. That's why I was so pissed off at the manuscript. It raises more questions than it answers. What happened to the child? What happened to the mistress? Why was the whole extortion affair so short lived?"

"Where did Sykes get all his information?" asked Peter.

"A lot of it came from B.B.'s correspondence with his bookseller. Chap named Benjamin Mayhew."

"Are you serious?" said Peter.

"As a heart attack," said Liz.

"Benjamin Mayhew is one of the names in the *Pandosto*."

"Well, that makes sense. So who the hell was B.B.?"

"He had to be Phillip Gardner," said Peter. "The evidence fits perfectly. Obviously Sykes never saw the box of documents or he would have figured out what the blackmail was all about."

"Did you tell him about the other documents?" asked Liz.

"No," said Peter, "just the *Pandosto*. Frankly, everything else paled by comparison."

"There's something else you need to know," said Liz, after they had driven a few miles in silence. The traffic had finally thinned out on the motorway and they were barreling toward Oxford.

"What's that?" said Peter.

"Well," said Liz, "you seem convinced that Thomas Gardner and Julia Alderson are the ones who killed Sykes and ransacked my house and office."

"It had to be them," said Peter.

"Well, it couldn't have been both of them," said Liz, "because I phoned Evenlode Manor this morning from a phone box in Hampstead on my way back from the heath and spoke with Julia Alderson. She can't have been in London ransacking my office."

"Why on earth did you call her?" said Peter, jerking forward in his seat for the first time since they had left London.

"Graham mentioned her in his acknowledgments as the person who had shown him B.B.'s watercolors. I wanted to try to talk her into letting us reproduce them for the book."

"And what did she say?" asked Peter.

"She's expecting me for tea tomorrow at three."

Benjamin Mayhew slipped into his usual seat in Sotheby's sales-room. Across the room, leaning in the doorway, was the familiar brooding figure of Reginald Alderson. Looking through the catalog of the day's sale, Benjamin reflected how disappointing the afternoon was likely to be for Reginald. Benjamin knew that Reginald collected documents signed by the kings and queens of England. He knew, too, that Alderson's collection lacked the signatures of only four monarchs, and all four were represented in that afternoon's sale—four documents that would be leaving Sotheby's with Benjamin Mayhew bound to Evenlode House and the collection of Phillip Gardner.

Benjamin glanced up at Alderson again and realized that he was not, after all, brooding, as was his wont during these fruitless appearances at Sotheby's. On the contrary, a sly smile played across Alderson's face as he brushed a hank of hair back from his forehead.

As the auction progressed, Alderson's behavior became even stranger. He did not move from his spot in the doorway, nor did he lift a hand to bid on the documents that Mayhew knew he so coveted. This must have come as a disappointment to the consignor, for the spirited bidding between Alderson and Mayhew had driven the prices of documents to new heights recently, and it was generally assumed among the antiquarians of London that today's auction would be no exception. Instead, Mayhew easily bought the four royal documents, as well as several other choice items, without a serious challenger. Alderson seemed amused by the whole affair. As soon as the final hammer fell, he tipped his hat to Mayhew and disappeared from the room, now buzzing with gossip about the sale. Mayhew accepted the congratulations of his colleagues perfunctorily, for pleased as he was to be bearing new treasures to his best customer, he had a nagging feeling that Reginald Alderson was up to something.

Two days after the Sotheby's sale, Phillip Gardner came up to London to claim his prizes. Far from being the gloating victor that Benjamin usually saw after a successful auction, Phillip slumped into the bookseller's office a picture of abject defeat.

"You do know that we won," said Mayhew, opening a large portfolio on his desk and displaying the documents that now belonged to Gardner. "Some spectacular acquisitions, and at an excellent price." Phillip did not so much as glance at the documents, but with a long sigh, he merely fell into a plush armchair under the window.

"Do you know of a fellow named Collier?" said Gardner. "John Payne Collier."

"I know of his work," said Mayhew, puzzled by the abruptness of the incongruous question.

"But you don't know him personally? He's not a customer?"

"No," said Mayhew. "Is he still alive? He must be quite an old man by now. He was living in Maidenhead, last I heard. There was always something of a taint to his work after that business with the Shakespeare folio."

"He forged the marginalia, isn't that right?" asked Gardner.

"So it would seem. I was a young man at the time, first starting out in the book business. It caused quite a stir, I can tell you."

"And he lives in Maidenhead, you say?"

"I suppose if he's still alive he may still be there. Why this sudden interest in Collier?"

"I've been thinking about starting a collection of books on forgery," said Gardner.

"That's quite a departure."

"Not at all," said Gardner. "It seems to me that a man who collects documents should know as much about forgery as he can, if only to protect himself." Benjamin knew enough about the eccentricities of collectors not to question the motivation behind a fresh passion, but merely to take that new interest as an opportunity for additional sales.

"Is it just the Shakespeare forgers you're interested in, or is it any forgery?" asked Mayhew.

"Any of them, I suppose," said Gardner. "Are there other Shakespeare forgers?"

"I think I might be able to get you a nice little collection of books on William Henry Ireland," said Mayhew. "He was the greatest. Forged manuscripts, letters, all sorts of things. He was absolutely shameless."

"And would these books tell how he did it?" asked Gardner, and for the first time in the conversation, Benjamin Mayhew suspected that he knew what his customer was thinking.

Ridgefield, 1987

The Ridgefield campus was a riot of dogwoods and azaleas and the students had returned from Easter break in shorts and T-shirts, when Peter pulled the last stack of letters from the last box of Amanda Devereaux's papers and finally found something he could not share with Sarah and Amanda—a correspondence that, unique among the papers he had cataloged, showed Amanda Devereaux not as a book collector but as a woman: the correspondence between Amanda Devereaux and her future husband, Robert Ridgefield.

They had met in the New York salesroom of Sotheby's, where Robert Ridgefield's first encounter with Amanda Devereaux had left him both outbid and smitten. She had just turned forty; he was twenty years her senior. They corresponded first about books—Ridgefield was not a serious collector, but occasionally bid on something that struck his fancy. They saw each other in New York, where Ridgefield lived during most of the season. Amanda liked to be in the auction room for important sales, and Ridgefield soon learned to follow the schedules at Sotheby's and Parke-Bernet so he did not miss a chance to encounter her.

Protestations of love gradually crept into Ridgefield's letters to Amanda Devereaux; her letters to him were concerned mostly with points of bibliography, but she did not rebuff his epistolary advances nor his increasingly frequent invitations to social events. This delicate dance between the aging banker and the brilliant book collector culminated in the spring of 1939. The final letter in the collection, which Peter felt compelled to hide from both Sarah Ridgefield and her daughter, was dated May 2.

My Dear Mr. Ridgefield,

I write to respond to your kind proposal of the twenty-fifth, for which I thank you. I have for many years considered myself a spinster and have had no thought of marriage—my books being both husband and children to me. However, as I approach the age after which such positions cannot be recanted, I begin to feel that not only a husband clothed in flesh and blood, but similarly attired children, if it be God's will, would enrich my life in a way that my books, precious to me though they may be, have never done.

It is my potential acquisition of the latter that compels me to write you. For years I have ignored the protestation of both family and friends that a woman's life cannot be complete without children. I fancied myself a "modern girl" above such things. However, in more recent years I have gradually come to agree with a great collecting compatriot who once told me that children were the greatest blessing of his life and that the absence of them in my own would be my great sadness.

You are not a young man, Mr. Ridgefield, and although you may represent my only opportunity to add a husband to my collection, I could not in good conscience accept your proposal without telling you this—at this late stage of my life, for I have completed four decades as you know, I have a deep yearning for motherhood, which I would expect any husband to honor. At your age, you may not relish the thought of becoming a father, and I would quite understand your feelings in that case. If, however, you are willing to give me a chance at motherhood, I will, with humility and genuine affection, accept your proposal of marriage.

Yours,

Amanda Devereaux

Ridgefield had obviously agreed to the terms of Ms. Devereaux's acceptance; eleven months later, Sarah Ridgefield had been born. But Peter's heart ached for Ms. Devereaux's granddaughter when he read this letter. No matter how much Amanda pretended not to be bothered by the fact that she could not bear children, Peter knew the day would come when she would feel that void in her life that her grandmother had felt. But for Amanda there would be no wealthy banker waiting in the wings to provide her with progeny. There would be only Peter, trying to help her cope with her loss.

Two weeks after filing the last of the folders containing the Devereaux papers in its archival storage box, Peter Byerly graduated from Ridgefield University.

"Another year and this will be you," said Peter, as Amanda found him in the crowd and admired his academic finery. Charlie Ridgefield clapped him on the back and Sarah kissed his cheek. Peter's parents arrived late and missed the ceremony.

For three years, Peter had successfully kept his own parents and Amanda's from coming face-to-face—an effort in which he was abetted by the apathy of his mother and father. The Byerlys had met Amanda twice—once on campus and once when she insisted that Peter take her home for Thanksgiving dinner. On both occasions he had introduced her only as Amanda, and made no mention of her wealthy family.

Though both the Ridgefields' mansion and his parents' farmhouse sat on several acres of undeveloped land, and though they were only eight miles apart, the inhabitants of those homes could not have come from more different worlds. Two hours after his graduation, at a reception given in his honor by Amanda and her parents, those worlds collided.

Peter's father, Joseph Byerly, looked stiff and uncomfortable in a pressed suit and ineptly tied tie, which his wife, Doreen, had obviously forced him to wear for the occasion. He lurked in the corner of the patio, within striking distance of the one thing in the world of the Ridgefields that he understood—the bar. His father's unobtrusive, if increasingly inebriated, presence was far preferable to that of Peter's mother, whose lime green concoction of a dress looked like something made from the curtains of a double-wide trailer. Doreen Byerly swept through the throng of professors, parents, recent graduates, and Ridgefields as if she were the hostess.

"That's my son, Peter," she would say to anyone who would listen, loud enough to be heard at the end of the drive. "He's engaged to Amanda Ridgefield, you know. All this will be his someday."

After an hour of this, Peter sought refuge in the guest room where Amanda found him. "Is the guest of honor hiding?" she teased, pushing him onto a bed and kissing him hard on the lips.

"Are you sure you want to marry into that family?" asked Peter, nodding toward the door. He was just imagining his parents living in the guesthouse and frightening the grandchildren when he remembered there would be no grandchildren.

"I'm willing to take the good with the slightly embarrassing," said Amanda.

"Don't worry, I'll tell Dad not to bring Mom back here again until the wedding. I'll tell him as soon as he sobers up," said Peter, now giggling as Amanda tugged at his belt. "That should be in about nineteen ninety-five."

"Parents are supposed to be embarrassing," said Amanda, sliding a hand into Peter's pants.

"You do realize that every socialite in Ridgefield is on the other side of that door," said Peter.

"If they only knew," said Amanda, "that prim and proper Miss Amanda Ridgefield is having her wicked way in the guest room with a college graduate." When Peter and Amanda slipped back into the party a half hour later, Mr. and Mrs. Byerly had left.

———

As it turned out, they would not come back for the wedding. Two months after Peter's graduation, his father drove his pickup truck, containing his wife and two empty scotch bottles, off I-40 at ninety-three miles an hour. The night after the funeral, as Peter lay in Amanda's arms on the narrow single bed in his childhood bedroom, he was overcome by the feeling that he was now a child without parents on the verge of becoming a spouse without children. Though his parents had been, for most of his life, either a burden or an embarrassment; though he had resented them for their neglect, at times even hated them, they were nonetheless his parents. As much as he had tried to pretend they were not a part of who he was, he knew he had lost a part of his own being.

"You never talked about them much," said Amanda.

"No."

"You can talk to me about anything, you know."

"I know that," said Peter, squeezing Amanda's arm. "That's why I love you."

"Did you love them?"

Peter stared at the ceiling for a long time before answering.

"I wish I knew."

About the time he and Liz were wending their way through Wood-stock, past the imposing gates of Blenheim Palace, Peter glanced in the mirror and saw Amanda sitting in the backseat. She winked at him, but when he turned to speak to her, she was gone. On the seat was nothing but Peter's satchel, containing his future—be it glory or doom.

"Oh, I forgot to tell you," said Liz, pulling Peter's attention back to the front seat. "I found out about W. H. Smith. I called Lawrence last night. He's the speaker I told you about. He's a great-great-great-nephew, it turns out."

"What did you find out?" asked Peter, who had almost forgotten about this line of inquiry.

"Well, if Shakespeare is part of this mystery, it's not surprising Smith is involved. He was one of the original anti-Stratfordians."

"You're kidding," said Peter.

"He thought Francis Bacon wrote Shakespeare's plays," said Liz. "He wrote a pamphlet in the eighteen fifties, I think, and then a book a little after that."

"And this is the same guy who ran the chain of newsagents and was . . . what did you call it, Lord of the Admiralty or something?"

"Sir Joseph Porter, K.C.B. in *H.M.S. Pinafore*," said Liz with a giggle. "The same man."

"Why would Smith think Bacon wrote the plays if he had seen the *Pandosto?*" said Peter.

"Did he see it?" asked Liz. "What did the inscription say exactly?"

Peter reached into the backseat and retrieved his bag. He carefully removed the book from its envelope. He cringed to think to what dangers he had exposed this potential treasure in the past two days. He gently opened the front cover and read the relevant entry in the list of owners. "B. Mayhew for William H. Smith."

"So I guess Mayhew sold books to B.B. *and* W. H. Smith."

"Maybe so," said Peter.

"It doesn't exactly say Smith owned it, though, does it?" said Liz.

"Even if he did," said Peter, "what if he found it after he was on the record for Bacon?"

"It could have been embarrassing," said Liz.

"Imagine this," said Peter, warming to his hypothetical tale. "Mayhew gets hold of the *Pandosto* somehow. The previous name on this list is Robert Harley, who would have owned it in the early eighteenth century. So it's been hidden away somewhere for a hundred and fifty years or so.

"Mayhew knows W. H. Smith—he's a customer—and Mayhew doesn't want Smith exposed to the embarrassment of having his Bacon theory refuted. So he has a nice folding box made, because he can't stand not to protect such a treasure. He was a bookseller, after all—he'd want to preserve the *Pandosto*."

"Yes, they're such a noble breed," said Liz, smiling.

"And then he hides the book away in Evenlode House, figuring B.B. won't realize what it is and it will stay safely undiscovered until after Smith is dead."

"Seems a bit risky," said Liz. "I mean, if B.B. was a document collector, he'd know what he had. And if Mayhew really wanted to hide it, why not destroy it?"

"He couldn't bear to do that," said Peter. "Not if he was a bibliophile. It's in our blood to preserve such things."

"Oh, right, I forgot how upright and moral you all are. But what if Mayhew was a forger and he made this phony Shakespeare relic so he could extort the extremely wealthy W. H. Smith by threatening to disprove his Bacon theory?" asked Liz. "Wouldn't that make more sense?"

"But we think B.B. was the most likely forger," said Peter. "He was the artist."

"He was also friends with Mayhew. It sounds to me like you just want a version of the story that lets the *Pandosto* be genuine."

"It would be nice," Peter admitted.

"What about this box you were talking about?" said Liz. "Where's that?"

"I left it at home," said Peter. "But it's definitely nineteenth century, so it had to have been made by one of the last names on the list—or for them, at any rate."

"So what are we going to do when we get to Kingham, exactly?" said Liz. "Walk up to Thomas Gardner and say, 'Hello, are you a murderer, and if so, why?'"

Peter recalled his last encounter with Thomas Gardner. He recalled, too, the rumors the old sisters in Kingham had spoken of—that Phillip Gardner had been murdered by his wife and buried in the family chapel, perhaps with his mistress.

"I'd sure like to see the inside of the Gardner chapel," said Peter, almost to himself.

"Wait a minute—I think Graham might have seen it," said Liz.

"You're kidding," said Peter.

"He said something to me about going through an old chapel in the country when he was doing his research. Said the whole thing made him nervous because the fellow who was showing him around carried a bloody shotgun the whole time."

"Thomas Gardner!" said Peter. "It has to be."

"Anyhow," said Liz, "Graham said he spent an hour going over every stone in this chapel with Gardner or whoever it was."

"And did he find what he was looking for?" asked Peter.

"No, he said it was a dead end. But he said he got the feeling this bloke with the shotgun was hiding something."

"I'll bet he was," said Peter.

"Well," said Liz, as she turned toward Chipping Norton, "whatever else we do when we get to Kingham, we're going to have to get into that chapel."

Personal misfortune was part of Benjamin Mayhew's stock-in-trade. Though he usually sold books to those whose lives were going well, he most often acquired new stock when someone had lost a career, a fortune, or a life. This morning was no different, he thought, spreading out the *Times* on his desk and perusing the obituaries. He was surprised to see the name of a certain nobleman whose library he had visited on several occasions. Benjamin had sold him a few books over the years, but not enough, perhaps, to be considered the family's bookman of choice. Still, he well remembered one visit to the stately home in Cambridgeshire when the eldest son of the family had stood in the library and said, "It shall need to be culled a bit after father is gone."

Indeed it was an overstuffed library, with books so heaped upon books that few could be either found when needed or appreciated as things of beauty when not. Benjamin was on the next train out of King's Cross. The son, whose remarks about the library Benjamin had recalled, recognized immediately the purpose of his visit.

"I'm afraid you're too late," he said.

"So I understand," said Benjamin with sympathy. "I shall miss my friendship with your father."

"You and father were never friends," said the son flatly. "And I meant that you are too late for the books. Father let me sell off nearly half the library three months ago." Benjamin winced internally at this news, angry that some other bookseller had beat him to what was doubtless a treasure trove. "You can have a look at the Shakespeare folios if you like, though. Father insisted we keep them until he died, but I'll be glad to get rid of them."

Benjamin remembered the deceased gentleman's attitude toward his Shakespeare folios. Family legend, he said, described them as a Second and Fourth Folio, respectively. But he, like his father, refused to allow them to be removed from the shelf, or even touched. They were a revered family treasure, a precious relic of past glories off-limits to present generations. If they were as the old man had described them, Benjamin could almost certainly sell them to one of his wealthy American clients with a single telegram. He followed the son into the significantly pared-down library.

"I shall expect a high price," said the son. "Have a look and I'll be back in half an hour. I've more important things to attend to than old books. They're on the bottom shelf, under the Gainsborough." He turned and left Benjamin alone.

With trembling hands, Benjamin gently pulled from the shelf one of the tightly wedged folios bearing the name W. SHAKESPEARE on the spine. It thrilled him to think that no other hands had touched this book for at least a generation. The binding was in remarkable condition, and Benjamin suspected it was an early eighteenth-century rebind. He opened the book carefully to its center and stared dumbfounded at the pages. He didn't know whether to laugh or be angry. They were completely blank.

He flipped through the pages to the back of the book, without finding a single line of type. Turning to the front of the volume, he discovered that it did have the title page of the Second Folio edition of Shakespeare's works, published in 1632. The works themselves, however, were missing. Following the title page there were eight pages comprising part of the third act of *Othello*. The rest of the volume was nothing but blank paper. No wonder the old man's father hadn't wanted anyone to touch the precious folios. Benjamin had seen this binding trick before used to make a pamphlet or other slim piece look more like a complete book. He couldn't believe that the lord of this manor had been so hoodwinked by his own father. He laid the book to one side and opened the second volume, the one that purported to be a Fourth Folio of 1685. Again the title page was correct, and as Benjamin fanned out the pages, he saw that they all contained type. Perhaps the day wouldn't be a total loss. But as he began to carefully page through the volume, he discovered several plays were missing. Without *Hamlet, King Lear, A Midsummer Night's Dream,* and *A Winter's Tale* a Fourth Folio was little more than a curiosity. Benjamin saw no point in doing anything but laughing, though he tried to keep as quiet as he could out of respect for the mourners.

He was just about to replace the folios when he noticed, far in the back of the shelf, a slim volume that had apparently been pressed between them. Judging from the way the back half of the binding was compressed, Benjamin guessed that the book had been there at least as long as the ban on moving the folios had been in place—possibly longer. This binding, worn and battered, looked like it could date from the seventeenth century, or even earlier. He gingerly opened the cover to see if it might contain anything that would make his trip worthwhile.

Benjamin knew the works of Robert Greene well—he had sold many of Greene's pamphlets to customers in Britain and America, but he had never seen a copy of this, the first printing of the romance *Pandosto.* It was not the book itself, however, but the marginalia that caught Benjamin's eye. It did not take him long to deduce exactly what he held in his hand. At a lecture given by his friend William Henry Smith, putting forth Smith's theory of Francis Bacon as the author of Shakespeare's plays, Benjamin had heard Smith say, "If anyone can present to me a single piece of contemporary evidence that links William Shakespeare of Stratford to the plays published under that name, I shall recant my position entirely." But afterward, as the two men were walking to Smith's club, he had confided in Benjamin, "It would be quite embarrassing, were it ever to happen."

"Don't worry," Benjamin had said. "It won't."

Now Benjamin sat poring over just such a document. How it had survived undetected for over 250 years he could not imagine, but he did not doubt that when this copy of *Pandosto* was made public, Smith's humiliation would soon follow.

If Benjamin tried to buy the *Pandosto*, no doubt the young man who would soon be returning to the library would realize what it was, and in no time every book dealer and collector in the world would be bearing down on Sotheby's for a very public auction. It was unlikely that he, Benjamin, would make a brass farthing off the book. If, on the other hand, he suppressed the book to prevent Smith's embarrassment, he might someday be rewarded by the First Lord of the Admiralty. He closed the book and slipped it into his newspaper.

"I couldn't offer you what these folios are worth," he told the new lord of the manor a few minutes later, reflecting that, in a way, this was true.

"Sorry to waste your time then," said the young man. "You can show yourself out."

"Don't get me wrong," said Charlie Ridgefield, taking a sip of bourbon. "I love my wife. You understand that because you love her, too, don't you?"

"She's the only mother I have now," said Peter, staring into his empty glass, "and she understands me better than my own mother ever did."

The two men sat in a dim corner of the patio behind the house. The other rehearsal dinner guests had gradually drifted off to bed, some to spare rooms in the house and the guesthouse, others to the Marriott in downtown Ridgefield. The wedding would cap three days of events that had begun with Amanda's graduation. Peter hadn't noticed the moment when he and Amanda's father were left alone, but it had been at least a half hour since anyone else had been on the patio. Whether Charlie Ridgefield had planned this pre-wedding confessional with his future son-in-law, or whether the conversation in which Peter now found himself was merely a confluence of opportunity, emotion, and Jim Beam he could not guess, but Charlie was speaking more freely to Peter than he ever had.

"It's just that being married to a Ridgefield . . . well, it's a challenge," said Charlie. "This is a small town, Peter, and the world of people as wealthy as the Ridgefields—it's a small world. I don't care how much you're in love, there are a lot of people who will assume you're marrying a Ridgefield for one reason and one reason only."

"Money," said Peter.

"Exactly."

"I know why I'm marrying Amanda," said Peter. "I don't really care what other people think."

"Don't you?" said Charlie. "I was a business major in college and I really like business. When I got married and settled, I decided to go into banking and I loved it. I loved the idea that I could start out at the bottom and work my way up and that every promotion I got would be something I earned with my own hard work. Well, as soon as they found out I was married to Sarah Ridgefield, all that went out the window. My boss assumed I didn't need a promotion because I was just working as a hobby. When I did get promoted, everyone else assumed it was because of who I was married to, not because I deserved it. I was damned if I did and damned if I didn't. I finally gave up and went to work for Ridgefield Bank. There at least I could keep moving up the ladder and if people wanted to think it was because of who I was, well fuck 'em." He took another swig of bourbon.

"But I'm not going into business," said Peter. "I think the world of antiquarian bookselling is a little different from banking."

"Is it?" said Charlie. "Tell me, Peter, why do you want to be a bookseller?"

"It's my passion," said Peter. "I know it might seem silly to some people, but it's the way I want to change the world. To bring books together with people who will love them and preserve them for the next generation."

"Your passion, exactly. And you deserve some respect for that, right?"

"I suppose," said Peter. "Like I said, I've never been that concerned about what people think of me."

"But how would you feel if these people that you're bringing together with books, the people who share your passion, think of you as a little rich boy just playing a game? The very people that you want to use to change the world look at you and don't see a passion—at best they see a hobby, something to pass the time between golf games and debutante balls."

"They'd be wrong," said Peter, more loudly than he had intended, for he suddenly understood what Charlie was saying—that his dream of being a well-respected member of the rare-book community could end the moment he said "I do."

"You bet your ass they'd be wrong," said Charlie. "You know that and I know that, but right and wrong don't matter in this game, son. All that matters is what people think, and the minute they find out who you're married to it's game, set, and match. Welcome to the Ridgefields." Charlie drained his glass and stood up. "See you at the altar, son," he said, and staggered across the patio into the house, leaving Peter alone in the darkness.

Peter and Amanda lay breathless and tangled in the sheets on their third night in London and their fifth night as man and wife. Amanda's parents had insisted on paying for the honeymoon, and the newlyweds had enjoyed first-class tickets to London and a suite at The Ritz. Through it all, Peter had tried, without success, to forget his conversation with Charlie Ridgefield.

"Beds are fabulous," said Amanda. "Beds are even better than the carpet in the Devereaux Room."

"We've made love in a bed before," said Peter.

"Yes, but these are, like, eight-hundred-thread-count sheets. I love you and I love this bed."

"Can I ask you something?" said Peter.

"You can ask me anything, Mr. Byerly," said Amanda. "After all, I'm Mrs. Byerly. I like the sound of that. Mrs. Amanda Byerly wrapped in the arms of Mr. Peter Byerly and a set of eight-hundred-thread-count sheets."

"Would you love me even without the eight-hundred-thread-count sheets?" said Peter.

"Of course. What are you talking about?"

"It's just something your dad said to me the other night."

"After the rehearsal dinner? God, I'm sorry. He was drunk, wasn't he? He doesn't get drunk very often, but when he does he tends to get morose."

"He wasn't morose," said Peter, "just honest."

"What did he say?" Amanda asked, tracing lazy circles on Peter's chest with her manicured fingernail.

"He said . . . well, I guess he said that people are going to think I married you for your money."

"But you know that's not true."

"Sure I do," said Peter. "But he said that people won't . . . they won't take me seriously—as a bookseller, I mean. They'll think I'm just doing it as a hobby, that I'm living off your money."

"Well, that's just silly," said Amanda.

"Is it?" said Peter. "If we live in a big house and drive nice cars and fly first class to England whenever we want, people are going to know it's not bookselling that pays for all that."

"What are you saying, that Daddy is a kept man?"

"He feels that way sometimes, yes."

"When he's drunk," said Amanda, rolling away from Peter.

"Look," said Peter, "it's great that we don't have to worry about money, that we can afford to live where we want and do what we want, but it's just . . ."

"What?"

"It's just that I'd like to know that we can make it on our own. That we would make it even if you weren't a Ridgefield."

Amanda lay silent for a long moment. "Peter," she said at last, "would you still love me if I wasn't pretty?"

"You know I would," said Peter.

"And would you still love me if I had some horrible disease or if I were crippled?"

"Of course."

"Of course you would. Because the way I look and the way my body works, that's all part of who I am. Well, being a Ridgefield is part of who I am, too. For a long time I tried to deny that, but you're the one who helped me understand it was okay. And now you're asking me to hide who I am."

"I'm not asking you to hide who you are," said Peter. "I love your family, you know that. And I want them to be a part of our lives. I just think it would be nice to try . . . well, living on the money we actually earn. Would it be so terrible to start out in an apartment like most married couples?"

"No," said Amanda softly. "That wouldn't be terrible at all." She slipped her hand into his. "Can I decorate the apartment?"

"You don't mind?" asked Peter. "I mean, if we just set the family money aside for now?"

"Peter, I can give up eight-hundred-thread-count sheets and first-class flights and fancy cars and houses and everything else that goes with Ridgefield money. I mean, those things are nice, but who cares about nice. It's not the money that matters to me, it's my family and you—especially you. I love you. You, Peter Byerly, are what I need."

"But these are nice sheets," said Peter.

"Yeah, I think if I'm going to be living in a tiny apartment and shopping at Kmart, I definitely need to make love a few more times in these sheets." She pulled him into her arms and Peter felt a surge of love so intense he thought he might explode.

Kingham, Tuesday, February 21, 1995

It was dark by the time Peter and Liz rolled into Kingham. Peter was afraid someone might be watching his cottage, so he turned off West Street after passing the green and drove on through the village, crunching to a halt in the gravel car park of the Mill House Hotel. Peter had never actually been inside the hotel, though he had passed it often enough on his way to the train station.

At a small reception desk in the stone-floored foyer, he asked for two rooms and gave his name as Robert Cotton. Liz had suggested that, if the cottage was being watched, the local hotel might not be entirely safe either. When Peter reached for a credit card, she pulled him away from the desk and whispered, "Don't you ever watch crime dramas? They can trace those, you know. How much cash have you got?"

As it turned out, Peter had only enough cash for one room, and was just thinking that the King's Head, a mile away in Bledington, might be less expensive when Liz stepped forward and said, in a remarkably convincing American accent, "One twin-bedded room, please. My brother and I are used to sharing."

Peter fell onto his bed exhausted as soon as they had closed the door, but Liz paced in front of the window, which she had opened to let in the cool night air. "All the answers are right out there," she said, peering into the darkness. "It's going to drive me crazy to just sit here all night."

"You could sleep," Peter suggested.

"Are you kidding?" said Liz. "I've never been so awake." She leaned out the window and took a deep breath. "By the way," she said, "thanks for coming to my rescue. That was very gallant." She sat on the edge of Peter's bed and gave him a kiss on the cheek.

Peter had not thought of himself as gallant, but he found the kiss surprisingly pleasant. Just as he felt himself beginning to blush, Liz stood up and said, "I think I'll go down to the bar and get us some sandwiches. Nobody in Kingham knows me, so it should be safe."

When Liz had left, Peter kicked off his shoes and pulled the duvet over himself. He was just drifting off to sleep when he saw Amanda lying on the other bed, gazing at him across the small gap. "Sleeping with another woman, I see," she said.

"It's not like that," said Peter.

"I don't mind," she said.

"I know. But it's not like that," Peter repeated, barely able to focus on Amanda's eyes.

"I want you to be happy, Peter," she said.

"I am happy," said Peter.

"Peter," said Amanda in a scolding tone.

"Okay, maybe not happy," said Peter, "but these last few days, I've felt more alive than I have since . . ."

"Alive is good," said Amanda. "Alive is a start." Peter lay for several minutes, struggling to keep his eyes open so he could take in the sight of Amanda. "Liz is nice," she said at last.

"She's just a friend," murmured Peter.

He had no idea how much time had passed when Liz shook him awake. Where Amanda had been he saw only a tray of sandwiches. "I've got news," Liz said, as Peter hoisted himself into a sitting position. She thrust a cheese and pickle sandwich at him and he began to nibble the bread.

"I think I met your sisters in the bar," Liz began. "The two old ladies you told me about. I didn't ask their names because I didn't want to look like I was prying, but it must have been them. Apparently

Tuesday is their night out. Well, they were just filled with gossip. It seems you missed quite the little country drama while you were gone. Evidently Thomas Gardner was hunting pheasants out behind what's left of Evenlode House, and pheasants aren't even in season, though I wouldn't have known that, but I guess everyone else in the village did, because they kept dwelling on that particular aspect of the story—that Thomas Gardner was hunting bloody pheasants out of season—not on what actually happened to Thomas Gardner while he was hunting pheasants out of season." Liz paused to take a breath.

"Is there a point here?" asked Peter hopefully.

"Sorry, sorry," said Liz. "I chatter when I'm excited. Anyway, this was two days ago and apparently Thomas dropped his gun or something and it went off, I'm not sure exactly how, there was some argument over the details, but basically he shot himself in the leg."

"Thomas Gardner shot himself in the leg?" Peter suppressed a laugh as he recalled running full speed down the drive from Evenlode House to avoid the business end of Gardner's shotgun.

"*Two days ago* Thomas Gardner shot himself in the leg. He limped out to the main road and collapsed on the verge where the vicar found him. He's been lying in a bed in hospital up at Chipping Norton ever since."

Peter exhaled loudly. "So he couldn't have killed Graham Sykes."

"Thomas Gardner and Julia Alderson both have alibis," said Liz, taking a bite of her sandwich and staring at Peter with a grin. "You don't see what else this means, do you?" she said.

"What?"

"Thomas Gardner is in hospital in Chipping Norton. Rumor is he may come home tomorrow, but for tonight Evenlode House is unguarded."

"The chapel," said Peter, feeling a surge of energy course through his veins.

"Exactly," said Liz. "If we want to see the inside of that chapel, to-night's the night."

By climbing his back neighbor's wall, Peter and Liz were able to enter Peter's cottage through the conservatory, well hidden from the street in case anyone was watching. They did not turn on any lights, but a pale moon gave enough light for Peter to find what he needed—a flashlight, an Ordnance Survey map, a plastic zip bag full of antianx-iety medicine, and his lifting knife. This last he found in the box of binding supplies that Liz fell over in the sitting room.

"You could have bloody well picked up before you left," she said.

"I didn't know I'd be sneaking back in the middle of the night," said Peter, "with company."

When he slipped the knife out of the box and into his satchel, Liz asked him what it was for. "I don't know," said Peter, "but it's the sharpest thing I own and it might come in handy." Just as they were about to leave, Peter noticed the flashing light on the answering ma-chine. He turned the volume down and pressed Play.

"Peter, it's Nigel at the British Museum. I've got those test results back for you. The paper is definitely late sixteenth century. The ink is more of a bother. Without sending it out for more extensive testing than we can do here, all I can say for sure is that it's not modern. Could easily be sixteenth century as well, but I can't say for certain. If you'd like, I can send it for carbon dating, but that could be a bit ex-pensive. Just let me know. Cheerio."

"So maybe the *Pandosto* is real," said Liz.

"Maybe so, maybe not," said Peter.

The second message was from Francis Leland. "I haven't found any-thing on Matthew Harbottle or Benjamin Mayhew yet," he said, "but you're going to laugh when I tell you about William H. Smith. Give me a call and I'll give you the details, but the short version is he started a chain of newsagents and he was one of the first anti-Stratfordians."

"Don't I know it," said Peter, clicking off the machine.

Back at the Mill House, Peter pored over the map and found, as he suspected, a footpath running toward Cornwall that skirted the bottom of the hill below Evenlode House. "That will be safer than going by road," said Peter.

"What about getting into the chapel?" asked Liz. "Don't you think it will be locked?"

"Too bad I didn't have a crowbar at home," said Peter. "It's not a standard tool of the antiquarian book trade."

"I've got a wheel wrench in the car," said Liz. And with this weapon added to their arsenal, they made their way back through the village and onto the footpath that led out of Kingham and across the dark fields.

Peter had never been on this footpath. Even in the light of day it would not have been easy to follow, with the frequent interruption of fences and hedgerows where gates or passages had to be found. In the dark it was nearly impossible, but they dared not use the flashlight. A light bouncing across the valley toward Evenlode House would be visible to anyone watching from the ridge—or from the windows of Evenlode Manor.

After nearly an hour of creeping along, they reached the gurgling River Evenlode. High on a hill to the left they could just glimpse the gloomy silhouette of Evenlode House in the pale moonlight.

"According to Louisa," whispered Peter, "the chapel is at the bottom of this hill. So it should be nearby." They made their way slowly along the riverbank until they reached a stone wall.

"The edge of Gardner's property?" asked Liz.

"Must be," said Peter. Liz nimbly climbed the wall and jumped to the other side. Peter was less agile and managed to rip the leg of his pants as he leapt to the ground. A short distance in front of them, a small clump of trees and bushes provided the only possible hiding place in the area for a chapel. "Louisa said the chapel was covered with vines," said Peter as he pulled Liz by the hand toward the trees. "It's got to be in here."

They ducked under low branches and into complete darkness. The limbs of the trees blocked out what little light the moon was still giving off through the mist that was wafting up from the river.

"Even if we find it, how will we see to get in?" Liz asked.

"We'll have to risk the flashlight," Peter answered.

He was just fumbling in his satchel for the light when Liz cried out, "Bugger! That was not a tree. What my knee just hit was not a bloody tree."

"What was it?" asked Peter.

"It feels like the corner of a stone wall," said Liz. "And yes, I'm okay, thanks for asking."

Peter turned on the flashlight and held the beam low to the ground. Emerging from the ivy next to Liz's left knee was a corner of honey yellow Cotswold limestone—not the ragged, unfinished stone of a dry-stacked field wall, but smooth, mason-finished stone. They made their way around the building, tapping the lug wrench against the ivy-covered wall but hearing only the *chink, chink* of metal on stone.

"There has to be a door somewhere," said Liz.

"Louisa said the chapel was crumbling, but this wall seems pretty solid to me." Peter reached to tap the wrench on the wall again and he fell forward through the ivy, hitting his hip on hard stone.

"That hurt," he said.

"Tell me about it," said Liz. "Are you inside? It's pretty dark where I am."

Peter looked around and realized he was in a small porch. The archway to the outside was almost completely covered with ivy, but on the opposite side of the porch was a heavy wooden door. "I've found the way in," said Peter, reaching back out through the ivy and grasping for Liz. "Give me your hand."

"That's not my hand," said Liz with a giggle, and slipped her hand into his so he could pull her through the vines.

"You could at least buy me dinner first," said Liz.

"Sorry," said Peter, blushing in the dark.

"It's okay, Peter. I was just teasing you. It's something friends do. Besides, you have no idea where you grabbed me, do you?"

"Well, I have an idea," said Peter.

"Perv," said Liz, swatting him on the rump. "Now please tell me the door is unlocked."

Peter turned the iron ring that hung from the door and raised the latch. "So it would seem," he said. He pushed the door open, and they stepped into the Gardner family private chapel.

The chapel was neither as small nor as dilapidated as Peter had expected, though whether it had been restored since the previous century, or Louisa's memory was faulty, he couldn't tell. The nave was ten strides long and four wide, with no transepts and two steps leading up to the tiny chancel. The pitched ceiling was perhaps twenty feet high and supported by wooden beams. High on the walls were narrow, barred windows. There were no furnishings, but in addition to the many memorials on the walls, there were three freestanding tombs on which stone effigies of Gardners past lay in endless sleep.

Peter and Liz walked slowly toward the one other structure in the room, the stone altar in the chancel. It was unmarked, except for a cross carved into the front. Peter set his bag on the smooth stone and pointed his flashlight down what would have been the aisle if there had been pews in the chapel.

"I guess we start reading gravestones," he said.

Peter stepped toward the largest of the three standing tombs and was just about to read the inscription when a loud scraping noise from the back of the chapel was followed by a sickening thud.

"The door!" cried Liz, running past Peter, who followed her. The heavy wooden door, which they had left ajar, was now firmly shut. "There wasn't much wind tonight," said Liz.

"The wind couldn't have moved this door anyway," said Peter. He tried to turn the iron ring but it would not move, nor did the door budge when they pulled on it. Leaning against the door of what was now, effectively, their prison cell, the two said nothing for a minute. Peter expected to feel the onset of a panic attack, and even slipped his hand into his pocket to feel the bag of pills nestled there, but instead he felt strangely calm. More calm than he had since Sykes's murder.

"It will take them a while to get the police here this time of night," he said. "We'd better get to work."

Kingham, 1878

Phillip dipped his quill into a pot of ink he had mixed from an old recipe in the ragged leather notebook that lay open on his table. The pen glided easily over the paper as he followed the contours of the script propped in front of him. Forgery, as it turned out, was a job for which Phillip Gardner was uniquely suited. For his entire career as an artist he had been accused of being derivative and unoriginal—little better than a copyist. But as a copyist he not only excelled, he was a master. Marks on a page seemed to flow directly through his eyes and out the tip of his pen. And with guidance from the notebook, he had solved the problems of obtaining pens, paper, parchment, and ink from the period of whatever document he happened to be forging. This morning it was a letter from Lord Nelson to his mistress, Lady Emma Hamilton.

The light from his candles glowed steadily—there was no air moving in this forgotten chamber, and Phillip had discovered that candlelight was sufficient for his work. As an artist he had occupied a wide room at the top of the house with windows facing in three directions. An artist requires light, but a forger is more in need of secrecy, and in the gloomy chamber Phillip had honed his craft.

It had been nearly a year since Phillip had received the blackmail letter from Reginald Alderson threatening to reveal both his mistress and his bastard child to Mrs. Gardner. Phillip had lain awake all that night, wondering what to do. He seemed to be caught between two unacceptable options—handing his collection over to his family's worst enemy, or losing Mrs. Gardner, and with her the financial ability to maintain Evenlode House. Either option would make him reviled in the annals of the Gardner family. Not until the predawn light pressed its way through the mist and into his window did Phillip consider a possible solution. If he was no better than a copyist, as the elitist establishment of the Royal Academy claimed, then why should he not use that talent as a way out of this predicament?

Handbooks on forgery were not easy to come by, but Phillip had read about the Shakespearean forgery of John Payne Collier years ago. Collier had eventually been unmasked by experts, but Reginald Alderson was hardly an expert. So Phillip had presented himself to Collier as a sympathetic scholar working on a history of nineteenth-century forgeries.

"I'm sure you were just the victim of someone else's deceit," Phillip had said to the aging Collier. "But I thought perhaps you might provide me with some insights into the world of forgery." His insincere flattery had netted much more than insights. Collier had presented Phillip with several of his books and, more important, with several minutes alone in his study while he went out to wash the tea things. In a lower desk drawer Phillip had discovered an old leather-bound notebook filled with notes on forgery techniques—how to make period writing instruments, obtain old paper and parchment, mix ink from different periods, and make new documents look old. It had been a simple matter to abscond with this volume. Whether it was written by Collier or someone else he neither knew nor cared; the important thing was that it worked.

Benjamin Mayhew sat in a corner of the drawing room of an exclusive club with a cigar in one hand and a glass of brandy in the other. His host, William Henry Smith, had been holding forth for some time now on his theory that Francis Bacon wrote the works of William Shakespeare—a theory to which he had given no public voice in many years but which, when prodded by Benjamin, he was happy to explicate. On the shelf of Benjamin's office, barely a mile distant, stood a book that could shatter Smith's theory. Smith was not only one of Benjamin's oldest clients, he was by far the most highly placed. Benjamin had come to enjoy his occasional evenings as a guest in a club he could never hope to join on his own merits. As a servant refilled his brandy snifter, he thought he might do more than just hide the *Pandosto* to protect the reputation of his old friend.

"Did you ever catch up with Mr. Collier?" Benjamin asked Phillip Gardner as the two sat in the room above Benjamin's bookshop.

"I did," said Gardner. "Interesting old man. He gave me copies of some of his books for my collection. Of course I told him I believed he was just an innocent victim. I think he was senile enough to believe me."

"Probably believes it himself," said Benjamin. "Still, he was a brilliant man in his day."

"You think forgery is brilliant?" said Gardner.

"It's an art form, isn't it?"

"If you can call fraud an art form," said Gardner.

"What if I told you," said Benjamin, "that one of these documents is a forgery?" He indicated with a sweep of his hand four items spread across the table—items that Benjamin had gone to great pains to obtain in order to pose this question to Gardner. There were two parchment court documents from the fifteenth century and two letters from the eighteenth. None of them concerned anyone of importance, thus Benjamin could trust that Gardner would look at them without an acquisitive eye, a condition that, he knew all too well, could lead to blindness.

Gardner examined the documents for several minutes, holding each one up to the light at various angles before laying it down and picking up the next. Finally he picked up a letter dated 1756, ran a finger across the surface of the paper, and almost immediately produced a short snort.

"Well, it's clearly this one," he said. "And I must say it's a pretty poor job."

"What makes you say that?" said Benjamin, convinced already that his suspicions about Gardner were correct.

"Feel the way the pen has scraped the paper," said Gardner. "That doesn't happen with a quill. This was written with a metal-nib pen and those weren't mass-produced until the eighteen twenties. It's an ordinary household letter, so I think you can safely assume it would have been written with something that was widely available, and in seventeen fifty-six metal-nib pens were anything but." Gardner tossed the letter back on the table dismissively.

"You sound like an expert," said Benjamin.

"As I told you, I've been collecting books on forgery. One has to protect oneself, you know."

"Yes, but books on forgery can't show you what paper feels like when it's been written on with a metal nib," said Benjamin. "But don't worry, your secret is safe with me."

"What secret?"

"There are only two sorts of people who could have detected this forgery so quickly," said Benjamin, holding the letter up. "Someone with extensive experience in the field of forensic detection or an experienced forger. You are not the former; I can only assume you are the latter."

"Are you accusing me of being a forger?" said Gardner.

"I wouldn't call it an accusation exactly," said Benjamin, "more of a compliment." Ever since the day when Reginald Alderson had first failed to bid against Phillip Gardner, Benjamin had suspected something odd was going on. Gardner's sudden interest in forgery had further aroused his suspicion. The only explanation he could imagine was that Gardner was passing off forged copies of documents to Alderson—for what reason he could not imagine.

"See here," said Gardner. "What are you playing at? Are you the one who told Alderson about Isabel?"

"I beg your pardon?" said Benjamin, who could see no connection between the young American whose letters he had been asked to hold for Gardner and the present conversation about forgery.

"He's blackmailing me, you know," said Gardner angrily. "Reginald Alderson's threatened to tell Mrs. Gardner. I need hardly tell you that if she found out, you would lose a very good customer."

"My dear fellow," said Benjamin, smiling. "I've no intention of telling Mrs. Gardner anything. And frankly I had forgotten all about your young female friend. I'm simply in the market for a good forger—a better forger than the man who wrote the letter you so quickly unmasked."

"I see," said Gardner, calming down. He picked up the forged letter from the table and chuckled quietly before wadding it up and tossing it onto the fire. "In that case," he said, "you've come to the right man. It just so happens that I am a superb forger."

Ridgefield, 1988

Within a few months of their return from the honeymoon, Peter had agreed with Amanda's proposal that, so long as they lived modestly, they could spend some of what she delicately referred to as her "independent income." His business was growing slowly, and Amanda was beginning to get work as an interior decorator, but a little extra income meant that after a year in an apartment they could move into a small house in an older neighborhood not far from campus. The house needed work, and Peter spent his weekends learning how to scrape paint, refinish floors, and hang drywall. "It's like binding a book," he said to Amanda one day when he came in for lunch covered with paint. "Only bigger." The summer before they bought the house they had traveled to England again. It was the first of what would become semiannual book-buying trips. They flew economy class and stayed in bed-and-breakfasts where the bathroom was usually down the hall. Amanda never complained.

In the spring of 1993, when Peter saw that their next trip to England would coincide with their fifth anniversary, he thought maybe the time was right to travel a little less frugally.

"You've got some new clients," he said to Amanda in bed one night, "and so do I. Why don't we stay in hotels this time?"

"I kind of like those little places in the country," said Amanda, "but we should definitely spend our anniversary night at The Ritz." And so they had. Peter had forgotten how good those sheets felt.

A week later, wandering the Cotswolds in search of bookshops,

Peter and Amanda happened upon the village of Kingham and decided to have a picnic lunch on the village green.

"It's just a perfect village, isn't it?" said Amanda, as they lounged in the grass after lunch.

"It's peaceful," said Peter. "We should stay here a couple of days."

"Do you think there's any place to stay?" said Amanda.

And so they had wandered around the village looking for accommodation and had found a FOR SALE sign in front of a terraced cottage. Afterward they couldn't remember who had first suggested it, but standing in the cool May breeze in front of that empty cottage they suddenly saw themselves inside.

"It needs work," said Peter.

"We come to England all the time," said Amanda. "It would be nice to have a home base."

"It would," said Peter. And he had an intense vision of a crackling fire in the grate, a cup of tea in his hand, and Amanda reading a good book on a damp winter day. It was as seductive as anything he had ever imagined.

"Why not?" said Amanda. "We can afford it."

"You can afford it," said Peter.

"I haven't given you an anniversary present yet," said Amanda.

And without further discussion it had been decided. They hadn't set foot in the cottage, they had been in Kingham for a little over an hour, but it felt right. Three months later Peter and Amanda owned a cottage in England; two months after that the slow process of renovation began.

"Thank you," said Peter to Amanda as they lay in their bed in Ridgefield on the night the sale became final.

"For what?" said Amanda.

"For the cottage," said Peter.

"You're welcome," said Amanda, spooning herself around him.

"It makes me feel like a real bookseller, to have a cottage in England."

"Do all booksellers have cottages in England?" said Amanda.

"Actually I don't know any who do," said Peter, "but it lends a . . . I don't know, a legitimacy to my putting myself out there as an expert on English books."

"Darling, you *are* an expert on English books," said Amanda.

"It's going to be great, isn't it?" said Peter.

"It'll take some work," said Amanda, "but yes."

"How long do you think the renovations will take?"

"Well, if British contractors are anything like the ones here, I'd be surprised if it takes less than a year," said Amanda. "Maybe next year we can go for Christmas."

"That sounds nice," said Peter. Amanda was running her hand up and down his chest and he lay quietly for several minutes, enjoying the slow arousal that came with the promise of lovemaking.

"These sheets seem awfully soft," she murmured, as Peter moved his hand up her side and across her breast.

"I was hoping you'd notice," said Peter. "They're a little present for you. They're eight hundred thread count."

Peter and Liz had been trapped in the Gardner chapel for nearly an hour and were no closer to discovering any secrets than they had been when the door slammed shut on them. They had examined every memorial on the walls as well as the three stone effigies, but other than tracing the Gardner family tree from the sixteenth century they had accomplished nothing. They had found no sign of Phillip Gardner.

They were sitting on the cold stone floor, their backs against the immovable door when Peter saw, as he played the flashlight around the chapel's interior, a discernable pattern in the scratches on parts of the floor.

"I think there are graves in the floor," he said, crawling forward and running his fingers along the fine lines.

"I can't tell what it says," said Liz, "the words are almost worn away."

"I doubt our friend Phillip has been dead long enough for his stone to be worn so smooth," said Peter.

"Here's another one," said Liz, and soon they were crisscrossing the chapel on their hands and knees, occasionally making out part of a name or date. They were in front of the chancel steps, Peter holding his flashlight close to a stone trying to read what came after the date 1705, when Liz dropped the lug wrench just outside the light's beam and the two froze as they heard a hollow *clonk*, which seemed to echo below them.

"What was that?" said Peter.

"Sorry, I dropped the . . ."

"Do it again," said Peter.

Liz picked up the wrench and dropped it onto the stone and again the eerie sound of hollowness hung in the air for a second. "There's something under there," said Liz.

"Or more to the point, there's nothing under there," said Peter. "Nothing solid at least. Let me see your wrench."

Liz handed him the lug wrench and he tried to fit the flat end into the floor at the edge of the stone, but the joints with the abutting stones were hairline—there was no room for the prying end of a lug wrench. "How are we going to get the stone up?" said Peter.

"Give me the wrench," said Liz.

"It's no use," said Peter. "There's no space for . . ." But before he could finish his sentence, Liz brought the wrench down hard in the center of the stone and a splintering, crashing sound echoed throughout the chapel. The stone shattered and the pieces fell away into darkness.

"That worked," said Liz.

Peter and Liz knelt at the edge of a hole less than two feet square. The darkness seemed to devour the beam of Peter's flashlight when he shone it into the hole, but he thought he glimpsed a floor far below.

"I'll go first," said Peter.

"Are you crazy?" said Liz. "You've no idea what's down there."

"That's why I'm going," said Peter. He was rather surprised at his own courage—it was not a feeling he had experienced since he lost Amanda. He dropped his feet into the hole and gradually lowered the rest of his body, wriggling to squeeze through the narrow opening. He managed to maneuver his arms above his head and found himself holding on to the floor of the chapel with his fingertips, dangling in space. Above him he could still see the concerned face of Liz Sutcliffe illuminated by the glow of the flashlight, but just as his fingers began to ache, her face was replaced with Amanda's, who blew him a kiss and whispered, "Trust me; let go."

Peter let his fingers slip from the stone and felt a rush of cold air as he plunged through the darkness and thudded onto a rough stone floor. He felt a sharp pain in his ankle as his legs buckled beneath him, but after lying in the darkness for a moment and panting, he stood up, feeling relatively undamaged.

"Are you all right?" said Liz, her voice edged with panic. Peter looked up at the surprisingly small square of light in the ceiling, perhaps ten feet overhead, and saw Liz's concerned face.

"I'm fine," he said. "Toss me my bag and the flashlight and I'll be able to see to help you down."

"I'm not going down there," said Liz. "It's bad enough being trapped up here. I have a little claustrophobia."

"I think it's a pretty big room," said Peter. "Let me see the flashlight." Liz leaned into the hole and dropped the bag and then the flashlight into Peter's waiting hands. He swung the beam quickly around the chamber in which he now stood. A few feet away stood a heavy oak table. He managed to shove this under the hole and climb atop it.

"Look," he said. "Now I can help you down. It's not any smaller a space than where you are."

"That doesn't make me feel better," said Liz. "On the other hand, you do have the flashlight." She sat on the edge of the hole, her feet dangling above Peter's head, then took a deep breath and slowly lowered herself. Peter grabbed first her feet and then her calves, and then as she released her grip on the world above, he let her body slide through his arms until she was standing safely on the table. She kept her arms wrapped around him for a long minute, and Peter felt her trembling. He hugged her tightly, to comfort her, he thought, but when she returned his embrace with equal pressure, he felt an electricity in his veins. For a second he forgot his quest and wondered if he should kiss her.

"So how do you plan to get out of here?" said Liz, breaking the embrace and climbing off the table.

"I'm sure the police will help us out when they come to arrest me for murder," said Peter, shaking the ridiculous thought of romance out of his mind.

"What is this place?" said Liz, when they had both climbed off the table. Peter had not looked closely at the room yet, in his hurry to get Liz safely down. Now he moved the flashlight beam slowly across every surface as they stood in the center of the chamber taking it all in. They were in the crypt of the chapel. The ceiling was highest directly overhead where they had entered, elsewhere low arches created a series of nooks. The first few of these into which Peter shone his light were furnished not with altars or tombs but with tools, bottles, tables, and chairs.

"It looks like some sort of workshop," said Liz.

"That's exactly what it is," said Peter. "Or what it was." He crossed to one of the tables and examined a series of corked bottles next to which lay a row of ancient-looking pens and quills. In the next alcove was a small hand printing press; beyond that another table with tools carefully laid out on it. Peter recognized a lifting knife among the other tools arrayed before him. "Now why would someone need a printing press, old pens and ink, and a bunch of bookbinding equipment?"

"Sounds like everything you'd need to forge a sixteenth-century book," said Liz.

"Exactly what I was thinking," said Peter.

"So you think the *Pandosto* really is a fake?" said Liz.

"It's looking more and more that way," said Peter, as he made his way through the alcoves that ringed the chamber. One was empty except for some old lumber stacked against the back wall; in the next was an unadorned stone sarcophagus. "Come hold the light for me," he said. "I think this is someone's tomb."

Liz shone the flashlight on the lid of the sarcophagus but Peter could not see what was carved there without climbing onto the tomb and running his fingers along the letters as he read aloud: "Having made his mark, Phillip Gardner eighteen thirty-two to eighteen seventy-nine, beloved brother, and all his secrets rest here."

"Beloved brother?" said Liz.

"B.B.," said Peter. "We've found him."

"What does it mean 'all his secrets rest here'?" said Liz.

"We've got to look inside," said Peter.

"But it's a tomb. You can't desecrate a tomb."

"I'm not desecrating it," said Peter. "But more than Phillip Gardner is entombed here, and as long as I'm sitting around waiting to be arrested, I'm going to find out his secrets. Hand me the lug wrench."

Peter's initial attempts to pry the top off the tomb resulted in little more than a few scratches on the stone. He tried banging on the stone slab with the wrench, hoping it might break like the entrance stone to the crypt had done, but this slab was much thicker. After fifteen minutes of straining to no effect, Peter slumped against the wall, panting and sweating.

"How are we going to get this thing off?" he asked, gasping.

"I don't think we are," said Liz.

"Don't you see," said Peter. "I have to know. If I'm going to rot away in an English prison for a murder I didn't commit, I at least have to know the whole story of the *Pandosto*."

"You're not going to prison," said Liz.

"Don't be so sure," said Peter.

"Besides," said Liz, "I thought what you really wanted to know about was a watercolor that looked like . . ."

"That looked like Amanda," said Peter softly. He had almost forgotten what had started this whole business. It had been Amanda who had led him here. What would she have done? When he looked up, she was sitting at the table where the bottles of ink and pens were laid out.

"You can't solve everything by force, Peter," she said.

"I know," said Peter.

"You know what?" asked Liz.

"That I can't solve everything by force," said Peter as he watched Amanda fade away.

"I was just thinking the same thing," said Liz, who was now on her hands and knees with the flashlight, examining the base of Phillip Gardner's tomb.

"So what do we use if we don't use force?" asked Peter.

"A key," said Liz.

"I beg your pardon?"

"There's something here that looks like a keyhole."

"I didn't see any keys down here," said Peter.

"Well, I doubt he'd just leave the key lying around."

"Wait a minute, what did the first part of the inscription say again?" asked Peter.

" 'Having made his mark,' " said Liz. "What does that mean? What sort of mark? Does he mean the *Pandosto*?"

"Having made his mark," Peter murmured to himself as he ran a finger along the table of bookbinding equipment. On a series of shelves above the table lay row after row of wooden-handled brass tools, like the ones he had used to decorate the binding of Amanda's *At the Back of the North Wind*. "I wonder if it could mean a binder's mark?"

"What's that?" said Liz.

"Bookbinders sometimes have a special mark that they put on all their bindings to identify the work as their own."

"So we have to go through all those tools," said Liz.

"No," said Peter. "I've just realized it. I've seen Gardner's mark. His copy of Collier's book, the one that was inscribed to him—it was a rebind. Gardner must have bound it himself."

"What was the mark?"

"Sort of a butterfly shape," said Peter. "He put it just inside the back cover. Give me the light."

It took Peter no more than five minutes to find the butterfly stamp among Gardner's tools. "Try this," he said, handing the stamping tool to Liz. He trained the flashlight on the tiny hole in the stone as Liz inserted the tool.

"It fits," she said, "but it doesn't turn."

Peter thought about how Hank had taught him to use the brass stamps on a piece of fresh leather. "Press on the handle with the heel of your hand," he said, "and then rock it back and forth very gently, starting from the right and moving toward the left."

"What makes you think that—"

"Just try it, okay?" Peter interrupted impatiently.

"Okay, okay," said Liz. "Don't get your knickers in a twist." Peter held his breath and watched as Liz's shoulders tensed while she applied pressure to the stamp. Nothing happened.

"Now gradually increase the pressure," said Peter, closing his eyes and remembering the sensation of the leather yielding to the stamp. "Not too hard, though, or you'll tear the leather."

"What do you mean I'll . . ." But Liz was interrupted by a loud *click* that echoed through the chamber. Peter opened his eyes and saw that a wide crack had appeared between the stone slab on top of the sarcophagus and the tomb beneath.

"What was that?" asked Liz.

"I think you just unlocked Phillip Gardner's tomb," said Peter.

"I'm sure he's going to be so pleased about that," said Liz, standing up.

Peter had already begun to push on the stone top and found that it

now slid easily off, so easily that before he could stop it, the slab toppled to the floor where it broke in two with a thundering crash. It
took several seconds for the noise to subside and several more for the
dust to settle.

"Wonderful," said Liz. "Now we're trapped in a crypt with a dead
body we have no way of re-entombing. I'm feeling more comfortable
all the time."

"There's no body," said Peter, shining the flashlight into the tomb.

"What do you mean there's no bloody body?" Liz asked, taking a
tentative step toward the tomb.

"There's no body in here. There's nothing but a metal box."

"A metal box? What is it, his ashes?"

"Doubtful," said Peter as he pulled the heavy box toward him. It
struck him that the box, scraping loudly across the stone as he pulled
it, was about the size and shape of a Shakespeare First Folio. He
hoisted it out of the tomb and carried it to the table in the center of
the room. There was no lock, and Peter pulled back the hinged top
with ease.

"A bunch of papers?" said Liz, gazing into the box.

"We've got some time before the flashlight batteries die out," said
Peter. "Let's read, shall we?"

Atop the pile of papers lay a sealed envelope addressed in a neat
slanting script only to "Phillip." Peter took his lifting knife out of his
satchel and slit the envelope open with one smooth slice. He pulled
out the contents, unfolded the four sheets of paper, and read aloud.
The first page was written in the same script as the outside of the envelope.

I, Phillip Gardner of Evenlode House, Kingham, here direct that my estate shall pass to the children of my brother Nicholas. I do not include
in this bequest the contents of this box, or other items from my collection of rare books and documents, which, wheresoever they may be, I

leave in their entirety to my son, born Phillip Gardner, or to his youngest living heir.

"That must have been the bastard child," said Liz. "Otherwise why the secret will?"

"So Sykes was right," said Peter, perusing the testament again. "And what's this about 'wheresoever they may be'?"

"Could that be because some of them were in Reginald Alderson's collection?" said Liz.

"It must be," said Peter. "I wonder if the son has any living heirs. I can't imagine John Alderson would be too happy to have the terms of this will enforced."

"But how could you prove that Alderson's documents really belonged to Phillip Gardner?"

"This might help," answered Peter, holding up a letter with the words EVENLODE MANOR printed at the top.

Mr. Gardner,

I have spent a most revealing evening with my dear friend Miss Evangeline Prickett and her young charge. Imagine my shock at discovering that Miss Isabel has given birth to a child and named it Phillip Gardner. I shall not bore you with the unsavory details of the affair that led to this bastard child—you are well acquainted with them already. However, I imagine that Mrs. Gardner would find the story most enlightening. Should you wish to prevent her from learning the truth about her husband, you will transfer to me your collection of historical and literary documents. I realize that the loss of the entire collection might arouse suspicion, so I think it best if you send them to me one or two at a time over the next few months. In that way you can be said to have lost interest and sold the pieces to finance your considerable construction at Evenlode House.

You will be pleased to learn that I shall not bid against you next week at the auction of royal documents. I shall expect the pieces to arrive at my home within a week of the sale. You should not expect a commission.

Reginald Alderson

"The blackmail letter," said Liz.

"Exactly," said Peter. He laid the letter down and excitedly reached for the next item from the envelope. It was a small sheet of correspondence paper, on which a letter was written in a cramped, shaky hand.

My Dearest Phillip,

I send this letter through your bookseller Mr. Mayhew as you asked, and I promise it will be the last, but I must tell you that your son and I are safely arrived in America. My family is more understanding than you might believe and so I have not, as you suggested, invented a fiction about a foundling. Both Miss Prickett and myself have been honest with my family about the events of the past months. All my father has requested is that young Phillip be raised with our family name, not the name of Gardner. With all the love and acceptance he has shown to his fallen daughter, I cannot but honor his request. Please know that, whatever I was to you, you shall never be replaced in my affections.

Always, your Isabel

"So she moved back to America," said Liz.

There was one more sheet of paper lying on the table. "This one is written by Gardner, too," said Peter, glancing at the signature. "But it's not addressed to anyone. It just starts." And Peter read.

I am not in the habit of making confessions, but if I have cared little in this life for my wife or what family is left to me; if I have proven a failure in both my career and my finances; if morals have never been high among my priorities, one thing I have nurtured and cared for: my collection. Whatever dark impulses first impelled me to collect, I have come to realize that in those letters and manuscripts and documents lies my one chance to impart something to the world. Despite the threat of financial and marital ruin that he held over me, I would no more pass these treasures to Mr. Reginald Alderson than I would destroy them. Thus I here confess that through the circumstance of my neighbor's blackmailing I discovered my true calling as an artist. Some may call it forgery; for me it was merely preservation—preservation of my own peace for a short time, preservation of my collection forever.

While this confession is for those of my heirs who may one day find it and resurrect that collection, I have written a companion to Mr. Alderson in which it was my great pleasure to inform him that the documents he has extorted from me these past two years are as worthless as my watercolors that he blocked from proper exhibition. A few of these hang on the walls of friends' homes, the rest I have destroyed, except for a select group I have sent along to Mr. Alderson. I relish the thought of his descendants one day singing their praises. To ensure that Mr. Alderson will not fool others as I have fooled him, I have included in each of my forgeries a clue to its origin; my technique is, I believe, undetectable, but a careful reading of the text of each document will reveal a flaw. Thus the Aldersons, in perpetuity, will be forced to live with my duping of their forebear.

For a few hours after my death, Mr. Alderson may believe he has won, and that he possesses a great literary relic—the book I shall deliver to him shortly. Then, my final letter to Mr. Alderson will arrive, and he will know the truth not just about this greatest relic, but about all the documents he believes are so valuable. Revenge shall be mine at the last.

I hope that whatever ancestor made the secret of this crypt did so to provide nefarious access to the Aldersons, not friendly commerce. In any case, I shall use that secret not just to deliver my final forgery but also to make a gift to Reginald Alderson of my small collection of books on that art. Whether he shall notice that they have inexplicably appeared on his shelves I may never know.

To Mrs. Gardner, I make no apologies. To my Isabel, should she ever see this, I profess that at the end, I thought only of you, my beloved. Forgive me my wrongs and be blessed.

Phillip Gardner, November 22, 1879

"No wonder the box at Evenlode Manor said 'not to be sold,'" said Peter. "Every document in there is a forgery."

"And these must be the originals," said Liz, pulling the rest of the papers out of the box.

"Exactly," said Peter, looking quickly through the stack of documents. "It's so bizarre to see these, because I've seen them all before."

"What about the *Pandosto*?" said Liz. "Could that be the 'great literary relic'?"

Peter pulled the book from his case and opened it on the table. "'A careful reading of the text of each document will reveal a flaw,'" he said. "I've examined the text pretty carefully."

"How about the marginalia? Without that it's just a rare book, right?"

"I read all that, too," said Peter.

"Yes," said Liz, "but you read it as someone who was excited to discover a great Shakespeare relic, not someone looking for a flaw." Liz began scanning the margin notes.

"What do you think he meant by 'flaw'?" said Peter.

"Something that's not right textually, I suppose," said Liz. "Some reference to something Shakespeare couldn't have known, or an anachronism. You know, Hermione wearing a digital watch. That sort of thing." Peter looked over Liz's shoulder as she turned the page and ran her finger slowly down the scrawled script in the margins. Though it seemed less possible every minute, a part of him still wanted to believe that William Shakespeare of Stratford-upon-Avon had written those notes. He had relished the thought of the day he would show the *Pandosto* to Francis Leland—the apprentice presenting the Holy Grail to his master. It was a fantasy he wasn't quite ready to give up.

"What year did Shakespeare die?" asked Liz, her fingertip pausing near the bottom of a page.

"Sixteen sixteen," said Peter. "Why?"

"Bloody hell! Listen to this. 'Death of Garinter unjust as in execution of Raleigh.'"

"We don't know what Shakespeare thought of Raleigh's execution," said Peter. "He might have felt it was unjust."

"You're wrong, Peter. We know exactly what Shakespeare thought of Raleigh's execution."

"Liz, trust me, I've read the literature, and . . ."

"Peter, we know what Shakespeare thought. He thought nothing. Because Shakespeare had been dead for two years when Raleigh was executed."

"Raleigh was beheaded in sixteen eighteen," said Peter, suddenly remembering the date from his English history class. "How could I have missed that?"

"It's subtle," said Liz, "and you weren't looking for it."

Peter watched the Holy Grail dissolve into a fascinating example of nineteenth-century forgery. Judging from the presence of a printing press in Gardner's lair, Peter guessed that not even the text was authentic, though it had probably been copied from a genuine first edition of *Pandosto*. It might fetch as much as a few thousand pounds at auction, so it couldn't be said to be worthless, but it was far from extraordinary. His burning question of the past week answered, he was suddenly struck by the harsh reality of his situation. He was trapped underground in a remote country chapel. He was the prime suspect in a brutal murder, with a raft of evidence implicating him.

And he was now the caretaker of a book that would make the tiniest ripple in Shakespeare studies, and pass completely unnoticed in the broader world.

"I'll bet Mayhew commissioned Gardner to make the *Pandosto* forgery," said Liz, who still seemed excited about unraveling the book's mystery. "He told Gardner to leave a textual clue just like he had in his other forgeries. He must have planned for it to surface and be revealed as a fake. That would have been an embarrassment to the Stratfordians."

"And it would make his friend William H. Smith look good at the same time."

"What was all that about 'nefarious access' to the Aldersons and secretly putting books into their library?" said Liz, picking up Gardner's deathbed confession.

"'I hope that whatever ancestor made the secret of this crypt did so to provide nefarious access to the Aldersons, not friendly commerce,'" read Peter.

"You don't think . . ."

"There must be a passage," said Peter. "A passage that leads from here to Evenlode Manor."

"But why?" said Liz.

"Who knows why," said Peter, grabbing the flashlight from her and shining it into the back of an alcove. "Even Phillip Gardner didn't know why. Maybe it was some sort of Romeo and Juliet thing." Peter found nothing but a solid wall and hurriedly moved to the next alcove. "Or maybe the feud between the families was just for show—at first, I mean. This chapel has to be at least four hundred years old, judging from the tombs. Here, help me move these boards."

He had come to the alcove that contained nothing more than a pile of old lumber leaning up against the back wall. It took him and Liz several minutes to clear the boards away, during which the quiet of the crypt gave way to the banging of wood on stone as they hurled the lumber from the wall. When the last plank had been cast to the floor, the quiet returned, though dust still swirled in the air and stuck to Peter's sweaty face. He picked up the flashlight and trained it into the alcove where it shone on the back wall. There, in the center of the arch, was a narrow door made of rough planks. Peter pulled the handle and the door swung open, revealing a flight of stone steps leading down into darkness.

Kingham, 1879

Every great artist, thought Phillip Gardner, has his masterpiece, and the forgery of the *Pandosto*, which took him nearly a year to complete, was his. True, there was a certain frustration that this masterpiece must go unheralded, but knowing that it would ultimately bring embarrassment to the Alderson family was reward enough.

Phillip had started by covering the endpapers of the book with new paper—concealing all evidence to the casual observer that the scribblings in the margins were those of William Shakespeare, for the proper forgery of the *Pandosto* would require outside assistance, and he had no wish to raise suspicions. Next he had the text of each page photographed. He was careful to choose a photographer who had no higher education and no connections to the book trade. A studio in Manchester fit his needs perfectly.

In the meantime, he began, with help from Benjamin Mayhew, to collect the paper on which the *Pandosto* would be printed. The book was a quarto, so by neatly slicing blank pages out of the backs of folio volumes from the same time period, Phillip was able to collect sheets on which four pages of the new *Pandosto* could be printed. He could then fold these sheets in half for binding.

The next step was to convert the photographs into zinc plates from which the text could be printed. After masking out the marginalia on the photographs, he told the owner of the workshop in Birmingham where he ordered the plates that he was making a facsimile of an obscure old book for scholarly purposes. Three weeks later he collected the photographs and the zinc plates. The former he tossed into the drawing room fire; the latter he used to print *Pandosto*'s text on the paper that he and Mayhew had collected. He had mixed a large batch of ink from one of Collier's recipes for this purpose, and Mayhew had helped him find and purchase a hand printing press, which he had spent some months learning to master.

Zincographic printing does not leave as deep an impression on the paper as hand-set type, so once the printing was complete, Phillip embarked on the most tedious part of his work. Taking a tiny, smoothed piece of bone, he traced each letter, pressing just hard enough to imitate the impression made by sixteenth-century movable type. He had practiced this technique for weeks on scrap paper before he learned to apply just the right amount of pressure—his early attempts had left the paper riddled with holes and tears.

When he had completed the forging of the text, Phillip set about the fun part—meticulously copying the marginalia using a quill, a batch of sixteenth-century ink, and his expert eye and steady hand. All his practice in document forging now came to bear, as he copied each smudge and smear to perfection. He made only a single change, adding the line that would be the undoing of both the *Pandosto* and Reginald Alderson: "Death of Garinter unjust as in execution of Raleigh."

In the course of his work on the forgery, Phillip had become interested in all aspects of the book arts, and while he was far from an expert binder, he had collected some binding tools and equipment and had some modest success rebinding several of his own books. To bind his *Pandosto*, however, he merely bought a book of similar size in an old leather binding and sewed the newly printed text block into the old cover. At the same time, he removed the false endpapers from the original *Pandosto*, revealing once again the list of owners.

"It's a beautiful job," said Benjamin Mayhew, paging through the forged *Pandosto*.

"It's not quite done," said Phillip. "I still need to scuff the edges of the pages. I almost hate to give it up to Alderson. It's become . . . well, I've become close to that particular bit of forgery."

"We shouldn't become too close to our books," said Mayhew. "They are only objects, after all."

"Ah, but you are a bookseller, not a book collector. Besides, this one is my own creation."

"That should bring you all the more satisfaction when Alderson is made a fool."

"What is your plan exactly?" said Phillip.

"I've made all the arrangements," said Mayhew. "A colleague of mine will offer your *Pandosto* to Alderson for an irresistible price. This colleague will pretend not to know what he has. When Alderson makes the book public, my friend William Smith will reveal it as a forgery, thanks to your little clue. Smith will be happy because the Stratfordians will be embarrassed; you will be happy because Alderson will be embarrassed; and I shall be happy because my two best customers are happy. Now, I've a little something to make *Pandosto* look even better to Alderson."

Mayhew showed Phillip a beautiful leather-backed case from which he withdrew an elaborate folder. Into this he laid Phillip's masterpiece, carefully refolding the flaps and then slipping it back into the case.

"Properly imposing," said Phillip, taking the sumptuous case from Benjamin. "But what did you do with the original?"

"I shall see to it," said Benjamin.

"It seems a shame to destroy it."

"No choice, my good man, no choice. Your forgery preserves all the real marginalia for future generations. Some enterprising scholar will ferret out that you couldn't possibly have made all that up."

"I wonder," said Phillip, "if you might provide me with a bill of sale. Just so I can know that I owned it, however briefly."

"I don't see why not," said Benjamin. "And as for the rest, leave it all to me."

Phillip wanted to feel triumphant as he mounted the steps of Evenlode House on his return from London and his meeting with Benjamin Mayhew. He had created a masterpiece, fulfilled his first commission as an artist, and ensured the eventual public embarrassment of Reginald Alderson. However, he had also been complicit in the destruction of a great literary treasure. He was one of only two men alive who knew with absolute certainty the true identity of that greatest of English authors, and he had agreed to take that secret to his grave.

He was just turning the handle when the front door jerked open. Standing before him, a letter clasped in her hand and a look of fury on her face, was a woman he had not seen in some days.

"Good afternoon, Mrs. Gardner," he said.

"Mr. Gardner, when we married I demanded only one thing from you in exchange for my substantial financial support of both you and your estate—fidelity. Perhaps it seems an odd thing to desire from a man whom I neither love nor respect, but call it my little eccentricity."

"Yes, I had a lovely trip to London," said Phillip, striding into the entrance hall past his wife. "Thank you for asking."

"Was it as lovely as the trips you took to London to see Isabel?" said Mrs. Gardner.

Ridgefield, 1994

Peter remembered with photographic accuracy the moment when Amanda told him she had a headache. It hadn't seemed important at the time so Peter didn't know why he remembered that moment so well, but he did. They had just returned from their final visit to London to find news of another delay in the renovations of their cottage in Kingham, and Amanda, who usually brushed off such delays with a laugh and a comment about contractors being the same the world over, had slammed her fist on the telephone table in frustration.

"I'm starting to think I'm never going to see this project done," she said.

She stood by the window, the afternoon sun glowing in a few stray wisps of hair, her brow knitted in consternation, her lips pursed. Perhaps Peter remembered the moment because he had so rarely seen Amanda angry.

"Are you all right?" he asked.

"Oh, I'm fine," said Amanda, and the tension seemed to flow out of her in a second. "I just have a headache, that's all." After a nap and a cup of tea, Amanda felt better, and neither of them thought anything more of it. That she had another headache on the flight home the next week was hardly unusual—Peter had one, too. Could anyone in that business-class cabin with that crying baby not have a headache? Peter thought perhaps he would let Amanda pay for first-class tickets the next time.

———

Sarah and Charlie Ridgefield threw a sixth anniversary party for Peter and Amanda a week after they returned home. "You were off buying books on your fifth," said Sarah, "so we'll just do it this year instead." Amanda hadn't felt well that morning, another headache and an upset stomach, and Peter had insisted she go back to bed, not daring to give voice to the secret fantasy he was now harboring— that she had, by some miracle, become pregnant. As Amanda dozed on the living room sofa with the curtains drawn that afternoon, he recalled the expression on her face when he had ordered Coke instead of tea at the Tate Gallery café two weeks earlier—how could her amused, loving, protective face have been anything but maternal? How was it possible that Amanda would not one day bear a child? Peter thought perhaps, if her latest symptoms were not indicative of a miracle, the time might be right to bring up adoption. He needed something to father besides his book business, he thought; Amanda needed something to mother besides her English cottage.

She had felt better by the time of the party, though Peter hadn't seen her much that evening. Cynthia, who was now writing for a newspaper in Virginia, was back in Ridgefield for the weekend. Amanda and Cynthia hadn't seen each other in nearly a year, and, despite weekly hour-long phone conversations, they were desperate to catch up and spent most of the evening huddled together in a far corner of the patio. As for Peter, after that unpleasant period of awkward reintroductions to family friends that he had not seen since his wedding, he settled down at a table with Charlie Ridgefield. His father-in-law had not mentioned the subject of money since the night before Peter's wedding. Tonight the two talked about European travel and Ridgefield's upcoming football season.

All evening Peter watched Amanda out of the corner of his eye and wondered what secrets she was sharing with Cynthia and whether they included a piece of joyful news that she would share with him when they got home. But when the party was over, Amanda was exhausted and she asked Peter if they had to drive home. "Couldn't we just crash in the guest room?" she said, and Peter said yes. She was sound asleep before he had finished brushing his teeth.

There are days when, without prior notice, your life changes in some fundamental way. When Peter awoke bathed in the morning sun on May 14, 1994, he suspected that today might be one of those days. He was convinced that Amanda had shared some earthshaking news with Cynthia the night before and that today she would tell him. By now the slim hope that she might be pregnant had solidified into a near certainty. When he got up, letting his wife sleep, he spent ten minutes in front of the bathroom mirror practicing expressions of surprise.

Peter, Sarah, and Charlie had eaten breakfast, and Charlie was just saying that he might go into the office for a couple of hours even though it was a Saturday, when a scream erupted from upstairs. Peter knew at once it was not a scream of fear or anger, but a cry of pain. He was first by Amanda's bedside, where she sat holding her head and rocking back and forth, moaning loudly, but Charlie Ridgefield shoved him aside and scooped his daughter into his arms.

Amanda screamed again as Charlie took the stairs two at a time, trailing Peter and Sarah in his wake. "Get to the car," was all Sarah could manage to say. Peter looked to see tears streaming down her cheeks and sprinted for Charlie's BMW parked in the front drive. Charlie was slipping into the backseat with Amanda, who was still crying in apparent agony, and before Peter could decide where he should go, Sarah jerked open the driver's door and jumped in. Peter barely had time to get into the passenger seat before Sarah sped off, spewing gravel behind them.

In the backseat Charlie cradled Amanda, who was quieter now—

Peter could hear the words "My head" every so often, but other than that her cries had been reduced to low moans. Sarah skidded onto the main road, tires squealing as she accelerated in the direction of Ridgefield Hospital. Peter felt utterly helpless—no more than a spectator in someone else's family drama.

Sitting in the passenger seat of Charlie Ridgefield's new car, Peter Byerly, who had started his morning with such hope two hours earlier, had a creeping dread that his life was over.

"Look," said Liz, "I got locked in this chapel with you and I came down into the bloody dungeon, but this is mad. I'm not going down those stairs into God knows what."

"We're not going out the way we came in," said Peter, shoving the contents of Gardner's tomb into his satchel. "So we might as well try this." Staring at the black hole before him, Peter immediately thought of Alice blithely following the White Rabbit down its hole. The claustrophobic picture of Alice from the manuscript in the British Museum flashed before him, but for now at least, curiosity and adrenaline seemed to be winning the battle with panic and claustrophobia, as he started tentatively down the damp stone steps, running the fingers of one hand against the rough wall while his other hand grasped the flashlight and the handle of his satchel ever more firmly.

"Peter," called Liz from above, "there's something else in the bottom of the box. Don't you want to read it?"

"We'll read it when we get to wherever this leads," said Peter, taking another step down.

"It's dark up here without the flashlight," said Liz, hysteria in her voice.

Peter stopped and pointed the flashlight behind him. "Well, come on then," he said. There was silence for a moment, and then he heard slow footsteps on the stairs above him. In another minute he felt Liz's hand on his shoulder, and he started forward again as she guided herself behind him.

"Did I mention I have claustrophobia?" said Liz. "Oh wait, I did—when you lured me into this hellhole."

"I have it, too," said Peter, but as he continued to descend he felt strangely calm. "This isn't so bad."

"That's what you think," said Liz.

The stairs curved slightly as they descended, so by the time Peter reached the bottom, he had no idea what direction they were facing. In front of him the flashlight revealed a low, narrow passage sloping down and disappearing around another curve. The tunnel was just high enough for Peter to stand up in, and barely wider than his shoulders.

"That was fifty-two steps," said Liz, her hand gripping Peter's shoulder tightly.

"You counted?"

"How deep do you think we are?" said Liz. "No, don't answer that."

Peter started forward but was jerked back by Liz grasping his shirt.

"Are you sure we should do this?" she said. "I don't like this, I really don't."

"It looks perfectly harmless," said Peter.

"I can't see," said Liz. "You're blocking out all the light from the bloody flashlight."

"Actually there isn't much light from the flashlight, so we better get moving," said Peter.

"Well, I feel so much better now," said Liz, but this time she followed Peter as he started forward, though she did not loosen her grip on his shirt. "At least you're taller than I am," she said, forcing a laugh. "So it will be your head that gets cracked on the ceiling."

Peter had actually considered this possibility, and he waved the flashlight gently up and down as he shuffled forward, illuminating the floor and the ceiling in turn. He pressed forward a bit more quickly, almost pulling Liz along behind him, hoping they might reach an exit before the flashlight completely died.

"I wonder if this is where they hid all those soldiers in the Civil War," said Peter.

"I wonder if any of them died down here," said Liz. After another minute of walking she added, "We're going down pretty steeply."

"Maybe we have to get under the river," said Peter.

"Bugger," said Liz, stopping again. "I can't do this. I can't walk under a fucking river. We have to go back."

"Haven't you ever driven through the Lincoln Tunnel?" said Peter.

"No I have not driven through the bloody Lincoln Tunnel," said Liz. "I'm from London. We have bridges."

Peter felt the envelope of pills nestled in his jacket pocket and wondered if he ought to give her one but decided it was best to simply keep pressing forward. "Come on," he said. "You can do this. I'm with you. Here, hold my hand."

Peter reached his free hand behind his back and Liz gripped it tightly, almost crushing his fingers, but Peter did not complain. If he could somehow communicate his calm to her through this contact, it was worth a little pain. "Ready?" he said.

"No," said Liz. "But let's go anyway."

They walked on without speaking for several minutes, Liz's shallow breathing and their shoes sliding across the stones the only sounds in the tunnel. Peter did not mention that the flashlight beam had faded to the point of uselessness and that only by holding his satchel in front of him could he hope to detect any sudden barrier. Every few seconds Liz would squeeze his hand sharply, and Peter found himself relishing her need for him. As long as she needed him to calm her, he thought, he wouldn't panic himself.

"I think we're starting to go up again," he said after a few more minutes.

"Toward the light?" said Liz. "Do you see any light?"

"Not yet," said Peter, trying to pull her along more quickly. He had felt a sudden chill, as if the cold of the river were seeping into the tunnel, but he hoped it had been only that they had reached the deepest part of the tunnel, where centuries of cold lurked.

"Why is it so dark?" said Liz a moment later. "It seems really fucking dark. Peter stop. Stop, it's too dark." She once again came to a halt, pulling hard on Peter's hand and, with her free hand, on his shirt. Peter felt her arm slip around his chest and her head press against his back as the flashlight finally faded away. They were in absolute darkness. He heard Liz begin to cry softly.

"It's okay," he said. "Just close your eyes and let me lead you." Peter took a deep breath and let his back relax into Liz. He suddenly remembered the way Amanda used to sneak up behind him and slip her arms around him, pulling him tight to her chest so he could feel her breasts pressed into his back.

"Keep going," Amanda said now. "You can do this. You can make it to the other end. You can make it out."

He stepped forward and let Liz loosen her grip on him, still holding her hand. Her breathing seemed to be steadier now.

"Eyes closed?" said Peter.

"Yes," whispered Liz.

"Now, you're just walking down the corridor of your flat late at night. Just take one step at a time." They walked for what seemed to Peter like an eternity. He didn't dare speak, for fear he would trigger more panic in Liz. The slope of the floor gradually steepened, but in spite of the climb he increased his pace as much as he dared. He tried not to think about the possibility that there might be no exit, that they would have to turn around in these cramped confines and retrace their steps.

"How far do you think we've come?" said Liz, her voice steadier than it had been since they entered the tunnel.

"We must be nearly there," said Peter, who had no way of knowing this but could think of nothing else to say. Had they come a mile? Two? Certainly if they had been walking this long aboveground they could have reached Chipping Norton by now. Peter had tried not to think about either time or distance, but he had to guess it had been over an hour since they had descended the stairs from the crypt.

"Peter," said Liz.

"What is it?" said Peter, still moving forward.

"It sounds different."

"Are your eyes still closed?" said Peter.

"Yes, and it sounds different. More hollow or something."

"Maybe we're coming to the end," said Peter.

"What if we can't get out?" said Liz, shaking Peter's hand in hers. "What if we come to the end and we can't get out?"

"We'll be able to get out."

"You don't know that," said Liz, her voice rising. "How can you know that? What if we have to go back? I don't think I can go back. Oh, Jesus fuck, we're going to die in here, aren't we? We're going to die in this fucking place." She stopped again, forcing Peter to stop as well, and now he could hear her sobbing in great heaves.

"We're not going to die," said Peter.

"How do you know?" wailed Liz, her voice echoing down the tunnel. "How can you possibly know?"

"I'll tell you how I know," said Peter, gently squeezing Liz's hand. "Just take a deep breath and listen and I'll tell you." He listened as her breathing slowed and the choking sounds of her sobs faded.

"Tell me," she whispered.

"I've never told anyone this before, but I can trust you, right?"

"Yes," said Liz softly.

"Okay," said Peter. Still holding her hand, he began moving forward again as he spoke. "Ever since Amanda, my wife, ever since she died, sometimes she talks to me. I don't mean that I imagine her voice or that I remember things that she said, but she just shows up and says things. Sometimes it's when I really need her, and sometimes it's when I least expect it. Like when we had lunch at that Italian restaurant, remember that?"

"Yes," said Liz.

"Well, she was there. Just for a second, she was standing across the room and she told me to tell you that story about going to the opera."

Liz was silent.

"I know it sounds like I'm crazy, but believe me I'm not. And whenever she tells me to do something, it turns out to be the right thing. Anyhow, she was here a while ago, not long after we started, and she said that we would make it. She said we would make it to the other side and we would get out."

"Really?" said Liz, and Peter was relieved to hear in her voice not skepticism or sarcasm but hope.

"Really," said Peter. And as he voiced the word, he hit something hard with his toe and nearly toppled forward.

"What is it?"

"I think it's another flight of steps," said Peter, feeling in the darkness with his foot.

"I can't go down again," said Liz. "I just can't do it."

"They don't go down," said Peter. "They go up." And they began to climb.

Peter hadn't felt out of breath during their whole underground journey, but he found himself gasping for air as the steps curved round and round, on and on.

"That's fifty-two," said Liz. "That's how many we came down." But still the steps went up and up in the darkness. Finally Peter stopped.

"I've got to rest," he said.

"Keep going," said Liz. "I can take the pain in my legs if we can just get out of here." And so they climbed on. "That was two hundred," said Liz a few minutes later. By the way, I have my eyes open now."

Peter lifted his foot for the next step and felt nothing. "I think we're at the top," he said, sliding his foot forward across smooth stone. He took two more steps forward and his satchel hit something solid. He stopped, and over the sound of his panting he could hear Liz.

"Let there be a way out," she said. "Let there be a way out."

Peter set down his bag and dropped Liz's hand. She grasped his shirt as he felt the wall in front of him.

"It's wood," he said.

"Is it a door?" said Liz.

"It must be," said Peter, though he knew it might just as easily be a solid wall. He ran his hands across the barrier starting at the top and working his way down, lightly touching the wood with his fingertips to avoid splinters.

"Come on," said Liz. "Find the way out."

Just as he heard her breathing speeding up again, Peter felt something cold and hard.

"Hang on," he said. "This feels like a handle." Peter pressed down on what felt like an iron latch and pushed his shoulder against the wood. In the next instant he was stumbling forward into warmth and blinding light as Liz pushed him through the door. For a moment Peter could see nothing and could hear only Liz crying and laughing simultaneously. Before his eyes had adjusted sufficiently for him to recognize his surroundings, he heard the voice of John Alderson.

"Ah, Mr. Byerly. How good of you to drop in. And I see you've brought a friend."

Peter did not realize he had been tensing his muscles for the past hour, but he felt a wave of relaxation wash over him as Alderson invited him to have a seat and then helped Liz to a spot by the fire. She was still shaking, but she looked up at Peter and smiled and he knew she would recover. He had not voiced to her his fear that if the pas-

sageway did lead to Evenlode Manor, they would be met by Julia Alderson brandishing her lover's shotgun. To be met, instead, by her
brother's kindness was relief indeed.

"You look as if you've had a harrowing evening," said John. Peter
realized he was covered in mud and scratches. The pain from his
twisted ankle, forgotten in the intensity of the underground trek,
now surged back.

"It's a tunnel," said Peter. "A tunnel all the way to the Gardner family chapel."

"Extraordinary," said John.

"My friend here is a bit claustrophobic," said Peter. "And we were
in there quite some time."

"I'd heard of such a passage," said John. "My grandfather used to
tell tales about secret commerce between the Aldersons and the
Gardners—cooperation going on underground while the feud raged
above. I never believed it until Thomas Gardner showed up drunk in
my library one night."

"Then you knew?" said Peter.

"Oh yes," said John, "though I never had the courage to take the
trip myself. Like your friend, I'm not fond of tight spots." He closed
the door to the passage, which disappeared seamlessly into the pan-
eling, and handed Peter his satchel. "Mr. Gardner used the tunnel on
several occasions, though he never found what I'd hoped he would in
his family crypt."

Before Peter could catch her eye to silence her, Liz, who seemed
much recovered, said, "Do you mean Phillip Gardner's document
collection? We found it."

"You did, did you?" said John, smiling. "I had rather hoped you
might when I locked you in."

"You . . . ," said Liz, unable to articulate the rest of her thought and
struggling to apologize to Peter with her eyes.

"I suppose you'd like to see them," said Peter, as calmly as if they had been discussing a simple business deal. He opened his satchel and reached in, gathering together the bulk of the documents and pulling them out.

"Feel free to set them on the table," said John, reaching into his jacket pocket. "And don't think about going anywhere." He withdrew a pistol and waved Peter toward the library table on which he had first examined the *Pandosto*. It hardly seemed possible that had been less than a week ago.

"You locked us in?" said Liz, curiosity and anger mixed in her voice. "You dirty bastard."

"I've been kept quite busy the past couple of days trying to stay ahead of the two of you," said Alderson. "Not everything has gone precisely to plan, but things worked out in the end—and you've brought me a nice little bonus." He nodded toward the stack of documents.

"But those don't belong to you," said Liz. "They don't even belong to Thomas Gardner. Phillip Gardner left them to the descendants of his illegitimate son. We found his will."

"My dear, no one but you will ever see that will, and it's common knowledge among several of the leading document dealers that I have an old family collection I'm ready to sell. I assure you there will be no question of ownership."

"But if you locked us in . . ." said Peter. "I mean, we thought that Thomas Gardner and Julia had . . ." Peter let his thought hang in the air.

"My sister Julia? Yes, she was to have helped out but then that fool Gardner went and got himself an alibi at the worst possible time. Not that I actually trusted Gardner to do the dirty work for me, but he would have made a lovely scapegoat. That's why I asked Julia to seduce him in the first place."

"So you knew about Thomas and Julia?" said Peter.

"Of course I knew," said Alderson. "It was my idea. Just as it was my idea to tempt you with the *Pandosto*. But you proved far too curious and steps had to be taken."

"So you're the one who . . . ." said Peter.

"I'm the one who killed Graham Sykes, ransacked this young lady's office and apartment looking for his blasted book—yes, I did all of that. And if Thomas Gardner hadn't shot himself, he would have taken the blame once Julia testified against him. Lucky for me you managed to leave a raft of evidence at the site of the murder. I should think it will be an open-and-shut case."

"I'll testify for him," said Liz, standing and taking a step toward Alderson.

"That won't be necessary," said Alderson, turning the gun on her and motioning her back to her chair. "There's not going to be a trial." Liz sat back down, her face suddenly ashen.

"Now," said Alderson, turning to Peter. "I believe you have something else that belongs to me."

"The *Pandosto*," said Peter.

"My sister gave you a week to arrange for its sale. Your time is about up."

"It's a forgery," he said, "but then I guess you knew that or you would have taken it to Sotheby's or Christie's."

"Yes," said John, "but it was so much easier to take it to you. I'd hoped that you had neither the resources nor the wit to prove it a fake. And of course your ego made you want to believe you'd found a great treasure. Am I wrong?"

"Not entirely," said Peter.

"It's a shame really. If you'd been a little less clever, some rich American would be drooling over the *Pandosto*, you and I would both be quite wealthy, and I wouldn't be forced to become a three-time murderer and start all over with a new bookseller."

"A three-time murderer?" said Liz.

"Well, I can't very well let you two live, knowing what you know.

When I tell the police that Graham Sykes's murderer and his accomplice came after me in my own home, naturally they'll have no qualms about my having defended myself. Shall we have a drink?" Alderson asked, waving his gun toward a cut-glass decanter. "I'm not entirely uncivilized."

Kingham, 1879

As the servants packing Mrs. Gardner's things banged and clattered unceasingly overhead, Phillip Gardner read again the letter that had brought an end to his marriage and to his hopes of saving Evenlode House from ruin. These losses paled, however, next to the pain that welled in his chest every time he read the words that swam before him. He realized only now that he could have lived with the shame of condemning the family estate to ruin, but to have first wronged and then lost the one woman he ever truly loved was more than he could bear.

His triumph over Reginald Alderson now seemed childish, and the pain of losing Isabel was twinned with the shame he felt for his complicity in the destruction of a great treasure. Only now did it occur to him that he might have made two forgeries, returning one of them to Mayhew as the original while keeping the true *Pandosto* for himself. It was not out of greed that he wished he had thought of this plan earlier but out of a sudden and intense desire to preserve a great piece of literary history. But Phillip had been blinded by hatred and arrogance.

As he read the words of Miss Prickett's letter again and again, his course of action gradually became clear. Gathering together a few papers and books, he left the house by the kitchen door and made one last trek to the lair in which he had plied his craft as a forger. As he was entering the chapel, Mrs. Gardner was stepping into the trap that would bear her to the railway station. They would never see each other again.

———

In the waning light of a short November day, Benjamin Mayhew strode down Piccadilly toward St. James's Street and dinner with William Smith at his club. He had disposed of the *Pandosto*, and though he knew it could have brought him fame, it might equally have brought him ruin and notoriety—he had, after all, stolen the book to begin with. It was technically not even his book anymore; he had provided Phillip Gardner with a bill of sale.

Only he and Gardner knew the truth about the *Pandosto*, and Benjamin thought perhaps he ought to write down the whole story of the book and what it really did reveal, just in case anything were to happen to him. If he did, he would of course contrive for the secret to be kept until after the death of William Smith.

Thus preoccupied with his thoughts, Mayhew stepped off the curb into Haymarket imagining the surprise of some future scholar's discovering that the famous *Pandosto* forgery was copied from a genuine relic. The image was strong enough in his mind to blot out the sound of approaching hooves, and it might rightly be said of Benjamin Mayhew that as he was struck down by the cab, he had no idea what had hit him.

As Benjamin Mayhew breathed his last on the stones of Haymarket, Phillip Gardner hoisted himself up through the hole in the floor of the family chapel, using the rope he had lowered into the darkness a few hours earlier. He had made his final preparations. He was proud of the way he had applied his artistic abilities to the job of carving an appropriate inscription on his tomb in the crypt. He had then sealed his collection of documents, along with his confession and letters from Isabel and Miss Prickett, in that vault. His tomb would remain otherwise empty. *Let it be a monument to foolishness,* he thought, *an empty tribute to what happens to a man who places money over love, rivalry over integrity, forgery over reality.*

It had taken him only an hour to put the finishing touches on the *Pandosto*. At the bottom of the list of owners' names, he made two additions. The first, he saw as an insurance policy. Should the *Pandosto* come to the attention of scholars, he wanted to direct them toward Mayhew, in hopes that the bookseller might admit that, but for Phillip's lone addition, the marginalia were copied from Shakespeare's own hand. So he added the inscription, "B. Mayhew for William H. Smith." Under this, he wrote in pencil and in his own hand, "B.B. / E.H." Though it would be meaningless to most people, to Reginald Alderson it would serve as a reminder of who had tricked whom.

Phillip hoped Mayhew would forgive him for the change of plans, but he knew from experience that private anguish could be more painful than public humiliation, and he wanted Alderson to know the extent to which he had been duped. Alderson would have one night of joy, when he found the *Pandosto* on his library table; tomorrow morning that would all be shattered with the delivery of Phillip's final letter. Should Alderson ever be foolish enough to reveal the *Pandosto* to the public, Smith would still get to have his laugh at the Stratfordians, but Phillip no longer cared about making Mayhew or Smith happy.

Before he made his surreptitious deliveries to Evenlode Manor, Phillip had returned to his only true loves—painting and Isabel. In only one hour he had created what he now knew to be his second masterpiece, and his only truly original work. He painted her as he remembered her best, brushing her hair before the mirror after they had made love. As he thought back on that glorious afternoon, it seemed to Phillip that that had been the only time in his life he had been truly happy. In summoning Isabel's face once more and letting it flow from his memory through the brush and onto the paper, he felt, for the first and last time, what it meant to be an artist.

For more than an hour after the paint was dry he stared at Isa-

bel—the only face that had ever looked upon him with uncondi-
tional love, the face he had betrayed and banished.

Even after he slipped the painting inside the book in which it
would remain hidden in Alderson's library, after he slid the false
grave marker that hid the entrance to the crypt back into place, Phillip still saw that face. He hoped his painting might eventually see the
light of day—not so he would be remembered, but so his blessed Isabel might once again smile upon some lucky soul years hence.

The house was silent when he returned, the servants gone with
their mistress, for they knew who paid their wages. Rain had just
begun to fall as Phillip climbed from a window of the main house
onto the top of a wall of the unfinished west wing. Three stories
below, through the mist, he could see stacks of freshly quarried limestone—the final delivery of construction materials that had arrived
just a few days earlier. Phillip wondered if Mrs. Gardner had paid the
bill.

Ridgefield, 1994

Sitting in the waiting room at the hospital hour after hour while Amanda underwent a battery of tests, Peter felt more alone than ever. True, Sarah and Charlie Ridgefield were there, sitting together on the other side of the room, one of them occasionally standing and crossing to look out the window, but they did not speak—to each other or to Peter—and Peter felt that they blamed him in some way for whatever had happened to Amanda. He knew rationally that this could not be true, that the idea of speaking before hearing the doctor's verdict was as abhorrent to them as it was to him, but reason was not likely to win a battle against emotion today, and as time slowed to a glacial pace, Peter wracked his memory for what he could have done to make Amanda sick. He could not even look at Sarah and Charlie and so did not see when Amanda's mother stood up and walked across the room. She slipped onto the sofa next to Peter and took his hand in hers without speaking. He still could not look at her, but he felt hot tears on his cheek as his emotions finally admitted what his reason had known all along—he was not alone.

Sarah's gesture of inclusion finally gave Peter the strength to do more than simply wait. From a pay phone in the corridor he called Cynthia.

"I'll be right there," Amanda's friend had said, and there was such sympathy and support and shared agony in those few words that Peter began to cry again.

"Would you do one thing for me first?" he said.

"Anything," said Cynthia.

"Would you stop by the house and bring me something?"

An hour later a doctor finally emerged to speak with them. "We're looking over the results of her MRI," he said. "We won't know anything conclusive for a little longer."

"What do you know that's not conclusive?" said Charlie Ridgefield. "What do you suspect? What's likely?"

"I'd rather not speculate until we get the results back," the doctor said.

"If you think you're sparing our feelings by not telling us what you're afraid of, you're not," said Charlie, a hint of anger creeping into his voice. "We can't possibly be more afraid than we are right now."

"She's had quite a bit of pain medication and sedatives," said the doctor, "so she's a bit groggy. But I think it would be okay if one of you came back to see her."

Sarah reached for her purse, but Charlie laid a hand on her shoulder. "It should be Peter," he said, and Peter knew then that his father-in-law didn't blame him, hadn't been trying to shut him out.

"Come with me," said the doctor.

She was beautiful, Peter thought when he saw his wife lying in the hospital bed. She had been so pale that morning when Charlie had carried her into the emergency room, but her color had returned, and though he knew she would say her hair was a mess, Peter didn't care. She was the most beautiful thing he had ever seen. He sat beside her and it took a moment for her to focus on him and to whisper, "Peter," and in those two syllables and in those eyes Peter saw it all—the girl sitting upright in the library reading room; the late-night talks in the snack bar; the tender lovemaking in the Devereaux Room; the trips to England, holding hands when the plane took off—in this beautiful woman he saw all that was good and right about his life.

"You saved me, you know," he said. "I never told you that before, but you saved me."

He was afraid she wouldn't understand what he was talking about, but she smiled and whispered, "I know." She slid a warm hand out from underneath the covers and said, "Hold my hand while I sleep."

Peter took her hand and watched her eyes close. Her breathing slowed and he leaned his head against her chest and listened to the sound of her heartbeat and prayed that the doctor would never come. He did not want to hear test results and a diagnosis and a survival rate, he wanted only to hold Amanda's hand forever and listen to her heartbeat go on and on.

"We can't make any promises about the surgery," said Dr. Owen, "but there is some reason to be optimistic." Peter was standing in a small consulting room with Sarah and Charlie and the neurosurgeon, who was pointing to a series of MRI images. They looked like modern art, was all Peter could think. Amanda would hate them.

"With a tumor of this type, there are cases of complete recovery, but I have to warn you the five-year survival rate is only about ten percent."

"She'll be in the ten percent," said Charlie, pulling his wife into his embrace.

"And of course there are risks of complications developing as a result of the surgery. Any time you cut into the brain you're taking a chance."

For the second time in his life Peter steeled himself to deliver a diagnosis to Amanda, this time to tell her that she had brain cancer, that she would need to undergo several hours of surgery and several months of radiation, and that even then her chances of survival were not good. She was awake when he entered her room, looking more alert than she had on his last visit.

"I have something for you," he said. "Cynthia brought it." He held out the copy of *At the Back of the North Wind* that he had bound for her eight years ago. Amanda always kept the book by her bedside, even when they traveled.

"It's so beautiful," she said. "I think you won me with this book."

"Hank says I never did as good a job on a binding as I did on that one."

"That's because this one was bound with so much love, you know that, Peter." She clutched the book to her breast and Peter bit hard on his tongue to keep from crying. She had always been the strong one, but now he knew he would have to be her pillar of strength and he wasn't sure he was up to the job.

"I've got some news from the doctor," he said.

Peter stayed in Amanda's room that night, sleeping fitfully in the chair by the bed. Deep in the night he felt her touching his hand and he sat forward to look into her eyes in the dim light.

"What is it?" he asked.

"Make love to me," she said.

"Are you crazy?" said Peter, stifling a laugh. "We're in a hospital room."

"I know," she said, pulling him toward her so hard that he had no choice but to rise out of his chair and lie on the edge of the bed. "But tomorrow they're going to shave my head and cut a hole in my skull and then they're going to spend six months shooting poison radiation at me, so I may not feel sexy for a while."

"But we can't here," said Peter, as she began to unbutton his shirt.

She slipped her hands around his neck and drew him to her, kissing him long and deep. "And I'm scared," she whispered into his ear. "I'm so scared and I need you inside me because when you're making love to me everything else goes away." And so Peter slipped under the covers with her and for an hour everything did go away and they were back on the floor of the Devereaux Room, crazy in love, giggly and hoping they wouldn't get caught, and they cried when they came and neither could decide, as they lay in each other's arms afterward, whether those had been tears of joy or love or fear or sadness or all those emotions together.

"It happened quickly," the doctor told them, "when she was in the recovery room after the operation. She was still under the anesthetic. She didn't feel a thing. Strokes are not an uncommon side effect with this type of condition. We did everything we could to revive her, but the patient expired."

Like a subscription to a magazine, thought Peter. *The period during which I am allowed to be happy has expired.*

Peter walked through the next week in a daze. He may have spoken to Sarah and Charlie Ridgefield, to Cynthia and Amanda's other friends who came to the visitation and the funeral, but if so, his body carried on these conversations without the consent or cooperation of his mind or his heart. Those parts of him were frozen—permanently frozen, he thought, and what was frozen could avoid facing the magnitude of the loss.

At the burial, Peter feared that permafrost might start to thaw, as he lay on Amanda's coffin a blue leather-bound book—her cherished copy of *At the Back of the North Wind* into which he had poured so much love. When he stood back up, Cynthia reached out for him, but he brushed her off and hurried down the hill to the waiting cars. Before anyone could catch up with him he locked himself in the back of a town car and gave the driver his home address. There he closed the curtains, unplugged the phone, and tried to find a way to live that didn't involve . . . well, anything.

There was no question of forgetting Amanda. Everything in the house reminded him of her—not just the furniture and the carpets and the colors of the walls, all of which she had picked out—but the glass from which she had drunk her daily orange juice, and the microwave popcorn she had bought for him to eat when they watched movies together. Amanda was everywhere, and she was nowhere.

And then she started visiting him. At first she would just watch him as he read a book or poured cereal in a bowl, but soon she started talking. He rarely talked back, but he listened. And when she told him to please go see Dr. Strayer, he washed some clothes and stepped outside for the first time in nearly a month. He had lost twenty pounds, his skin was pale, and he squinted in the unfamiliar light of the sun, but he drove the three miles to keep the appointment that he had made with Dr. Strayer the previous day.

Peter refused to use the word *recovery*—to say that he was beginning his recovery would be to admit that Amanda was gone. And so because Peter was not ready to take the steps necessary to deal with his grief, Dr. Strayer, who feared his patient might retreat back into his darkened house for good, made him a list. Ten things Peter needed to do to save his own life.

Peter had taped the list to the refrigerator, but three months after Amanda's death he still paid it little heed. His curtains stayed drawn, his phone remained unplugged, and he ventured out only to see Dr. Strayer and on late-night trips to the grocery. He had seen Sarah and Charlie only once since the funeral, when he had been summoned to a lawyer's office to sign the papers relating to the distribution of Amanda's estate. Despite their obvious concern he spoke to them curtly and left the office before the ink was dry. No one who saw the hollow man hurrying across the parking lot would have guessed that he had just inherited slightly over fourteen million dollars.

Just after Labor Day, when undergraduates were settling back onto the Ridgefield campus, Peter went through the daily motions of opening his mail and discovered a bill from the contractor who had been renovating the cottage in England. "Final statement," the invoice said. The work was complete. Leaving Ridgefield suddenly struck Peter as an obvious thing to do. Three days later he had packed up his reference books and arranged for them to be shipped to Oxfordshire, and a taxi was waiting outside to take him to the airport. He stood in the kitchen next to his suitcase and took one last look around before turning out the light. As the taxi honked impatiently, he glanced at the refrigerator and saw Dr. Strayer's list. He ripped it off the door and stuffed it into his jacket pocket.

Kingham, 1879

As the rain streaked down the tall library windows, Reginald Alderson reread the extraordinary collection of marginalia in the copy of *Pandosto* that had appeared on his library table the previous evening. The parcel had not been posted; he assumed Phillip Gardner must have delivered it by hand, though he'd not had a chance to ask the butler about this. He shuddered to think that he was now the guardian of such a treasure, for he had read enough about Shakespeare to know how truly spectacular a document the *Pandosto* was. He had never imagined that his blackmailing of Gardner would be so fruitful.

He was so distracted by the book, and its potential to make him the most famous collector in the land—the "Alderson *Pandosto*" the press would call it—that he did not notice a row of ten books on a lower shelf of his library that had not been there the previous day. He was just imagining delivering a lecture in a packed Egyptian Hall when the butler arrived with the morning post.

Reginald was used to seeing the slanting script of Phillip Gardner on the parcels that contained documents from Gardner's collection. Today's packet was thick with what Reginald supposed were new treasures, and he slit open the envelope and withdrew the contents. When a dozen mediocre watercolors spilled out onto the table, Reginald felt a sense of foreboding. He picked up the letter on top of the pile of paintings and read. Gardner's words brought a pain to his chest that did not abate when he began to breathe again. All thought of presenting his precious *Pandosto* to an adoring public evaporated.

He was on the verge of dropping the worthless book into the fire when the butler returned, this time leading the local constable into the library.

"Sorry to disturb you, sir," said the constable, "but there's been a death over at Evenlode House. Mr. Phillip Gardner." Among his many responsibilities in the parish, Reginald Alderson had served for the past three years as coroner, a largely ceremonial post, as there had not in all that time been a single suspicious death in the parish.

The inquest into the death of Phillip Gardner was held in the drawing room of Evenlode House. Reginald Alderson had arranged for fires to be lit, as the servants had mysteriously disappeared. He did not dwell on this fact or on the disappearance of Mrs. Gardner during the course of his questioning the one witness—the builder who had found the deceased's body on a pile of limestone blocks. Aside from the constable, the assistant constable, and the witness, the deceased's younger brother and heir to the estate was the only other person in the room to hear Reginald's quickly rendered verdict of accidental death. Reginald thought such a verdict would be the best way of preventing further investigation that might reveal his collection of forgeries or even his blackmailing of Gardner. Since Reginald had in his private possession the only evidence that Gardner had, in fact, committed suicide, no one questioned the verdict.

Phillip Gardner was buried just outside the family chapel. The single mourner, Nicholas Gardner, saddled with the debts of an estate that he had never wanted, had neither the money nor the inclination to erect a headstone.

Reginald Alderson placed first the *Pandosto* and then the rest of his ill-gotten collection of forgeries into a wooden box that he labeled NEVER TO BE SOLD and locked in a cabinet in his library. For the rest of his days, which were many, he wore the key to that cabinet on a leather cord around his neck—a constant reminder of how he had been fooled.

He would not be fooled again. Reginald spent the rest of his life moving from one shrewd business deal to another, building up the coffers of the family estate while Evenlode House, abandoned and neglected by Nicholas Gardner, fell into disrepair. During a gale on Boxing Day, 1898, all of Kingham and people as far away as Chipping Norton heard the great boom of the unfinished west wing of Evenlode House collapsing. Reginald Alderson walked over the next day to silently gloat over the Gardners' downfall.

Three days later, Reginald, who should not have ventured out in the cold at his age, lay on his deathbed. For the first time in nearly twenty years he untied the cord that held the key around his neck, solemnly presenting it to his son. He then told Edward Alderson the story of the *Pandosto* and the forged documents, making him swear to guard the key with his life and to share the secrets of the hidden box only with the heir to Evenlode Manor.

Edward Alderson lived to be nearly ninety—long enough to see his son killed in the Great War and his grandson killed in World War II. Not until 1955 did he finally pass the secret of the Evenlode documents to his great-grandson, John Alderson, who had just turned eighteen. John had always been rather fond of the watercolors that hung in his childhood bedroom, and had been shocked to discover their place in a family secret.

For forty years John had kept that secret, but in the early 1990s he had lost a fortune in junk bonds, and as debts on the family estate mounted and his own son began to ask about his inheritance, John considered the possibility that the long-hidden box might prove his salvation. And then Miss O'Hara had returned from the shop one day and mentioned in passing that an American rare-book dealer was living in Kingham.

The bells of St. Andrew's tolled midnight as John Alderson waved the gun lazily toward Peter. "Perhaps you'd better pour," he said. "I'll keep the gun on your girlfriend in case you decide to try some foolish heroics."

Peter rose and crossed the room. There were two crystal glasses on the silver tray next to the decanter. Peter was glad to have his back to Alderson for a moment. "Whiskey?" he asked as he took the stopper out of the bottle and slowly set about the job of pouring the drinks.

"I find it settles my nerves when I'm in a tight spot," said John. "Perhaps it will do the same for yours."

"Who said I'm nervous?" said Peter, still surprised that he wasn't.

"Facing death most people are a bit jittery," said Alderson.

"So you have experience with this?" said Peter.

"Only Graham Sykes. I wouldn't describe him as nervous so much as belligerent, though. He actually bit my arm before I was able to dispatch him."

Peter tried to hide his disgust as he pictured the stubborn old man fighting for his life. He turned and handed a tumbler to his host.

"You misunderstand," said Alderson. "The drinks are for the two of you."

"She doesn't drink," said Peter, shooting Liz a silencing look that had exactly the effect he intended. "And frankly I'm not sure I should myself. How do I know you haven't poisoned the whiskey?"

"You're just like every other American," said Alderson. "You've read far too many murder mysteries set in old English houses. What Agatha Christie has done to the image of this country!"

"Still," said Peter, offering a glass to Alderson.

"Very well," said Alderson. "Cheers." He drained the glass at a single go and set it down hard on a table by his chair. "You see—no convulsions, no foaming at the mouth. Just a nice stiff jolt of scotch."

"I notice you didn't drink to my health," said Peter, sipping his drink and setting it back down.

"That would have been a bit hypocritical, don't you think? Now, you will please return my *Pandosto*."

Peter reached into his satchel and withdrew the book whose history he had been chasing for the past several days. Pulling it from its protective envelope, he held it out to Alderson. "Maybe the forgery really is yours," he said, "but I'm sure there will be quite a debate over who owns the original."

"There is no original," said Alderson, snatching the book from Peter. "That is to say, there was one, but it was destroyed long ago."

"On the contrary," said Peter. "I've held the original in my hands. It's not far from here."

"I doubt that," said Alderson.

"Doubt all you wish," said Peter "but it's true." Liz looked at Peter with a questioning expression and he shook his head imperceptibly at her.

"It's true, I've seen it as well," said Liz.

"Now I know you're lying," said Alderson. "Listen to the way your voice is shaking."

"Maybe that's because you're about to kill me," said Liz.

"Actually she is lying," said Peter evenly. "But I'm not."

"As it happens," said Alderson, rising and crossing to the desk in front of the curtained windows, "I have proof right here that the original was destroyed." He opened the drawer from which his sister Julia had taken the key to *Pandosto*'s cabinet the previous week and withdrew a small, browning envelope. "The last letter from Phillip Gardner to my great-great-grandfather. Perhaps you'd like to read it." He flung the letter toward Liz, still keeping the gun steady in his other hand. As she picked up the envelope from the floor, Alderson returned to his chair.

Liz slipped the letter out of its envelope, unfolded it, and paced in front of the fire as she read the now familiar script of Phillip Gardner.

Mr. Alderson,

By the time you read this, I will have ended my life, and so there will be no way for you to take your revenge for what I have done. Each of the documents you have so viciously extorted from me over the past two years is a forgery. I must thank you for helping me find my true calling as an artist. The proof is in my masterpiece, the *Pandosto* that you recently received.

Each document in your collection includes a clue to its own falsehood, and should you or your heirs ever attempt to sell any of these items, they will undoubtedly be revealed for what they are. The originals are safely put away for my own heirs. The exception to this, sadly, is the *Pandosto*. Although the original did belong to me, it was destroyed by Benjamin Mayhew, he wishing to protect the reputation of another client.

And so, Mr. Alderson, I have won. I now go to my rest, and you shall be left to live with the knowledge that your blackmail has been for naught.

"So it was destroyed," said Liz.

"Sadly yes," said Alderson, who seemed quite relaxed in his chair now.

"Balderdash!" said Peter. "All that letter proves is that Gardner *thought* Mayhew destroyed it."

"It was destroyed," said Alderson, in an almost dreamy voice.

"Bollocks," said Peter, trying out the English idiom. "Mayhew was a bookseller. He may have wanted to protect William H. Smith's little fantasy about Francis Bacon, but he was still a bookseller. You can't possibly understand him the way I can."

"Because you're a bookseller, too?" sneered Alderson.

"Exactly," said Peter. "And I'm telling you that no bookseller, even one who was involved in forgery and cover-ups, would ever destroy a treasure like the *Pandosto*."

"You're so arrogant," said Alderson. "You think everyone in the world thinks the same way you do. You're such an American."

"I may be," said Peter, "but I'm also right, and you know I'm right. If you didn't think there was at least a chance that the original had survived, you would have killed me by now." Peter sat on the edge of the desk, forcing Alderson to turn slightly in his chair in order to keep the gun trained on him. It seemed an effort for Alderson, whose arm wobbled as he tried to aim the gun.

"If what you say is true," said Alderson, "if booksellers are so keen to preserve treasures, then you'll tell me where the original is, even if you know I'm going to kill you. You'll do anything to be sure the *Pandosto* is discovered and survives."

"That's true," said Peter, standing and pacing in front of the desk as he nodded discreetly to Liz. "And so I'm going to tell you. But in exchange I want you to spare the life of my friend here."

Alderson turned toward the hearth to see Liz, but he was too late. As Peter had talked, she had crept up behind Alderson's chair. In the second before she took action, Alderson seemed to be trying to stand up, but his body wasn't responding and his hand flailed wildly, still clutching the gun. Before he could wrench himself around to see her, Liz brought the iron poker down hard on his arm, making a sickening crunch. Alderson howled in pain as the gun fell from his hand and skittered across the floor toward Peter.

Peter picked up the gun just in time to point it at Julia Alderson as she came rushing into the room. No longer the mousy girl he had met the previous week, Julia, self-possessed and tensely alert, seemed ready to take command of the situation, but when she saw the barrel of her brother's pistol pointing at her, she turned for the door. Peter took two quick strides across the room and grabbed Julia's arm, dragging her back into the room and shutting the door.

"You're not going anywhere," he said. For a moment there was no sound but Liz's panting, the even breathing of the others, and an occasional crackle from the dying fire. John Alderson had lost consciousness.

"Miss Alderson," said Liz at last, "I'm afraid I'm a little early for tea."

"I've rung the police," snapped Julia. "You may have outsmarted my brother, but you'll still be convicted of murder."

"That seems unlikely," said Peter, releasing Julia's arm, but keeping the gun trained on her. "I think this will tell the police who the real murderer is." Peter reached into his open satchel and withdrew the mini-cassette recorder he had used to take notes at the British Library. He pressed a button and the squeal of the tape rewinding filled the room. He hit another button and the squeal was replaced by the voice of John Alderson.

" 'I'm the one who killed Graham Sykes, ransacked this young lady's office and apartment looking for his blasted book—yes, I did all of that.' "

"That and the imprint of Graham Sykes's teeth on your brother's arm should be more than enough to get a conviction," said Peter. There was another lull in the conversation as the implication of the tape settled onto the room.

"Can we take my brother to the hospital?" said Julia at last, her entire demeanor deflating in defeat.

"Call an ambulance," said Peter to Liz. "Tell them Mr. Alderson has had an overdose of anxiety medication."

By the time Peter and Liz had given their statements to the police, the southern sky was beginning to lighten. John Alderson had been taken to the hospital, where he would be arrested a few hours later for the murder of Graham Sykes. Julia Alderson was marched out of the house and charged with conspiracy to commit murder. The police had taken all the documents—forgeries and originals—along with Peter's recording of John Alderson's confession into evidence.

"There's more than just a murder here," an officer had said to Peter as he loaded the documents into the back of the car. "Someone has to decide who all these things belong to."

"Don't forget this," said Peter, handing the officer Phillip Gardner's brilliant forgery of *Pandosto*. He felt only a slight pang of loss as the officer tossed the *Pandosto* into the car and it disappeared from view.

The police offered to drive Peter and Liz back into Kingham and drop them off at Peter's cottage.

"What about our room at the Mill House?" said Liz as the car pulled away from Evenlode Manor.

"I have a very nice guest room," said Peter. "It's never been used."

But neither of them felt much like sleep when they arrived at the cottage, so Peter made a pot of tea and poured them each a cup.

"You know you saved me back there," said Liz, after taking a long drink of tea.

"I did?"

"In that bloody tunnel. I never could have made it through that without you."

"You never would have been trapped down there without me," said Peter.

"Nevertheless," said Liz, "you saved me. So thank you."

"You're welcome," said Peter. "And thank you for breaking Alderson's arm."

"It was nothing," said Liz, laughing. "I do it all the time. So what was that stuff you slipped him?"

"It's a sedative," said Peter. "I have a panic disorder."

"You could have fooled me," said Liz. "Seems like I was the one who was panicking."

"Wait until tomorrow when the adrenaline wears off," said Peter. "Anyway, I had an envelope of pills in my jacket pocket and I guess they got crushed when I was wriggling through that hole in the chapel floor. I thought about giving you one in the tunnel—that's when I realized they were nothing but dust. So when Alderson offered me a drink, I just imagined myself in an Agatha Christie plot and slipped the powder into the glass."

"And then challenged him to drink it."

"I really didn't think he was stupid enough to fall for it," said Peter.

"I guess he doesn't read enough mysteries," said Liz, laughing again.

"I wonder what set him off?" said Peter.

"Who, Alderson?"

"No, Phillip Gardner. Why did he decide to commit suicide? Do you think he felt guilty about the *Pandosto*?"

"Probably it was Miss Prickett's letter," said Liz.

"What letter?"

"You never let me read it to you," said Liz, pulling an envelope out of the pocket of her overcoat. "Remember I told you there was something else in the box you found in Gardner's tomb? It was this. I read it while you were talking to the police."

"What's it say?" asked Peter.

Liz unfolded the thick paper. "Well, on one side Gardner has written another confession." She read.

On receiving this letter I reposed to my workshop where I painted the only true work of art that has ever flowed from me, a portrait of my beloved Isabel. Like the rest of my creations, I shall hide her in the library of Reginald Alderson. There, until some lucky soul looks into her eyes once more, she shall stay, safely escaped from Evenlode House, and as immortal as I can make her.

"So my portrait . . ."

"Is of Isabel," said Liz. "Phillip Gardner's mistress."

"What does the letter say?" asked Peter.

Liz turned the paper over and read:

My Dear Mr. Gardner,

I write to share with you news of great sadness to us both. A month ago Miss Isabel fell ill and last night she slipped away from this life, which has brought her such joy and such grief. I spoke with her in confidence a few hours before she left us, and her thoughts were only of you. You must know that she does not blame you in any way for what happened, and she asked me to write and tell you that at the last she felt only love for you. Should you ever wish to contact your son, you may write to him through me, for the Devereaux family has graciously agreed to keep me on as Phillip's governess. I know that you loved Isabel and she loved you; I loved her, too, and I hope you will know that I share in your loss.

Yours,

Evangeline Prickett

"What was the name of the family?" said Peter.

"Devereaux. Why, have you heard of them?"

"Oh my God," said Peter. "You remember Gardner's will? How he said he left his books and documents to his son's youngest living heir?"

"I remember," said Liz.

"I think that might be me."

As soon as she had said the name, Peter remembered the family tree he had found among Amanda Devereaux's papers. Amanda's father was Phillip Devereaux; his mother was Isabel and his father had been listed simply as "unknown."

"You could be the legitimate owner of all those documents?" said Liz.

"Not just of those, but of the *Pandosto,* too."

"But the *Pandosto*'s a fake," said Liz. "We proved that ourselves."

"Not the one the police have," said Peter, "the real one."

"Yeah, what was all that back there about knowing where the real *Pandosto* was? You were just bluffing, right?"

"I don't care how crooked Benjamin Mayhew was," said Peter. "No bookseller would destroy anything as spectacular as the *Pandosto*. And I wouldn't say I know where it is, but I have a pretty good idea."

Peter reached into his bag and withdrew his lifting knife. On the table in the conservatory lay the elaborate folding box in which the *Pandosto* had been stored. It seemed months ago that Peter had identified this box, built up to make the *Pandosto* look like a much thicker book, as a Victorian construction. He opened the innermost folding flap and inserted the lifting knife into the joint where this flap met the body of the box. With one swift motion he sliced cleanly through the cloth. He turned the box and repeated this motion on two other sides, leaving a flap of loose cloth attached on one side. Peter lay down his knife and peeled back the flap. There, snuggly nestled where it had been placed over a hundred years earlier, was a brown and battered book, the same size and shape as the *Pandosto* that Peter had been carrying around England for the past several days.

He turned the folder over and the book fell out onto the table. The binding was more worn than that of the forged *Pandosto* and Peter gently opened the cover. Liz leaned over his shoulder as they read a list of names on the endpaper—a list that included Wm. Shakspere, Stratford, but that made no mention of Mayhew, Smith, B.B., or E.H.

The final name on the list was Phillip Gardner. On page sixteen there was no mention of the death of Walter Raleigh.

In the center of the rear pastedown was a rectangular impression. "What's that?" said Liz.

Peter slipped his lifting knife under a loose edge of the pastedown and pulled the paper away from the binding. He held up the rear cover and a folded piece of paper fluttered to the table. Peter set down the book, unfolded the paper, and read:

Harbottle,

Pardon the messenger, but I have business in Stratford. I think you will find something of yourself in *A Winter's Tale*. I beg forgiveness for defacing your *Pandosto*, but return it herewith with my thanks.

W. Shakespeare

"It's the real thing," said Liz in whispered awe.

"So it would seem," said Peter, smiling. "So it would seem."

Kingham, Friday, June 23, 1995

Peter straightened his tie one more time in the mirror before running downstairs for a quick breakfast and a cup of tea. The train for London didn't leave for an hour but it was such a lovely summer morning that he wanted to walk to the station.

It had taken four months for teams of lawyers and genealogists in Oxfordshire, Louisiana, and North Carolina to reach the same conclusion that Peter had reached that morning in his cottage—that the youngest living heir of Phillip Devereaux, illegitimate son of Phillip Gardner, was none other than Peter Byerly. According to a bill of sale found among the papers in his tomb, Phillip Gardner had been the legal owner of the true *Pandosto*; the forgery was determined to have been his property as well.

During that time Peter had returned to North Carolina for a long stay with the Ridgefields. He and Sarah had taken walks together nearly every day in Ridgefield Gardens, watching the daffodils blossom and then the dogwoods and the azaleas. Sometimes they spoke of one or the other of the Amandas, but often they spoke of nothing important. They were friends, Peter discovered, and he liked that.

Peter had brought the *Pandosto* to Ridgefield to show to Francis Leland, who had been properly awed. With the help of Hank Christiansen he had done some minor repair work on the volume so it would be ready for this morning. The forged *Pandosto* he had given to Francis to be shelved in the Devereaux Room along with forgeries of Thomas Wise. Peter had also donated Gardner's portrait of Isabel Devereaux to the Special Collections department, where it was now displayed in the case below the significantly more imposing portrait of Isabel's granddaughter, Amanda.

Cynthia had come to visit at the end of April and she and Peter had stayed up late watching old movies on television. One night she sidled next to him on the sofa and slipped an arm around him, pulling him toward her and kissing him gently. It was pleasant enough, thought Peter, but he had no desire to take things any further.

"Is it Amanda?" said Cynthia.

"No," said Peter, "it's just . . ."

"You don't like me," said Cynthia.

"No, I like you. As a friend I like you. You've been great, Cynthia."

"Well it doesn't have to be anything more than friends having a little fling. I mean, it is the nineteen nineties."

"I know," said Peter. "It's just that—"

"Oh my God, there's another woman, isn't there," said Cynthia, grinning and punching Peter on the shoulder. "You've got a girlfriend."

"Well, I wouldn't exactly call her a girlfriend," said Peter.

"Okay," said Cynthia, "tell me all about her."

When Peter had returned to England in June, there were still only a handful of people who knew of the existence of the *Pandosto*, but that would all change in a few hours at an internationally televised event where he would present the volume to the British Library as a memorial to Amanda Byerly. After the ceremony it would be housed in the library's permanent exhibit, in a case including items from the collection of Robert Cotton. Cotton, after all, had been the last legitimate owner of the *Pandosto,* as far as Peter could tell.

In the years to come some of the older anti-Stratfordians would continue to deny the authenticity of the *Pandosto* marginalia, but it passed every test, including the ion migration test that finally exposed Mark Hofmann's forgery of "Oath of a Freeman." Professor

Kashimoto did, as promised, recant his position, first in a private phone call to Peter and later at a literary conference in San Francisco. Many others followed suit, and the few who continued to proclaim the Earl of Oxford or Christopher Marlowe or Francis Bacon as the author of the plays dwindled in number as the years went by. The English majors of the world, most of whom had seen the *Pandosto* either in person or in one of its widely published facsimiles, no longer offered fertile recruiting ground for the anti-Stratfordians, and by the end of the decade those who denied William Shakespeare his rightful place were only a handful of eccentrics, guilty of just what they had accused academia of for so many years—reaching conclusions without regard for the evidential record.

Sarah and Charlie Ridgefield had flown to London the previous morning and were staying at the Russell Hotel along with Francis Leland, Hank Christiansen, and Cynthia. Peter had insisted on paying for suites for everyone.

Peter was just finishing washing up the breakfast dishes when he saw Amanda standing in the corner of the kitchen. He hadn't seen much of her in the past few months, though they had had a chat after Cynthia had kissed him.

"It's a big day for you," she said.

"For us," said Peter. "It's a gift in your honor."

"It's what you always wanted," she said, "to find a book that would change literary history."

"I wish I could share it with you," he said.

"I'll be there," said Amanda.

"I miss you," said Peter, "but it hurts a little less than it used to."

"You won't see me anymore," said Amanda.

"I know," said Peter.

"I'll always love you," said Amanda, "but I have to go now, and so do you."

And she was gone.

Peter took a deep breath and then had one more look around the kitchen. After the ceremony Liz was coming up for the weekend and he wanted everything to be perfect. The counters were clean, the dishes put away—the only bit of clutter was the curling paper of Dr. Strayer's list pinned to the message board. Peter read quickly over the list and chuckled. In one deft motion he yanked it from the board and threw it into the rubbish bin.

Two minutes later he was striding toward the station, the *Pandosto* under his arm, and the warm summer breeze sweeping him toward the center of life.

ACKNOWLEDGMENTS

I am grateful to scores of people who helped inspire, grow, and hone this book, particularly to my mentors in the world of book collecting, Bob Lovett, Stuart Wright, the late Stan Marx, and Justin Schiller; to those who nurtured my writing life, especially Phyllis Barber, Chris Noël, Walter Wetherell, Diane Lefer, Sandra Adams, and Peggy Elam; to early readers Janice Lovett, Stephanie Lovett, and Nina Weigl for their excellent advice; to David Lovett for introducing me to my agent; to Anna Worrall for her early support; to David Gernert for his faith in the book and his insightful advice on revisions; to all those at the Gernert Company who have helped bring the book to the world; and to Kathryn Court and Tara Singh for their kind guidance and brilliant editing.

Thanks to all those librarians around the world who inhabit places like the Devereaux Room and who have assisted me with research and welcomed me into their sanctuaries over the years.

I would like to thank the people of the real Kingham, which is a more lovely, welcoming, and peaceful place than I could ever hope to portray in its fictional counterpart. In particular thanks to the Stockwell family for their love and friendship over many years.

Just as scores of people are responsible for the book you hold, so did scores of sources help create the historical sections of the novel. I am particularly indebted to the following—for details on William Shakespeare and his fellow Elizabethan writers, Judith Cook's *Roaring Boys: Shakespeare's Rat Pack*, Stephen Greenblatt's *Will in the World: How Shakespeare Became Shakespeare*, and Bill Bryson's *Shakespeare*; for her descriptions of book repair, restoration, and binding, Annie Tremmel Wilcox's *A Degree of Mastery: A Journey Through Book Arts Apprenticeship*; and for the saga of Mark Hofmann's forgeries, Linda Sillitoe and Allen Robert's *Salamander: The Story of the Mormon Forgery Murders*. All the books quoted in the text were, needless to say, important sources and those quotes are, with minor editing, taken from the original sources.

Above all, I wish to express my gratitude to my children, Jordan and Lucy, for their love and inspiration, and to my wife, Janice, whose love and faith supports me daily.

AUTHOR'S NOTE

All the published books mentioned in the text and their bibliographical details are real, though obviously some individual copies, inscriptions, and marginalia have been invented for this narrative. No complete copy of the first edition of Robert Greene's *Pandosto*, upon which Shakespeare based *A Winter's Tale*, is known to survive. Only two copies of the bad quarto of *Hamlet* are known.

I have invented scenes, actions, and dialogues for historical characters, but the basic biographical details of the following real people are more or less as stated in the text: the Elizabethan writers and their acquaintances William Shakespeare, Robert Greene, Christopher Marlowe, Thomas Nashe, George Peele, John Lyly, Emma Ball (and her son Fortunatus), Mrs. Isam, and Richard Burbage; the book collectors and librarians Robert Cotton, John Bagford, John Warburton, Humfrey Wanley, Robert and Edward Harley, and Henry Clay and Emily Jordan Folger; the forgers William Henry Ireland, Thomas Wise, John Payne Collier, and Mark Hofmann; and the bibliographers and scholars Edmond Malone, John Carter, Graham Pollard, William Henry Smith, and Charlton Hinman.

It is a sad truth for English literature that the combination of the carelessness of John Warburton and the ignorance of his cook Betsy Baker led to the destruction of over fifty manuscripts of Elizabethan and Jacobean plays, only five of which were preserved through separate sources. The rest were lost forever.